BLOODSPORT

A FICTION-ATLAS PRESS VAMPIRE ANTHOLOGY

C.L. CANNON   K. MATT   AIMEE SHAYE

DEVORAH FOX   D. FISCHER

LISAH JAYNE WALDEN   HELEN GLYNN JONES

L.B. CARTER   DORA BLUME   LYNN MULLICAN

TAYLOR J

FICTION-ATLAS PRESS LLC

BLOODSPORT

A FICTION-ATLAS PRESS VAMPIRE ANTHOLOGY

**Thank you for supporting
The International Red Cross
by buying this anthology!**

100% of all proceeds from the sale of this book will be donated to **The International Red Cross**.

The international Red Cross and Red Crescent network is the largest humanitarian network in the world with a presence and activities in almost every country.

All Red Cross and Red Crescent activities have one central purpose: to help those who suffer, without discrimination, whether during conflict, in response to natural or man-made disasters, or due to conditions of chronic poverty.

VAMPS WILL BE VAMPS

BY C.L. CANNON

Silas smirked at his reflection in the car mirror, running a hand through his dark locks before smoothing them down again. He struggled to hide his excitement. He always got a little antsy before outings like these, but today was special. Of all the venues, this was his favorite. The Flesh Fair was back in town, and as always, it proved the perfect hunting ground. Hundreds of impressionable young things practically throwing themselves at him. Sating his hunger would be all too easy. He had to remember to draw this one out. Often, he jumped the gun and spooked his companion before he'd had enough time to play. Not tonight.

The sun had just settled over the horizon, and that meant one thing, showtime. Silas took one last cursory glance at himself, exited the car, and began the trek to the main entrance. The queue was already wrapped around the side of the building, and as he passed the waiting patrons, he already saw a few contenders. There was a tall, dark-skinned woman sporting fake fangs and yellow contact lenses. She could be fun, definitely into role play. Of course, the large man standing with a possessive arm draped around her waist could prove a problem. A little further up the line, he glimpsed a petite pale thing with dark lines drawn around shocking blue eyes and a tight black fishnet top that pushed freckled breasts to the sky. She was a little too noticeable, perhaps. Harder to disappear a girl with so many admirers. No matter, as he arrived at the main doorway, he spotted the perfect match.

Stella could almost feel the electricity in the air as she approached the amphitheater. It wouldn't normally be a welcome place for her. Too many people, too many eyes judging her, but tonight, The Flesh Fair was in town. This is where they came—the outsiders, the unwanted, the ones who didn't fit in. Here they eagerly donned their dark lipstick and eyeliner, even the boys. Their black clothes and cold metal jewelry were praised rather than whispered about. Here, her paleness would be marveled at, and her queer way of observing might be mimicked instead of questioned. Here she could belong.

She'd heard the rumors about Flesh Fair for years, but she hadn't really believed them until she'd run into a girl who'd been there. A girl who described her experiences in detail. The tale was, the later you stayed, the realer the show got. That's when the real monsters showed their faces without shame. And if you weren't careful, they just might steal you away. After listening to the girl's story, Stella made up her mind once and for all, if it was the last thing she ever did, she was going to seek one of these demons out. She didn't know what truths she would discover, but seeing was believing, and Stella had always been a seeker of truths, even frightening ones.

And so, with this mission in mind, she stepped up to the main entrance and waited for her turn to be admitted. Twenty or so minutes later, she finally reached the doors only to be greeted with a scowl from the burly security guard.

"Oh, no, girl. Let me see some ID. I know you ain't eighteen."

"Oh, I, um," Stella pretended to thumb through her purse, but she hadn't even thought about bringing any identification.

Just as she was about to make up an excuse, a tall, dark-haired man came striding forward to her rescue.

"She's with me," he insisted.

The guard didn't seem to buy his story and began to protest, but the man insisted once more, lowering his sunglasses down the bridge of his nose to look the other man directly in the eye.

"I said, it's fine. She's with me."

The guard looked annoyed for a second before stepping aside to let Stella through the doorway.

The dark-haired man took Stella's arm, and together they walked across the threshold.

"I don't want no trouble," the guard called after them.

"My dear man, I assure you, we'll be no trouble at all," the mysterious man called over his shoulder.

"Thank you so much!" Stella beamed. "I completely forgot my ID, and I didn't know what I was going to do. I've been waiting for this for a whole year, and dumb me almost got kicked out, but you were just amazing!"

"Oh, no worries, it turns out I was due for a good deed," he said, performing a mock bow in her honor.

"Well, thank you, again…um, sorry, I didn't catch your name," Stella said, suddenly aware that she had no idea what to call her savior.

"Silas," he supplied.

"Nice to meet you, Silas. I'm Stella. Stella Anderson."

"So, Stella, what's a girl like you doing in a place like this?" Silas asked. His eyes roamed up and down her body as if he was a lion and she a piece of meat.

"It's kind of embarrassing," Stella admitted. "I'm here because I heard there were real monsters here. Not just people pretending or posers trying to be the next Damon Salvatore."

"Ah, so you've come to slay a demon then?"

"Something like that," she confirmed with a small nod.

"Well, I don't know much about these real monsters you've heard about, but there are plenty of cool things at this con. I'm sure we can find something to pique your interest."

There was a twinkle of mischief in his eye that excited Stella. Maybe she could afford to hang out with him a little longer. There was plenty of time to explore, and judging from the exhibitor badge hanging around his neck, Silas might know a thing or two about the people of The Flesh Fair.

A few hours later, and they had gotten to know a little more about each other. Stella let Silas know that she was not only legal, but nineteen, a whole year older than necessary to get in.

"I'm young looking for my age," she confessed. "Always have been."

She also filled him in on a rather substantial fight with her roommate, which meant she was currently living by herself in an apartment just outside her college campus. Despite it being lonely, she was happy for the extra living space. Silas regaled Stella with tales of Flesh Fair's past and some of the amazing artists and musicians he'd had the pleasure to meet while working the con the past three years.

"You haven't lived until you've heard Deathknot live," he insisted.

They both took part in some Edgar Allen Poe trivia and sat in on a panel about the spiritual journey of life after death. Stella had to admit she was having more fun than she'd expected. Other than the first salivating once over, Silas had been the perfect gentleman, but she wasn't sure if that was true to his nature or an elaborate act. He had charm for days and a smooth way of talking that she was sure could make any girl turn permanently red-cheeked. Once she'd assured herself of his intentions, she excused herself to the ladies' room to gain her composure. She splashed some water on her pallid face, psyching herself up for what would inevitably come. This was it. She could do this. She would not let this pass her by. Only a half-hour of tonight's con remained. It was showtime.

. . .

He'd been right. This girl was entirely too trusting, and it seemed very much alone. Now all he had to do was get her alone, and she'd be his for the taking. If he could just get her out of the bathroom. What was taking her so long? Finally, after a few more minutes, she emerged, her face betraying a smile when she spotted him.

"Stella!" he called, sprinting to her side once more. "You'll never guess what I heard."

"What? Tell me," she urged, looping her arm through his.

"Well, while you were gone, I got to thinking about what you said earlier...about the real monsters. So, I asked my buddy, Jacob. He's been working this con for years and years." Silas was pretty sure he hadn't known anyone named Jacob since primary school, but he continued his ruse. "Anyway, he said he heard that there was a secret after party where all the weird stuff goes down."

"Weird stuff?" She halted, abruptly pulling her arm away.

"Yeah, all the spooky, scary shit. He gave me an address. Wanna check it out?" Silas pushed.

"He just gave you the address, just like that?"

"Well, I'll owe him later, I'm sure, but don't you see how awesome this is? We can see for ourselves. You did want to know, right?"

He knew this girl. She'd cave under the pressure. She was weak-willed.

"Of course I do, it's just...do you think it's really real?" Stella asked, a bit of disbelief lacing her words.

"Only one way to find out," Silas said, dangling his keys in front of her.

Stella's unease faded, replaced with an adventurous smile. He had her.

"Lead the way."

Silas escorted the girl to his Mustang on the far side of the parking garage. Once she was securely fastened into the passenger seat, he slid the keys into the ignition and let it idle for a moment. He took a moment to revel in his work as the engine warmed. Only a matter of time now.

A few moments passed as Silas drove the car further toward the outskirts of town, and Stella absently swiped at her phone. His stomach lurched, making a loud, garbling sound in the silence. Who was she talking to? He'd been sure this girl was a loner.

"Sorry," he apologized, "I guess I'm a little hungry. Who are you texting?" he asked, trying to level the anger in his tone.

"Oh, I was just checking my grades. I had a test yesterday. B minus, but I guess I'll live."

"I'm sure it's a fluke," he said. "You don't need to tell someone where you're at, do you?"

"Oh, no," she protested. "I'm a big girl. Besides, I don't think my dad could work a cell phone to save his life."

"Good. I just want to make sure you're safe," Silas said, doing his best to sound like a convincing knight in shining armor.

"I feel safe with you," Stella assured him.

"I'm glad. Hey, you don't mind if I stop by my house for a minute, do you? I need to pick up a few things. Yah, know, stakes, holy water, stuff like that," he quipped.

"Of course, maybe you should get something to eat. That stomach grumble sounded serious."

A few minutes later, the Mustang pulled into the gravel driveway of a small Cape Cod.

"Won't you come in with me?" Silas asked.

"I don't know," Stella began, but stepped out of the car anyway. She looked from side to side, perhaps, assessing the danger, then finally followed Silas up some rickety steps and into his house.

Silas shut the door behind Stella but didn't make a move to turn the light on. There was no escape now. He'd stalked his prey, he'd played his part, and now, it was time for his reward.

"Stella?" Silas whispered in the dark.

"Yes?"

At once, his hands were on her body, fingers pinching and grabbing, his body pressed firmly to her own. She could feel the formica of a kitchen counter digging into her back as he pinned her against it. Rough hands ceased pinching to gather her wrists in a tight hold above her head. Teeth bit at her earlobe like a ferocious dog rather than a lover.

"Silas, you're hurting me…"

"Shut up," he spat. "Shut up, you whore."

"Silas, let me go!" she screamed.

A hand reared back to strike her, but she caught it deftly, turning the wrist until it snapped.

Silas cried out in pain, not quite registering what had just happened.

"You bitch, you'll pay for tha-"

But Silas never had a chance to finish his threat. In a flash, Stella pushed Silas's head back and sunk her teeth into the flesh of his neck, drinking deep. She felt the fight in him slowly fade and then dissipate with the last beat of his heart.

What luck, she hadn't had to go searching for trouble. It found her before she'd even gotten through the door. If she hadn't been sure after the first lustful gaze, Stella had been sure she'd found her monster after the next hour of narcissistic boasting and fake compliments. Silas also fit the description Maddie gave when she met the frightened girl in a back alley last year. Maddie had been one of the luckier girls. Over the past three years, seven other girls had gone missing. She'd managed to track down two, but they weren't willing to talk openly about their experiences. The other five had never been heard from again. Silas had been careful when picking his victims. He deliberately sought out loners. Mousey, slight girls, he could easily overpower and intimidate and who had few family connections. By the time someone realized they were missing, most of the girls had no chance of being discovered. Of course, Stella knew what had really happened to them. The ones who failed to escape lay buried beneath this house. She could smell the faint smell of decay eeking through the floorboards. Too subtle for a human to detect, but a good dog or a curious vampire could smell death a mile away.

The sound of the front door banging open reverberated around the apartment and a booming voice called out in the darkness. "Yo, dude, I hope you didn't go home with that girl you had me let in tonight. What was with that eye thing, anyway, man?" The kitchen light flickered to life, revealing quite a bloody mess, but the man still had his back turned as he placed his coat and keys on the rack by the door.

"And don't even try to make excuses. I know she's got to be under-age, bro. Not cool!" he continued, finally turning to face Stella.

"Well, at least one of you has an intact sense of morality," Stella mused, her tongue gliding over one sharp fang.

She watched as Silas's friend, the security guard, looked from the blood dripping down her chin to the corpse of his serial raping buddy, lying face-down on the floor. The man's mouth transformed into a wide 'O', but not a sound spilled from his lips. In a flash, Stella was across the room, positioning herself between the guard and the door.

"I don't think so."

"Wha…what hap…what are you?" he finally managed to stammer out."

"A monster," Stella replied, grasping the man by his thick neck.

There was a loud snap, and she disappeared once more into the night. There was no telling how many more monsters like Silas were out there. No telling how many secrets they kept. Stella would find them all. Stella had always been a seeker of truths, even frightening ones.

C.L. Cannon is a USA Today Bestselling Author, publisher, publicist, editor, designer, and lots of other occupations with the -er sound at the end! She is a woman of many talents who never gives up or stops improving. She enjoys writing about love and friendship. She loves it even more when she can add fantasy and science fiction aspects to those themes! She's a self-proclaimed Harry Potter freak (Slytherin Pride people), lover of anything Joss Whedon (Spuffy forever), Tolkien fiend (who enjoys second breakfast), and addict of classic literature (Social class struggles turn me on... literally ;) yah see what I did there?) She spends her days trying to #bookstagram (and probably failing), helping other authors grow and succeed (I love my job), and loving on her two babes (velociraptors), Seth and Petey.

You can find her basically everywhere on the net (man I just aged myself). Visit her website or join her street team for more content!

https://clcannon.net
https://facebook.com/groups/clcannon

f facebook.com/clcannonauthor

𝕏 twitter.com/clcannonauthor

⃝ instagram.com/cl_cannon

CURE THE ENEMY

BY D. FISHER

There is trouble brewing in Dirth, a brass city where the smog from factories drifts through the streets, and dreams belonging to wild dreamers rise to the bright wishing stars. This trouble is between two supernatural creatures, the vampires and the werewolves, who prowl unnoticed into the night. But they won't be unnoticed for long. Not if the war that threatens their peaceful days truly unfolds in the forest that surrounds the tall factories whose gears grind from dusk until dawn.

"Isobella, your deadline has passed," Romaine Silver mumbles behind her, disrupting her thoughts. The vampire coven leader has been lurking there, watching her work from the shadows of her crypt – her home. He hovered when she made the cure for vampires against sunlight, too, and it had annoyed her just the same.

The gears – both large and small – of all her inventions grind in the cluttered space, and the fire that fuels them heats to a stifling temperature. Isobella Baxter ignores him in favor of impenetrable concentration and swipes at the sweat beading on her temple. The gears she can block out, but his gravelly voice is rather difficult to disregard. How is she expected to work if she continues to be bothered?

The heel of his leather boot clicks against the stone floor as he invades her space. "Are you listening to me, love?" Placing a hand on her bare shoulder, right next to the hem of her leather vest, he squeezes her skin.

The gesture halts her fiddling with her instruments, and he turns her to face him. A concoction of chemicals bubbles in a flask, licking the side of the sloped glass while trying to free itself. Steam rises from the top, the scent of sweet roses and cold steel mixing with the crypt's stale air. Below, the flame strokes the flat glass bottom, cooking the contents to the exact temperature she needs to make the elixir she's been tasked with.

Romaine watches the steam rise from the lip of the beaker and into a brass tube that travels and winds to the smallest vial he's ever seen. Some might say it's a potion bottle, but Romaine doesn't like to indulge superstition even though he's a vampire himself. As the steam travels through the tube, it turns back into a liquid and slowly drips into the vial, blood, red in color. It's his favorite color.

Isobella leans over her unbalanced worktable, her tight-fitting vest constricting the air inside her lungs. She flicks a knob at the end of her contraption, and the tiny flame becomes smaller. "It's almost finished, Romaine," she whispers while bending to the vial. Her eyes sparkle with hope like a persistent northern star. She grips her fingers on the edge of the wooden table, pale knuckles turning a snowy white. Splinters dig into her palms.

She's spent hours on this formula, days of restless sleep dreaming of numbers and equations, chemicals, and possible reactions. The stone walls of her dimly lit crypt are lined with crisp vellum that's been accidentally burned around the edges. Her ideas scrawl across them. Most are rubbish ideas that she happened to scribble down on evenings where she had little sleep. Chemicals mar and blend the ink, though, but it matters not. She remembers every invention and elixir she's ever thought of with ingenious ease.

Romaine bends to peer with her, his eyes narrowing as he watches more drops drip from the brass tube. "You've said this before," he reminds her. His patience is thin. It always has been despite his immortality.

Sliding her hand into the discolored glove, she turns the smallest of gears on the right. The flames extinguish entirely, puffing out of existence.

"So you keep telling me." She lifts the vial, brings it to her nose, and takes a sniff. A ghost of a smile plays at the edges of her ruby red lips, tugging them upward and brightening her cheeks with palpable glee.

At first, this was a cure for herself, an attempted escape from coven life and what Romaine had made her. But somewhere along the way, as the rest of the vampires caught wind, it had become Romaine's obsession. If vampires can be cured – can become immortal – then so can the werewolves squatting in the factories of the city. Isobella wanted to live a normal life. She wanted to return to the humans as one of them, marry a handsome man, and grow a family. As a vampire, she'll have none of those things. Somewhere along the way, through her pathetic excuse for a life, she became a prisoner of sorts. A prisoner to the very thing she used to love: Chemistry.

"And each time, you haven't found the cure. This was your idea, remember?" Romaine stands fully erect, straightening his slick, black vest. He smells of oiled leather, an aroma Isobella has never liked. The brass buttons against his chest twitch as the fine fabric moves about, the large pocket-flaps rubbing against his white, long-sleeve shirt underneath.

"So distrustful," she growls, her emotions thin as she endures his half-truth. It may have been her idea, but it most certainly wasn't her idea to use the cure against the werewolf clans so that Romaine and the coven may take over Dirth. Remove a werewolf's immortality, and they're easy to kill.

Isobella never wanted this.

She watches him adjust his short-topped black hat to prevent him seeing the hate in her eyes. A brass band runs around the base of the hat, and it catches the dying sunlight's reflection for a split second as it seeps through the small window of the crypt. Her anger gets the better of her, however. Her fangs slide past her lips and poke the edge of her chin.

"Careful, Isobella," Romaine whispers. He folds his arms behind his back and quirks an eyebrow. "I understand you're a bit . . . touchy. We all are, but let's not do anything you'll regret. Save your rage for the werewolves. Help us take them down, and I will let you be mortal once more."

Isobella recognizes his subtle threat and internally recoils. *Ultimatums*, she grumbles into her mind. She's never done well with them, and she's not fool enough to ignore the way his words dance around a threat. He may be far older than she is, better adept at the monster he's become, but at times like this, she sees him for what he truly is even if her vampire siblings do not.

Holding the flask in trembling hands, Isobella glances away to the vellum on the walls. Her fangs retract, her unspoken words bitten off at the edge of her tongue.

Satisfied, Romaine continues, "If our coven is to defeat our rivals, we must remain composed. And you?" He pauses, glancing at the instruments sprawled across her worktable. "You must finish this 'cure' before a war breaks out, and the humans suffer for being in its path. Do you want that, my love? Is that what you wish for? For your precious humans to die?"

Isobella's fingers clench into fists at his threat. She glares at him and squares her jaw. "If you were so intent on ruling this city – a city you truthfully despise – then you should have been more selective over whom you chose to become enemies with."

Dirth hasn't always been plagued with vampires and werewolves. A hundred years ago, marked yesterday, Romaine had set foot in this city, intent on building a home – a future – by creating more of his ilk to rule humans and dip his hands into their purses of meager wealth. There had been something about the gears and the never-ending smoke that drew his interest. Or maybe it was because, at the time, he had thought Dirth was unclaimed territory.

Damon, the head of the werewolf clan, had been the first to

befriend him. Neither knew what the other truly was until Damon had stumbled across Romaine feeding from his sister's neck. Damon had begun to transform to defend his sister's corpse, but Romaine fled, shocked by this other superior species he had known nothing about. Since then, both leaders have been adding to their numbers in hopes of one day winning a war over the rights to the city.

Isobella has never met Damon, but she knows he and his were-wolves live on the other side of Dirth, somewhere around the leaning and smoking tower on the East end. It's an area no vampire dares go.

Romaine returns Isobella's glare, his body tensing. "It was not a choice. They are the scum of this city, and I plan to rid it of them."

"With war comes casualties. Some of your sons and daughters will die. Do you love them so little?"

"I love each of those I create," he responds through clenched teeth.

"And me? You call me *your love*. What am I truly to you, Romaine?"

His features soften at her words, and he takes a step closer to her, unfolding his arms to cup both of her warm cheeks. "You are my wolf, Ms. Baxter, in this world of unfortunate dreamers." Leaning forward, he touches his lips to hers, a dispassionate kiss. He releases her so soon that Isobella finds herself disappointed as his words ring false to her ears. Lying is one of the many talents of Romaine Silver.

Romaine releases her face and steps away, the click of his leather boots pulling at the taut silence. He clears his throat, uncomfortable with the lack of returned endearment from Isobella. Or perhaps, he now understands that Isobella is aware of his ruse.

Sighing, Isobella slides on a padded glove and picks up the small vial full of hot red liquid. She holds it up to her eye.

"Did it work this time?" he asks.

She returns it to the edge of the table. "I don't know. There's only one way to find out."

"Shall I leave and return with a test subject?"

Test subject? She hadn't realized there was one. Nodding once, she says, "Yes."

"Very well." He grins charmingly. "Wait here."

Rolling her eyes, she exhales loudly through her nose. As if she would – could – go anywhere. Romaine hadn't seen her expression, however. He had abruptly turned on his heels and marched toward the large wooden door. Isobella keeps her back to him as he opens it and slips out into the cool evening air like the predator he truly is.

She raises her gaze to her small window. Through the soot-covered pane, the sun dips over the horizon, bathing the rising smog in bloody orange. She can see the tops of the city's factories from here, too. They cast the sky's reflection along their brass chimneys.

She walks to the window and brushes her fingers along the soot. She was a lonely woman before this life – a life sustained by the blood of others. Before, when she knew nothing of vampires and were-wolves, she hadn't been content with her life as a meaningless and overlooked chemist. Her mother had died shortly after her birth, leaving her father alone to raise her. He was often not present because of his occupation. Her father had run the trains through the city, carrying scraps of metals, gold, and brass to each factory when he wasn't holding a bottle of scotch between his legs. She remembers the slurping sound he had made when he lifted the bottle to his lips and gulped greedily.

On the day her father had died, she had been walking home from the funeral. Romaine had found her in an alley – a short cut she normally took. He had bumped into her, dislodging the papers from her arms, and then charmingly helped her pick them back up. She thought him handsome at the time, and when he grinned at her, her heart had filled with glee from the attention of an attractive man. He turned her into a vampire that night – sunk his teeth into her neck, drained her blood, and fed her his own. She woke with an insatiable hunger, and her life has never been the same. Romaine had made her into a beast, feeding her sweet words of nothingness to fill her lonely heart and feasting on her insecurities to indulge his appetite for power.

Her vampire siblings are happy with their lives. She's the only one of them who isn't, and she's the only one who hasn't let bloodlust make them into a monster. It makes her wonder who truly is the monster –

the werewolves or the vampires. The werewolves live among the humans, protecting them from the vampires who prowl the streets for their next meal. She knows Damon isn't pure and innocent. She knows that during an evening with a full moon, he and his clan turn into terrible beasts, but she also knows that it's uncontrollable. Blood drips from his hands, too, but . . .

Darkness is cast into the crypt. Isobella picks up the box of matches on the window's sill. She opens it, plucks a single gnarled match from within, and strikes it to life. Then, she lights the wicks atop the candles along the wall. The flame licks the air, holding her attention as it consumes the wood of the match. It sways this way and that, the tip constantly changing shape, changing direction, as the breath leaving her nostrils moves it about.

She peers at the elixir that was only ever meant to be hers. She must find a way out of this.

The door bursts open, and Isobella startles by the elixir's table. Romaine strides in, his steps confident as he adjusts his white sleeves with a certain air of pride. He cocks the brim of his hat parallel to his sideways grin. "I have a good feeling about this, Isobella." Romaine never calls her *his love* in the presence of others.

Entering behind him, two of her vampire brothers carry another man held up in the crook of their elbows. They follow Romaine across the crypt, and the bruised and beaten captive struggles in their grip. The captive is a werewolf, and his white shirt and leather pants are stained by his own blood. They roughly place him in the metal chair that's bolted to the floor.

"Is this one of Damon's?" Isobella asks as Romaine comes to stand beside her. She places her hands on the wooden table, making the flasks atop it rattle against one another as she steadies her weight and calms her shaking knees. She hadn't realized they were going to injure the man she was going to cure.

"Yes," he answers with glee, rocking on the toes of his polished leather boots. "We found him a few days ago, spying on the coven home. One might think it fate."

"I see," she whispers, crossing her arms. Discomfort pricks at her every nerve. She hadn't heard they had caught anybody. She had ignorantly assumed he had a willing subject.

Romaine grabs the heavy chains from underneath the worktable, and the back of his vest glints in the candlelight as he bends.

"How are you going to get him to transform?" Isobella asks reluctantly. "It's not a full moon." One of the brothers helps Romaine drag the heavy chains across the floor while the other holds the werewolf down. Together, they wrap it around the struggling man's middle. A lock clicks, sealing the chain and the werewolf's fate.

"Do you still have it?" Romaine asks, standing upright and brushing off his stomach.

Blinking, she reluctantly nods. She should have never told him about any of her experiments. Heading over to the cupboard on the far wall, she closes her eyes and strokes the corroded iron double doors. Grasping the handle, she yanks it open. The hinges squeal. She reaches for the vial with regretful, trembling fingers and heads back to Romaine's side, placing it in his hands.

"Open his mouth," Romaine orders her brothers.

They oblige, forcing the man's jaw open. He struggles, his lips parting before their grip becomes too much, and a scream leaves his mouth. Romaine pours the clear contents inside while Isobella backs away, her rump bumping the table and rattling her equipment again.

As soon as the liquid lathers the werewolf's tongue, they close his mouth and pinch his nose, forcing him to swallow. They release him and not a moment too soon. The werewolf slumps forward, grunts, and groans. His limbs elongate, his jaw unhinging, and his canines poke through his upper lip. He squeezes his eyes closed as the pain convulses his body. His chest expands, and soon, dark hair pokes through every pore along his skin.

Fully transformed into a large wolf who walks on two legs, the werewolf opens his eyes, and yellow irises meet Isobella's frightened gaze.

Her breath quivers. She's never tested that particular elixir, nor has she ever seen a werewolf in person. Feeling vulnerable and unprotected, she swallows thickly, her lips bunching into a tight rosebud as she stares.

"The cure," Romaine demands, holding out his hand.

Tearing her eyes away from the beast, she walks back to the table and grasps the small vial of red liquid. Abruptly, the werewolf howls and all the vampires cover their ears against the loud sound that vibrates against the confines of the crypt.

"Now, Isobella!" Romaine yells, his voice barely heard above the ruckus.

Isobella shuffles her feet, stepping as close to the beast as she dares before reaching out and placing the flask in Romaine's waiting hand. He doesn't waste time.

Her brothers grab the fur at the top of the werewolf's head. The werewolf snaps his jaw and struggles against his chains. Romaine rushes forward, tips the vial, and pours the liquid into the beast's chomping jaws. Her brothers release him, and together, they watch as the werewolf takes on a curious and confused expression. His body begins to vibrate, and his fur ripples. Soon, fur covers the floor, and his canines detach and tumble to the stone. His yellow irises turn red as they fill with blood, and more blood dribbles from his mouth as his bones reset.

"We're killing him!" Isobella yells, rushing forward.

Romaine holds out an arm, stopping her from aiding the beast. "Wait!"

Within a few blinks, the werewolf's skin returns to the pale white it had been when he entered, and his heavy, labored breathing quiets. Sweat covers the man's skin, and he curls his shoulders and head forward, exhausted. Blood still fills his eyes, however, and as he raises them to Romaine, a chill creeps over Isobella's skin.

"What did you do?" the captive croaks.

Romaine is silent, his facial muscles set in an awed gape. "You're human," he says, sniffing the air for confirmation.

"He's human," she echoes in a whisper.

Turning to Isobella, Romaine grins wide and bright and then grips the collar of her vest. "You did it!"

"I –" She clamps her mouth shut and silently seethes.

"You're all fools," the captive says in place of what he assumes is Isobella's excited speechlessness. Romaine turns back to him, and the man's voice becomes steel, commanding the room's attention. "You, Mr. Silver, have your coven of leeches fooled. You're a monster – a creature who has to feed on the life of others to survive. You rule with lies and trickery and manipulation. But we know differently. The werewolves know differently. We know who you really are."

Romaine invades the man's space. "That's enough out of you." He glances at Isobella's brothers. "Kill him."

"What?" Isobella squeals. "Kill him? But he's human now. He's no longer a threat. We can keep him here until –"

"No," Romaine interrupts without looking at her. "He's aware of the werewolf cure, Isobella. He knows who created it, and he knows where it's made." He nods to one of her brothers. "Do it."

Isobella glances over her shoulder nervously while attempting to lose herself within the crowd on the busy streets of Dirth. With each step, the small metal box clutched to her breasts rattles the vials within.

Crowds of people mill about on the sidewalks, hand-in-hand or side by side, unaware they're assisting Isobella as she tries to blend in. It's hard to blend in, though. She can hear their blood thump through their veins, and her stomach growls loudly because of it.

To distract herself, she studies the back of the many dresses that flap in the wind. Machines with metal legs like spiders, gears rotating each step forward, share the dirt road with horses and carriages. Some carriages aren't pulled by horses. These particular carriages puff great clouds of black smoke as the fire in their engines rotate the iron wheels to carry them onward.

Isobella wildly searches the faces of many as she weaves in and out of a crowd of men smoking pipes outside of a factory. Last night was the last night she'll ever endure being Romaine's puppet. He had gone too far with killing that man. She had the realization that once the werewolf clan is cured and dead, she would certainly be next. The mortality Romaine had promised will be swiftly followed by her death. So, she had spent the rest of the evening secretly making more cures, destroyed everything inside the crypt, and then fled at first light.

She rounds a corner, walking through the smog of the crooked East factory. Keeping her strides purposeful even as the crowd thins, she continues to her destination. Isobella plans to turn the tables on the monster who created her, and this thought alone is what keeps her moving forward.

Soon, she reaches an area where there isn't a single person in sight. The skin along the back of her neck raises as gooseflesh peppers her skin to the abrupt change in atmosphere, her hunger completely forgotten. She slows her pace when she feels eyes watching her every move. Before she can pass an alley, a man steps in front of her, blocking her path with his broad stance. She halts as he crosses his meaty arms.

"Excuse me," she whispers, side-stepping in an attempt to pass him. He grabs her arm, and the air stirs. She gets the full whiff of his scent, and if she had a beating heart, it would have skipped a beat. *He's a werewolf.*

Isobella looks at his hairy fingers curled around her upper arm, then raises her gaze to his. "Damon's clan?"

His grip tightens as he inhales. She yanks her arm from his grasp, causing her metal box to clink.

"You're a vampire," he growls.

"I am. But I have business with Damon."

His eyes zoom to her chest, where the box is clutched. "What's in there?"

Isobella straightens her shoulders. "Like I said, I have business with Damon. I'm not here to cause trouble. I'm here to fix your problem and my own."

Ticking his jaw, he eyes the box once more. Then, he studies her expression in an attempt to search for the truth.

"I swear it," she adds, her voice as strong as the buildings around her.

He releases a breath and rubs the back of his neck. "Follow me." Turning on his heel, his long coat whips to the side as he marches back inside the dark alley.

Isobella follows him, side-stepping chunks of metal and gears that litter the dirt path. Curiosity piques her interest – she isn't privy to exactly *where* Damon's clan lives by the crooked East factory. And she certainly hadn't realized that it was *in* the factory itself.

Her chauffeur turns a sharp right, grasping the knob of a metal door that Isobella hadn't noticed. He twists his wrist and pushes the door open. Once he's inside, he gestures for her to enter. She gulps as she follows him into the depths of the factory.

"This is where you guys live?" she asks, eyeing the end of the hallway he leads her through. Along the way, she doesn't fail to notice that there are no other doors and no other exits or entrances.

The werewolf doesn't answer. The heels of her boots clicking against the floor fills the silence, and soon, the hallway opens ahead. When they step through, Isobella hesitates.

Dozens of eyes turn to her – eyes that belong to many werewolves seated on broken couches and chairs. They don't seem surprised by her appearance, and Isobella wonders if they knew she was headed this way since she stepped into the city.

Isobella tries to look past their stares and studies the rest of the room's furnishings. There's a steel bar with glittering bottles of liquor tucked in a corner, and low hanging pipes drip water to the ground, creating various puddles. Smog covers the ceiling, filling the room with the smell of burning coal.

Before she's finished with her perusal, her werewolf escort leads her through the room. She tries to remain confident in a crowd who could easily kill her. Indeed, this could go very wrong, and she breathes a sigh of relief when they enter another hallway where the stares no longer prick the back of her neck.

They don't travel far. The werewolf stops in front of a large and metal sliding door and taps his knuckles against it. Without waiting for an answer, he slides the door to the side. Light spills into the dark hallway.

"In here," he mumbles, moving aside for her to enter.

Isobella tentatively steps inside, and the door slides closed behind her. Her stomach churns as she blinks at the many candles lit within the room. Books line each wall, shelves of them adorning multi-colored spines in a variety of sizes. Two couches, patterned red and orange, are situated on a western rug. Gears are finely stitched into this rug, and she notes the beauty of the craftsmanship that must have gone into it. The two couches face each other in the middle of the room, and a large flat-topped chest is placed between them. The chest is leather, bordered with leather straps and gears that have no purpose other than décor.

She raises her gaze to peer at the far end of what she can only assume is an office. There, a large floral-etched oak desk takes up the space, and behind it, a man sits.

Startled and ashamed for not having seen him until now, Isobella clears her throat. "Hello."

The man leans and props his elbows on his desk, steepling his fingers as he studies her. Isobella wishes she could see his eyes, but his wide-brimmed hat shadows most of his face.

"My name is –"

"I know who you are," the man – Damon, she assumes – murmurs. "Everyone knows who you are. Or, I suppose, what you are." His voice is low and deep, and a scar runs the length of his jaw. Blond hair sticks out from under the hat in a boyish sort of way.

"You do?" Isobella asks suspiciously. "How?"

He bobs his shoulders in a lazy shrug. "Spies. You're the one who is always in the crypt, working on concoctions."

Isobella inclines her head. "I am. My name is Isobella Baxter."

He leans back in his chair and taps his fingers against his desk. "What I'd really like to know is what a vampire from the Silver coven wants with me."

Could this man really be so cold? Perhaps it's because, until this very moment, vampires have always been his enemy. She fidgets with the box in her hand and steps onto the rug. "May I sit?" she asks, pointing to one of the couches.

Damon inclines his head, his chin dipping toward the collar of his jacket. When she's comfortably seated on the firm cushions, she sets the box on top of her lap and angles her body to face his. "As you assumed, I am a chemist. I was trying to come up with a cure for myself to become human again, but Romaine twisted my success into something else."

"Shocking," he comments sarcastically. "And you don't approve?"

"No." She shakes her head. "I was given an ultimatum because of it."

A grin spreads across Damon's lips. "And that ultimatum led you to me."

"It did."

"Smart woman." Standing from his chair, he makes his way around his desk to the couch opposite hers and sits. "What is Romaine Silver up to? And what does it have to do with you and that box, and why should I trust anything you say?"

"Damon," she begins, tucking a stray hair behind her ear. "I never wanted to be a vampire, and I've despised every day that I've been one. My only purpose here is to rid the city of monsters." Damon waves a hand in the air, a gesture for her to answer his other questions. She blows out a breath and opens the box.

"Vials?" Damon asks, raising an eyebrow.

"Cures," she whispers, tentatively correcting him. "For werewolves and vampires. I had created it for myself, but Romaine had used it against one of your own and . . ."

Sorrow firms the corner of Damon's lips. He leans away and scrubs at his jaw. "Augustus. He's been missing for days. I assume he's been cured, but now he's dead?"

"Yes." She glances away, ashamed of having had a part in it. "I'm sorry. I didn't – this wasn't – Like I said, this cure was meant for me and no one else. But now, he's going to use it against all of the werewolves, and I didn't know what else to do. You have to believe me. I'm not here for nefarious reasons."

He holds up a hand. "I believe you. You don't have to explain." The cushions of his couch squeak as he settles back into them. "What do you want from me, Ms. Baxter?"

Wetting her bottom lip, she picks up the box and holds it out to him. "I want you to use them. Not for you or for me but against the Silver coven. But when it's over, I do want to be human again."

He slowly takes the box from her. "You do know what you're asking, right? By giving this to me, you're sealing the fates of your brothers and sisters. There is no going back."

"I know," she whispers meekly, twisting her fingers in her lap.

Weighing the box in his palm, he asks, "And how do you propose we 'cure' your coven?"

"Tomorrow," she answers with more confidence than she feels. "It's a full moon." His grin widens as she spends the next half hour explaining how they'll accomplish the task without losing anyone's life. She may be turning her back on the Silver coven, but she doesn't want anyone dead.

The injected sheep bleat as they leave the motor-powered carriage, skittering away from its smoke and loud engine as soon as their tiny hooves are on solid ground. Dusk has approached, and a full moon rises high into the sky while the unmanned machine chugs back the way it came.

"All the sheep are injected?" Isobella asks from the tree trunk she seeks shelter behind. Their fur is slathered in blood, a lure to any vampire for miles.

Damon is standing to her left, watching the bloody sheep nibble the grass in the field surrounded by a dying forest. "I made sure of it," he mumbles, swiveling his head to survey the quieting atmosphere. It's almost as if, after years of living under a loud factory, he hadn't realized the world could be so tranquil.

After Isobella had made her proposal for curing the vampires, Damon had taken one of the vials for himself. Like her, he hadn't wanted the life he'd been given. He had swallowed the cure before she could stop him, and it was then she learned he didn't need to be in his beast's form to be rid of his full moon curse.

Feeling some sort of obligation toward the man, she had stayed by his side as the elixir worked its magic and then stood by his side when he spoke to the clan. There wasn't a single one of them who wanted to remain as a werewolf. It had touched Isobella that she wasn't the only one in the city sick and tired of being a predator – of being a wolf to a bloody flock.

She took the cure with the other werewolves, and now, the thrill of humanity once again courses through her human veins.

Everyone is tucked and waiting in the forest for the vampires. This is the clearing the coven normally takes when they're on the way to feed in the city. She prays that the vampires won't catch their scents instead because they'll have no way to stop them from feeding from their own necks.

"It's almost time," she whispers while gazing at the moon. The vampires are punctual creatures.

"I never thought I'd see the full moon with human eyes again. I never thought –" His gaze meets hers, and there's a certain sort of rare peace within them. "Thank you, Isobella."

Never in her life had she been thanked for anything, and deep down, her racing heart calms, knowing she made the right choice in curing her true enemy.

She grins back at him just as a twig snaps. Damon whips his head to the sound and points into the trees across the way.

Through the darkness, the pale skin of the vampires blur into view as they race into the clearing. Their fangs are elongated, and Isobella can practically feel the echo of their insatiable hunger. She hugs herself to the tree as the coven attacks the sheep while Damon watches on with a clenched jaw. She blocks out the sounds by covering her ears and squeezing her eyes shut.

Seconds pass. Minutes? Someone touches her arm, and she flinches into awareness. Damon's eyes peer down into hers. "It's done," he whispers, his tone full of hope. He points into the clearing, and there, among the massacre of sheep, are groaning humans.

"It worked," she whispers, peeling herself away from the tree. The humans – those whom she used to call brothers and sisters, begin to pry themselves from the ground. She notes Romaine among them, and he locks eyes with her, her name whispered angrily on his lips.

She leans toward Damon. "Now what?"

"Now. . ." Damon squeezes her shoulder. "Now, we live again."

Bestselling and award-winning author D. Fischer is a mother of two very busy boys, a wife to a wonderful husband, and an owner of two sock-loving German Shorthair Pointers. They also have a cat named Geralt, but since Geralt adopted them and not the other way around, the cat is more of a tenant who occasionally purr-purrs for his rent, if he's not too busy murdering nerf darts. Together, they live in Orange City, Iowa. When D. Fischer isn't chasing after her children, she enjoys freeing her creativity through worlds that don't exist, no matter how much we wish they did.

We hope you have enjoyed Cure the Enemy.
Want to binge read? D. Fischer's novels connect to one another. For their series' order, visit dfischerauthor.com.

Take a moment and follow D. Fischer on social media or Email. If you'd like to connect more exclusively, join her Facebook group, D. Fischer Reader's Group.

f facebook.com/dfischerauthor

🐦 twitter.com/DFischerAuthor

📷 instagram.com/dfischerauthor

THIRST FOR VENGENCE

BY L.B. CARTER

*Old Welsh lore tells of the **Gwrach y Rhibyn**, "the Hag of the Mist."*

*Often conflated with stories of the **Gwyllion**, one of the five subsets of **Tylwyth Teg** ("fae folk"), and the **Cyhyraeth**, something of a Celtic banshee, she is a mystical spirit and vampire in one. This terrifying creature is generally seen near forest streams or ponds, lamenting the loss of her husband and/or child, and subsists, in some versions of the myth, on the blood of sleeping children. For those who hear her cries, death follows.*

Chapter One

Landing gently on the roof, *Gwrach y Rhibyn* folded her membranous leather wings, which spanned nearly the entire width of the quaint bungalow. She tucked a greasy strand of thin black hair behind a hunched shoulder with gnarled claws and let out a low, keening moan toward the moon.

She could scent the child on the faint breeze passing through the valleys. It wasn't as delectable as the sharp tang of blood sliding luxuriously down her throat, but the musk of human was like an appetizer, taunting her with the succulent nectar that was to come. Fresh saliva pooled in her mouth and dripped unheeded down pointed, slender, onyx fangs.

"Too long," she rasped to herself. "Too long. So thirsty."

Weak, the being that some humans called a vampire stumbled toward the edge of the roof above the child's bedroom from memory. Her bare-footed steps were louder than usual on the clay tiles. The house frame creaked beneath her slight weight, belying its age. Likely, it was younger than the terrifying creature of the night crawling toward the corner above the child's bedroom. She'd waited too long between feedings.

The child would sleep soundly, undisturbed by the bumps in the night; a deep sleeper, the human never once awoke during the vampire's visits. The child had a unique flavor that *Gwrach y Rhibyn* could not resist. Her favorite source had dominated her thoughts that night when the hag finally succumbed to her thirst.

Dragging her emaciated body from a starved stupor, she'd emerged from her hidden river cove high in the Welsh forests ready to hunt for blood. It was almost less safe to have waited because now her attention was scattered and blurry from deficiency. She would not notice if anyone snuck up on her, so focused was she on her own target.

Twitching a glance over her shoulder, the vampire scanned the dark of the residential street in the sparsely populated town up. Only the trees moved, swaying slightly in the wind. Moonlight played on the shadowed leaves as they danced, generating a shushing sound like rushing water.

Her stomach clenched painfully, long past the point of growling, and *Gwrach y Rhibyn* dug her claws into her midsection until warm blood flowed dark over pale, nearly translucent skin. The aroma, less sweet than that of any child or even adult human, snaked into flared nostrils. Her lust for blood went berserk, escalating her desire into an uncontrollable craze.

Grimacing, she urgently dropped to a crouch, wrapping her nails instead around the lip of the roof, feet spanning the apex. Sliding onto her stomach, *Gwrach y Rhibyn* snapped her wings out again, letting the sharp talon at the curve of each black appendage hook between roofing tiles, then she slid over the edge. Lowering her upper body, her hair dripped like black wax ahead of her descent. Her own blood rushed to her head, dizzying her for a moment. After a few breaths that incentivized her further with the lure of the child, she stretched her wings until her view lowered past the top frame of the window.

The hag's ragged breath caught as she took in the lump curled in the bed. So small. So innocent. So delectable. She could almost taste the lifeblood already, warm and heady. Another hunger pang stabbed through her belly, and a wanton moan slipped from her thin lips.

The child tossed and turned.

The monster in the window watched and waited until her prey was still for several minutes before stretching out her narrow arms and pulling up the window. She knew just when to pause and ease it over a particularly creaky segment. When it was no wider than a foot, she slithered inside, her wings tucking tight to her skeletal body to fit through the narrow opening.

Bent low, *Gwrach y Rhibyn* felt a gust of wind skim across the top of her hair, fresh air flicking around the otherwise stale scene. Keeping to the shadows, she circumvented the spotlight of the moonbeam. The lock clicked in the bedroom door with a quick turn of her wrist. Then the hag crept toward the bed. Her crooked back slid up the wall beside the bed as she rose, her gaze on his peaceful form. A different ache burned her core.

Age-old grief gripped her heart. Her baby. Her child. Ripped from her. "Too early, too early," she whispered. A shaking hand stretched out, barely visible in the gloom, and her palm gently brushed the child's rosy cheek, plump and warm beneath her fingers. *Gwrach y Rhibyn*'s breath skittered out in a rush.

The child stirred again.

Bending low over the child's chubby form, she inhaled talcum powder and lavender soap. A drip of saliva plopped on the blanket tucked up under the child's chin. *Gwrach y Rhibyn* pulled it down to expose the girl's neck and fixated on the pulsing artery. There was no evidence there of past visits, the punctures long since healed.

"Too long," she murmured.

A frown marred the child's face, and *Gwrach y Rhibyn* paused until the girl settled once more. Then, she dipped and opened her jaws wide, the full row of thin black teeth poised over the rosy skin.

Quickly, she pierced the flesh, and the divine taste flooded her mouth, cascading down her parched throat. She moaned again, sucking hard, gulping back thick swallows of rich blood. The child had fully revived after her last encounter with the hag.

A tap on the window snapped *Gwrach y Rhibyn*'s awareness away from her meal.

Whipping her head around, huddled over the girl protectively, teeth displayed in threat, the vampire stared at a pair of large green eyes, sharp white teeth, and gleaming silver hair. The hag inhaled hard in a hiss that expressed annoyance, and the scent that filtered through the open window confirmed the identity of the voyeur. *Gwrach y Rhibyn* snarled softly.

"*Tylwyth Teg*," she growled. Another fae. The appearance told her this was an elf. Here. Trying to take her source.

She knew what those fae did in the human realm, those thieves. Many times, *Gwrach y Rhibyn* had returned to a source to find that the child had been replaced with a changeling. Stolen. The fae had taken her husband and her child from her, and in so doing, they had turned her into what she was, a broken wraith instead of a mother and a wife. She had been human once… in another life.

And the *Ellyllon* had realized their mistake. The elves had created all of the *Gwyllion* spirits by taking and destroying, and then tried to exterminate the beings borne from their selfish annihilation, *Cyhyraeth* included. Survivors had fled Underhill, forced to hide from both fae and human, belonging to neither.

Now, this elf wanted to wrench her source from her? This child? *No.* They had taken enough. This elf would die before the hag let her take this child. It wasn't simply an intention. It was an inevitability, a truth. Because as soon as the thought congealed in *Gwrach y Rhibyn*'s mind, a scream expelled from her throat, foretelling the elf's end.

The *Ellyllon* had already infiltrated the precious space, unwelcome, intruding in the child's domain, so *Gwrach y Rhibyn*'s deafening pitch caused the fae to pause for a split-second in a wince as she withdrew the wooden stake at her hip. The space was too confined to allow her to draw the bow off her shoulders.

In that moment of hesitation, the vampire's claws slashed first one way, then the other, across the elf's chest, leaving several crisscrossing streaks of mauve and backing their fight away from the child.

The elf sucked a breath in through her teeth but withheld further noise.

Unfortunately, the sanguineous color and the spicy fragrance distracted *Gwrach y Rhibyn*, her dire thirst unquenched due to the interruption to her feeding. Involuntarily, driven blindly by her thirst, she dipped her head, spiked tongue flicking out to lick the enticing droplets trickling down the elf's leather clothing most enticingly.

Gwrach y Rhibyn cried out as a stake pierced her side, wrenching away and flicking her hand out in retaliation.

"Bran? Branwyn! What's wrong?" The frantic voices of the child's parents accompanied a sudden banging on the door. The first scream had woken them. The second brought them running to their baby. The door rattled in its frame as they attempted to open it, the lock clanging within the mechanism in the doorjamb. "Bran, open the door! Is it a nightmare?"

The child herself cowered in the corner of the bed, sobbing and shivering.

None of them need worry. The child would be safe. The vampire who frequented their home would ensure it. A few drinks of the child's special blood sang in the hag's arteries, strengthening her like she hadn't been in months. A cruel grin pulled at the wraith's cracked lips, causing the frail skin to split. She lapped up the seepage of blood.

A second hit to the *Ellyllon*'s face sent her to the floor in a satisfy-ingly boneless heap. Slow to roll over and get to her feet, the elf remained slumped. The hag raised a hand to slash fragile gossamer wings and stopped.

No wings.

The *Ellyllon* appeared old enough that she should have developed them. The elf must be defective; she had no means of quick escape from the window. If she jumped, she wouldn't survive the fall. The vampire grinned with delight. This fight would be hers.

"Death comes," the being some called a banshee predicted.

This way was preferable. Dropping on her victim like a suffocating blanket, *Gwrach y Rhibyn* hovered above the fae, who rolled her head in a daze and blinked one unfocused eye, the other covered in blood and swollen shut. The vampire's claws bit into the elf's shoulders, and a finger dipped to swipe up a smear of missed blood. She lifted the finger and dipped the tip into her mouth. The taste exploded across all her senses.

Lured by the tease of one droplet, the vampire dipped her head and pulled. Sucking the life of the fae was like a hit of the most potent and fulfilling source. It was tantalizing. Never before had the hag had the chance to consume the power of a fellow *Tylwyth Teg*. The elf tasted a bit like Underhill, like its magic, earthy and vibrant. Absorbing it greedily, she shook and shuddered, the surge enthralling and over-whelming. The sound of the child's parents' desperation vanished from her awareness, and the groans of her victim as she neared death became white noise.

Something heavy thumped into *Gwrach y Rhibyn* from the direction of the window, knocking her off her victim and halting the transfer. The hag felt bereft. She snarled, spinning on her knees to face the new threat.

A great dragon swelled in the space. A *Ddraig*? They persisted? She should not be surprised; the *Cyhyraeth* were also thought to have been hunted into extinction.

The child was distraught now, and her parents sobbed. Sirens sounded through the gap the wraith had opened in the window.

How had the dragon come in through such a small entry?

As she watched, *Gwrach y Rhibyn* got her answer: the dragon shrank, scales smoothed into grey skin, hair sprouted, horns turned into pointed ears that stuck out from a round face, wings became short arms, and rear legs retracted until they were as stout as a child's but thick as stumps. The goblin protected the incapacitated *Ellyllon*, displaying the sharp teeth all fae bore. Another *Tylwyth Teg*. One that shouldn't be working with the elf.

The *Pwca* rarely involved themselves with the affairs of the fae court, which was run by the *Ellyllon*... before the goblins that humans sometimes called will-o-the-wisps betrayed all other fae to the powerful elves.

"*Pwca*," the vampire spat.

They faced off. The wraith was energized, despite the loss of the elf's full power. The child's blood had brought her back from the brink, exhumed her from weakness, and the small drink of elf blood was doubly potent. Their combined provisions zipped like lightning bugs through the hag's emaciated muscles, and she flexed her claws and stretched her lips wider to expose more teeth.

The *Pwca* did the same, his teeth wider, more designed for sawing through bone and ripping apart tendons and muscle rather than puncturing flesh. He had no other obvious weapon, but his ability to shift into any creature was an advantage. *Why hadn't he taken her on as a dragon?* He might have won the fight that way. When he shifted slightly, the hag realized the goblin was afraid of his partner becoming collateral damage.

That would be his weakness. "Death comes," she told the traitor.

Without warning, the door behind *Gwrach y Rhibyn* crashed open before she could pounce. She peered over her shoulder, turning her head unnaturally far around. The human bobbies in the doorway blinked in astonishment, and in that pause, the vampire spread her wings. She turned to the window, which was now shattered.

While she'd been distracted, the *Pwca* had removed the elf by taking a dragon's form once more.

The vampire bid a silent farewell to her source. Another child lost.

Infuriated, the Hag of the Mist ran for the window and, flattening her wings against her body, dove out into the night, flapping once and flying high over the trees, leaving the humans to gape after her.

Whether it was their imagination — a vivid nightmare superimposed on a normal human burglar — or if they believed in the supernatural, the myths would be perpetuated. Either way, humans would continue to fear the fair folk.

So they should.

If it was the last thing she did, the first and the last of the spirits, the hags, the vampires, the banshees, *Gwrach y Rhibyn* would win this battle with the oppressive fae. The Underhill War was not yet over; the centuries-long ceasefire was now defunct.

Chapter Two

I was tempted to crumple the letter. The moment my fingers curled, however, it fizzled out of existence, raining sparkles that zapped my skin gently. The summons was gone before I could tip it closer to the faint glow emanating from the window to glean a few more words.

I couldn't have taken it to Jac to ascertain the reason I might be compelled to court anyway as the parchment bore my full name. Dread cramped my stomach upon seeing my true name for the second time in my life.

"*Madalch,*" I swore under my breath.

A whimper came from the other side of the window in response.

I pulled myself up by my fingers, hanging on the bending flower box, to peer through the pane. Long distances were worse, so I barely discerned the shivering outline of a small form curled on a bed. The child's features would be indistinguishable, but I suspected, given its gradual curves, that it was huddled beneath a blanket.

I snorted, fogging the glass for a moment. One hand lifted free to wipe the condensation away with my glove. Then I tapped the glass with a nail. "A fabric covering could not stop me if I wanted you, human. Fortunately for you, I have other requests from my superiors."

The word 'superior' was vile, almost as much as 'Uncle.' I knew he felt the same. He'd rather we weren't related.

I dared not think that, barring that connection, he might have wished the *Cyhyraeth* had succeeded in draining my blood and taking my life. Instead, I had survived and become more of a blight to his lineage. I considered that he was hoping one of these humans might be a worthy heir. I certainly wasn't suitable to inherit his role.

Small fingers, chubby enough to allow me to distinguish their appearance, wrapped around the edge of the blanket, lifting it just enough to expose a pair of wide, terrified eyes.

I grinned widely, wiggling my pointed ears to draw the little boy's notice. As if by intention, the wind picked up, tossing my silver-white hair around my head. The moon glinted off the strands. If my glamour had developed, I would have adopted a more fearsome demeanor than my natural appearance. Being a late bloomer — a very late bloomer — I had to settle for the otherworldly and unexpected features that caused fear. Nevertheless, the preternatural mixture of teeth, nails, ears, and coloring was sufficient.

The child screamed as he vanished beneath the covers again, too terrified to flee the room and find sanctity with his parents, not that they could defend themselves against me. But we tried to remain folk-lore. Given the child's paralyzing fear, the full taking would have been easy.

I paused, debating completing the mission. I could simply scoop him up and head back to Underhill with our target. But the summons tugged in my navel. My nail tapped the window again, this time, wistfully. "You're safe, little one. For now."

"Elly!"

The hissed whisper caused me to whip around, drop into a crouch, and bare my teeth in a snarl. "Jac," I admonished as I saw the squat outline emerge from the trees. The twinkling glow above one upon palm ensured it was my partner and friend. "Extinguish your light." My tone was more brusque than usual, a combination of the surprise, breach in plan … and the lingering worry about the cause for the summons.

His lure dissipated with more of a fade than the summons' sizzle. "Take too long," he grumbled by way of explanation for his unwelcome presence. "May something happened to Elly."

My scowl deepened. "I'm fine. I got a summons. We need to go back." Glancing over my shoulder at the target, I said, "We'll return another time." Contrary to Jac's assumption, this one was guaranteed to be conflict-free. It was a simple human. There was nothing hidden at this residence to threaten my life.

"No take?" Jac confirmed.

I shook my head and began pacing away. Jac jogged to keep up in the grass. "Not tonight. Uncle requests my presence."

As soon as we disappeared into the dark cover of the glen, Jac shifted into a steer and bent a front knee low.

My gloves creaked as my fists clenched. I was on edge tonight. It wasn't my first acquisition after the accident. However, it was another chance to prove I was fine, that I could still track.

No one besides Jac knew about the damage that the *Cyhyraeth's* pull had done. My prayers that my glamour would manifest and heal me were innumerable — nearly a constant litany in the back of my mind. The arrival of my ability to wield my own magic would also unveil my wings and enable me to transport myself, rather than relying on the *Pwca's* shapeshifting.

With self-disgust, I mounted Jac and tried not to grip his antlers with too much loathing. He was trying to be of assistance, not rub salt in my wounds. Jac reared, nearly dismounting me from his back, and took off in a full gallop, leaping wildly over logs and darting around the trees with a whimsical skip in his step.

My frown quickly morphed into a free laugh as he'd intended his antics to do. When he twisted his long neck to look at me over his shoulder, I smiled. "Not bad, but I still think one of these days you should try shifting into a *Ddraig*." Riding a dragon through the skies would be even better than flying myself.

His visible eye rolled, head returning to focus on our path through the brush. We began to climb a slope, and I leaned forward to keep seated.

"I know what you wish you could say," I commented in his ear. "But, I'm only half-goblin." With the looks of my elf half, to Mum's relief. Mum blamed her decision to try mating with a will-o-the-wisp for tempering my ascension to full capabilities, neither *Pwca* nor *Ellyllon* magical abilities.

Therein lay the primary insult to my uncle. My only uncle, he was not; a mysterious member of Jac's family also held that privilege. I was impure — a great shame for the Keeper of Names, the most honorable and powerful role in the fae's ruling court.

Jac skidded to a stop, quickly dropping his forelegs to his knees. I tumbled over the top, my outfit catching on his antlers as I rolled into a heap against a tree trunk.

I flipped my hair aside and narrowed my eyes on him, rolling to my hands and knees. "Rude."

He seamlessly morphed back into his regular form, a grin stretching his wide lips. "Funny," he objected, then his wide lips pulled down. He pointed behind me. "Saw something."

I looked, but nothing was visible in the little clearing, illuminated by moonlight. No other *Tylwyth Teg* should be using that gate tonight; the monitoring system ensured no two groups hunted in the same area to avoid raising suspicion amongst the humans. I tapped the point of one of Jac's ears with a questioning expression.

He held my gaze for a moment as he listened then shook his head.

"Me neither. Probably an animal," I suggested, heading toward the portal. "And for bucking me off, I'll leave you out here to get eaten by it."

Jac laughed, waddling quickly to catch up to me. We both knew any animal would become his dinner, not vice versa. "Rude," he parroted.

I rolled my eyes and focused on the fairy ring. I could not retort as the task required clear and precise thoughts.

Once Underhill received my formal request to enter and recognized my essence, we stepped into the circle of toadstools, entering our realm. Jac followed behind me.

Lesser fae could enter and exit Underhill, but their passing was logged and required approval. With me, Jac could come and go freely; it was part of why he'd joined the Acquisitions Team. What we acquired was of no advantage to his people.

Unlike my partner, I'd been drafted, a punishment for what I am — a way for my uncle to manage my every move as well as portray me in a positive light. This was my redemption amongst our people, proof that I was loyal to the courts and disavowed my *Pwca* nature. That first summons to join the Acquisitions Team had been a way to ensure he appeared benevolent, merciful, and powerful, to remind the *Ellyllon* to revere him.

Since then, I'd embarrassed him with my run-in with that *Cyhyraeth*.

We walked straight toward the courts; if I detoured or dallied, Uncle would know, and I would feel pain for resisting the summons. I bit my lip as we neared town.

What would this summons bring?

Plentyn Aestylaneru o Ellyllon a Pwca yn nheulu'r Tylwyth Teg fewn Dany-bryn. My full name resonated in my mind, the Welsh lilts turned austere.

I withheld any reaction to the compulsive control that felt like a hook in my mind and a tingling in my limbs. Theoretically, one *could* resist the power of a name — but it would result in debilitating pain that would lead to death, whether self-induced to end the torture or due to a long-suffering fading as the will drained one's strength.

I leveled my chin and kept my gaze direct, though I could make out little more than the Namekeeper's silhouette, shadowed in the elevated recesses at the front of the courtroom. My uncle was not alone.

Focusing on the queen, however respectful it may seem to provide the reigning head my undue attention, was forbidden. But my periphery was slightly better than my ability to see those directly in my line of sight, and I was certain she was napping. It was possible she considered this audience unworthy of her consciousness. Or perhaps she knew nothing of Uncle's summons. No one knew how much direction she deigned to have over the court's decisions.

Some suspected she appointed the court to lead the fae and the refugees left in Underhill, trusting them to ensure the survival of their kind. Others suspected she had more power than any of us realized and whispered that she was omniscient of all ongoings, omnipotent in her control. It was not a topic discussed often, though. It was not anyone's place to question the queen's ways; that would be treason.

Personally, I did not believe Uncle was a puppet that diverted attention from her and hid the extent of her hold over the People, held in her thrall by his own name. However, I could not confirm or deny either option, so I tended to err in the middle area between the two suggestions. She may have a hand on Uncle's, but he had some autonomy.

Generally, I refrained from contemplating too much on any hypotheses because whichever was the truth did not nullify the fact that if a Namekeeper had access to my thoughts, the queen of the fae certainly did.

Uncle, known and addressed here as *Prif* Namekeeper, continued aloud. "You have a new task as duty to Her Highness."

My eyelids twitched. I had assumed as much. The anticipation of the task to which I was being reassigned churned in my gut. Outwardly, I remained stoic.

He responded to my inner question. I hadn't intended to think it; he might have just guessed my objection. "Jac will carry out your scheduled acquisitions alone until you return."

I blinked. We never sent anyone alone. Our targets might often be children. But the *Cyhyraeth* incident was evidence that other dangers might be present that calls for backup. Without Jac, that creature would have done considerably more damage — or defeated me. Sending Jac back to work without a partner displayed some disregard for the *Pwca*'s wellbeing.

"I believe he is capable of handling any potential dangers. He has proven himself able."

I understood. Simultaneously complimenting my partner, the inference dissed me.

"You have a more important task that requires urgent attention." His long hair slid over his ear tips as he cocked his head, studying me. "You will use your tracking prowess."

I swallowed, chin lifting higher. "The treasure?"

"Information."

A flicker of surprise slipped across my features before I recovered. "*Prif?*"

"There is a threat to the throne."

"*Prif?*" I repeated with more shock than curiosity.

"A rumor of a threat," he corrected himself. "You will follow the rumor and acquire the identity of the threat, if it exists. You are not responsible for punishment or questioning." He leaned forward to pin me with a glare that I barely made out. "Just bring me the *Tylwyth Teg* to name. You may begin your search with Puc."

My mouth unwillingly fell open. Jac's dad? The spokesfae of the *Pwca?*

"That is all."

Dismissed, I turned to leave, mind reeling.

"*Aestylaneru,*" he called before I reached the massive doors.

Stunned, I flipped back to face him involuntarily, my body responding to the power of my name. My eyes flicked to the queen. If she didn't know my true name before, she would now. Sleep appeared to hold her.

"This task is for you alone. You may discuss it with no one but me and your contact."

Bowing my head, I retreated and waited until I was far from the court, marching up my favorite knoll, before I tipped back my head, let out my breath, and collapsed to the ground, forehead landing on my knees. Then, I let myself internalize the situation.

There were two reasons my uncle may have chosen me for this task. One: I was being tested to confirm whether I should or should not lose my status as an Acquisitions Team agent after my failure. Or two: I was being sent on my own to face a significant threat with the acceptance that the probability of my survival was low — but hopefully, I could provide information as my last use.

Worst case scenario of Uncle's arrangement: I and Jac both died, and an assassination attempt was made on the queen. Best case: I solved the mystery, Uncle handled the accused, and Jac successfully acquired all our targets.

I laughed sordidly, amending my assessment to note that my survival might be the worst-case scenario for my uncle, who would delight in the removal of my disgraceful presence from his family without him being directly implicated.

That I was forbidden from letting anyone know what I was doing, including my partner and best friend who would be covering our joint duties solo, meant I could not say goodbye if the latter were likely.

Lifting my head, I stared at the tree to which humans were tied when we first brought them into Underhill. There were scorch marks on the charred trunk, outlining many forms who'd pressed up against the wood during the initiation process. Frayed ropes coiled around the base, draped innocently over the exposed roots. It was there where other members of the court determined whether the treasures we brought from the human realm could survive mating with us, creating or carrying a fae baby to term. That was what mattered; the survival of our race.

"I will survive," I decided aloud. Just to spite Uncle. "We will survive."

I'd do my duty quickly and get back to Jac, though I was equally as confident as my uncle if not more that he would be fine alone. I wasn't sure I was.

Being a tracker with a dwindling ability to see was not a recipe for success.

Chapter Three

Gwrach y Rhibyn had lost them.

She had dropped low, that fateful night when she met the disfigured elf, hugging the trees as she soared on the updrafts coasting through the valleys. The canopy could always be trusted to hide her presence at night, concealing her, should the fae glance back. But they neither had they checked behind them nor had the Jack O' Lantern flared his bioluminescent light; he retained a massive dragon form, flying fast ahead of the vampire. The *Ellyllon* had appeared to be unconscious, pale hair hanging like a draped curtain over the beast's flanks as he carried her through the wood to safety, far outpacing her with his extraordinary wingspan.

The memory of that sight drew *Gwrach y Rhibyn* to bare her teeth as envy drove an imaginary stake into her abdomen in her now-healed wound. She'd had that support once from her husband. Before the elves took it all from her. Before the *Pwca* surrendered the rest of the races to the *Ellyllon*, letting them overpower all other *Tylwyth Teg* in Underhill, erasing those who countered their blasphemous ideals.

Humans were precious, not fertility tools to be used and discarded once dead. The *Gwrach y Rhibyn* spat in disgust. The elves' desperate attempts to revive their decimated ranks — those half fae-half human abominations — deserved to be destroyed while the hag's family lived.

They had complemented each other in the past, the *Cyhyraeth* and *Pwca*. The vampires consumed the liquid that flowed through their prey's veins then left the victim to stumble back onto their path. Weak and susceptible, the humans were easily lured by a will-o-the-wisp, with whom they would find their grave in an off-road swamp or marsh. The two had shared the spoils... before the goblins became traitors.

This *Pwca* was due a painful death, and *Gwrach y Rhibyn*'s greedy lips wanted to impart the sentence with glee.

However, at some point, the shape-shifter's silhouette dipped into the forest far ahead.

The vampire had stalked toward the spot, bare soles crunching over twigs and rocks, but by the time she had arrived and searched the grounds, they had disappeared. The rage surged all over again as she recalled the disappointment.

Infuriation at their escape and the thrill of the hunt urged her after the elf and goblin. Long fingers sifted the ground, blood coating her hands and leaving a stain that confused her sense of smell. Some of it was her own blood from the burning wound in her stomach that she could not ignore. The stab wound from the Ellyllon's *stake sent a sharp shooting pain through her body with each breath she took, and the impact of the dragon's arrival at the scene caused a persistent ache in her shoulder.*

Snarling, the hag once again took to the skies. Passing over the house surrounded by red and blue lights, she mourned. She circled once, taking one last glance to say a final goodbye to the child who'd nourished the vampire so. The hour was late, and the options scarce. Finding a new source would be a challenge.

Beginning to tire, Gwrach y Rhybin *spotted a small brook meandering down a nearby hillside. She landed and shuffled to the edge of the trickling stream. Lowering her hands into the cool, clear water, she began to wash them clean of blood.*

The motions raised bitter memories, and her gritted teeth reflected back in the ripples.

"My child, my child," she muttered in a rasp, remembering the blood of her family sifting into the mountain waters. Rocking back and forth to try to soothe the hollow feeling, she sniffled back a ragged sob. "My husband, my husband."

"Hello?"

The spirit stopped. Her hands were spotless and rubbed raw.

"Someone there?" The words were slurred.

The sadness washed downstream with the scarlet swirls, and the wraith smiled a malicious grin, returning the question with silence: a false response.

When no answer came, the human appeared to believe her ruse. He unknowingly sent an alluring faint whistling tune tripping into the little clearing in which she knelt.

The hungry blood-sucker took flight to scan the area. Quickly, she spotted a man stumbling home along a winding hedge-rimmed road from the town pub.

She flew ahead and dropped down near a fork in the road, settling into the shadows to await her prey.

"Death comes," she whispered in delight, her thirst renewed but soon to be sated. From this source, she would take all he offered and leave nothing behind.

Then, she would hunt fae.

Now, a week later, the vampire was skulking around that same location by the light of a crescent moon. She felt more vitalized than she had since before the war, having drunk enough to quell her thirst, which had led to several coma-like days of rest.

Now, she was ready to hunt.

She hadn't scoured the forest floor for long for footprints or other telltale signs of the fae's trail before the sound of hooves thundering through the wood reached her ears.

Hunched over, *Gwrach y Rhibyn* craned around at the waist and squinted into the dark through loose strands of hair that fluttered with each heaving breath of hatred. Skirting around the back of the tree, she hissed softly when she saw the *Pwca*. Equal parts delight, and malevolence raged within her; they had come to her.

The elf sat on the back of the *Pwca*'s deer form and laughed gleefully. After a while, the deer slowed his gallop to a canter, then a trot, eventually pacing to a stop in the shadow of an immense, old tree. The hag smiled when he playfully tossed the elf off, and she rolled with a thump into the trunk that was wide and tall, tipped with boughing limbs, neatly hiding the vampire.

Gwrach y Rhibyn's forked tongue flicked across her teeth, catching on a fine point and releasing a splash of blood that dripped onto dry leaves before she sucked it back in, alighting her rage with its flavor. It was nothing compared to the spicy delicacy of the *Ellyllon*. The lingering need for the elf's blood rumbled through the vampire.

The shapeshifter and elf made inane comments to each other that the vampire missed, the urge to leap out, and drain the two fae rushing unrestrained into her limbs and whooshing through her ears. Leaning around the tree to identify their locations, she hesitated.

The pair she hunted stood a respectful distance and bowed low, not to the tree but the circle of mushrooms that sprouted between its roots. The broken elf stepped forward and closed her eyes. A moment later, the fairy ring glowed bright, flaring in a pulsing rhythm that continued like a heartbeat. They stepped inside the circle of mushrooms and vanished. The glow abated.

A gate. A gate to Underhill.

Gwrach y Rhibyn stared in shock and triumph.

Vampires were not permitted within its borders. Not anymore. So long ago had the fae banished their creations, stalking and murdering those they caught fleeing and those who remained behind.

Now, they had led her home.

Eagerly, the *Gwyllion* abandoned her niche and circumvented the roots. Pausing before the ring, the *Cyhyraeth* closed her eyes, curtseyed, and mentally asked Underhill for admittance.

The despised Fae Court who controlled the gates would not permit her passing, but Underhill was fond of vengeance. It had enjoyed the war, breeding violence, feasting on death, harboring those who thrived on causing humans pain in particular. Humans poisoned Underhill and pushed back her boundaries.

Underhill also knew the *Cyhyraeth* did not belong in the human realm. Unlike the rest of the *Tylwyth Teg*, *Gwyllion* were not weak to iron — humans had iron in their blood, where those from Underhill had magic in theirs — and could exist without getting sick in this realm. However, the fae used this realm as their hunting ground, and fear of discovery by fae and humans alike kept *Gwrach y Rhibyn* confined to her mountainside caves.

She felt the release when the portal unlocked, the magic passing over the vampire's face and skin with a change in pressure that popped her ears. A grin stretched her dry lips and exposed her onyx needle teeth.

The hunt continued.

She would kill the *Ellyllon*, who had threatened her child and taken her source from her, and for dessert, she would destroy the traitorous shapeshifter who helped the elf.

With the power of their magic to fortify her strength, the vampire would take on the ruthless Fae Court. She would bathe in the blood of the fae the way they did on the battlegrounds, drenched in the lifeforce of her family.

Pausing, she prepared herself for the possibility that she might not find the *Ellyllon* on the other side, reminding herself that time coursed independently in Underhill, not synced to this world. *Gwrach y Rhibyn* hissed. If something or someone else had taken the privilege of ending the elf's life, the hag would realign her aim onto that being for its thievery.

Cackling with a throaty cough, the hag stepped into the ring after her prey.

The sudden feeling of comfort, of home, of settling into place pacified her yet stirred her cravings. She scented brimstone, decay, and loam. There was even a faint copper tang that lingered from the war; Underhill was loath to let go of that scrumptious scent. The magic in the ground throbbed in pace with the vampire's footfalls.

Ready to take back her rightful place in the supernatural world, *Gwrach y Rhibyn* entered the fae's realm with a thirst for vengeance.

· · ·

Chapter Four

"Mum?" I called when I stepped inside our small abode, pausing to lean on the doorjamb.

Hiding the exhaustion was part of my routine. The ladders were installed on the tree trunks beneath each family's dwelling when a child was born, and they remained there until the child sprouted wings. The wooden slats remained longer than usual on our tree, a reminder of our family's shame.

There was no answer.

Breathing steadied, I ventured in further. The living room was empty, as was the kitchen. Opening a door, I peered into the sunroom at the back of our cozy tree-top hut, but her studio was also vacant. I detoured up the next set of planks nailed to the trunk to the landing overlooking the living room. My bedroom door, on the right, was shut. The door on the left was also closed. I presumed Mum had decided to go to bed early. She would hear about the new task from her brother before I awoke.

Unlike the queen, I suspected the mystique of motherhood was partly at fault — she was overprotective, always keeping a close eye on my comings and goings, perhaps more so than Uncle. I might also blame Uncle's telepathy. He could well osmotically impart my latest news into Mum's mind while she slept, given how she seemed to know exactly what was happening before I got out of bed each evening.

Slipping into my room, I began removing my gear, starting with my bow and quiver, which crisscrossed my chest, the leather strap of the quiver buckled beneath the bowstring. The fingerless gloves came next, tossed on a dresser as I walked toward the en suite bathroom.

My ears suddenly picked up on a noise in my room.

I froze, listening hard, my eyes scanning and seeing nothing out of the ordinary amongst the shadows, the sun not yet having risen high enough to breach the treetops outside the window behind me.

A second creak told me my wardrobe door had just swung open across the room.

"Mum?" Was she putting away my washing?

There was a bright glint, then something slammed into my chest, and with a shattering crash, I was shoved out the window.

Air whipped my hair, removing any ability to see, and I screamed as I plummeted toward the ground, our tall tree absent of branches between the limb on which our house perched and the forest floor. Too soon, I hit hard with an abrupt stop that wrenched my body.

But it wasn't the ground that ended my fall.

My limbs continued their momentum, swinging beneath my body, and my head flung back with painful whiplash. My eyes squeezed shut at the wrenching pull twanging through me, and I registered a secondary, sharper pain in my stomach.

I pulled my chin down to my chest to relieve the immediate ache on my neck and opened my eyes. Two blurry hands gripped the leather covering my stomach.

Shutting my lids again, I focused on my other senses. The air had stopped rushing past and was now moving past me the other way — the sensation of being lifted overwhelmed me. I heard a repeated whoosh that preceded an extra blast of wind on my face by a few seconds. The whoosh came with a familiar scent: lavender with a touch of bitterness that I associated with magic-infused herbal mixes. A sniffle reached my ears.

"Mum?"

She didn't respond, just carried me back into my bedroom, the bright light of the sunrise behind my eyelids vanishing and the air around me stilling. Her sniffles continued as she gently deposited me on my bed, my muscles finally able to relax. My heavy and throbbing head and limbs went limp against the mattress.

I heard her feet back away and cracked an eye just as the tip of her glistening wing disappeared and my door clicked closed behind her, leaving me alone. Sighing, I stared at the hazy ceiling.

Mum wasn't disappointed in me the way her brother was; it was her actions that caused my existence. She was disappointed that the trauma hadn't been enough of a shock to my system to jolt my glamour out of its shell. She thought of it as locked in my core by the *Pwca* genes.

When she realized she'd misinterpreted the healers' vague comment that I wasn't the same as before the incident, she was crushed. I couldn't bring myself to tell her that they meant my eyes, not my magic abilities. With the idea implanted, however, she had taken it upon herself to surprise me at unexpected opportunities and place me in seemingly dangerous situations to coax my powers out to no avail.

I blew out a long-held breath.

Heights were comfortable for the *Ellyllon*. Without wings, however, I had some … reservations. I would not permit myself to call it acrophobia. But those related to my other half, the *Pwca*, were ground-dwellers. Though they could shift into beings with wings, their natural forms were as flightless as I was.

Unable to move without setting off a rattling explosion in my throbbing head and lacking the magic to relieve the aches, I closed my eyes against it all. I had a job to do in the morning.

When I woke, it was to the tinkling sounds of glass.

"Mum?" I croaked, rolling to my side to avoid craning my neck to look around.

She paused in her efforts to sweep up a few shards from the shattered window, holding a crouched pose. The curtains were drawn behind her, so I wasn't sure if it was night yet or if I had awoken early at the noise. "Aetyl." Her eyes were red from weeping, though she smiled. "How do you feel?"

She was asking if the trick had worked with some kind of delay, not whether I was injured. I did not answer.

"Your uncle told me about your new task." Her attention remained on the dustpan in her hand as she stood. There wasn't much to gather. Given that we had tumbled out of the window, most of the debris would be in the hedges and flowerbeds below. "This is very important." Her gaze flicked to mine then, and she took a step toward me. I couldn't make out her expression from across the room. "Very important. We must keep the peace. We must remain united as we have been for these past centuries. To stand strong against the humans."

If she knew I had an important task to accomplish, why did she not offer me one of her concoctions to soothe my pain? "I know." I could not restrain my answer; she was informing me of validities of which I was well aware, so I did the same in return. "That's why the Acquisition Team was brought into existence: to repopulate our people such that we might survive the war with the humans as we did the Underhill War. That's why you had me."

She flinched, and her head turned to the side, her wings twitching.

I continued. "Humans are the enemy now with their iron and their expansion into nature — the destruction and compression of Underhill." I barely restrained the rest of the lesson my school teacher had spoken years prior.

The *Coblynau* had died out, the tommyknockers defending Underhill's boundaries and gateways for years as human miners came close to breaking through into fae territory. The *Bwbachod* had also been a casualty of the war, though the brownies' tale was much more tragic. The *Gwragedd Annwn* reverted to their rivers and lakes, leaving others alone minus the wayward fishermen the nymphs invited into their waters for sustenance. The *Gwyllion*, spirits created as a result of the bloody war, had retreated to the mountains where they were hunted by Uncle himself and the rest of the *Ellyllon* war-clean-up task force. As one of the *Gwyllion*, the *Cyhyraeth*... well, they were mostly extinct.

Mostly, I thought darkly with coiling hatred.

If I ever ran into that *Cyhyraeth* again... That was why I was determined to survive this task. If I could escape death herself, then I could do this task for the queen to keep the peace in her realm. Perhaps the current quiescence was why the queen could nap guiltlessly.

And then it struck me what I was thinking, what Mum was getting at.

"You think there is unrest? Because of the *Cyhyraeth* and this… threat?"

If there was dissent amongst those the queen governed, whisperings of mutiny, war might return. And, still recovering from the last of Underhill's battles and the simultaneous advances by humans, this time we might not win.

"It's not that," she corrected in a soft voice. "I just … I worry about you. With other *Tylwyth Teg*."

Ah. I understood. She felt I was at a disadvantage. My job with humans had never worried her, but if I had to face off against another fae who had use of magic where I did not, I wouldn't be able to affably defend myself… as I'd learned the hard way.

I sighed, knowing her heart was in the right place. It didn't matter. I had no choice but to overcome my handicap, to show my family — and the rest of society — that one isolated error, which was more the result of surprise than fallibility, did not define me.

Really, it was the vampire who should suffer the scrutiny, having breached our unofficial ceasefire.

"I will succeed," I told Mum, keeping my voice strong and steady. Biting down on a wince, I carefully pulled myself into a sitting position, staring boldly toward her while holding my neck immobile.

She observed me for a moment, then her head lowered. Padding closer, avoiding looking in my direction, she left her eyes on the tray of glass clutched tightly in her hands. "I hope you will." She could not speak with any more conviction than that and retain the truth a *Tylwyth Teg* always spoke.

Her loss of faith pained more than the ache in my neck.

I caught the unprovoked sharp motion, but I couldn't quite see what had transpired until an array of sharp points came into focus as their flight was frozen inches from my face.

Jerking back, I managed an inhale, my heart flitting like a butterfly's wings as my arms instinctively flew up to cover my face too late, useless eyes squeezing shut.

The moment hung suspended for a moment. Then I heard the

sound of glass tinkling to the floor, and a sharp sting peppered my thighs. A crunching sound told me Mum had stepped closer.

I lowered my arms out of respect as well as to dismantle my obvious cowardice in the face of dismay. A hand landed on my shoulder.

"You must learn from your mistakes, Aetyl, from your wounds. My daughter, you must learn and overcome."

So, that was why she did not heal me; I was to take from her throwing me off a treetop and slicing my skin with broken glass a lesson in building up resistance to suffering and attacks.

Had I not experienced enough damage from the *Cyhyraeth*? Mum knew not of my deteriorating vision, though. To her, my reactions were driven by fear.

Fear was a weakness for a tracker, for any fae. She could see my external scars, the branching pink lines of scar tissue left behind as if I'd been struck by lightning. But the scars I bore were not signs of bravery; I had not emerged from that battle victorious. Mum picked at the inner scars so that they bleed afresh.

"Yes, Mum," I whispered, lowering my eyelids to shield the vacancy in my gaze.

I heard the sigh, felt her fingers squeeze my shoulder from which a new wing had again not revealed itself. She departed in a whirl of lavender.

When she was gone, I did not permit myself to linger. I plucked the shards from my legs without a sound, tossing them to the floor to be swept up with the rest of the debris. Ripping off my shirt, I flung it aside to don a new outfit. A bright splotch of red on my stomach reflected in the wardrobe mirror stilled my movements.

Streaks crossed my stomach that almost mirrored the puckered slashes from the death monster's claws — four of them... from Mum's nails when she'd caught me mid-fall.

They, too, would scar, a reminder of all wrong I had achieved.

As instructed, I would learn from these scars, and I would prove that they did not define me. In fact, my handicap would make me a better tracker. Something I'd been realizing was that my other senses were growing stronger without my eyes to rely on, somewhat thanks to Mum's surprises, though she hadn't intended them to be useful in this way.

I was going to find this threat against the throne. No other option would be permitted.

Chapter Five

As night descended, the vampire, sitting in the boughs of a nearby tree, watched the abomination without wings descend from the elves' canopy village using hands and feet as if she were human. *Gwrach y Rhibyn* flapped open her wide leather wings, proud of that difference between herself and the deformed *Ellyllon*.

The elf turned from her home and paused. She looked small, frail, weak without her wings. Her head tipped back, and she seemed to soak in the moonlight. Pivoting toward the wood, the fae kept her eyes closed as she broke into a jog, pale hair bouncing against her spine like a beacon for the sharp eyes tracking her.

Flapping her wings once, *Gwrach y Rhibyn* rose from her perch, tattered gowns billowing against her ankles, then she pursued her prey.

The elf started slowly, first tripping and stumbling, hands continually flinging in front of her, sometimes touching an obstacle before detouring around it, sometimes catching her as she fell. She stepped on large, vibrant blooms, crushed sacred toadstools, kicked up carefully constructed piles of twigs that woodland creatures had erected.

The hag grinned, realizing that more was wrong with the elf than her flightlessness. The *Ellyllon* was blind or almost blind. This would be easy pickings now that they were finally alone.

It was comical watching the elf fumble, and the vampire alighted on a branch nearby to watch with mirth. The struggle was like a show before dinner.

The elf stopped for a moment, shaking her head and muttering to herself. "Focus," she heard the fae tell herself. "Use your other senses."

The girl cocked her head, spinning in a circle, sniffed an exaggerated inhale, and dropped to her behind to pull off her leather boots and her deadly gloves. The boots, she slipped beneath her quiver against her spine, and the gloves were tucked in a pocket of her jacket so that her hands could burrow into the soil. When she stood back up, the elf wiggled her toes in the dirt, then slid one set of toes forward, tapping and sweeping across the ground. She put it down, transferred her weight, and slid the next foot in front, getting a feel for the terrain with her bare soles.

Gwrach y Rhibyn's own bare feet were wrapped over the rough bark of the branch on which she hid, and she snorted at how belated the ruling fae were to realize that nature was their companion; Underhill would always guide its people.

Once she'd gotten a feel for the earth, the elf broke into a sprint, zig-zagging around tree trunks, leaping over boulders, cushioning her falls, or rolling through them without stopping when she hit a root or plant. But the forest floor tore up the bottoms of her feet, the skin supple after years of being coddled behind the protection of boots.

The vampire used the rich aroma as a guide and flapped harder, flying faster to catch up, a growl gurgling up her throat. She wanted that blood. Needed it. "So thirsty." She extended her arms, claws reaching to snatch her target.

Suddenly, the elf grabbed a hanging vine, swinging up and over the hag's head.

The vampire flapped hard to stop, then arced up and over, tracing the fae's loop. The elf, once again right side up, landed on a branch. It was the perfect opportunity. But *Gwrach y Rhibyn* needed to be quick — ahead, a bright glowing orb disappeared, and a clip-clop sound commenced.

The fae heard it too.

Her prey dropped from the limb just as the stag appeared below them, and the hag's claws slid through the ends of long pale hair, closing around air.

The girl landed with a laugh on the ground, the goblin having instantly morphed into a small bat to dart out of the way of the falling elf.

Gwrach y Rhibyn perched on the same limb the fae had just vacated and hissed internally at the insult. Not only had she missed the only opportunity that had presented itself, but the *Pwca* mocked her form with miniature versions of her leathery wings. And it chirped merrily.

When his chirps turned toward the hag as he flitted in play around the elf's head, *Gwrach y Rhibyn* pressed against the tree trunk to avoid being detected by his echolocation. The *Pwca's* wing-tip brushed the elf's cheek, causing her to giggle before landing on her shoulder.

"A bat," the elf breathed in a peppy, happy voice that made the hag's blood boil and her fists curl. "Blind like me." The friendly laugh nearly made the vampire's ears bleed.

The *Pwca* shape-shifted again, this time his appearance mimicking that of a male elf with pointed ears — but notably lacking the iconic wings like the girl he faced. He held out a hand to the true *Ellyllon* to help her to her feet.

She shook her head, and her next words were so soft, *Gwrach y Rhibyn* almost couldn't discern them. "I like you when you're you," were the words that reached her ears. "We can be ourselves with each other."

Gwrach y Rhibyn's teeth revealed themselves. As if the cuteness of the interaction burned her, with a silent glare at the couple, the hag scrubbed at her ears until they bled.

The goblin took his own stout shape, and only then did the elf girl take his hand, allowing him to pull her up as best he could, being shorter than her.

The only thing that enraptured the vampire to the interaction was the blush staining the elf's cheeks as blood flowed to her face. "So tantalizing."

The arrogant fae girl's eyes glittered in the moonlight as she leaned down toward the shape-shifter's mouth. And that fiend of a *Pwca* let her.

Gwrach y Rhibyn focused on the sky. She could not afford to scratch her eyes out, too, over what happened next. Launching herself toward the moon before dipping back under the canopy of trees, she dallied before flying silently behind the pair as they resumed their wander through the woods, hand in hand.

They ambled slowly, keeping to the elf's slow wingless pace, innocent love, and idiocy, making them blind to the threat on their tail. The goblin directed them, helping the blind fae over obstacles, leading her toward the old swamp — his people's territory.

Anger roared through the hag. "*Pwca* traitors," *Gwrach y Rhibyn* rasped viciously. There were too many in this area to take on at once without having yet consumed the fae's blood for power. "Later." The vampire holed up in a nook in a tree to wait for them to return. Later, she would make all of the goblins pay.

The *Pwca* left quickly, retracing the elf's steps through the woods, but the *Ellyllon* remained in the swamp, so the vampire did as well. She needed that blood first, craved it even. She wouldn't rest until she had drained that elf.

She took out a few natural bats due to impatience, imagining them to be the *Pwca*, delighting in their sharp squeaks that cut-off quickly. She lorded over their small furry bodies, weak and insignificant compared to her might.

Underhill didn't seem to mind the morbid game. In fact, there was a distinct pulsing that seemed to encourage the vampire's collection.

She didn't bother tasting the bats' blood, though it might carry traces of magic from simply living in Underhill. Instead, she left a mound in the middle of the trail of their bodies, hoping that without the *Pwca* to steer her, the elf might be likely to overlook the unexpected hurdle and fall to her knees where she belonged. Then the vampire could snatch her from behind like the elf had been planning to do to the child. She'd grab her where her wings should be, and she'd take her high, let her feel what it was like to fly... before she ripped out her throat and drank her dry.

When the elf reappeared, she was not alone. A different goblin accompanied her. This one was stout and wide, hairier. "Too hairy," the vampire told herself; he was old. Taking him out would send a message to his people, but it would be a feat. And he would protect the elf, his body language conveyed.

Irritated, *Gwrach y Rhibyn* snatched another bat from the air. It gave a pitiful squeak as her grip crushed its body, claws slicing through delicate wings. She breathed in the aroma of its blood, then threw it aside and took off, stalking her prey from above further into the early hours.

When the pair stopped at a different gate, she dropped to the forest floor, using her wings to lower herself gently and soundlessly behind them. Still, the elf half-turned as if sensing the hag, but turned back, seeing nothing, and they vanished into the human world.

The vampire hesitated for only a second. She didn't want to leave Underhill after just finding her way back. If she didn't follow, though, she'd lose her prey... again. In the human realm, the elf would be separated from other magical help. In what had become the hag's territory — if she could get the girl away from the *Pwca* — there would be no one to save her.

With the time difference, *Gwrach y Rhibyn* couldn't afford to wait. Her irritated shriek startled the remaining bats in the area before the vampire slipped back across the gate into the human world.

Chapter Six

Puc led me through the twisting winding tunnels of an abandoned mine, our footfalls echoing in the rock-lined cavern. Dust-laden air billowed in and out of my lungs loudly in the cramped space; *Ellyllon* and *Pwca* were both shorter than humans, the latter shorter than the first — and I fit right between the two — but *Coblynau* were much smaller beings. Once we stepped out into fresh air, we trudged down a mountainside in the dark of night.

This particular gate was new to me. Unlike in Underhill, I could not feel the pulsing of nature here, and I found it hard to get in sync with my surroundings, even opening up my other senses. Puc held back tree branches and helped me over fallen logs as we traversed the dense wood at the base of the hill. I knew Jac had not betrayed my secret to his father, but the elder will-o-the-wisp was observant.

This side of the veil, the forest lost its rich tang of magic. The bittersweet floral aroma and heady scents of life were replaced with the musk of rot, the swampy, and fetid funk of decay. The air was thicker as well, old and heavy, polluted. My feet pounded into dry and hard earth. The ground lacked any springy rebound, and shock waves splintered through my shins and knees with each stride. A spiderweb, too finely spun to catch my notice, caught on my face and hair. The celebratory songs of crickets, frogs, and birds carried, the crunching of frolicking hooves and paws absent. A lone owl hooted in the distance.

I was beginning to regret my lack of boots at this point but persisted without resheathing my feet out of pride. I needed to get used to it if I was to use my sense of touch effectively.

Jac had been encouraging me to use my other senses since my vision first began to deteriorate without me, even realizing that was what he was doing.

The inclination to slap myself in the face rose again. I had been blind in more ways than one until he grew blatant with his hints, turning into a creature that not only survived but excelled without relying on vision: a bat.

I blushed, hoping the dark masked the flush, thinking of what happened after that. I hadn't planned to kiss him; it had just sort of happened, my giddiness over finding my rhythm and my appreciation for his support spilling over.

But I didn't regret it. Jac was more than a friend. He was the only one who knew everything about me, actually rescued me in my moment of downfall, and he never once made me feel any less for it.

When the sharp, acerbic taste of iron in the air first singed my tongue, I realized we were nearing civilization. We slipped through the shadows and clung to the dark silhouettes of trees for cover. My white strands picked up all faint touches of light from the human residences, even without my *Pwca* companion using his glow to brighten our traverse.

I'd sent Jac on a fool's errand to find my gloves at my house, which, of course, were in my pocket, and I felt somewhat bereft without him. Not because of our evolving relationship, but because I'd grown so accustomed to working with him as my partner. Jac had assured me, "Elly will be fine" with whatever task *Prif* Namekeeper had assigned me, never once pushing me for information before he left me with his father.

"This way," Puc said, and I followed the sound of his voice, trying to drag my mind from thoughts of his son, my cheeks heating more. Puc, being our informant, was already involved, so I was breaking no promise by traveling with him to our destination.

"How did you encounter this human?" I asked. Even now, I was having trouble internalizing that it was someone in the *human realm* who was threatening the queen, as Puc had revealed in his subterranean home. The news had caused me to smack my head on the shape-shifters' low rocky ceiling, which had revived all my aches from Mum's window surprise.

How did a human know about our existence, let alone that of the queen of the *Tylwyth Teg*? She — we were mere whispers in the night, ghost stories, haunting legends to the humans of Wales. They could not pass through the gates or see Underhill. Those with whom we interacted would never speak of it, either taking the knowledge with them to their grave or through the gate to the realm of magic.

"Jac," Puc finally answered me.

I faltered and, in so doing, lost my footing. Puc quickly transformed into an elephant to catch me with his trunk. His sudden size expansion caused a nearby sapling to bow out of the way. Once I was righted, he returned to his natural state.

"Jac told you about humans threatening our queen?" I asked, not understanding.

"We here." Puc stopped walking. I nearly bounced off him, not seeing him until I was nearly on him, but he had turned to face me and gently put up a hand to catch my shoulder.

With gentle pressure, he twisted me around him and pulled aside a few vines that had formed a wall I'd have run into without Puc's caution. Beneath the vines was a wooden fence. Puc directed my eye toward a small hole.

Holding my breath, I chose the slightly better eye and pressed the outer edges of my eye socket against the opening rim, which was so perfectly ovular it had to have been a knot that rotted out. Peering through, I scanned the area on the other side of the fence. Obviously, Puc expected me to learn something from what I saw.

I couldn't.

Air leaked from my lungs in frustration. "I can't see anything." I pulled back, scowling at the fence as if it were to blame for keeping me at a far enough distance to discern clear objects.

I'd gotten some glimpses of colors in my periphery, a shadowy mass at the center that I suspected to be the house of the human in question, but it could very well be another fence or a massive hedgerow.

"Come." Puc shifted into a giant Tawny owl. He could easily have blended in with the wooded area, were it not for his disproportionate size, which was closer to that of a car than the other birds of prey hooting in the night. He splayed out one wing, allowing me to climb on his feathered back.

I did so, trying to push aside the shame for not having my own wings — or *Pwca* shifting abilities for that matter. His people were kind to me, considered me one of them, but also respected me as an *Ellyllon*, a stark contrast to Uncle, who would not recognize my cross-bred blood.

Puc's head rotated almost entirely around to check that I was settled with massive, luminous eyes that reminded me of his people's glowing orbs. Reassured, he faced front and easily took a few flaps to lift us both over the fence.

The closer we got, the more I was able to see. My other senses were able to pick up on more details as well.

There was a garden filled with fragrant plants and bright paving stones, even a faintly trickling fountain that was home to a few croaking toads. Hedges lined the front of the garden. A fence enclosed a side and made a ninety-degree turn to enclose the rear of the quaint two-story cobblestone house. The fourth side of the rectangular perimeter was bordered by a thick wood — a familiar thick wood.

"No," I gasped, clutching the owl's feathers without regard for the pain I might be causing Puc as I leaned over to get a better look.

Overlooking the woods was a window — a new window, freshly replaced.

Puc's massive wingspan helped us glide easily onto the roof, where we landed with the quietest tinkle as his talons clacked against the ceramic tiles. I immediately slid off his back and whipped my bow over my head, gripping it tight in front of me as if I might run into the *Cyhyraeth* again at any second. The stake at my hip had proven worthless last time; I wouldn't let her get close enough to need to resort to that form of close hand-to-hand combat again.

"Here?" I asked Puc in incredulity.

Hearing a noise, I quickly spun, grabbing an arrow and drawing my bow. When nothing revealed itself in the direction I faced, I tried to relax, my paranoia obviously getting the best of me. Mum would be so disappointed if I didn't keep my head.

Relaxing the string, I worked through the logic aloud to Puc. "They saw us. The humans who live here. Last time we were here. They now believe. Truly. That we exist. That our queen of lore exists."

The spokesfae of the *Pwca* blinked large round eyes at me, unable to speak through his short, curved beak.

My nostrils flared as I huffed out a breath. "Easy enough." I just needed to take out the humans and take the child with me.

Uncle's voice spoke in my mind, reminding me just to acquire information and let him dole out the sentences. But it would be a win-win. I'd accomplish this task and close the loop on my failed mission. I could just imagine Uncle's sour expression when I not only came back alive but successful in what he asked and more, redeeming myself and our family name.

He'd have no choice but to accept me. And Mum might finally acknowledge that I was capable of great things without the standard wings other *Ellyllon* sported.

"Can you take me to the child's bedroom?" I asked Puc, swinging my bow back over my head.

In response, he crouched. I mounted, and he easily looped into the sky, arced once, and without warning, bucked me off his back. Holding back a scream, my stomach vaulted into my throat as I fell, the movement reminiscent of the night prior with Mum. Puc's talons scraped raw skin as he caught my shirt and then tossed me unceremoniously toward the window.

Rolling in the air, I caught the edge of the dark window before my feet slammed into the grass, cushioning my fall. Shifting my weight to one hand, fingers turning white at the pull, I tried to leverage the window open.

It was locked. The humans had learned their lesson.

Lifting myself up, my nose pressed against the cool of the glass. "Just a reminder," I whispered. "Do not presume you are safe. I have returned for you." My nail tapped on the window.

No one moved in the room in response to the click of my nail. The child slept soundly in her bed, a sliver of yellow from the hall that leaked through the cracked bedroom door, allowing me to make out her small, huddled form.

Tonight, there was another form in the bed with her.

I blinked at it, trying to clear my blurry vision, but of course, it did not improve. The second lump shifted, and I shoved myself closer, knuckles whitening on the plant box as I tried to make out what it was.

A pair of wings unfolded. They spread wide — bat wings, not gossamer.

Jac? Had Uncle given him the case alone to spite me? It was unexpected; Jac was a better lure for adults. Children were my area of specialty. Usually. The creature turned toward me, the light from the hallway catching on a row of glinting teeth, dripping blood.

My brain revolted, and a chill shivered down my spine. My breathing shallowed until it no longer fogged the pane, and I strained my eyes. I could not tell if it was a hallucination. My lips curled.

"Death." The whisper slithered to me, muted through the window-pane, speaking either to me or the child. It mattered not.

The *Cyhyraeth* was here. She had returned to steal our treasure... again.

I dropped from the window, rolling softly in the grass to cushion the fall.

"Elly?" Puc, in his natural form, appeared at my elbow, scurrying to keep up to my long strides as I marched around the house to the back door.

"I'm going inside."

It wasn't a detour. Puc had brought me here. I would take out the humans and the monster. The *Cyhyraeth* was involved in the treason. The blood-sucker was why we had been forced to reveal ourselves before the humans.

I paused at the back door.

Given my magical shortcomings, it was Jac who typically provided the strength in our pairing when I hit any barriers. If I struggled to enter a child's room, he would simply take a larger shape and force the opening. Mammoth was a favorite of his. Or, if opposable thumbs were required, something akin to what humans called Bigfoot or a Yeti. He relished the human's squeals in the night.

But I didn't want to ask Puc for assistance. Asking felt like admitting weakness; Jac never waited for me to ask. Besides, this was my mission. Puc had led me to the right location; his part was complete. Fortunately, my excursions into the human world had taught me some about their habits.

In Underhill, we had no locks. Humans are selfish, isolated creatures, whereas in Underhill, we worked as a community... at least within one kind. The war changed how much we interacted with each other. My existence as a mix of two was now more taboo than ever before.

I pulled on my gloves. Lifting a mat revealed no key, so I checked the other likely locations: a food grill, a plant pot, an electrical outlet — the human equivalent of magic as far as I understood. When I could find nothing, I decided not to keep messing around in front of the leader of the *Pwca*.

Taking a chance, I closed my eyes and wrapped my fingers around the doorknob, praying that the humans would think a window lock might keep the monsters at bay, but such night stalkers wouldn't use a door.

It turned under my hand, twisted from the other side.

As if burned by the iron in the metal through my protective glove, I ripped my hand away and backed up, bumping into Puc as the door swung open into the interior of the house. I ripped my bow off my head and knocked an arrow, drawing it back to my cheek just as a woman stepped out the opening into the light, walking right toward the stone tip of my weapon.

I didn't release my hold, but I did hesitate.

Expecting to see the *Cyhyraeth*, I was surprised at the revelation of a fairly normal woman, eyes wide and palms extended toward us. She was short for a human, closer to Puc's height than mine, and bony to the point of being nearly skeletal. Her eyes were rounded at the sight of my threat, though they were oddly large to begin with and set wide on her round face. A wide mouth that reminded me of a toad was pulled down beneath a knob-hooked nose. Most humans in this country were pale; this woman's skin was leathery and tanned to the point that she would camouflage in the wood around her house.

"Please," the woman squeaked. "Don't take my daughter..." Puc was right. The woman knew me, understood my job. She was a threat.

I took a deep breath. "Help me with what stalks your child," I said, evading her request. I would kill the vampire first, then the humans.

Her head cocked, and her eyes seemed to lose focus for a second, pupils dilating wide enough to overcome the green irises then shrinking. Her body shuddered once, perhaps chilled by the night breeze filtering through her loose t-shirt and sleep pants. "Help you. Yes," she muttered in a distant tone. Then she stepped back without complaint, allowing me to pass.

Puc stepped toward the woman, and asked in a voice filled with awe, "*Na, Bwbachod?*"

"A brownie?" I repeated, dropping my bow toward the ground and relaxing the string. "They were wiped out during the war." I was told. I'd never seen one.

Bwbachod were harmless, simply caring for human abodes upon request at night when humans slept... and before the war, they were enslaved. Their need to fulfill requests had put them against the *Ellyllon*. When they returned to Underhill to support other lesser fae in battle, they were easily overpowered.

The brownie blinked at Puc, taking in his odd form. She nodded, attention flicking between Puc and me. "*Pwca a Ellyllon?*"

"Yes," Puc said. "Elly, no can kill." Puc was concerned. "Keep brownie safe."

My nostrils flared. The best I could do was let the woman live. Their kind were manipulated; I did not know their true loyalties. But I didn't need her; I needed the humans she served. Besides, I had a more concerning enemy here.

I tried to peer behind her to determine if the blood-sucker hid in the shadows, using the brownie as a shield, hoping to distract me and pounce once I had lowered my defenses.

My bow rose again. I would take no chances this time. She had bested me before. Not this time. That evil spirit was going down.

"Whose house is this?" I queried. Their names were what I sought.

"My husband works a night shift," she replied in a high-pitched, squeaking voice. "But, my daughter..."

Puc noticed the same thing I did about her answer to my question. "Husband... human?" he asked.

She nodded, eyes casting down. "I had to. I was the last."

There was a tense silence after her admission.

"We hide you," Puc defiantly told the brownie. "You need leave before *Ellyllon* know here."

I swallowed. Treason. Puc spoke of treason against the elves, against the court.

Looking at the frightened woman, I said nothing, though. Uncle only wanted the name. He did not direct me against this. This *Tylwyth Teg* was doing as their peers, the *Ellyllon,* were doing and repopulating her people how best she could.

Suddenly, I realized that the humans weren't the threat. This brownie was. By repopulating the people who fought against the elves, she was building a threat against the queen. Apparently, that was how Uncle saw it.

But... I was a half-breed just like that child.

"You need hide. Call husband." Puc was trying to hide his peers from Uncle.

That too was not my concern. "What's your husband's name?"

"Dylan. Dylan Blood."

I would give Uncle that name — Namekeepers had no power over humans. Secretly, I hoped Puc got them somewhere safe far away. "Stay here," I told the brownie, the rasp in my voice more pronounced.

Puc understood my concern and said to me, "Get child. I stay with *Bwbachod.*"

I nodded my thanks and entered the dwelling.

Chapter Seven

No lights had been turned on in the interior, and I cursed my poor vision in the inky blackness, trying to scan my surroundings for movement, my bow following so that I could loose the arrow as soon as my gaze alighted on the *Cyhyraeth.*

I proceeded toward the part of the building that housed the child's bedroom, switching my focus to what my ears and nose broadcasted to my awareness. The blood-sucker's animalistic growls and gluttonous moans of bloodlust abraded my memory. The scent of blood and death that clung to the hag was not one I would soon forget.

I passed down a creaky hallway, keeping my barefooted steps light, grateful I'd removed my boots, and began to ascend a staircase. Pausing when one wooden plank protested my weight, I skipped the last few steps in a single soft-footed leap. The landing opened into a shorter corridor on the second floor. The yellow light I'd seen from the window had been extinguished.

Did the *Cyhyraeth* know I had lost my night vision? Did she revel in the damage she'd done to me?

Keeping Jac's encouragement in mind, I used touch to guide me, elbows extended wide to skim the walls of the passage and keep me moving down the middle. When an elbow lost contact, I whipped to the left, pointing my arrow at a closed door.

If my mental map was correct, it was not the room belonging to the child, so I stepped farther into the gloom. The door to the child's room was ajar, and from within, I could hear soft sobbing.

With the arrow tip, I pushed the door farther open, immediately pointing my weapon where I'd last seen the winged shadow. The bed was empty, the sheets thrown down. The child was nowhere to be seen, but I could hear her faint whimpering.

A sudden shout from the kitchen, caused me to whip around in surprise. That's when the *Cyhyraeth* let out a shriek that flash-froze my core as much as the feel of her claws wrapping around my throat from behind did.

Ditching my traditional hold, since keeping the arrow along my sightline was nebulously effective with my vision anyway, I tipped my bow up and, with some difficulty, fired over my shoulder.

The vampire screamed in my ear, the sound tugging faintly on my soul, and causing a ringing that blocked other noises. But she also released her grip around my neck, so I was able to flip around while knocking a second arrow drawn from my quiver and dropping to one knee to get a better angle on the shadowy corners of the room.

I inhaled in quick and shallow breaths to scent her out.

"You cannot have her."

I spun toward the closet from whence the hiss emanated.

The vampire stepped from the dark depths, and I loosed an arrow. It went wide, my aiming off.

"*Madalch*," I swore as the vampire crouched, and I braced for her next move.

"No, no!" the child wailed as the vampire pulled her from under the bed. The girl's little fingernails scratched on the floor audibly as she was dragged from her hiding spot, sliding on her stomach.

I stepped around the bed to get a more direct view. But when the vampire rose, she held the half-brownie child against her chest, wings wrapped, so the girl's terrified face peeked out the top, the rest of her hidden.

I hesitated in releasing my third arrow, unsure if I trusted my eyes to hit the vampire and bypass the child. For one, Puc would be displeased. I felt some kinship with the girl that stated my reaction, too. Treasures were for acquiring without harm, and my uncle's warning to do nothing to the offending party than ascertain a name nagged at my mind. Did that include the *Cyhyraeth*?

"I do not want the child," I told the spirit, whose black eyes were indistinguishable to me, giving her a skeletal appearance with dark craters punctuating a pale face. I inched further into the room.

"Lies," the hag hissed, her forked tongue flicking out. She mirrored my movements, keeping me beyond arm's reach from the child. "You came for her before."

"That's true," I admitted. "This time, I'm here for you." That was a trade I was willing to make. Acquiring the child was no longer one of my court-appointed tasks; it was Jac's. "Let the child go."

"Like I let you go?" The *Cyhyraeth* laughed a coughing cackle. Blood trickled down her chin. She'd already fed from the child. "You can have her if you give me your blood instead," she taunted.

"No." No negotiation. She was distracting me. I would do the same in return.

Quickly snapping the elbow of my cocked arm sharply upward, the leather of my jacket snagged on the light switch, and the room was flooded in incandescence. The *Gwyllion,* created from the dark deeds of war, were creatures of the night. Elves may have been nocturnal hunters, but we thrived on moonlight the way night jasmine did.

The *Cyhyraeth* screeched, wings rising to block her eyes. My foe backed toward the window, seeking escape as I blocked the door. But she didn't drop the child, who screamed at the sight of my teeth, now illuminated, and burrowed into the spirit's chest.

Rage fueled me as I stalked toward the *Cyhyraeth,* my arrow ready to pierce her treacherous flesh. Not only did the artificial light make her stand out with her dark coloring and attire, but the window behind outlined her shape perfectly despite my imperfect sight. I wasn't going to let her leave with the child.

"Death comes," I told her savagely, a smile crooking my face as I relaxed my fingers on the string.

Chapter Eight

Gwrach y Rhibyn smiled back, not moving from her spot.

The elf thought she'd found her perfect opening. The bow pinged.

At the same moment, the vampire flung the child into the air. The woman who'd been sneaking up behind the elf jumped between them to catch her baby.

"No!" the child's mother screamed, diving forward. She caught the child, but the arrow pierced her back, the close range giving it such force that the woman jerked, and the tip penetrated through her chest. The woman dropped to her knees, eyes wide in shock as she stared down at the protrusion. Then she fell to her side, the fletch of the arrow breaking off as she collapsed.

Wanton desire filled the vampire as the fragrance of blood leaked into the room. She dropped to the ground next to the woman, unable to help herself; it was reminiscent of the child, but so much more pungent.

A hulking form crashed through the window behind her. "Elly!"

"Jac?!"

The vampire was shoved roughly off the mother and child by a massive male body coated in fur.

"No!" the hag snarled as the child cried out.

The elder *Pwca* had followed the woman upstairs and scooped the girl from the mother's drooping arms, running from the room.

She scuttled after them too late; the elf blocked the way with another arrow tip and the newcomer whaling on her with meaty fists.

The child screamed from down the hall, being carried away. The vampire moaned as the child was taken from right under her hands. "My child, my child."

Enraged, she tossed off the beast and surged forward, ready to end the elf and chase her child. The younger goblin grabbed her from behind, wrapping his oversized arms around her torso. She shot out her wings, breaking his hold and knocking him off balance, leading him to topple out the broken pane that failed to take him out when he shifted midair into a small bat.

Hissing at his reprised insult, the vampire dove after him, pursuing him by air. They danced around the house and flew over the roof.

Ditching the strange flight pattern, the vampire dipped toward the garden. Landing, she turned, ready for the bat to pursue her instead. She got her wish, but he shifted into a dragon as he descended.

Crushing her with his weight upon impact, she would have suffocated. However, she had positioned herself appropriately, and the rusted prong of the hoe pierced his hide. The dragon roared and became a goblin once more, the iron ripping through his magic destructively.

"Death comes," the vampire tittered, rolling out from under him. She crouched, watching as he took ragged breaths, the metal poisoning his system. His eyes rolled toward the house, and in the back of her awareness *Gwrach y Rhibyn* heard the elf screaming.

This was the wrong order, but the vampire would take what she could get. The vampire's fangs pierced the goblin's flesh and drew heavily. She didn't hurry; the elf's wingless state forced her to traverse all the way back through the house and down the stairs to reach the garden. The goblin's blood was less flavorful than his love. Nevertheless, the vampire took greedily, and the magic in his blood sang through her veins. She lost track of the scene around her.

With a banshee wail, she siphoned out every last drop, and he took his final breath.

Something clanged against her skull as she swallowed, and she dropped onto the empty husk of the goblin, dazed. The elf had shown up more quickly than anticipated. Before the vampire could focus, an arrow pierced her back.

She let out a roar of fury. As she struggled to stand, she caught sight of the elf running into the woods.

The elf thought the vampire was dead, but with the magic in her system, she sat up and ripped out the arrow, the ringing in her head dissipating. *Gwrach y Rhibyn* flapped her wings, rising into the air to get a better view of her prey.

Movement across the garden distracted her. The family — child and father — led by the older goblin, sprinted into the opposite wood.

"My child, my child," she cried, reaching out her claws in want.

The vampire stalled, intentions wavering. Torn, she hesitated for a second longer, then took off after the *Pwca* who had her child.

The cheetah outpaced the hag at a rapid clip. When it vanished into a mine, so too did the vampire. Once in Underhill, the shapeshifter did not head toward the fae domains, where she hoped to track down the elf once the goblin was taken care of and the child restored to her.

Instead, he veered a new direction, and *Gwrach y Rhibyn* paused again.

"Death comes." But for which fae?

Chapter Nine

Prif Namekeeper was not happy. The court was thrown in shadow as if a thunderstorm coiled beneath the roof, and his glamour crackled around him in a dark cloud. The queen was undisturbed by his display of rage.

"You have failed me. You have failed the *Ellyllon*. You have failed your queen."

My chin raised higher. "I have brought you the name, *Prif* Name-keeper, as requested," I dared to disagree politely.

"Dylan?" Uncle spat. "Dylan Blood? A human? That is useless to me. Her highness is not threatened by humans."

"The woman is dead," I reminded him.

"There remains the child."

My suspicions were correct. When Uncle requested a hunt for trai-tors, he meant it as a guise for cleaning the last of the "lower" species he found distasteful and below him. He specifically sought out *Tylwyth Teg* themselves, hoping to eradicate any vestiges of the fae we had deci-mated in the war. He feared a revival of our enemies. Uncle wanted genocide.

But I had seen the fear in that child's eyes and the plea in the woman's. They simply wanted to survive... as I did. They did not seek to harm us. They did not seek revenge.

Not like I had with the *Cyhyraeth*.

I struggled to contain my triumphant smile at the recollection of the arrow piercing her back. Then it dipped when the memory shifted to show the blurred form of a very still Jac beneath the blood-sucker.

Tears pricked my eyes again. My sight was all but gone now, so the haze of liquid did little to alter my uncle's appearance.

His exhale was audible across the courtroom. "We cannot let an enemy of the crown go free."

Uncle had not even cared that I'd taken out the last of the *Cyhyraeth*, getting my revenge. He did not care while other "lesser fae" escaped and thrived.

"Least of all, a crossbreed," he finished with a sneer.

My jaw clenched. I was a crossbreed. Many of us were technically crossbreeds, though our magic tended to dominate over human genes. It was a time when intermingling was necessary for the vitality of our kind. And it made us no less; I had developed powers in the end. My wings were a weight on my back I had not yet gotten used to.

Uncle was unimpressed by that either.

"You will complete this task," he decided with finality.

"*Prif?*"

Plentyn Aestylaneru o Ellyllon a Pwca yn nheulu'r Tylwyth Teg fewn Danybryn.

I stood up straight, compelled by my name. "Yes, *Prif?*"

The rest, he spoke aloud. "You are a disgrace. You will not return until you have removed the threat against the queen."

"But," I couldn't help but spit out, stepping back in shock, "they went to the mortal realm."

The silence was almost enough of an answer, though the queen gave a gentle snore in the midst of it. "Correct. You may be welcomed back once you have proven yourself worthy, but until then... You are hereby exiled to the mortal realm."

I was permitted time only to say goodbye to Mum. Nothing could be brought with me that was not on my back. So, I changed into a new outfit, donned my weapons, and walked out of my bedroom without a backward glance, ignoring the magically repaired window.

"This is good, Aetyl," Mum said, standing at the bottom of the stairs. Her distress was impossible to miss, even for me. "You have a chance to redeem yourself after everything..." Her hand shot out and paused before she could touch my back. The dark, leathery wings obviously made her uncomfortable. "We will be here when you return."

"Yeah," I scoffed and turned away to the door.

I had no qualms that Uncle wasn't trying to get rid of me once and for all. The mortal realm was poison to elves, teeming with iron that would slowly integrate in my system and none of Underhill's magic to combat it. I'd embarrassed him enough with my failures and the nature of the powers that had at long last revealed themselves during my final confrontation with the *Cyhyraeth*.

Mum did not need to throw me from the tree this time, so I felt no worry in turning away from her.

She had been right and wrong; it had been a shock to my system that had snapped the barrier on my dueling abilities, letting them both explode out of their cage. But it had not been a fight for my own life that had done it. It had been the desperation to save Jac, my friend, my partner… my future no longer.

But it had come too late.

Choking back the grief, I turned to look over my shoulder. "Goodbye, Mum." She could mistake the thickness in my voice for sorrow at leaving her.

Truthfully, I was glad to be rid of a place where I didn't belong, where no one wanted me. Jac had been the only one to give me trust, support, and love.

The wings that had finally unfurled as I'd looked down on the fight in the garden resembled those of the *Cyhyraeth* that I had finally vanquished without ado. However, I chose to believe it was because of the creature Jac had mimicked when he sparked a change in me… and our relationship. My new permanent appendages were a tribute to his memory and a dis to the *Cyhyraeth*'s.

Given that the wings remained regardless of the shape I shifted into, I gladly took the form of a bat. Blindly, I made my way toward the gate Puc had led the brownie child.

Epilogue

Noel Jones knew it was a mistake to break the seal. But after four shots and two pints of beer at one bar alone, no one could expect him to hold out. And that was after the three previous stops with — He consulted the permanent marker tallies slashed across his left forearm. — *Shit*, with eleven drinks already drowning his system.

His bladder was so full to the point of bursting that it was painful.

He'd have pissed his golf slacks if he waited for the next "hole" on the bar crawl. But, of course, after relieving himself and stumbling back toward the dim bar, his buddies were gone.

Assholes. He knew tonight was going to suck, but it was his wife's soon-to-be brother-in-law. For her, he'd suck it up.

Noel ripped his phone from his pocket and, his fingers, too clumsy to type a text, hit the call button. He leaned heavily on a stool while listening to the ringtone. The chair slid back under his heavy weight, skidding loudly on the floor before finding support against the wooden bar. Noel barely caught himself before his ass went down. He turned around and rested his elbows on the sticky bar top instead.

Someone who was not his wife's sister's fiancé answered. "Yo, you've rung the line of the soon-to-be-whipped Vince. Leave one, and he'll get back to you when the wife says he's allowed to." A chortle of laughter from several males concluded the slurred fake voicemail.

Noel heard Vince say from far away, "Hey, man, give it back. It might be Angela."

"It's not fucking Angela. You're whipped already, bro."

Noel interrupted in exasperation. "Dave."

"Oh, hey, man." Dave turns away from the phone. "It's Noel. Guess he's done pissing." More snickering preceded the return of Dave's voice to the speaker. "You think you can keep up with us? World's smallest bladder. I seriously thought Vince was fucking joking when he said you were coming. Isn't it past your bedtime, old man?"

Noel covered his eyes with one palm to stop the half-damp coaster below him from swaying as if the bar were on a boat. "Just tell me where you are. I'll come meet you."

"He wants to know where we are," Dave reported back to his drunk cronies with an audible sneer.

"C'mon, Dave. That's Angela's brother-in-law."

"If I tell him, then you'll hear where we're going, and that'll ruin the fucking surprise."

Vince sighed in the background.

"Listen, *Noelle*," Dave started with condescension. "You probably won't like where we're going next anyway, so why don't you head to Rainey Street in an hour, and we'll meet you there for the final hole once we're done."

Noel echoed Vince's sigh. "Vince requested no strip clubs, Dave."

"Listen, man, thanks for the fatherly advice, but I got my own dad. Vince made me best man so that means I plan the bachelor party, not you. Enjoy your hour-long break. Maybe use the time to piss so you won't hold us up again later."

Noel wanted to object to that statement — he didn't hold them up; they left without him — but the line had gone dead.

The sound of a glass hitting the bar surface caused Noel to wrench away the hand covering his face, ready to protest more alcohol. A cool pint of water sat before him like the gates of heaven. Noel smiled at the young bartender in thanks. He appeared closer to Dave's age than Noel's middle-age. The bartender gave a nod and sympathetic twist of his lips.

"Keep 'em coming," Noel mumbled. "I've got an hour to sober up."

Unfortunately, when you've had seventeen drinks and five shots— which was sixteen drinks more than he's had in any one night since his daughter was born seventeen years ago and eight more than his own bachelor party twenty-four years ago—then three glasses of water (and another trip to the men's room) was like a band aid on a bleeding artery.

Noel got to his feet when the bartender removed the third empty glass and kindly informed him it had been an hour in case he had somewhere to be. Observant guy. Noel's phone had died half an hour into his wait. It wasn't used to being up this late either.

"You gonna be okay?"

Noel nodded, though he took a few steps to the side when he stood from the stool. "I'm walking." He tipped the man for the care and stumbled into the street.

It had gotten very dark out, though the populated Texas city was still full of bright lights. He was used to nights at home in the countryside near the vineyards where there weren't any streetlights. How did anyone get any sleep here?

The sidewalk was as crowded as the bar, answering his question: They didn't.

Thankfully, it was less noisy with the chatter no longer echoing off the cramping walls and wrapped up in dreadful noise some call music. The bass from several nearby clubs continued to thump in his chest.

Noel did not belong on Austin's "Dirty Sixth," as his daughter had said when she found out where he was going, her tone infused with mortification. Most patrons were her age, in fact. Actually...

A girl was standing in a group of guys with the same hair as his daughter's best friend. He squinted, trying to tell if it was her in that inappropriate situation. What was her name? "Rachel?"

The girl startled, stared at him in horror, then grabbed the sleeve of the nearest guy, towing him down the sidewalk while the guy tried to look over his shoulder to see who he should beat up for upsetting his girl.

Noel ran a hand down his face, trying to get his act together and not embarrass his teenager. If Dave hadn't decided the hotel should be a surprise too, he'd head there.

"Excuse me," he said to a group passing him. "How do I get to Rainey Street?"

They just looked him up and down, cracked up, and kept walking.

Noel longed for his armchair, even the sound of his wife bickering with their daughter about her curfew that night over the faint chatter of some cop show on the TV. At least he could be certain his daughter wasn't at any of these clubs; she wouldn't be caught dead here for fear of running into her old man.

His best bet, he decided, was to follow the chattering and gamboling crowd down the street. There were really only two hubs for nightlife in the city; he wasn't too old to know that much. Tonight, he would be a lemming, following the kids to the second place at which he probably shouldn't be and certainly didn't want to be.

"Rainey street?" questioned a voice.

Noel blinked blurry eyes, slowing his lumber. An old woman stood near a trash can, an empty grocery cart in front of her. "Yes, ma'am. Do you know how to get there?"

She nodded. "Headed that way myself."

"To Rainey Street?" Noel couldn't hide his surprise. If he was accused of being too old to play with the crowd, he couldn't imagine what Dave would say if he saw this woman at their final hole. By the look of her stooping frame and withered face under the shawl wrapped around her head and mouth, loose strands of thin, unkempt black hair hanging about her gaunt cheeks, she was probably ten to twenty years his elder.

"Need a drink." She let out a cackle that turned into a cough and wheeled her cart around, shuffling away. "Out of milk."

He trotted after her. She was surprisingly quick. "It's —" He peered blearily at his watch. When he looked up, she was several feet ahead of him. He picked up his pace. "— just gone midnight. Will the store be open? Couldn't you go in the morning?" He's a little worried she wasn't all there. "Do you have anyone waiting for you at home?"

The squeak of one of the cart's wheels penetrated Noel's hearing, piercing through the evening revelry. He winced. His wooziness was quickly giving way to a thrumming headache and pure exhaustion.

She flapped a bony hand covered in a very thin layer of pale skin that looked more easily ripped than paper. "Thirsty now."

"Well," he tries again. "Can I escort you home after you've gotten your milk?" He raises his voice so she can hear. She's quickly outpacing him. Noel decides he might need to ease up on the fast-food on his lunch breaks during the week like his wife suggested.

"This is your turn," she tells him, her voice barely carrying on the night air. An index finger extends out. "Four streets yonder to your left."

There are a lot fewer people down this end of the street, but a freeway looms ahead, crossing their path, trucks honking and cars zipping past loudly even at this time of night on a Friday.

"Down here?" He turns back, but the old woman is gone on her way, presumably swallowed up by the shadows under the overpass.

Noel stares down the direction she pointed then back at where she vanished. He's in no state to help her — he needs to figure himself out. She seemed to know what she was doing. She'll be fine. He starts down the sidewalk alone, paralleling the freeway. He should have gotten her name. He berates himself. That way, he could have called the cops to check up on her from the hotel phone later and make sure she got home all right.

He slows as he reaches the fourth street. Did she say take the fourth or take the one after the fourth?

Turning around in a full circle, he sees a woman bicycle by in a full motorcycle helmet, one leg of her overalls rolled up to avoid getting caught in the bike chain. There are enough neon lights in her wheel spokes to light the bar he came from. She seems like someone heading to Rainey.

He heads that way. Some ways down the street, he hears a noise from a park on his left, like a groan. "Hello?" That must be where the biker went. He didn't see anyone else around. "Are you hurt?" Did she fall off her bike? Maybe, like him, she'd been drinking on Dirty Sixth before heading this way.

Another moan responded. "My husband, my husband."

"Ma'am? Is your husband hurt?" He hadn't seen a second person.

The park seemed empty, but partway down the street, he started over a little bridge crossing a stream. Trees on either side of its steep banks rustled in the night breeze, and Noel wrapped his arms around himself. Heading under the canopy of leaves, following the trail, he began to make out the sound of more thumping music. He hadn't found the biker, so maybe she was okay. Perhaps it was the music he heard. His head was swimming. Perhaps he'd imagined the words. Either way, he was on the right track. Rainey and the assholes it was harboring couldn't be far ahead.

The rustling picked up in the gully to his left. Some nocturnal animal out scavenging, no doubt. If he were nocturnal, his eyes wouldn't be drooping as they were. Startled by his presence, the animal gives a shrill scream, in turn sending Noel's heart hammering. Without warning, something flew out of the dark and clamped down on his shoulder, snatching him into the foliage with claws piercing his flesh.

He screamed as he tumbled down the embankment, branches scratching his skin and rocks bruising flesh. Tree trunks smacked into his shins and forehead. He hit the shallow stream at the bottom with a loud splash of chilly water that sobered him quickly.

Noel promptly vomited, having churned up the beer in his stomach, but in the back of his awareness, he distinctly heard a second splash to his right accompanied by a menacing growl.

If this was another prank by Dave, Noel was going to be pissed. Or had the bike girl come back to help him?

Pushing onto his hands and knees amongst the rocks as water rushed around his thighs and forearms, he looked up, trying to get his bearings and clear his vision after the tumble shook the dizziness in his head like a snow globe.

His eyes widened as a silhouette loomed, massive bat-like wings bracketing its hunched figure, which rippled and sloshed the water as it moved closer.

"So thirsty," it rasped in a familiar female voice. "No need for milk when there's delicious blood to be had."

The *vampire* — the term dragged itself into Noel's mind, foreign and unwelcome — lisped the lasciviously delivered words that chilled him more than the night air or water through a full row of long, black teeth dripping with saliva. Thin pale arms reached for him, arthritic hands grasping.

"Death comes."

The water between his legs warmed.

THE END.

L.B. Carter is a multi-award-winning, internationally bestselling author, bookworm, scientist, and cat-mom who loves hot chocolate, fairy lights, and foxes. Her books are a mix of haunting paranormal urban fantasy, gripping suspense, chilling horror, and dark humor with a dash of light romance. Expect unique contemporary twists on magical lore told by quirky anti-heroes.

Follow L.B. Carter on social media, join her reader groups, and subscribe to her newsletter at LBCarter.com to learn more about her books and download exclusive free stories.

Find all L.B.'s links at:
https://linktr.ee/lbcarterauthor

f facebook.com/lbcarterauthor

twitter.com/lbcarterauthor

instagram.com/lbcarterauthor

WHITE NIGHTS, BLACK DAYS

BY HELEN GLYNN JONES

"Evening, Nicky. You out again?"

Mrs. Govalenko, small and round like a pile of dumplings, her bosom straining against her flowered dress, looked up from sweeping the landing as Nikolai came out of his apartment.

He nodded, smiling with lips closed. "I am," he said. He liked the old lady. She took his rent every month and didn't ask questions. Not important ones, anyway.

"You should go out earlier, get some sunshine." She smiled, revealing gapped teeth. "You're too pale."

He snorted a small laugh. If only she knew. "I'm all right."

"You're looking thin," she went on, pinching his cheek. "All these nights out and no sleep isn't right for a young man." She shook her head. "I'll leave some of my pirozhki outside your door, something nice for you to eat when you come in."

"Thank you," he said, bending to kiss her wrinkled cheek. She giggled, soft, like the girl she once was. He patted her shoulder, then started down the stone stairs.

"Did you lock up, Nicky?" she called after him, the swish of her brush starting once more. "Don't want anyone breaking in now."

"It'll be fine," he said, waving his hand. "I'll be back in a bit."

Anyone who broke into his apartment would regret it, anyway. He would track them down before the sun rose.

The heavy wooden door closed behind him with a bang as he stepped into the street. He winced, squinting at the pearlescent sky from behind his sunglasses. He liked to leave the house at sunset, once the lamps had been lit, the dying sun painting licks of fire against the clouds. It hurt to be outside at such a time, but it was worth it to feel his soul twist and open against the beauty of the world, a reminder of something he could no longer have.

But at this time of year, when the sun never properly set, the sky eternally dusk and gold, he hated it. Hated lurking beneath trees, on the edge of the groups who thronged the wide boulevards, dancing beneath the curving glow of the White Nights, or strolling along the Neva, hand in hand. He wished for darkness, for the sweet oblivion of night, a cloak beneath which he could wander freely, rather than keeping to the shadows. He stopped beneath a tree whose green branches stretched out thick and full, sheltering him from the bright sky. Nearby, a young man played violin, a rousing tune, his foot tapping time on the pavement. On the ground in front of him, his open violin case was already filling with coins and even a few notes. Couples danced and laughed, their voices drifting in the perfumed air. Nikolai closed his eyes and let the music wash over him, let it take him to another time.

"Are you waiting for someone?"

The words were pert, flirtatious, like the speaker. She was achingly young, her skin smooth and sun-kissed, hair as golden as sunset. He smiled, enjoying the effect he knew he was having on her. He knew he was beautiful. Eyes like the ice-bound seas to the North, high cheekbones, a wide full mouth. She had used to tell him so, when they first met, her red lips pressing against his, her twisting scent like old roses, her long white hands pushing the dark hair back from his brow.

"Perhaps I'm waiting for you," he replied, moving closer. "After all, I can't dance alone, can I?"

He preferred brunettes, but she would do. Taking her hand, he let her lead him into the dance, let her help him forget, for a little while.

"Heads or tails?"

Those had been her first words to him, spoken in the red-black depths of a nightclub just off Nevsky Prospekt. He'd chosen tails, half-mesmerized by the golden coin, as it flipped through the darkness. She'd laughed, saying he had a lucky face. Her name was Tatiana, she'd told him, like one of the lost young duchesses. She'd looked like her as well, her face, the expression on it, slightly out of time, like a faded photograph come to life. He'd been drawn to her immediately, entranced by her stories of troika rides with dashing noblemen, of sapphire bracelets and jeweled eggs that opened to reveal surprises. Of palaces with painted walls and carved archways, of silk and song and silver goblets. Of a lost time, glittering like a fairy tale, like the ice on the Neva the next morning when she'd left him, disappearing like smoke.

He'd gone looking for her the following night, vodka in hand, wanting to be drawn into her web of stories once more. He hadn't realized he was already ensnared. She'd taken his arm, pulling him into the night, to a theatre where they'd watched ballet dancers, their skirts like white paper fans, spinning across the stage. She'd whispered to him of what she wanted to do to them. He'd thought she was joking, a weird game to turn him on.

He was to learn, later, that she was not.

He left the girl on a bench beneath the tree, her soft limbs draped over the painted wood. She'd wanted him to stay, had begged him to take her, but he'd been gentle in his refusal, willing her into sleep. She would wake soon and remember only a dance with a handsome stranger. It was better that way. Crossing the square, he continued into the night, letting memory lead him.

"Watch where you're going, hey?"

Nikolai blinked, stepping back, his nostrils assailed by the scent of tobacco and sweat and darker things. The old man shuffled past him, hands in pockets, stained black cap pushed down on his feathers of greying hair.

"Sorry, Grandpa," he said. He had no appetite for trouble tonight. He had no appetite for much at all these days. His skin burning, he headed for the darker shadows beneath the trees, where young lovers kissed, and old couples held hands, dreaming of times past when their fires still shone bright. Hands in pockets, he wandered along Nevsky Prospekt, crossing over into Liteiny Prospekt, past the old church of Ss Simeon and Anna, the grey domes and yellow walls lit by fading sun. He crossed the river, the last light of day glinting from the water, past the ornate wedding cake façade of the Bolshoi State Circus, along the Sadovaya and past the Mikhailovsky Palace, the city gleaming as the sky shaded to pearl. He pushed his dark glasses up his nose, ducking his head, shoulders hunched, the beauty of his surroundings lost on him.

He wondered, sometimes, why he bothered. What it was that drove him out, night after night, searching for her. There was a whole world out there for him to explore, endless victims, waiting for his embrace. But the city held him in his grip, just as she once had, a vice both beautiful and full of pain, from which there was no escape.

He'd never met anyone like her. She'd opened his eyes to a whole new world, twirling beneath chandeliers in underground rooms, running through darkened gardens, laughing and loving, experiencing life with such intensity it hurt, even now, to think of those glittering nights. Once, she'd broken into the Peterhof, grabbing his hand and laughing at his protests as she'd pushed open the iron gate, dragging him past the fountains with their gilded statues and, finding an open window, taking him inside. They'd wandered the halls where tsars once ruled in blood and war and jeweled excess and made love on the polished wooden floor, the ornate painted ceiling swirling above them.

But each day, she'd disappeared, despite his efforts to follow her, to find where she went at the first hint of dawn. He hadn't stopped trying, though. And one day, he'd found her.

He hadn't realized, at the time, how dangerous her love was.

Or what the price of discovery would be.

He'd thought himself a revolutionary. Oh, not like the green-suited red-starred ones of old, dealing death and oppression in the name of equality. If asked, he would describe himself as a dreamer who longed for change, for the wheel of power to turn once more, for his family's faded fortunes to be restored. They'd had a country house once, now a shattered shell, and a palace in the city, long lost. His relatives were scattered across the globe, but he was one of the few who remained in the embrace of Mother Russia, his great-grandparents choosing to weather the storm, wanting to cling to the old places, the old ways. They had paid, of course, as had all who thought that way.

He'd been brought up on their stories, though. Whispered tales by firelight of days gone by, of riches stolen, of lives lost. And later, once he'd gone to bed, the grown-ups thinking him asleep, he'd heard more. Tales of darkness and betrayal, violence and injustice. Tears flowing and voices rising as the level in the vodka bottle fell.

He'd grown up with the fire of those stories in his soul. They had kept him in the ancient city on the Neva with its glittering dark winters, its bright summers. Driven him to take an apartment in the palace his family had once called home. Thinking it was a beginning, a way back once the wall had fallen and Russia began to emerge from the shadows.

When he'd met Tatiana, with her stories of noblemen and sleigh rides, it had seemed like the next step in his quest. A sign from his ancestors that he was on the right path.

But then the path had twisted, taking him somewhere unexpected.

. . .

It had hurt, at first. Then there had been light-headedness and white light, exploding behind his closed eyelids. Then blackness. He'd thought he was dead. Which, in a way, he was. When he'd woken the next night she was already there, her skin that had previously felt ice-cream cold now soft and warm as his own.

She'd shown him in the mirror what he'd become. The iridescent shimmer to his eyes, the more prominent cheekbones. The red lips. And, behind them, fangs, diamond-sharp and white.

And the thirst.

She'd taught him to hunt, to use his beauty as a lure, clapping her hands like a child at his first success. It had felt like flying, the sweet tang of blood, the heat and rush, and pulsing heartbeat more potent than the strongest liquor. He wanted more, more, more.

Together, they had haunted the dark nights and gleaming streets, loving and feeding and dancing. Despite the fact that he was dead, he'd never felt more alive.

Until the moment on the bridge, when everything had changed.

He entered the cool green of the Summer Gardens, one of the few places that still had the power to move him. Heading down to the riverbank, he sat in the cool grass with his arms wrapped around his knees. The great river flowed past, silvered by the half-light, heading for the sea. He closed his eyes, remembering hours spent lying under blue skies, golden sun warming his skin. Lazy drifting summer days, the ice-cold kiss of vodka, the sharp-sour taste on his tongue. The way the ocean shifted hue with the sky, the bright green of sunlight through leaves, the miraculous colored arc of a rainbow.

All that was lost to him now. His fingers strayed to the cord around his neck, where a single coin hung. Another reminder, the most painful one of all.

He got up, running through the gardens as though he could leave the memory behind. But it followed him, no matter how fast or how long he ran for. He stopped, smashing his fist into one of the trees, the branches shivering and shaking, leaves cascading.

"Hey!" A young man nearby, lounging on the lawn in incongruous yellow trousers, waved his hand. "Stop that! The gardens are for all of us."

"Even me?" He wanted to snarl, to see the young man back away like a crab across the grass, green staining his ridiculous trousers. But instead, the words came out like a breath. He had no fight left in him, not anymore.

He was so lonely.

That's what no one ever mentioned about immortality. The utter, crushing loneliness. The strangeness of seeing the world change and move forward, yet being left behind, like an old photo in a frame. Vampires were supposed to live glamorous lives, weren't they? That's how it always was in books and films – their impossible beauty seducing others, their lives filled with opportunity and wealth. Yet Dracula had lived in his castle alone, mourning his lost love. He knew how that felt.

"All baby birds need to leave the nest. You'll thank me," she'd said. Her last words to him, barely heard over the gurgle of water, the crack of ice. He'd cried out as she'd pushed him, tumbling down past the unforgiving stone bridge, past the tiny bronze bird, the dark river closing over his head. A single coin, flipping over and over in a mockery of their first meeting, drifted down towards him. He'd caught it, holding on as though it was her hand, the last trace of her. Her silhouette had remained on the bridge, a dark shape seen through ripples, leaning over for a few minutes more. He'd called to her, but his voice was taken by the rushing water. Then she was gone.

He'd lain at the bottom of the river for a day and a night, his blood drifting like clouds, the dark shapes of ice creaking and groaning above him as he'd told himself she hadn't meant it, that she still loved him.

The only thing that had made him get out of the river was his dream of finding her again.

It was what drove him now.

He turned, taking one of the paths ran beneath the trees, past rows of statues that gleamed like bone in the strange almost-night. He needed to keep looking, despite how hopeless it seemed, despite the memories that rolled over him, like a tortured film of someone else's life. Flickers of color seemed to dance between the black tree trunks, like her skirts swirling in a pillared ballroom as she had spun in his arms, her dark hair streaming. Roses scented the air, just like her perfume, teasing him, just as she had. He stopped, his head back, eyes wide on the shimmering sky, mouth open in a soundless scream, fists clenched at his side. He longed for darkness, for the winter nights when the sun barely rose at all, where he could walk the streets, frost creaking beneath his boot heels as he searched. For the sweet tang of blood taken in an alleyway or nightclub, for the shadows that carved his face into beauty while also hiding his transgressions.

Summer, with its roses and green leaves and gleaming skies, depressed him. His fingers went to the coin at his throat, to the last piece of her, as he cried his sorrows to a heaven that was no longer open to him.

Then he started along the path once more.

A quarter of a century had passed since he'd pulled himself out of the river, a coin clutched in his cold fingers. A dark, wasted figure, dripping, half-frozen, but still alive. It was like a virus, this burgeoning life inside him. He could starve it, stab it, freeze it, but nothing would take it away. Other than the bright light of sunrise. And he wasn't quite ready to face that yet, not without seeing her, one last time.

And so he'd lived through endless long days, dark nights made darker by loneliness. He'd spent a year or so just sitting after she'd left him, unable to face anything. Precious time lost when he could have been searching for her.

Eventually, he'd gone out again, walking the streets where they had once laughed and loved, the seasons changing around him though he barely noticed. He'd gone to the old palaces, the places where his ancestors had lived before war and revolution forged a new Russia. He'd danced in the ballrooms, imagining sweet music, candlelight on snow, rippling silks and furs. All gone now.

Just like her.

He'd heard rumors, of course; she'd been seen in Morocco, splendid in jeweled kaftans and kohl, or up north among the tigers and bears, one more predator leaving footprints in the snow. He'd followed her trail up there, but instead found a loneliness so vast his mind couldn't take it, so far from the glittering lights, the jeweled palaces, the bustle of people with their scent of blood and flowers and ash. Eventually, he'd returned to the ancient city that dreamed by the sea, with its canals and bridges and green parks filled with shadows where he'd hidden his sorrow, hoping she might come back to him.

He left the gardens by a different route, past one of their favorite haunts, a nightclub just off the Kutuzov Embankment. Once a noble-man's palace, now the ornate rooms were home to lasers that pulsed, heated bodies dancing and downing tiny glasses of vodka, cloudy with cold. It had long been a place of vampires, but most of the old ones were gone, either headed south to where the nights were still long and dark, chasing an endless winter, or replaced by a new brood of brash young things, loud and thuggish in straining suits, roaring, expensive liquor flowing like the blood of the young women they fed on. It was a Russia he didn't recognize anymore.

Still he liked to check-in, to see if there was any news of her, despite all the times he had been laughed at or sent away. His name still had currency, even among the new Russians building their own aristocracy, so they humored him, listening to his pleas, to his stories, before sending him out into the night empty-handed.

It was getting close to dawn, the skies becoming more pearlescent, and he picked up his pace. Perhaps there would be no time for vodka and tears this night. But as he passed the club doorway, a hand shot out, grabbing him and pulling him into the shadows.

"I hear you're still looking for someone." The voice was low, growling.

Nikolai nodded. He reached up to untwist the fingers holding his shirt. It was silk, after all. He still had some standards.

"What of it?" If his heart still had the ability to beat, it would be hammering, a call from his soul to hers.

"If you visit the lucky bird, tomorrow night, maybe you toss a coin, you might find her."

"Who told you this?" Not hammering, fluttering. Like the wings of a captured bird who senses freedom. This time it was Nikolai's fingers twisting in the other vampire's shirt, shoving him against the wall. A heavy hand landed on his shoulder.

"We tell you this out of respect for your advanced years," said another voice, even darker than the first. "But our goodwill only goes so far, Grandfather."

Nikolai stiffened. Grandfather? But he knew who it was who spoke, knew of the atrocities that went on in a room deep below the night-club, committed against vampire and human alike. He let go of the other vampire's shirt.

"Of course," he said. "I am grateful." Depression stole over him again like a blanket, comforting and stifling all at once.

"Off you go then," the voice said, a big hand shoving him, so he stumbled back into the street, wincing in the pre-dawn light. He made his way quickly home, their laughter still ringing in his ears.

"You know the children's song," she'd said, laughing, her hand in his, back when he was still human, and she was still a mystery. "Chizhik-Pyzhik, where've you been? Drank vodka on the Fontanka." Her voice was like silver bells, and he'd laughed too, singing the old folk song with her, both of them dancing, their heels keeping time on the paving stones.

They'd peered over the side of the bridge to the dark rushing waters of the Fontanka River and, just visible, the little bronze bird statue sticking out from a curve in the wall below.

"If you can get a coin to land on the plinth, it's good luck," he'd said, fumbling in his pockets for some loose change.

"Stories for tourists," she'd said. But she was still laughing, cheering him on as he flipped coins into the dark water, grabbing him and kissing him until he was breathless when he'd finally succeeded.

"Lucky indeed," she'd murmured against his lips. Smitten, he could only agree.

He got home just before dawn, flame already streaking the horizon with gold. He climbed the stone stairs slowly, but his heart was lighter than it had been in so very long. A small parcel, wrapped in paper, sat on the mat outside his front door. He picked it up; it was still warm, grease coming through the wrapping. Mrs. Govalenko's pirozhki. He wished he could taste them but knew they would make him sick. Still, he tucked the parcel beneath his arm as he unlocked the door, stepping inside.

His apartment was dark, which suited him. Deep velvet curtains covered the long windows, the walls painted the color of old blood. He didn't have a lot of furniture – he didn't need it. A small desk stuffed with papers. A table and a single chair. In the small bedroom, a double bed, the sheets unused. And his one extravagance; a long red velvet sofa, tasseled, with ornate gold trim. He had bought it in an old junk shop that wasn't there anymore, back in the days when such things were still seen as rubbish, decadent reminders of a no-longer-needed past. He'd loved it, liked to imagine who might have sat on it, when it had been in a palace, liked to see her white skin against it, pale in the gloom of his room...

He shook his head. Soon, now. So soon. One more day and he would see her again, and the endless nights of waiting would be over. He knew she would be there – she wouldn't have sent the message, otherwise. And what better location to meet him than the last place they'd been together? He pushed her betrayal from his mind, not wanting it to weigh him down.

He went into his kitchen, putting the parcel on the counter – the pirozhki wouldn't go to waste. He knew a family, a few streets over, who would be glad of them. He opened the fridge, taking out the single carton of milk and pouring some into a saucer, placing it on the floor next to the oven. Something for his domovoy, to keep it happy. It was easier to feed the house spirit than it was a cat – he'd had one, back in the days when he was first turned, but the bloodlust had been too strong. Heartbroken, he'd never got another. The milk disappeared every day, still. He didn't ask why. He already knew there was magic in the world.

Then he went to his desk, searching through the tangle of papers, finding what he needed. He scratched out a short note on paperwhite as her skin, the pen bleeding black ink across the page. Putting it in an envelope, he left it there, where he knew it would be found.

Then, smiling a little at the thought of her red lips, her dark hair, he went to his bedroom, lying down on top of the bedclothes. His hand at his throat, the coin clutched between his fingers, he closed his eyes and waited.

Sunset came, and with it, something he'd not felt in decades. A small tendril of excitement, like a ray of sunlight cutting through deep gloom. He left the house as soon as he was able, pausing to kiss Mrs. Govalenko on both cheeks as she paused from her sweeping. He'd left money for her, with his note, as well as the deed to all his things— small payment for keeping his secrets for so many years.

He danced through the pearlescent night, his steps taking him through familiar streets towards where she waited for him. Passers-by laughed, some dancing with him, young women and men taking his hands, blowing him kisses. It felt almost like the old days, and he hoped it was an omen. In his pocket, no longer on the knotted cord, was a single coin.

Finally, he reached the bridge. The river gleamed like mother-of-pearl beneath the shimmering skies. A lone figure in a long black coat leaned against the railings, overlooking the little bird statue. Her dark hair blew in the breeze. At his step, she turned.

He stopped, sorrow lancing his heart.

She was still beautiful, still a sculpture in snow, a perfect ice-maiden. Her lips were still red, her hair long and satin-sleek. But the scar that bisected one perfect cheek spoke of a troubled existence, as did the deep shadows beneath her eyes. Like his.

She obviously hadn't fed in a while.

And then she was in his arms, bird-light and fragile, her lips on his. He sighed her name, letting the years of longing wash away from him, like the river rushing below them.

Beneath the longing, surprising him, was anger. He pushed her away.

"Why?" His voice cracked on the words, a raw cry from the heart.

She shook her head, her hands clasped together, long fingers almost translucent.

"I had no choice," she said. Her voice was no longer silver bells. Instead, it was smoke.

"There's always a choice!" His fists were clenched. "If you knew what I've been through!" He turned away.

"I made the choice to save you," she said. Her hand rested on his shoulder, the scent of roses twisting around him once more. 'It was the only one I had. And I knew I had to make the break so strong you would never want to see me again.'

He turned back to her. Pearly light glinted on her high cheekbones.

"Save me?" He shook his head. She held his gaze, a vestige of her old strength and fire still visible.

"Yes. You didn't know what I did, who I was. Or who I worked for. They'd sent me, you see, to watch you. I never expected to fall in love."

"Love?" A whisper, but it held a quarter-century of sorrow.

She nodded.

He blinked. "Who was it?"

But he didn't need to know, really. Who else could it have been, who would have used a vampire as a spy, who would have carved their mark into her beauty? There were several choices, none of them pleasant. And he had been a young man with thoughts of a different world, of possibility, at a time of turmoil.

"So, what now?" He chewed on his lip and then huffed out a laugh, looking down, then up. "I brought a coin, you know."

Her face lit up, in the familiar smile that still tugged his heart.

"Let's see if we can be lucky again, hey?"

She broke into the Peterhof again, although he had to help her with the gate this time. They wandered through the ornate gardens, past fountains, and waterfalls, up marble stairs. Once inside, they raced along the wide corridors, dancing in the ballroom, Tatiana humming the old songs with her eyes closed, her hair streaming out behind her in inky ribbons. Then they found a room on the top floor, long deserted, and made love as they used to until stars danced behind Nicky's eyelids.

Afterward, she lay there, pliant as silk in his arms, her skin so soft against his own. "What happens now?" she whispered.

"Everything."

A few hours later, they sat on the roof, their arms around each other, watching the sky change.

"Are you sure?' she said, her head on his shoulder, the scent of roses all around.

"It's the only way, isn't it? To be free? For you to be free of them?"

"My own freedom, yes. But what about you? There is still a world out there for you."

"My world is here," he said, knowing it to be true with every fiber of his being.

She laid her hand against his cheek. A single tear, ruby-red, lay on hers. "I never meant it to be like this, you know."

"I know you didn't."

He wouldn't change it, though. Not now. Not after finding her again, after all the lost years. The sky shimmered like a mirage, the colors changing as night turned toward day.

"It's not too late to leave," she whispered.

"I'm not leaving you," he said.

She turned to kiss him, her lips lingering. Then she took something from her finger, something that glittered in the pale dawn, and laid it on the roof tiles. A ring made of gold, engraved with a crest bearing a double-headed eagle, studded with diamonds.

"It's good to be back here again, Nicky," she murmured, her skin already starting to smoke. It was strange, but he wasn't sure she was talking to him anymore, even though he was the only other person there. She reached her hand out, and he took it. There was a rushing noise, brightness all around him, but no pain. He thought he heard her say something else, something about being back where it all began, but he was rising up, his hand leaving hers, the unbearable brightness of dawn all through him, the great city, with its palaces and towers and rivers, spread out below him and gleaming as though made of gold.

He was free at last.

And as the city woke, something glinted on the plinth of the small statue of Chizhik-Pyzhik. A single golden coin.

Helen Glynn Jones is a prize-winning author of six novels, writing for middle-grade, young adult and adult audiences. She's been published in magazines and anthologies, written for the Writers & Artists website and The Guardian, and created regular content for a variety of businesses and publications in Australia and the UK.

Born in the UK, Helen has since lived in both Australia and Canada. A few years ago she returned to her native England where, when she's not writing stories, she likes to hunt for vintage treasures, explore stone circles and watch the sky change colour. She now lives in Hertfordshire with her husband, daughter, and wonderfully chaotic cockapoo.

Find out more at helenglynnjones.co.uk

f facebook.com/authorhelenglynnjones
🐦 twitter.com/AuthorHelenJ
📷 instagram.com/helenejones33

LICENSED TO KILL

BY DEVORAH FOX

Chapter One

Gretel trudged toward the office's refreshment cart, her boot heels clicking on the hardwood floor. She reached for the coffeepot, changed her mind, and grabbed a beer from the mini-fridge instead.

Her brother Hans looked up from his desk. "A little early in the day for drinking, isn't it? It isn't even lunchtime."

Gretel popped the cap and plopped in the small guest chair.

"I take it you fought a tough battle," Hans said.

Gretel cast a downward glance. A dark blotch stained the Grethans Exterminators logo on her tee-shirt. She nodded and took a swig from the beer bottle.

Hans tucked in the paper ends and set a roll of quarters next to the banded bills. Check- and credit-card transactions were more convenient, but the business took cash, even barter, if that was the clients' preference. She knew Hans didn't mind. To him, remittance, in whatever form it was made, meant a job well done.

Gretel laid a folded check on top of the currency.

Hans smiled. "I see from the payment that you got it done, and we have a contented customer."

"Yup," Gretel said. "Old Man Swiggert's bluebirds won't be bothered by that squirrel again. My newest trap worked. I caught the varmint, took him way out past the village limits, and released him in the woods. He'll have a distance to travel if he takes it into his furry head to come back. If the hawks and the coyotes don't nail him first." She drank more beer. "Nothing Swiggert couldn't do himself with a live trap, the right bait, and a little patience."

"Except for the releasing-in-the-woods part. Folks around here are—"

"Afraid? And with good reason. Evil lurks in those wild places, as we found out. But we do what has to be done."

Hans narrowed his eyes. "Yet, I get the impression you're not happy."

Gretel stood and paced before Hans's desk in their parlor, repurposed as an office, stopping now and then to drink. "Nah, it's okay. Really. It's part of the job."

"Swiggert will tell his friends and neighbors. We'll get more work."

"Right."

"Just not the work you want to do."

Gretel dropped into the chair without comment.

"I'm guessing eradicating roaches and rodents is something of a come-down from besting a cannibalistic witch," he said.

She shrugged. "You're happy enough with how the business is progressing."

Hans stamped the reverse of the check with their firm's endorsement. "We're building a company doing what we learned we can do—rid Hip Deep of pests. Solve problems for our neighbors, remove threats to their security. Improve the quality of their life."

"And you like your role." Gretel flicked her index finger at the papers piled on his desk. "Pushing numbers around."

Hans folded his long fingers over the ledger book and grinned. "I do."

"You always were the brainy one. It was your idea to scoop up those precious metals and jewels the witch hoarded. We put them to good use, didn't we?" Gretel glanced at the framed business license hanging on the wall above Hans's National Honor Society diploma and the certificate naming Gretel the Sportslurp Player of the Year.

Hans tapped the ledger with a pencil. "Fear not, dear sister. We got a job that you can sink your teeth into."

"Oh?"

Hans folded his hands on the desktop. "Mr. Robert says something is attacking his animals."

"Robert? James Robert? The one with the gentleman's ranch in the country?"

"That's the one."

"Something? Like what?"

Hans shrugged. "He doesn't know. One of his goats has an injury he can't explain. He'd like us to look into it."

Gretel snorted. "I suspect a coyote or a wild dog. James needs to do a better job of looking after his flock."

"Maybe so, but I told him we'd check it out. C'mon, we can use every bit of business we can pick up."

Gretel sighed and got to her feet. "Okay, fine. I'll change into a fresh tee-shirt and see the man."

Gretel steered her white Jeep Wrangler up the tree-lined graded lane leading to the Roberts' country home. Small white goats grazed in the pastureland, stretching away on either side. Gretel parked in the driveway and walked up to the colonnaded front porch. The gravel crunching under her boots must have announced her approach because James's daughter met her at the door.

"Hi, Sybil," Gretel said, noting the young woman's leisurewear. "No classes today?"

Sybil shook her head. "I don't feel well."

Gretel could see that. Sybil's face was pale and drawn. In contrast, her eyes were unusually dark.

Sybil stepped forward to open the screen door for Gretel, then winced and retreated out of the wash of sunlight as if the brightness was too much for her. "Come on in."

Lucy Robert came down the hallway. Over her house dress, the woman wore a pink sweater vest so soft and silky that Gretel barely resisted stroking it. Mohair, Lucy had knitted it with yarn milled from the fleece their Angora goats produced.

The woman's warm smile was welcoming, but creases between her eyes spoke of stress. "Gretel, I'm so glad you came. James is at wit's end about this. May I offer you a refreshment? Iced tea? Lemonade?"

"Thanks, but I'd just as soon get started. Is James available?"

"He's in the loafing shed, the little barn set back to the right of the house."

Rectangular with a pitched roof and an overhang above the board-and-batten double doors, the building was more shed than barn. The odorous air was thick with dust, dander, and pollen, and Gretel suppressed a sneeze. She found James Robert inside stacking farm implements against the wall alongside the feed sacks and hay bales. He pulled off heavy work gloves and extended a hand in greeting. A retired accountant, James still served a few clients but spent more of his time at the country home than in his downtown office. What had once been a desk worker's soft pale hands were rough and reddened. "Gretel, thanks for coming."

"You told Hans that something attacked your herd."

"Let me show you." He led Gretel to where a single goat munched hay. Its curly white coat had been shaved at the base of its neck, revealing a patch of bare skin.

"Is it shearing season?" Gretel asked.

"No. I routinely do a little shearing of their nether parts. Otherwise, urine wicks into their fleece and ruins it." He gave her an apologetic smile. "TMI? Oh, you mean the patch at Cherie's neck. I had to do that for the vet, so she could examine and treat the injury. That's what I want you to look at."

Gretel moved forward with temerity.

"You don't need to be shy. These Angoras are the sweetest critters. Calm, quiet, gentle."

The little goat pointed its pink nose at her, gave her a bucktoothed smile, and gazed at her with black button eyes. It didn't flinch when Gretel drew near.

The wound was hard to miss. Two red spots stood in contrast with the pale shaved skin. "Oh, I see.

"What do you make of it?"

"I'm no vet, but it doesn't look infected to me."

"It isn't. The vet took care of that so it wouldn't fester."

"It looks like a puncture. I'm guessing you don't think it was an insect bite. What caused it?"

"Good question. I'm baffled. The vet was baffled."

Gretel leaned closer to examine the marks. "Could she have bumped into a protrusion, some pronged tool, or a piece of wire?"

James shook his head. "I can't think of a thing around here that could cause that type of injury. It had to be an animal."

Gretel frowned.

"What animal, I couldn't say, though. This little girl is never out in the pasture alone. She's with the other goats, and let me tell you, they are protective of their young'uns. Even when the older ones spread out to browse, at least one mom stays behind to mind the babies. I can't picture a scenario where a predator could get close to just one long enough to create this damage." He scratched his head through his feed cap. "If it did, it wouldn't stop with a tiny nick. A wild dog, a coyote or fox or a wolf would tear out the throat, pulled away flesh." James shuddered.

"Maybe all that fleece gets in the way and discourages further damage?"

James shrugged. "Possibly. I'm still discounting a canine predator. How one would access the pasture in the first place is beyond me. I installed high-tensile electric fencing to keep predators out."

"A snake?" Gretel suggested. "Those marks look fang-y. An electric fence wouldn't keep a reptile out."

"I thought about that. A snake would have released venom. Neither I nor the doc found any sign of that. Cherie here acted fatigued for a couple of days, but she's bouncing back." James shook his head. "I don't understand it."

"I'll be honest. I'm stumped." Gretel said. She held up an index finger. "Never fear, I'm on the case. I'll identify the attacker and come up with a plan."

James nodded.

"Meanwhile, consider getting a livestock dog. Breeds like Great Pyrenees give good herd protection."

"I'll look into it. Thanks."

Gretel left James Robert to his chores and traipsed through the pasture, arousing only mild curiosity among the grazing goats who glanced at her then returned to munching. She kept her eyes and ears open for anything that seemed out of place. Horizontal wires, plastic vertical struts, and PVC posts made up the electric fencing, and Gretel spotted no breaks in the mesh. Nowhere did she see grass torn up by a struggle. The goats themselves kept close in a tight clutch.

She had to agree with James. At first glance, she couldn't detect what could have injured the little goat.

Gretel gazed out over the pasture. Well-maintained green trees bordered the fence. Regularly spaced with their lower limbs trimmed away, they didn't afford much coverage in which a hunter on the prowl could hide. Beyond the trees, a narrow meadow fronted the densely wooded foothills of the distant Mount Gofrbye. Anything could lurk in the thick dark forest, but it would need to traverse the meadow to access the pasture. The exposure called for something swift and stealthy. Gretel could picture a cougar emerging from the forest and skulking low across the open ground, its tawny coat blending with the sunbaked grasses. It would leave puncture wounds, except the electrified fence would stop it in its tracks before it got anywhere near its prey.

Gretel's movements flushed a flock of crows that took to the sky. Hmm, she thought, the fence wouldn't deter a winged predator.

Perhaps a hawk or eagle harmed Cherie. Birds of prey were known to carry off small game such as mice, squirrels, even rabbits. Would one try to snatch up a kid? A hawk's talons could leave the kind of mark found on Cherie's neck. A hawk might have found the animal too heavy and released it.

She returned to the barn where James and Lucy enjoyed a break with lemonade and sugar cookies. Gretel was glad to accept a glass of the cool beverage and balance its tartness with a sweet.

"You're right, James. I couldn't find anything mechanic or structural that could have hurt Cherie. It was likely a natural enemy, but to come up with a defense plan, I need to know what I'm dealing with. Was Cherie the only one of your animals that was hurt?"

James nodded. "So far that I've found."

"When did the attack happen?"

"My best guess would be during the night. She was fine when I brought them in from the pasture three days ago. At least she didn't show any signs of having been injured. The following day I noticed she was sluggish. When she didn't improve, I called the vet. She prescribed antibiotics to counter any infection and supplements to restore her energy. Cherie's going to be fine but—"

"You're worried, I'm sure. I'm going to research what could have done this to her. Meanwhile, could you keep a close eye on the herd—"

"Tribe. A group of goats is called a tribe."

"No kidding?" Gretel chuckled at the unintended pun. "The tribe then. Where are they kept when they're not in the pasture?"

"In the loafing shed or just outside it if the weather's pleasant. I can't figure out how an intruder got near them."

"Let's hope this was a one-time occurrence. Tonight, if you notice any disturbance, any kind at all, make a note of the time. Call me if it becomes critical. Otherwise, I'll contact you tomorrow."

"Sounds good." They shook on it. With thanks, she handed the lemonade glass to Lucy and returned to her car.

Gretel looked up with a start. "How long have you been standing there?"

"Just a few minutes." Hans smiled. "I didn't want to ruin your concentration." He hoisted himself onto the stool to her left. "I took the deposit to the bank, saw your Jeep in the parking lot, and figured I'd join you." He waved to the bartender. "What are you working on?"

Gretel set her smartphone on the counter. "Our new case. Something did injure one of James Robert's flock, er, tribe. It wasn't immediately obvious what. This is a tough one."

"No kidding," Hans said with a mischievous grin.

Gretel groaned.

"Got your goat there, did I?"

"Hans!"

"At least we don't have to worry about James Robert trying to fleece us."

"Hans, stop it!" Gretel laughed and bopped him on his bicep. "I thought I'd ask around if anyone else is having the same experience." She glanced right and left. "No ranchers here." Two ladies with shopping bags occupied one booth, their hands wrapped around tall drinks with curlicue straws. Four men in suits and ties held down another booth; plates holding lunch remains lined the table's edge. A lone man sat at the end of the bar nursing a draft beer.

The bartender said, "It's not like our Wild West days. These days the ranch hands aren't punching cows so much as time clocks." He asked Hans, "What can I get you?"

"A cola. With lime." To Gretel, Hans said, "No rum." He winked. "I still have work to do."

The bartender placed Hans's drink in front of him. "Business will pick up later. This is the first night of our karaoke contest." He grabbed two fresh coasters, plucked a ballpoint pen from his shirt pocket, and wrote on the back. "Come back tonight, be my guests. Show this to the server and have a drink on me."

"Sounds great. Thanks."

With a thumbs-up, he stepped away to collect the lunch plates.

"I've been researching predators," Gretel said. "Something canine would fit the bill, but if it got close enough to bite, why didn't it do more damage?" She tugged her ear lobe. "I don't know. Could it have been an insect?" She shrugged. "For everyone's sake, I hope this was a one-time thing, but I almost want it to happen again. I need more clues."

Hans drained his drink and laid a bill on the counter. "If it doesn't reoccur and no one else is bothered, we don't have a case, do we?"

"I guess not."

"Meanwhile, Mrs. Wilson called. She found a scorpion in her bed."

Gretel shuddered. "Scorpions, ugh." She finished her beer. "I'll check it out."

Chapter Two

The karaoke competition did bring out the crowd, Gretel discovered as she and Hans entered the bar. Extra tables filled the floor with all the seats taken, and every booth occupied. They weaved around the four-tops, the air thick with the smell of alcohol and scores of assorted perfumes and aftershaves. They grabbed the last vacant bar stools. From her high perch, Gretel not only had a good view of the stage but also of the entire room. She couldn't remember it being quite so packed.

The couple in one booth was having an altercation if their strained postures and hand gestures were any clues. It looked like a lovers' quarrel, except it couldn't be, she decided. One of the participants was James Robert's daughter, Sybil, the other, a man whom Gretel didn't recognize. Gretel found his white shirt, black suit, cravat, and fedora an atypical but pleasing change-up from the tee-shirts, ball caps, and cowboy hats popular among the local men.

"Well, will you look at that?" Gretel nudged Hans. "I saw Sybil just hours ago, and she was feeling unwell enough to take a sick day."

"Looks like she's feeling better," Hans said.

Gretel wondered if perhaps Sybil had an out-of-town boyfriend. In any case, they weren't getting along. Sybil popped up, turned, and stomped away, leaving the man alone in the booth. A foursome approached. After a brief conversation, the man tipped his hat and yielded the booth.

Hans redeemed their signed coasters for drinks and sprang for jalapeño poppers.

The manager strode to the stage's center and tapped the microphone. The general din quieted a decibel. "Greetings. For those who don't know me, I'm The Saloon's owner, David Kramer. I want to personally welcome you to the first night of our competition. Now, many of you are familiar with and participate in our regular karaoke nights, but this is special. In addition to the usual applause and adulation, there are prizes to be won: cash and coupons for free eats and drinks here at The Saloon. The winners of tonight's elimination round will compete again tomorrow night for the prizes. You're in for some fine entertainment, but first, we want to introduce our judges."

Kramer bid the judges stand as he named them. The contest outcome would be decided by what passed for luminaries in Hip Deep: Squib, a twenty-something known for penning a popular blog reviewing indie music; Luigi, the telecom engineer who wired nearly every edifice in the village; and Hector Escamillo, a manager for The Ranch, a huge cattle operation at Hip Deep's outskirts. The karaoke-equipment operator wheeled a monitor into place next to the microphone stand, stepped to the player at the back of the stage, and gave Kramer the high sign. "Looks like we're ready," Kramer said. "Allow me to present our first contestant." The singer took the stage to cheers and whistles from a crowded booth.

Hans and Gretel sipped and munched through covers of contemporary hits, classic rock tunes, and country favorites.

Sybil Robert mounted the stage and performed Roberta Flack's "Killing Me Softly with His Song" with aplomb, to Gretel's amazement. Sybil sang with emotion that made the lyrics sound personal. With her focus fixed on someone in the audience, she appeared to sing to him alone.

"I am impressed," Gretel said. "What do you think, Hans? Hans?"

He swiveled his chair to follow Sybil's dismount from the stage. His head jerked back. "Huh?"

"You liked her performance, didn't you?"

His lips parted, and his eyes glazed, he nodded. "I'm going to go tell her how much."

"I'm sure she could use the ..." Gretel said, but before she could finish, Hans slid from his stool and dove into the crowd.

Gretel chuckled and ordered another drink.

David Kramer stepped up to the mic. "Okay, folks, you've enjoyed some great singing. Your regulars gave it all they've got, and I daresay you may have a new favorite. Our final presentation tonight is by a newcomer. He may be a stranger to Hip Deep, but he's no stranger to the karaoke circuit. Paul Zavare, the mic is yours." Kramer descended the steps, and the performer took his place.

As much as Gretel was startled by Sybil's appearance, the last singer was even more of a surprise. It was Sybil's out-of-town boyfriend or whomever it was she argued with in the booth earlier. When he stepped into the spotlight, and Gretel got a look at his face, she recognized him as the lone drinker who held down the end of the bar earlier that afternoon.

Paul Zavare stood silently for a long minute. The dramatic pause captured the audience's attention. He signaled the player operator and launched into an even older popular tune, Simon and Garfunkel's "The Sound of Silence." While he sang, his eyes swept the audience, engaging the listeners. His gaze caught Gretel's and clung. She couldn't look away. Zavare stared straight at her as he sang. The images of darkness and loneliness were more than words, they described Zavare's desolation. It was as though he talked to her and only her of his anguish.

He ended the song, but she was so captivated she forgot to clap until the applause brought her back to her senses.

Zavare left the stage. Kramer returned to thank the singers for their performances and the judges for their attention. "Okay, folks, don't forget. Tomorrow night, same time, same place. Come and learn which singers made the finals and hear them sing for their supper—or rather, prizes."

Hans appeared at Gretel's side, his expression both eager and anxious. "I offered to take Sybil home. She was going to cadge a ride from a friend but—"

"You'd like the opportunity to inflict more of your charm on the poor girl."

Hans rolled his eyes. "Since you put it that way—"

"I'm teasing. Go for it. I can tell you're smitten."

"Do you want to come with us? Or I could drop her off and come back for you."

"Don't worry about it. I can get myself home. Good luck, Lover Boy."

The thanks he tossed behind him were lost in the crowd noise.

Shaking her head, Gretel smiled and polished off the last jalapeño popper. She laid down a tip for the bartender, slid off her chair, and headed for the door.

She started down the street. After hours spent in the bar's close atmosphere, the outside air felt alive with movement, snaking around her ankles and ruffling her hair. Moonless and starless, the night sky was monochromatic black. No one traveled the dimly lit residential side streets, and Gretel felt vulnerable. It occurred to her a stroll along deserted streets in the wee hours might not be the wisest choice she ever made. Maybe she should have called for rideshare. Gretel told herself she didn't need to go far but accelerated her pace, none-theless.

She spotted the headlights washing the road first, then heard the purr of the motor. She turned her head to see a car creep close to the curb. The white Rolls Royce, with its long hood and curved fenders, could have been lifted from a vintage car catalog. It slowed to a near stop. The passenger window slid down.

"Would you like a ride?" came a throaty voice from the vehicle's dark interior.

"I'm fine," Gretel replied. She moved farther from the street and lengthened her stride.

"My apologies. I didn't mean to startle you. If you prefer to walk, I'll be on my way. I simply thought to offer you a lift." The car stopped, and the driver's face appeared framed by the open window. Gretel recognized Paul Zavare from the karaoke contest.

She didn't usually climb into cars at night with people she didn't know, although now that she thought about it, how would this be any different from getting a lift from an unfamiliar rideshare driver? Though Paul Zavare was a visitor to Hip Deep, he wasn't a stranger. His performance had communicated so much emotion, she felt as though they were acquainted. "I wouldn't want to take you out of your way."

He shrugged. "Unless you need to go to the next county..."

"Nothing like that. I'm not going that far. I've walked it in the daytime."

"At night, though? Maybe not the wisest decision. Especially here."

"What's wrong with 'here,'?" Gretel asked, sounding more defensive than she would like.

"I meant no offense. Simply that it's dark. And you're alone."

He was right about that, she thought.

"Would it put you at ease to be introduced by David Kramer?"

"That won't be necessary. I appreciate your offer. That's kind of you." She approached the car.

"In that case, Paul Zavare, at your service."

"From the karaoke contest, I know. I am—"

"Gretel. You and your brother Hans run Grethans Exterminators, am I not right?"

"You've heard of us?" Gretel asked, surprised the business was so well-known that a visitor was aware of it. Hans would be pleased.

Zavare circled to the passenger side, opened the door, and waved her in. "When you're new in town, the bartender at the local hangout is a good source of information. He told me the two of you would tackle anything imperiling life in Hip Deep."

"Pretty much." Gretel settled on a leather seat that, while not cracked or torn, had a soft burnished texture from years of use. She detected a faint fragrance of leather and tobacco. The seats were too old to emit an aroma, and since The Saloon had a no-smoking policy, they hadn't taken away any cigarette smoke on their clothes. She spied a pack of cigarillos on the center console.

"Head down the street," she said. "I'll tell you where to turn. Unless you have GPS. I could give you the address."

"I'm afraid I'm old-fashioned. I have none of those fancy modern devices. The vehicle even predates airbags. Fear not, though. I have safety equipment." He patted the dashboard, which held a St. Michael figurine. He chortled. "Nothing like having an angel on one's side."

His deep voice reminded her how much she had liked his singing. "I enjoyed your performance," she said. "You sing so well, it made me wonder if you've had a professional career. Turn left here."

"Why, thank you, but no. Following the competitive-karaoke circuit is the closest I've come to professional singing."

"I didn't know there was competitive karaoke. It certainly brings out some world-class amateurs. Right at the next corner. I'm guessing you and Sybil are the finalists."

"It appears Sybil has already walked off with the prize."

"You mean my brother?" Gretel laughed. "The opposite might be more the case. I doubt he chose to come to The Saloon tonight in hopes of scoring. But, I'm glad for him. He could use some fun. He's been putting a lot of work into growing the company."

"Ah, the entrepreneur's obsessive passion. I know it well. When you own a business, the business is you. They are inseparable. It's what you contribute to the world. It becomes your legacy. Some don't retire until circumstances force them to."

"You don't say. Well, this is it. Thanks for the ride."

"You're welcome. I hope you'll both come tomorrow night for the finals."

"If Sybil will be there, I'm sure we will too."

Zavare opened his door.

"Oh, don't bother. I'll let myself out."

"I would like to see you safely through your door."

"You don't need to do that."

"In that case, please take this." He handed her a small object wrapped in tissue paper.

She opened the package to find a pendant necklace. Strung on a chain was a white-gold medallion picturing Saint Michael centered on a yellow-gold cross. "Oh, I couldn't possibly."

"Please. For the next time you walk home in the dark. It would be reassuring to know you have protection."

"An angel on my side?" She tossed the pendant in her palm. She narrowed her eyes. "This doesn't mean I'll root for you tomorrow night."

Paul Zavare gave another throaty laugh.

Gretel noticed he lingered at the curb until she entered the house and closed the door behind her.

"Well, what's on the docket for today?" Gretel poured her second coffee of the morning from the office beverage cart.

"A second attack," Hans said. "James Robert called while you were in the shower. The same victim but a fresh injury, similar to the first. The goat survived but is feeble."

"Did he find any sign of the attacker?"

Hans shook his head.

Gretel sighed. "Okay, I'll go talk to him."

At the Robert farm, Gretel headed straight for the loafing shed. Cherie lay on the straw, her eyes barely open. The shaved area on her neck glistened with fresh medication, the skin immediately around the new wound red while the rest was sickly white.

"The vet told me to apply more ointment and a spray-on bandage," James said. "Cherie's not running a fever. Quite the opposite, her temperature is low, so I don't think she has an infection. The injury is similar to before."

"Do you know where or when this occurred?"

"I would say sometime last night, and here in the shed. That's what's got me stumped. She hasn't been in the pasture at all. I've kept her here. I fed and watered her here. She was rallying when I called it quits for the day. Now she's sluggish again. I don't understand how it happened. I had her in the goat house all day, and I worked nearby. Had there been a ruckus of any kind, I would have heard it."

"This is the crime scene, then? Let me give it a closer look."

James stepped aside, and Gretel scoured the small barn inch by inch. The doors, the walls, the roof were undamaged with no sign that anything had broken or burrowed in. She looked for fur lost by a predator in the skirmish, but there wasn't any. Splotches of dried blood would be no surprise, but she saw none. She expected the straw to be tossed and crushed by a struggle. All she spotted were matted patches where Cherie lay. Cherie's attempts to stand and move left pairs of crescent-shaped prints stamped into the straw. The only other marks were human shoeprints. Large ones likely matched James Robert's boots, and smaller ones were probably Lucy's. "You worked in here yesterday, I presume."

"Till suppertime. And this morning, of course."

"Just for the sake of argument, could you take off one of your boots for a moment?" Gretel asked.

James complied, and Gretel matched some prints to his footwear. "What would Lucy have worn out here?"

James frowned. "Lucy wasn't in the goat house yesterday. She was busy all day. Errands in the village and chores in the house. And in the house was where we spent the night."

"Not at all? You're sure?"

"I'm positive. We can ask her if you want."

Gretel laughed. "I'll take your word for it." *For now, at any rate.* "Sybil, then?"

"Sybil either, that I'm aware of. She was in the house, resting so she could compete at The Saloon. She went with some friends and was there until your brother brought her home. Well after closing time, I might add." He sounded stern, but he offset it with a wink. "She's inside. She says she's saving her strength for tonight. She's a finalist. Oops, did I speak out of turn?"

"I'm not surprised. Her singing took my breath away. Did you say the vet was out here this morning?"

"No, we consulted over the phone. She said she would come out if Cherie takes a turn for the worse. I'll keep an eye on her throughout the day, check on her between my other chores."

"I'll come back later today and take the night watch."

"You're going to a lot of trouble for this."

"Not at all. Whatever it takes. We said we would find and stop this menace." Gretel wondered who made the small footprints in the goat shed.

Chapter Three

"Look at you all duded up—jacket, tie. Let me guess. Karaoke contest finals?"

Hans nodded. "Sybil Robert is—"

"One of the finalists, I know. Her father mentioned it."

"I offered to pick her up and treat her to dinner before the contest starts. Do you want to join us?"

"Don't worry about it. I'm not going."

"No?"

"I'll be at the Robert place. James thinks the attacks occur at night. I want to stake the place out. That way, if it happens again, I'll be able to identify the culprit."

Hans narrowed his eyes. "Is that something you want to do alone? Shouldn't I come with you?"

"No, don't break your date with Sybil. I'll observe only, and I won't intervene unless it's perfectly safe. But I need to know what we're up against."

She armed herself with a travel cup of coffee and snacks. Not that she was superstitious, but she stashed the St. Michael cross in the Wrangler's glove box. Having an angel at her side couldn't hurt, and it might help.

Gretel arrived at the farm and found James wrapping up for the day. "How's the little patient?"

"About the same. I kept a close watch on her all day. She's not any worse. She didn't improve either. I did ask the vet to bring the big van, the one with all the diagnostic equipment. She ran tests, took a bunch of samples. Cherie's anemic, but there's no obvious cause. Now the vet's considering internal bleeding. We won't know what's causing it until the results come back." He glanced at the house. "Maybe she caught something from my daughter," he said with a dry laugh. "She's also a bit peaked, the way she was the other day."

"I'm sorry to hear that."

"She was in the house all day resting because she doesn't want to cancel her plans for tonight."

Hans would glad of that, Gretel thought. "How about I park over there? The tree will hide my truck, and I'll have a good view of the lane, the shed, and the front of the house."

"We appreciate everything you're doing. Don't hesitate to holler if you need help."

Gretel no sooner got situated than Hans arrived to pick up his date. The listless way Sybil dragged her feet led Gretel to think her performance might suffer.

Dusk deepened to evening, and Gretel saw James leave the animals' shed. Behind closed curtains, lights in the house switched on and off as James and Lucy moved from kitchen to dining room and back to the kitchen. A blue light flickered along with the yellow light of table lamps in the parlor for several hours of television viewing. The first floor went dark, and the second floor brightened briefly. Then, save for the front-porch light, the house was quiet.

To avoid lighting the Jeep's interior, Gretel shielded her phone under her shirt to call Hans. His phone rang and rang. She was about to give up when he answered, shouting to be heard over the bar noise. "How's it going?"

"Quiet here. Not a creature is stirring, not even a mouse. How about there?"

"Great. The Saloon is packed. Half of Hip Deep turned out to hear the finalists. Sybil, of course."

"How's she doing?"

"Terrific, especially since she seemed kind of low-energy to me. I hope getting something to eat perked her up."

"Wish her good luck for me."

"I will. The same to you."

Gretel ended the call and powered off the device so that any incoming calls or texts wouldn't make lights flash. She flexed her feet and flapped her arms. Staying alert sitting in the Wrangler proved harder than she would have thought. She caught herself nodding off several times.

A sweep of light on the lane announced a vehicle's approach. Gretel recognized Hans's car. Lover Boy bringing his date home; they'd stayed for last call and then some. Hans stopped short of the corona of light from the front porch fixture. In his front seat, two heads overlapped. Had the night been any colder, Gretel was certain the windows would have fogged up.

Okay, no, she thought. She did not want to sit in the dark watching her brother neck with Sybil. She swiveled in her seat and fixed her gaze on the animals' shed.

Hours of vigilance had yielded nothing. The only thing that could have preyed upon poor Cherie would have been a biting fly. Deciding to call it a fruitless exercise, Gretel made a mental note to research predatory insects in the morning.

Out of the corner of her eye, she saw the dome light in Hans's car come on. She turned her head to catch Sybil closing the car door behind her and walking to the house. Hans remained in the car. *Not walking his date to the door? No goodnight kiss?* Gretel snickered. They must have gotten their fill during the make-out session. Sybil let herself in, closed the door, and turned off the porch light.

Hans's car remained stationary. Gretel wondered if he was considering angling for a nightcap after all. More than mere minutes passed, and the car didn't budge. Gretel couldn't suppress her curiosity. She crept to her brother's car.

Her brother lay slumped against the seat, his head lolling. *Was he asleep? Did the lateness of the hour or the evening's amorous exertions wear him out?* Gretel had the sneaking suspicion that all was not right. She tapped on the windows. "Hans?"

He neither replied nor moved.

Gretel knocked a little louder. Hans still didn't respond. She opened the door. Hans collapsed across the console.

"Hans!" she cried, no longer worried about causing a commotion. The dome light showed his jacket open, his tie loosened, and his shirt half unbuttoned. It could have been the quality of the car's interior light, but Hans's face and neck looked white as a full moon. A dark blotch stained his collar, and on his neck, two dark spots stood out against his pallor. They looked enough like the little goat's wound to make Gretel gasp.

She grabbed Hans by the shoulders and shook him. "Hans, talk to me. Are you all right? What's wrong?"

His moan was feeble, and he was limp in her grasp. Gretel lowered the seatback and laid him stretched out. She raced back to the Wrangler, powered up her phone, and called 911. "Send an ambulance," she shrieked and sped back to Hans.

"Sybil," Hans murmured, then his head lolled to one side.

"What about Sybil? I'll get her just as soon as the ambulance arrives." Gretel cast desperate eyes to the lane and the deserted landscape. *Where was that ambulance? What was taking so long?* "Hans, say something!" She tried to rouse her brother. Gretel leaned on the horn and flashed the headlights. "Help! Help!"

Lights came on in the house. The front door opened, and Lucy and

James appeared, belting robes over their pajamas. James trotted out, his wife following. "What's going on?"

"I don't know. Hans is sick. I don't know with what."

The couple peered into Hans's car then stepped back, their faces pinched with worry. "I'll call an ambulance," Lucy said.

"I did. Oh, thank God, here they come."

Gretel saw headlights turn off the road and onto the lane. Lights flashing and a siren wailing, the emergency vehicle hurried toward her.

The ambulance crunched to a stop, and a technician sprung from the vehicle. "Who called in the emergency?"

"I did," Gretel said.

The technician quizzed her for details while her partner tended to Hans.

"Do you want to bring him inside? Can we help?" James asked.

"Thanks, no." To his partner, the second tech said, "His pulse is thready. He's barely breathing. We need to get him to the hospital. Let's move him into the ambulance."

The assessment made Gretel's eyes sting, and she blinked back tears.

While the EMTs transferred Hans to their vehicle, Sybil emerged from the house and drifted toward them, still in street clothes.

"Sybil, something's wrong with Hans. You were with him all evening. Did you notice anything? Did he seem ill?" Lucy asked.

"You had dinner together. What did he eat? Drink?" Gretel wanted to know. "What did he have in the bar? Tell me!"

Sybil smiled gently. "Nothing unusual. He'll be fine."

Sybil's nonchalance didn't comfort Gretel, it had the opposite effect, but before she could grill the young woman further, one of the EMTs said, "We're ready to go."

"I'll follow you."

"We'll throw on some clothes and be right behind you," James said.

"I'll go with you," Sybil said to Gretel.

Gretel hesitated. She hadn't invited Sybil, but Hans had whispered her name. Maybe her presence would help when he regained consciousness. "C'mon."

Gretel had jumped into her seat, fastened the safety belt, and started the motor before Sybil opened the passenger door. Gretel barely gave her time to pull it closed before charging off after the ambulance.

She found herself leaning forward over the steering wheel as if that would somehow propel the Wrangler faster and resisted matching the emergency vehicle's speed. "You never did say what Hans ate or drank or if he behaved strangely."

"He didn't," Sybil replied, calmer than Gretel thought she should be. "He took me to Kramer's Dining Room. Very elegant. That was so sweet of him. I confess I ordered from the right side of the menu. I had asparagus and lobster."

I don't care about you, Gretel wanted to scream. "What did Hans eat? Did any of it make him ill? Did he have a drink? Did he drink too much?"

"I wouldn't think so. We split a bottle of wine at the restaurant. I drank the same thing. I felt fine. I thought he was enjoying himself. We eased off at The Saloon. He had a Cuba Libre—one, just one—he wanted a clear head to drive home. I had a brandy. It warms the throat. I had just one because I needed a clear head too, for the competition. I was stunned that I made the finals. You know, I spent all day working out what to wear, what I should sing, what order to sing them in."

Gretel ground her teeth so hard her jaw hurt. She was about to bark "shut up" at Sybil. She didn't care what she ate or drank or wore or any of the evening's details but bit her tongue before the words left her mouth. Sybil was, no doubt, equally nervous and upset. The mind-less babbling was her way of handling the stress of the situation. She was so distracted she failed to fasten her seat belt; a small red warning icon on the dashboard display glowed.

"Don't worry, Gretel, he'll be fine," Sybil said, her voice oddly subdued. "Better than fine when he comes around. And he will. I stopped myself just in time before I went too far."

Stopped herself? What was the woman talking about? Gretel forced herself to focus on the ambulance's rear lights, mere dots miles ahead.

"I practiced on one of Dad's goats. She recovered, as you well know. So will Hans. Not just recover, be better than ever. Be one of us."

Gretel risked taking her eyes off the road to face Sybil. Sybil smiled. In the dark, her teeth looked very white, her eye teeth markedly long. And pointed.

Goosebumps paved Gretel's arms, and she shivered. She flashed on the wounds in the goat's neck, in Hans's. The spacing of the punctures —those marks could have been made by those sharp teeth. Gretel's world shrank. There was no night sky, no road, no truck, only her and Sybil and those teeth. "You …?"

"Yes, me. 'Vampire,' some like to call us. I prefer 'immortal.' Because now I am and Hans is, too. I didn't drain him. I could have, but I took only what I needed. And I gave back. I shared with him the elixir that now courses through my veins." Sybil's eyes were wide, alight.

Gretel pictured Sybil and Hans parked in her brother's car, locked in an amorous embrace. Only one of them had been necking. The other was getting necked. Gretel realized with a paralyzing chill that Hans didn't say Sybil's name because he wanted her near. He was naming his attacker.

"You can join us. It will take only a moment. You won't feel pain. In fact, you will find it quite enjoyable."

"I, uh, I'm sure, but uh, now? Not now. I, uh, want to go to the hospital. To see how Hans is doing," Gretel stammered, stalling for time to plan her escape.

"I'm telling you, he'll be fine. He'll regain his strength. There isn't anything the doctors can do for him now anyway." Sybil scooted toward her.

"Don't you touch me!" Gretel squeezed against the driver's door, but the armrest and console between the two front seats would hardly deter Sybil, who leaned toward her, her lips spread wide. Gretel yanked the steering wheel to the right and left, making the vehicle swerve.

"Don't do that," Sybil cooed. "You'll only cause a wreck. You'll die in the crash, but I'll survive. I will live. I will live forever."

Growing brightness told Gretel downtown was near. A blue-and-white H sign on the shoulder meant her destination was moments away.

Gretel stomped on the brakes, and the Wrangler screamed to a halt. Inertia threw the occupants forward. Gretel's seat belt dug into her skin, but Sybil never fastened hers. She smacked her forehead on the steering wheel and crumpled into a stunned heap.

Gretel pulled off the road, unsnapped her seat belt, and rifled in the Wrangler's cargo compartment. She unearthed a cargo net and cam-buckle straps and lashed Sybil to the seat, then resumed her sprint to the hospital.

Sybil moaned and wriggled against her bonds. "What have you done?"

"I can't deal with you now. I've got to get to Hans."

Sybil cackled. "These bindings won't hold me. I can simply turn into a bat and fly away."

Gretel rounded a corner. Mercy Hospital's lighted sign directed the way to the emergency entrance. Gretel swung into the parking lot and screeched to a stop. "You can?" Well, you just try that, she thought. She once nabbed a bat for a client who thought it was rabid.

"No, not really. That's just a myth."

"Then you'll stay put. I'll take care of you later." As an afterthought, she dug out the St. Michael's cross from the glove box and looped the chain over the rear-view mirror. "There, that'll hold you." With a growl, Sybil shrank back.

Gretel raced into the building, charged to the Admittance desk, and demanded information about Hans. He had been transferred to an intensive care room. Weak but breathing and stable, he was still uncommunicative. Gretel took a seat in the corridor. By the time the doctor had a minute for her, James and Lucy arrived.

"He's suffering from acute anemia due to blood loss," the doctor told them. "We've got him on fluids and oxygen. We need to ascertain the cause of the bleeding to determine the best treatment. He may need a transfusion or possibly simply iron to help build new red blood cells. We'll let you know as soon as we do, and we'll keep you apprised of any changes in his condition," he said before returning to his patient.

"Anemia. Blood loss," James echoed. He and his wife sank into their chairs. James shook his head. "Cherie's been anemic, and the vet didn't diagnose internal bleeding. What's going on?" He looked around. "Where's Sybil? Didn't she come with you?"

"Uh, about that ... I believe I ID'ed the predator." As gently as she could and struggling to sound rational rather than raving, Gretel told the Roberts of her battle with their daughter and Sybil's confession.

Mouths agape, they sat stunned for a long moment. James spoke first. "Sybil, a vampire?"

"I'm afraid so. You can ask her. She's, uh, safely in my truck." *At least she would be unless she had turned into a bat and escaped.*

James's brow wrinkled. "Sybil was feeling poorly. Then Cherie was, and Sybil improved. Then Sybil had a little relapse, and so did Cherie. Then Sybil rallied ..." He looked at Lucy.

"Who ... what could have done that to Sybil? Someone did. You don't just wake up one morning, and you're a ghoul." She grasped Gretel's hands. "You must find out."

James nodded. "There has to be a way to fix her. Can a vampire be cured? You have to find out."

Gretel glanced at the door behind which lay Hans, Sybil's latest victim. She didn't know the answer, but James and Lucy were right. She would have to find out. And quickly.

Chapter Four

Walking James and Lucy to her Jeep, Gretel said, "Please don't be startled by what you're about to see. I had to restrain her. You under-stand that, don't you?"

Though James and Lucy nodded, Gretel couldn't help but think they'd protest at the sight of their daughter trussed up with a heavy-duty strap. "I can release her into your custody." *Not that she had the authority to detain Sybil in the first place.* "You have to keep her, uh, confined. I know she doesn't mean to harm anyone. I know she thinks she's helping. But she isn't in control of this anymore. She won't hesitate to attack either of you or both."

In the parking lot's floodlights, Lucy blanched.

"She should be, uh, sated, for a while. She got what she, uh, needed, from Hans." Her Wrangler within sight, Gretel turned to face the couple and stopped them. Lucy peered over Gretel's shoulder, recoiled, and clutched at her husband. Gretel swung around. Her body twisted against the net, Sybil's face was pressed to the passenger window. It looked like Sybil except for her crazed expression. She spotted her parents and smiled, baring her fangs.

"Ohmigod," James breathed.

Her voice choked with tears, Lucy said, "But she's still our daughter."

"Maybe it would be too much for you. I would be tempted to be lenient. Would you rather that I keep an eye on her until I get to the bottom of this? She could stay in Hans's room. He won't be using it for a few days."

"No, we'll look after her. You've done so much already, and you have Hans to worry about," James said. "We need you out there to catch who did this and stop him or her before he hurts anyone else. And find a cure, if there is one."

"I'm sure there is," Gretel said, although she hadn't a clue.

The three of them transferred Sybil, netted and subdued from the prolonged exposure to the cross hanging from the Wrangler's rearview mirror, into the back seat of the Robert car. Gretel grabbed the necklace. "Here, take this. You'll need it."

"No, you keep that," said James. "We're good." He and Lucy reached into their shirt necks and pulled out crucifixes of their own.

With misgivings, Gretel waved to the departing Roberts and hustled back to the hospital.

The medical staff had done everything possible for Hans at the moment. "He's still unconscious, but you may visit him," the doctor said. "We'd like you to wear a face mask as a precaution, although we don't suspect a risk of contagion."

Unless he bites me, Gretel thought, then shook the idea from her head. She couldn't. She wouldn't think him a threat, not Hans, not her brother.

"Go ahead and speak to him. He may be able to hear you, and it might help him to come around."

Gretel settled in the easy chair next to Hans's bed. Mumbling as best she could through the mask, she related what had transpired since he brought Sybil home after their date. She didn't realize she fell asleep until the nurse on the morning shift came to check Hans's vitals. "It looks like his red blood cell count is improving," she reported. "I'll tell Doctor the good news. Our guy here may not need a transfusion after all."

Sybil had said she didn't drain Hans. Gretel thanked the nurse, straightened in the chair, and stretched to work the kinks out of her neck and back. "C'mon, Hans. Wake up. You've got us all worried."

The heart monitor registered activity. Hans's eyelids fluttered. "Sybil," he moaned.

"Yes, Hans, I know. I took care of her."

Hans opened his eyes. "You killed her?"

"Kill her? No. Can a vampire be killed?"

"I don't know," he answered, his voice faltering. "You gotta find out. Then come kill me." Hans tried to rise on his elbows and collapsed against the pillow. "Where am I?"

"The hospital. You were perilously anemic. They're working to bring you back to health."

"Take me out of here. They're trying to keep me alive. They should let me die."

Gretel clutched his hand. "Don't say that. I'm on the case. I'll figure out a way to save you and Sybil."

Hans whimpered, his eyes closed, and he slipped back into unconsciousness.

Promising she would return with good news, Gretel exited the room. She gave her contact information to the nursing staff, accepted a foam cup of coffee, and left the building. She got in her truck with no idea of where to go next or what to do and drifted to the office. At Hans's desk, she researched vampirism on the Internet. The display kept blurring, replaced by the image of Hans lying in the hospital bed, white as, well, white as that damn bed sheet.

She uncovered a lot of lore but nothing definitive and much contradictory. A wooden stake could be lethal, but should be it aspen, ash, hawthorn, or oak, and should the weapon be driven through the head, the mouth, or the chest? Decapitation was another option. A silver bullet could be fatal. Or maybe not. It was a moot point since Gretel didn't have a firearm, and anyway, she didn't want to kill Hans or Sybil. She just wanted to un-vampire them. She was about to launch a search for a cure when the desk phone rang. "James! How are you holding up? How are Lucy and Sybil?"

"They're fine. Tired, of course. Well, Lucy is. Sybil says she's running out of ... energy."

"Don't let her persuade you to release her. She'll be fine for a few days and by then I will have an answer," Gretel said with a confidence she didn't feel.

"We didn't free her. That's why I'm puzzled. Cherie's been attacked, again."

"No!"

"I assure you, not by Sybil. Believe me, s. She's been confined the whole time. Either Lucy or I can attest to that."

Unless she can turn into a bat and fly away. "Do you have any idea when it happened?"

"The wounds look fresh to me. I'm no expert, but my guess would be in the wee hours when we were with you and Hans. It would have been easy enough to sneak into the loafing shed with no one here."

"Is Cherie going to be all right?"

"I'd say so. She's behaving the way she did the other two times. Lethargic, but not critically. It couldn't be Sybil."

"Nor could it be Hans. He was in the hospital all night. I was there with him."

"How is he doing?"

"Still very weak, but I'm told his red blood cell count is rising, which is a good thing."

"We'd go visit him—"

"No, you keep a watch on Sybil. I'll let you know as soon as I learn something." Another attack meant there was still a vampire at work. *The one who inoculated Sybil days ago?* She didn't morph of her own volition. "Can you recall where Sybil was, the day before Cherie's first attack? No, wait, the day before that. And the night. Can you account for her whereabouts?"

There was silence at the other end of the line.

"James?"

"I'm thinking. During that day, that would have been school. That night she was out. If I recall correctly, she met her friends at The Saloon. Yes, that's right. It was karaoke night. Their regularly scheduled one, not the competition. I remember her saying how much fun it was that they had stayed way longer than they planned. When she felt so sluggish the next day, I scolded her for partying too hard. She perked up the day after that. The day you first came out."

"Thanks, that helps." Gretel would have to backtrack, uncover Sybil's movements, and consider with whom she came in contact.

Gretel spent the day tracking Sybil's steps just before being "turned," a fruitless exercise. The young woman had been where she was supposed to be when she was supposed to be there, according to witnesses who, as far as Gretel could tell, had no reason to lie. It was unlikely she met a vampire during the day. They didn't go out in sunlight. Gretel talked with a couple of the pals who were with Sybil in The Saloon that evening.

"Oh, she was captivated by the karaoke," one friend related. "We weren't at all surprised when she said she would enter the contest."

The gang had arrived separately that night and left separately. All of Sybil's friends assumed she went straight home, but none of the women could say for certain.

Gretel phoned for a report on Hans and learned his condition remained unchanged. She continued to The Saloon, where she quizzed the bartender, the manager, and the wait staff. They remembered Sybil and her friends being there that night but had nothing to add about where Sybil went once she left.

Gretel sighed. She seated herself on a barstool and ordered a beer. She sipped so slowly it became warm before she finished half of it, and she still had no idea what to do next.

"Good evening. I would offer to buy you another beer, but you don't seem to be enjoying that one," came a voice at her shoulder.

She turned to see Paul Zavare. "Oh, hello."

"I didn't catch you last night at The Saloon."

"No, I, uh, had somewhere else to be. How did it turn out?"

Zavare mounted the barstool next to Gretel. "I won first place."

"Congratulations. No wonder. How did Sybil Robert do?"

"She came in last."

"That surprises me. She did so well in the first round, I figured it would be a tie between the two of you."

"Yes, I was impressed by her at first. I'm sorry to say that she didn't live up to her potential. I expected more of her."

"It may be because she was struggling with a ... health issue. Now that the contest is over, I gather you'll be moving on?"

Zavare nodded. "Another town, another contest."

"Wise decision. Hip Deep has become an unusually dangerous place to be lately. We have a predator on the loose. That's how I spent this morning. Tracing its movements, trying to pin down its location, so I can restrain it and remove the threat."

"Sounds ambitious. And dangerous. You have taken on a serious responsibility."

"It's my job. It's what we do at Grethans Exterminators. We get rid of pests. Solve problems for our neighbors, remove threats to their security." Hans had said that. Poor Hans! Gretel wondered how he fared. She wasn't accomplishing anything here. She might as well go visit him in the hospital.

"Your bravery and commitment are commendable. Those are qualities not seen in many people these days. I'm glad I gave you that medallion."

It had come in handy in subduing Sybil, Gretel thought. "I do keep it in the truck." To which, in light of the existence of an unidentified vampire at large, she had added a weapon: an ash stake. Not a stake so much as a cracked softball bat. Composite and metal bats had their advantages, but nothing matched the sound of a wood bat smacking a ball. She ruined hers hitting that championship-winning home run. Though no longer useful for play, she had been too sentimental about it to discard it.

"You should wear the necklace. That way, you'll have its protection no matter what you encounter."

"Good advice. Now you'll have to excuse me; I'm going to see how my brother is doing."

"Is he unwell also?"

"Yes. It's serious."

"Hans and Sybil both ailing? Weren't they together last night? Do you think he caught something from her?"

"I'm certain of it." Gretel drained her drink and slid off the stool. "If I don't see you again, safe travels."

"Why, thank you, but you haven't seen quite the last of me."

Chapter Five

Gretel stopped at the nurses' station for a report.

"He's regained consciousness," the nurse said. "His red blood cell count continues to increase. For some reason, he's still lethargic. We have him on nutritional supplements, so that should bring about an improvement."

Gretel found Hans sitting propped against the pillows, the bed's head elevated. An IV tube delivered solutions to his arm. She wondered if the supplements would make any difference or if he needed an entirely different liquid. "I'm so glad you're awake."

He gave her a weak smile. "Sybil—?"

"She's at home." Gretel held up her hand to stop Hans's protest. "James and Lucy are keeping her restricted."

"Her parents? Can they be trusted?"

"I believe they can. I saw the look on their faces."

"Like the one on yours?"

"Hans!"

He dipped his chin. "I'm okay for now but for how long?" He raised his head. His eyes pleading, he said, "I'm not in control."

"I realize that. There must be a way to fix it, you and Sybil. I've been working on it all day. I'll stay on it, but I needed to see how you are."

"This is probably the safest place for me now. Should I behave ... erratically, they do have a locked ward where they can secure patients who become ... disruptive." His grimace squeezed Gretel's heart.

Grisly images presented themselves. Gretel shuddered and tried to think of something reassuring to say. Her phone chirped, alerting her to a text message. *Saved by the bell.* She hoped one of the people she interviewed today had new and useful information.

She didn't recognize the number. "Leaving soon," the message read. "Have something vital 4U b4 I go. Meet me @midnight @the ball field" and was signed "Paul Zavare." She showed Hans the message. "Odd. I just saw him. I wonder why he didn't give it to me then."

Hans shook his head. "I don't like it. Sounds suspicious."

"He didn't ask to meet in a dark alley. Or the cemetery," she said with a nervous laugh. "The ball field is open space. Plenty of light." Gretel shrugged. Zavare had given her the protective medallion. "He says it's vital. It can't hurt to check it out. He's on his way out of town." She rose and headed for the door. She spotted the cross mounted on the wall facing Hans's bed and paused, recalling the effect her necklace had on Sybil. The cross could explain why Hans's energy was at low ebb. "Would you like me to take that down?"

"No," he said, his voice feeble. "It's keeping me in line."

Gretel gulped a sob and hurried from the room.

Though deserted, artificial light bathed the softball field, an effort to deter crime and keep wild animals away. Gretel spotted Zavare's white sedan in the parking lot and pulled up next to it. She plucked the necklace from the rear-view mirror. Should he ask about it, she wouldn't want him to think her unappreciative of his gift.

She found him sitting on the bleachers just inside the park.

"You have been searching for answers to two questions: how did Sybil become a vampire, and can she be cured?"

"How do you know that?"

"I have lived a long time, in many places, and I have seen many things."

Despite Zavare's placid tone, Gretel felt the prickle of menace. "And would you happen to have the answers?"

"I do. The cure is not a simple thing to make or to endure. It is a potion made from the blood of the sire, the one who turned the human. Combined with garlic and sage, it is a pungent and strong-smelling brew. It forces the turned to vomit the vampire's blood from their system until they lose consciousness, a brutally painful process but necessary. They are often sick for days, as it can take time to purge them of any remaining traces.

"Its effectiveness depends on whether the turned has drunk any human blood. In that case, the cure may not work at all."

Gretel's head swam as she evaluated the options. "Hans was turned by Sybil. He's been in the hospital since then. Assuming he hasn't assaulted a nurse or an orderly, he would be a candidate for a cure prepared from Sybil's blood, right?"

Zavare nodded.

"Sybil, however, drank Hans's blood. Even if I knew who turned her, the potion might not be effective."

"It might not. Assuming that was the only occurrence, possibly her vampire blood could still be purged. It would be worth the risk if she wants to be cured and is willing to undergo the treatment.

"That answers one question. What about the other?"

"Ah, yes. The sire. As you said, Sybil is Hans's sire."

"And Sybil's? I ran around all day trying to learn who she came in contact with. It had to be when she was at the bar. I'll have to go back, identify everyone who was in or near the place that night."

"No need. I was there. I can tell you."

"Well?" Gretel asked, tempted to shake the answer out of the man.

"It was I."

"Y … you?" Gretel suddenly became aware of the pendant against her chest.

"Yes, Gretel, it was I."

"You're a vampire?"

Zavare inhaled deeply. "Partly. I am mostly a Hunter. I seek out and destroy vampires. Like many with my calling, I am driven because I have vampire blood. It is a constant struggle to constrain my impulses. Sometimes animal blood will suffice."

"Cherie! You preyed on Cherie last night."

"I took only what I needed. Cherie will recover."

"But Sybil. You failed with Sybil."

"Not failed, exactly. It was deliberate. I had the best intentions. You see, Gretel, I am dying. I have not enough vampire blood to be immortal, and my human body is failing. Someone must take up the fight. I hoped it would be Sybil, and I sought to induct her into the fold. To give her just enough reason to make it her mission. It became clear that she was not up to the job."

"So, when you said she was a disappointment, you didn't mean as a singer. You meant—"

"As my heir. Correct."

"The argument in The Saloon?"

"She was angry that I turned her. In vain, as it turned out. I tried to convince her of the advantages, but …" Zavare shrugged. "All is not lost, however. I have found a much better candidate."

The prickle of menace engulfed Gretel's body in a cold wave.

"Yes, you. You are strong and brave, committed. You take on a task and stick with it to the finish."

"Oh, no. Forget it. Find someone else."

Zavare frowned. "Vanquishing vampires fits in with your mission, to rid Hip Deep of pests, to improve lives."

"Not if it means becoming one myself."

Zavare sighed. "If you don't do it this way, it will likely happen anyway. Despite precautions, vampire hunters are bitten by their prey. Sometimes severely, thoroughly, irredeemably. At least this way, it will be under controlled conditions. You would still be part human."

Gretel shook her head. "Grethans Exterminators is not the least bit interested in taking on this job. "

"In that case, Hans and Sybil will have no hope of being cured. They will remain vampires."

Hot anger burned off the chill of fear. "You're blackmailing me? My cooperation in exchange for your blood? For the cure?"

"A fair bargain, it seems to me." He reached into his jacket and withdrew two glass vials, one filled with a tinted liquid, the other with a dark fluid. "These are what you need. You will obtain a sample of Sybil's blood first and add it to the vial with the cloudy solution. Give that to Hans. The other vial is my blood mixed with the necessary ingredients. Give that potion to Sybil and hope for the best."

A cure for Sybil and a cure for Hans, but there would be no remedy for Gretel. She would be cursed for eternity, unable to bear sunlight, forced to roam the night in search of innocents to victimize to sustain herself. What kind of life would that be? "Um, give me some time to think it over."

"There is no time. They must be treated now. Both Sybil and Hans will have to feed soon. Then they will no longer be curable. Decide now, Gretel. Or I am leaving." He waved the two vials.

Sybil's and Hans's lives for hers. Her fury seeped away, leaving Gretel cold as stone. She heard her strangled voice say, "What do I have to do?"

"Are you wearing the necklace I gave you?"

Gretel nodded.

"You will have to remove it."

Zavare stepped closer. His leather-and-tobacco scent filled Gretel's nostrils and flooded her brain. Sybil had said that being inoculated wouldn't hurt. Nevertheless, Gretel tightened every muscle.

She squeezed her eyes shut, lifted the chain from around her neck, and fingered the pendant. Zavare moved as if to embrace her.

"Stop!" Gretel held the medallion in front of Zavare's face.

He cringed. "What are you doing? Throw that away."

"I won't. I won't do it." Zavare backed away, and she matched him step for step, keeping the cross in his view.

Zavare stumbled. Gretel grabbed the vials from his hand.

"No," he growled. He spread his lips, exposing his fangs.

Gretel ran for her truck, Zavare, at her heels. She heard his panting, turned, and flashed the cross. He fell back, and she seized the advantage, sprinting ahead. She tucked the vials in her bra, reached the Jeep, and tore open the rear door.

Zavare grabbed her left arm and yanked her toward him. A drop of saliva splashed against her cheek.

She pulled loose, snatched the softball bat from the cargo compartment, whirled, and swung at Zavare. The bat connected with a resounding crack. Less resounding than her home-run hit, it nevertheless drove Zavare to knees. Gretel thrust the bat's splintered tip into Zavare's chest. His bellow shattered the air.

Gretel didn't waste a minute to assess the damage. She tugged out the bat, tossed it in the truck, and slammed the door closed. She flung herself into the driver's seat and roared out of the parking lot.

One hand on the wheel, Gretel used the other to put in a call to James Robert.

After several rings, he answered, his voice strained.

"I know I'm calling in the middle of the night—"

"That's okay. We're not sleeping much. Napping in shifts."

"I'm on my way with a remedy to try. You're certain Sybil hasn't been out."

"I'm certain. We've taken turns guarding her."

"Good. That will improve the chances this will work."

Gretel arrived at the Robert place to find the lights on and Lucy waiting on the porch. Dark crescents underscored her eyes. She looked drawn but not drained. Her cross pendant twinkled in the porch light. She led Gretel to Sybil's room, where James sat at his daughter's bedside. Sybil lay against the pillows, exhibiting the same enervation that Hans did. Gretel figured the wall-mounted cross was a contributing factor.

Gretel explained about the emetic and its side effects. "Not only is this going to make you feel wretched, but it also may not work. But it's the only chance."

Sybil nodded. "I'll take it. I can't go on like this."

"First, though, we need something from you. You haven't, huh, fed, since—"

"Attacking your brother? No. I am so sorry I did that." Tears filled her eyes.

"You can apologize by giving a sample of your blood." Gretel produced the vial with the cloudy solution.

"How?"

Lucy darted from the room and returned with a bottle of rubbing alcohol, a cotton ball, and a sewing needle. She dabbed Sybil's fingertip with the antiseptic then pierced the skin. Gretel wondered if, under the circumstances, sterilizing against infection was necessary but before she could comment, a blood bubble sprouted from Sybil's finger. Gretel held the glass steady while Lucy squeezed Sybil's blood into it. "Is that enough, do you think?"

The liquid became as dark as the other preparation. "For Hans's sake, I hope so." Gretel capped the vial. She handed Sybil the other preparation. "This is yours. Down the hatch."

Wrinkling her nose at the odor, Sybil swallowed the contents. No one spoke a word as they waited for her to react. Tense moments passed when the loudest sound was everyone's shallow breathing.

Lucy's raised eyebrows asked an unspoken question, and James said, "Maybe it isn't working."

"It could take time to be effective," Gretel said with more assurance than she felt. "It has to permeate her bloodstream. But I … I have to go and deliver this to Hans. I don't know how long it lasts before it spoils."

"Go," James said. "We'll stay with Sybil."

"And pray," Lucy said.

"Keep me posted," Gretel called as she dashed from the room. Running to her car, she dialed Hans. "I'm on my way with what I hope will be a remedy. You have to get yourself released. This is an emetic. The doctors will misinterpret your reactions and try to counteract the cure's effects. I'll meet you at the Discharge Office."

Though tempted, Gretel did not break the speed limit racing to the hospital. Now would not be an opportune time to be pulled over. She screeched to a stop in the Visitors parking lot and raced to the Cashier, where she hoped to find Hans finalizing the discharge process. No one was aware of him being released, so she hurried to his room. He sat on his bed in the street clothes he wore when admitted.

"Why are you still here?"

"There's a bunch of paperwork to process, and I have to meet with the doctor and a planner. I'm guessing it's easier to break out of jail."

"We're going to have to get you home. Here, swallow this. It can work while we're sneaking you out of here."

Hans guzzled the vial's contents. "Ooh, nasty stuff. I could use a chaser."

"When we get home, I will fix you the biggest Cuba Libre you ever had. C'mon, let's go before anyone shows up to stop you."

They took the stairs, hoping to encounter as few people as possible. Feeble, Hans faltered. Gretel pulled his arm over her shoulder to support him. Puffs of his breath tickled her neck, and she realized he was near enough to bite her. She cinched up her courage, pulled him closer, and half-carried him down the steps.

"Wait," he gasped. "I gotta sit. Queasy."

"Maybe that means the cure is working!"

"Maybe I'm allergic."

"Ever the pessimist, Hans. Let's keep moving. We're almost there." She opened the door to the first floor, peered out, and spotted a red exit sign at the hallway's end.

She escorted him along the corridor. An orderly pushing a wheelchair gave them a second glance. He parked the cart. "Need some help?"

"No, thanks," Gretel replied, trying to hustle Hans along."

"He doesn't look well. Let me help you take him to Admitting."

"Thank you, no. We'll be fine."

"We were just leaving." Hans smiled, the creases around his eyes the only clue to his discomfort.

The orderly glared. "You're supposed to have an escort to the door."

"Well, we, uh, waited a long time, but no one came."

The orderly sighed. "Some days ..." he grumbled and shook his head. "I haven't received any directives, but take a seat."

Hans looked a question at Gretel, and she nodded.

Hans sat upright, but his arm wrapped around his belly told Gretel of his distress.

"I'll bring the truck around and meet you at the door," she said.

She got Hans loaded into the Jeep, peeled out of the parking lot, and headed for home, switching lanes and running yellow lights so as not to have to slow or stop.

Hans groaned. "Better hurry, Gretel, or I'll be messing up your truck."

"Don't worry. I can clean it. I can get a new one. I can't get a new brother."

Hans belched, rolled down the window, and barfed. He pulled his head back inside and wiped his mouth on his sleeve, leaving a red streak on the white fabric.

They limped home in fits and starts with stops to let Hans retch. A call from James reported that much the same transpired at the Robert house. "I swear, she's throwing up everything she ever ate and then some," James said, his voice choked with tears.

"I'm sorry, but that could be a good sign. It means the remedy works. I was afraid that it wouldn't."

"Should we call for an ambulance? Take her to the Emergency Room?" Lucy asked.

"What if they attempt to reverse the process? Hans is experiencing the same thing if that's any consolation. Gotta go. I'll check in with you later." Gretel turned into their driveway and helped Hans limp into the house, where they made a beeline for the bathroom.

Gretel cracked open an eye to a bedroom bright with sunlight. She lay on her made-up bed in clothes she put on the day before yesterday.

Hans! She stumbled to the bathroom where she had left him kneeling before the porcelain throne. The room stank. Towels with grisly stains littered the floor, but there was no sign of her brother.

The door to his bedroom was ajar. Gretel peeked in. He sprawled on the bed in shorts and a tee-shirt, so inert it made her heart race. She took a step inside. She was about to try to rouse him when she noticed the objects on the nightstand. A cola can lay on its side next to a bottle of rum and a glass tumbler empty save for a lime wedge.

Hans let out a perfectly normal burp and rolled over.

Chuckling, Gretel returned to her room.

Chapter Six

Gretel trudged toward the office's refreshment cart, her boot heels clicking on the hardwood floor.

Hans looked up from his desk. "I can tell from your expression that you do not bring good news."

Gretel slumped into the armchair. "The windowsill damage that Mr. McArdle thought was due to dry rot? It proved to be nothing of the sort. He has termites. This is a much bigger job than we thought." She shook her head. "I don't know. We could try boric acid if the wood isn't too dry. Or diatomaceous earth if I can find a way to distribute it and achieve adequate coverage." She winced. "Orange oil, maybe?" She frowned. "Not all that effective, and it could damage the wood."

"Don't worry. We can handle it." Hans sprang to his feet and fetched a beer from the mini-fridge for her. "Here. You deserve it. Have I thanked you enough for rescuing me?"

The bottle to her lips, she dismissed his apology with a wave. "Don't mention it. That's just what big sisters do. You look pleased with yourself."

"Pleased with us. You took off for McArdle's before you had a chance to read the latest issue of the Hip Deep *Crier*." He passed her the broadsheet.

The Paul Zavare incident had made the front page, albeit below the fold. Gretel scanned the part reporting where she led police to Zavare's car, abandoned in the ballfield parking lot, and to a strange pile of ash, yet to be identified. She skipped ahead to where James Robert accused Zavare of being the bloodsucker who preyed on his livestock and menaced his daughter. "The Robert family will forever be in Grethan Exterminators' debt for ridding Hip Deep of this threat." Not a mention was made of the parts Sybil and Hans played.

Gretel snorted. "That's one version of the story."

"I'm going with it," Hans said. "And you're gonna like what came in the mail. They fast-tracked it in response to what we did to remove Paul Zavare."

Hans handed her an eight-and-a-half-by-eleven-inch sheet of paper topped with the Hip Deep council's official letterhead.

Gretel squinted then grinned. "Our license!"

Hans nodded. "This will make our work so much easier. I told you the McArdle job won't be a problem. Like the business permit, we're required to display it where people can see it. That way that the public is advised that we are authorized to use pesticides and other dangerous chemicals."

"Display it? I want to frame it! It means that we're—"

"Yup. I already ordered updated company stationary and tee-shirts.

Here's a print proof." Hans held up another sheet. Printed across it was the business's name, Grethans Exterminators, and below it, a second line: Licensed to Kill. "We might need it, too. We've got a new job. One you can sink your teeth into." He snorted.

Gretel groaned. "Really, Hans?"

"Yeah. Not like the last one. This one doesn't suck."

"Hans!"

"Or maybe it does. Seriously, this sounds interesting."

Gretel straightened in her seat. "Tell me."

"Hector Escamillo called. It seems something is attacking the cattle at The Ranch."

Gretel gaped. "Okay, wait a minute. We took care of that."

"This is different. This was a serious attack. The cow wasn't merely bitten. It was killed."

"I'd guess a coyote or a mountain lion."

Hans raised his hand. "Now hold on there. Hector knows his business. He gave the surrounding area a thorough examination. He knows coyote tracks when he sees them. Mountain lion, too. There was nothing like that anywhere near the dead animal."

"Please, don't tell me. He found footprints?"

"Not exactly. The attacker appeared to be bipedal, but the prints were the strangest thing Hector has ever seen. Three-toed. With claws. What's more, the cow was dead all right. Its flesh wasn't torn, but the animal was drained of every drop of blood."

Gretel rolled her eyes. "I suppose now you're going to tell me that cow's neck had two punctures from fangs."

"No."

Gretel sighed with relief. "Not a vampire, then. So, the cow bled out from the injury?"

"Nope. Hardly any blood was spilled. Hector's stumped. One more thing. About the bite, it wasn't two fang punctures. There were three perforations, arranged in a triangle."

"What?"

"Hector didn't want to jump to conclusions. He wants confirmation from us."

"Confirmation? Of what?"

"Something he heard about when he worked a ranch in Puerto Rico. Heard but never saw for himself. Until now."

"I give up. What?"

"A chupacabra."

It's said of Devorah Fox that she writes outside the box. Its feelings hurt, the box gets up and stomps off. So she writes about that, too. A multi-genre author, she has written "The Bewildering Adventures of King Bewilliam," a best-selling epic fantasy series, as well as an acclaimed mystery and a popular thriller, and co-authored a contemporary thriller with Jed Donellie. She contributed short stories to a variety of anthologies and has several Mystery and Fantasy Short Reads to her name. Born in Brooklyn, New York, she now lives on the Texas Gulf Coast with rescued tabby cats ... and a dragon named Inky.

Visit the "Dee-Scoveries" blog at:
http://devorahfox.com/http://devorahfox.com
Sign up for the free e-mail newsletter:
http://eepurl.com/LrZGX

facebook.com/DevorahFoxAuthor

twitter.com/devorah_fox

amazon.com/author/devorahfox

DON'T TAKE ANY WOODEN DIMES

BY LISA JAYNE WALDEN

Dempsey's eyelids fluttered, tear ducts releasing moisture in annoyance from the rising sun as it blanketed cascading rays over the hills of New York's Southern Tier. He loathed this plot of land, wanted to move away from this county, but now drove through it with that brazen sun in his eyes. He aligned himself with fog from the previous night, watching the mist attempt to hide from the sun's intrusive glare.

"We are the same," Dempsey said as he watched the fog flitter about, the denseness of it settling, reserving itself to the underbrush of weeds. He did not feel the birds awaken with song but rather believed they squawked at the intrusive light, reminding them of their daily ardor. "We are in this labor together," Dempsey said, gripping the steering wheel firmer.

The song of these birds was not the chime of the delicate creatures who graced his childhood home. That pleasant serenity had turned into his young adult home. A new wife, who would, hopefully, bring to his family new life. He remembered them, the cheerful chirps that always awakened his wife first. Her jovial, he sullen as he pulled the woolen blanket over his shoulder. She kissed his cheek and giggled. He grumbled. She smiled, then flitted off to check on breakfast.

Dempsey took in the angry sound of the birds flying over his vehicle. Well, at least now Belinda would be happy. Dempsey had finally found himself aligned with nature. Perhaps it was because there was something different in the song of these birds. They were edgy, almost hungry. It was not a song of blissful awareness, but rather a chime, a death toll of voracious hunger.

That is what Dempsey heard as his car barreled on. He did not hear the Laughing Gull, nor did he see the scarlet red of the Cardinal. He did, however, hear the call of an Osprey as his car drove over a bridge.

"Killy, killy, killy," it beckoned.

That call was high pitched and delicate as he remembered, but for some reason, Dempsey heard, "killy, killy, killy."

He had to take a second look. He pulled his car over and expected the bird to take flight, but it stayed put on the shoulder of the road. He looked closer. Yes, it was an Osprey. The brilliant white feathers at its breast and abdomen, similar white plumes around its head, and the streak of black about its eyes. The massive wings were brownish-black. Yes, that was the raptor, river hawk there before him on the side of the road. But was it here calling out to nothing but dirt and gravel? The river was miles away.

Dempsey's ponderings were interrupted by the loud squawk of a murder of crows. They bellowed as if they were answering the Osprey. The cluster of crows gathered in the sky above him. They hovered and circled, then, to his surprise, descended on the Osprey. Dempsey knew they were both birds of prey. His father, being an avid bird watcher, had schooled him in the varying species, much to his great distaste for the study. This sight was nothing he had ever witnessed under his father's watchful eye. The Osprey spread its mammoth wings to take flight, but the crows surrounded it.

The relentless pecking and squawking ensued as the Osprey screeched out once again, "killy, killy, killy."

Dempsey bore witness to the annihilation, the high-pitched chirps drowning in a throat pecked and filling with blood. White feathers stained crimson-rose into the air. The Osprey's once beautiful form and chirping voice became darkened by black feathers.

Dempsey stayed a moment longer as the murder pulled the flesh from the once beautiful raptor. He watched them as they turned their heads upon him and began to spread their wings. He at once decided to shift the gears of his vehicle and continue with his journey.

The crows raised their wings, as if their squawks turned to laughter, knowing they had taken out the first morning call. What would be the next call? Dempsey didn't want to think of their next prey as he sped off the shoulder and returned his car to the highway.

The thick fog, which had been discarded to the underbrush, had returned to the highway upon the next turn encircling his Packard Twin Roadstar. All he could hear was the call of the crows echoing in his memory as he blazed through the dense dew of this dreadful morning hour. His vehicle sliced the fog at every turn, and in those turns of fog and calling crows, he saw his wife's face.

That once pure face contained no powder, no pomp. But with all that absence in toiletry, she persisted to relish in the rebellion she displayed to her father and him. She did not need rouge. Her cheeks were constantly flushed at the next argument. He remembered the way her vein pulsed in between her brows when she demanded the right to march, to stand with those women.

That face, Dempsey was always a sucker for it. At least with her father at his side, he felt emboldened to stand against her. She had no real property. She was married to him and, as his wife, had to obey his wishes. That was the law. When her father had passed on, and Belinda an only child, her father's property became hers, which under the law, became Dempsey's. Yet, he remembered reaching for her arm at the wake. He swore he saw a smirk on his wife's face underneath the black lace shroud.

Soon after the funeral, she ignored his pleas and scoffed at his threats of discipline. He saw her, dressed in white with that damn sash across her chest. He found himself canceling meetings to chase after her only to arrive too late. Held at bay by patrolmen, he saw her as she marched. He saw her as she was hit with batons and dragged away.

He accelerated the gas, trying to clear his head of the images. Yet as the fog rolled on, he became transfixed, almost lulled into the memories of his mother's voice in his ear. His mother always gave him the eye, that disapproving, how have I failed you, look. The fog he once felt sorry for was now wearing on him. It was no longer hunkered down in underbrush but rather right in his face. He squinted as he drove through it, that damnable fog. Maybe he was tired, finally tired. He had been searching for her, and now he would find her. Maybe this angst in him was settling, a chapter he could close for good. He sucked air in then slowly dispelled it. With every breath, there was the fog, and in that fog, the disapproving eye, or were there eyes in that fog? At first, he saw Belinda's brown eyes. They were young and innocent, those eyes that beseeched him when he first courted her. Shaky eyes. Scared eyes. Expecting and excited eyes. If he could, he would have those eyes forever. Keep them on his person at all times. Not the eyes which had last looked on his stature and made him feel incredibly small. No, not those eyes. Dempsey blinked again, but the eyes were still there in the fog. No longer his wife's loving eyes, but rather, his mother's. Cold and blue, they were, not the gentle, burning embers of brown from his wife, before she had become so impassioned and emboldened. Those ice blue, cutting eyes, always judging. He blinked again. Now they both were there. They both disapproved. Both scoffing for opposite reasons. Dempsey felt ripped in two.

Dempsey realized that he had begun to cry. "Damn fog!" He grabbed his handkerchief and blotted his eyes. Then he screamed again, "What man does this for his wife? A woman?" He shifted in his seat. "And this fog! This damnable fog!" It was deep now, covering the roadways and blanketing the fields. He swore he heard voices coming from the fog. It couldn't be voices, could it? Dempsey shook his head and gripped the steering wheel so tightly he felt the skin of his knuckles stretch. He almost felt them crack. He released his grip and took another deep breath. No matter his breathing. No matter how he readjusted himself behind the wheel, that fog was present, and those voices persisted. He wanted Belinda's voice. He wanted to see her eyes. His wife, when they were happy and content. He concentrated on the mist of white as if calling for her. He envisioned her again before him, those beautiful brown eyes, the delicate cheekbones. She even had adorable freckles that kissed her skin.

To his horror, that face melted in front of him. The eyes faded from brown to gray and then turned to an ice blue. The cheeks, full and plump, became shallow, sunken in as if eaten by age and decay. The hair turned gray, and all he could see was his mother.

Soon, all he could hear was his mother bashing her words round and round and round again in his head. "My darling boy, what a trollop you've chained your carriage to. First, she will be fighting for niggers then she will be putting these devices into her body to not have children! Where will it end?"

"Mother, please." Dempsey struck the steering wheel. The past played out in the fog before him.

"Don't you beg me, my dumb-witted son!" That scene played out before him. The fog taking shape. He heard the hiss of his mother as she held up her cane and lifted the negligee. "No corset. No binding!".

"It's a different time. Clothing has changed," Dempsey said, repeating the words he had uttered years ago.

"No binding. And she won't be bound to you!"

Dempsey pulled over. He felt the liquor rise up from his stomach. He tried to push the bile down. He heard the call of crows and violently vomited on the side of the road. He heard his mother's voice in his head and attempted to push her words from his mind. As his thoughts drifted, the fog rose. He did not like the thickness of the mist. He wiped the spittle of vomit from his chin and sat back in his car. He had to get going. Now. He had to reach his wife before she picked up and moved again.

He looked around his car as the fog filtered into his vehicle. When would this god-forsaken fog end! He turned on his wipers. The blades pulled away the beads of moisture from his windshield, then sent the pearls of wetness cascading into his sleep-deprived vision. How much sleep had he gained over the past few nights? How could he remember? As he set his car in drive, he thought of her letter, Belinda's letter, stating she was going to a cousin's. A cousin, to be precise. Was it Margaret? Anna? Perhaps Gladys? Who knew! And all of this after he got her ass out of jail. He checked all her cousins. Nothing. He made calls to her friends. Negative. Lies. All lies. The wind whipped up, forcing the tendrils of water on his windshield to congeal into a figure. He looked at it. He reached to his steering wheel and gripped it. Why weren't his wipers moving this image from his sight?

First, it formed her eye. The wipers still didn't swipe this beautiful image from his face. Then from the eye fell droplets of moisture forming tendrils of her hair. He turned the wipers off then on again, wanting nothing more than to destroy her frame, destroy the women who took any chance of him having children. She made sure of that the last time she crossed him. It was her fault for crossing him. Her fault that she fell down the stairs. It was her fault. He saw the blood flowing from between her legs, saw that as he drove his car towards where she should be—her fault. No baby. Gone. That baby was caught in her gown in a clot of blood. It was her fault he struck her and... and... Yes, it was her fault, her clumsiness that sent her toppling down the stairs. It was her weak frame that lost their baby. Yes. *Her.*

He grimaced and grasped the steering wheel harder. He cursed the windshield wipers. He cursed her image. He sucked in the air around him, filling his lungs. He exhaled and laughed at the image that would not disappear. Let her preach at him about liquor now. And to find out that after all of this, she, his wife, his whore was at a club.

The fog was so deep now, he could barely see. He adjusted his footing on the clutch when something smashed his windshield. He jumped from the striking of it, the smack against the glass, fracturing his shield into spiderwebs. There was a beak in the center of the glass. He pulled over his car and cursed. It was a baby crow, not full-grown, its beak buried in the glass of his windshield. He looked at the bird, beak buried in the windshield. He pulled the body of the bird from the glass. He held the twitching animal as it died in his hands. As he looked at the broken beak and dark feathers, he saw Belinda's face behind the dark funeral shroud smiling at him once again. His mind went back to the Osprey and the bloody white feathers, the falling chirp, the gurgling scream of, "killy, killy, killy."

He looked at the dying baby crow. It opened its eyes. He threw it to the road as bile, once again, rose in his throat. Dempsey looked at the baby crow on the side of the road. The creature fell into the death throws on the dirt and clay gravel. He drew in another deep breath and exhaled, "There is a place for all of God's creatures."

It was when he had wiped his hands on his handkerchief and placed them on the steering wheel again that the fog lifted from his memory. That fight. The reason for it. It was before he struck. He remembered it vividly, as he sat in his car watching the wipers go back and forth, and forth and back. The numbness of that repetition lulled him as if hypnotized to that day, and all the while, those wipers refused to erase her face. He had checked the wipers before he got in the car. No debris. No reason for the streaks. But as he sat in his seat, he laughed as they swished and swooshed and yet still allowed his dear Belinda's face to show on his windshield.

He drove through the feeling of that image. At first, he saw the violence. He felt his fingers in her shorn hair. He saw her terrified eyes filled with dread as he smashed her skull into her vanity mirror. He felt his biceps twitch as he hoisted her body out of her room and to the stairs. He felt his foot connect with her fallen torso as he kicked her over and over again until she toppled.

No. She did this. Back from jail and shame on his family, she did this. Those women—they did this. He was a man. He is a man. "I am a man," Dempsey said. He tried to reassure himself of his status as the head of a household, a great and formidable, but now waning house-hold. "I am a man," he found himself saying again. He punched the clutch, shifted, and sped on. "I am a man!" he lifted his voice up. To whom was he lifting his voice to? The bleak morning sky had given him so much blood. The feathers, streaked in blood. That chirping voice fallen into death throes as flesh was pecked away. Was he crying out to his wife now? Was it the Osprey he was hearing? He couldn't be sure. All he could be sure of was the way she looked at him when he forced open her bedroom door as she sat at her vanity, cutting her hair.

He remembered the feeling of her flesh on his foot as drove the pedal in gaining speed. His foot wasn't the first thing of his body that had taken her in. It was his eyes. His eyes saw her and drank that image in of his beloved sitting there in front of her vanity with a pair of shears as she shorn her hair. He remembered screaming at her, but not the words he said. He just remembered her laughter and how it stirred him. He attempted to grab the shears from her hand. She thrust them out, the edge of the shears catching his forearm. He looked at the blood that soaked his cotton shirt. Again, that smile, once hidden behind the black shroud, but there was no shroud now. Dempsey looked about her room. He looked at the blood that fell from his arm. He struck her. She merely laughed.

"Funny!" he remembered screaming as he looked at his shirt sleeve. "You find me comical?"

"Oh, husband, yes. I find us all comical," she said as she pulled herself up, blood dripping from her lips. He saw her in her shift, that cotton gown. Breasts displayed beyond the buttons, more swollen than before. How could he know? He didn't see the swollen breasts, nor did he see a belly rising. He saw the hair she had shorn. After all he had done. All he had done, to protect their name, to get her out. How could she with this…this hair? He walked up to her and delivered a swift kick to her side. She grimaced at his kick, then laughed as she picked up her hair on the carpet. She held it in her hands and licked it as he kicked her again. She grabbed the shorn hair on either side of her and threw it in the air. Belinda laughed again. "Catch my headdress, husband," she had said to him. "It is all you care about!"

This drove him into a rage. This woman he had rescued after her ridiculous cause. Her abhorrent jail time. The stain in his family name. He remembered how he grabbed her by the scruff of what hair she had left. He dragged her against the walls, and the pictures of the halls, the pictures of those who came before, pictures she cared little of. He remembered smashing her head into one of them before he slammed her to the ground. He was proud to do that. Let her come face to face with *his* ancestors. Then, with one last act, he kicked her in the belly and sent Belinda flying down the stairs. He watched her form fall head over heel down the stairs. He stood at the top of the stairs breathing in deep and short breaths, as he did now, trying to see through his windshield. Anna, the maid, came rushing in. She saw Belinda huddled in a mass of broken bones and averted her eyes.

"Go!" Dempsey yelled as he held the railing of the staircase. He yelled as he gazed upon his wife's tattered body at the bottom of the stairs. He yelled as dust motes rattled off that railing in the noon sun. Time held its breath. Time paused that dust in the air. They danced in the golden rays, looking like birds spreading their wings, looking like elements wanting to escape, to take flight. They took to the sun and froze. Time dallied and delayed, and then time laughed.

Dempsey attempted to push these thoughts from his mind as he was reaching Rochester, New York. He tried to banish the image of her crumpled body at the bottom of the staircase from his vision as the wipers swooshed back and forth. But he couldn't do it. He was there trapped in that time, trapped in what brought him here now. All he saw was his form stepping step by step down the staircase towards her. Her face still beautiful. The delicate freckles on her cheeks. Her neck. No. Her neck was not right. It was bent, and a bone almost thrust through the skin at the left. Her eyes were open. Glassy.

Dempsey knew the directions to the bar. He refused to write it down. By all accounts, he had killed her. Yet, she did exist. He pulled into the town of Rochester, New York. Already the streets were bustling with commerce and traffic. He accepted the interaction, almost smiled at it. The fear of seeing her once again made Dempsey want to hit the bottle, but that bottle was long since dry. This bustle around him was a needed distraction. He almost felt close to normal. No wife to chase again. No dead wife. To chase. Again.

He was here. He was where he needed to be. Being. Present. Here. He parked his car and sat for a moment wanting to lose himself in time, to wander down the hallways of his mind's regret. He wanted to push the image from his head. That bone jutting from the flesh of her neck. He wanted to forget her face. He remembered how he walked down the staircase, one step feeling like a judgement as he came closer to the fallen body of his Belinda. The bone, that disgusting bone, and the way it jutted against the flesh of her throat. Everything around him whirled. He was trapped in a tunnel vision, the dark mahogany of the stairs whirling together with her cotton shift, and the blood, and the bone. He was lost, caught in her body as he touched her beautiful face, how beautiful she was now, that she was silent and still. He held her face. He kissed her lips. He kissed her dead forehead. He kissed her unmoving cheeks. He let his tears fall on her open eyelids. Then he heard her, felt her move.

She did move. Slightly at first. There was a low gurgling in her throat. She reached up a slow, shaking arm, attempting to caress his face with her frail hand. "Dempsey," was what she said.

"Oh, my sweetheart," he said. He pulled her close. He looked into her brown eyes and saw them fade into a dull silver, a dull dead eye look. "No, don't leave me." He began to cry as he pulled her body to him. He ran his fingers through her course cut hair. "I'm so sorry. So sorry."

He felt her go limp. He kissed her lips. He laid her on the landing. Dempsey looked around them. He saw the sunlight peeking through the stained glass. He saw the dust motes dance and float about. He accepted their tiny beauty. He looked back at Belinda. He kissed her lips again, but now they were cold. She coughed. She took a hand and pushed him away from her. That pushing, that movement did not upset him. Dempsey was delighted. She wasn't dead. She drew in a breath and again pushed away from him. She was gasping with the bone pushing through her neck. He tried to calm her to make her lie still. She brought up her shaking legs and shoved him. Then she brought her hands to her throat and thrust the bone back. "You will never gain this beauty again," she said as she cleared her throat. She still had the hair in her hands. She opened her fists and threw what was left of her blonde locks at him. "Take your headdress!" She then began to try to stand.

He heard the bones of her legs crunch. They had to be broken, but she stood up regardless. He looked at her legs and saw the bruising from her fall on the stairs. He also saw the blood from between her legs. Her body shook as if taken by a fever. She then felt her belly. She reached up and down her abdomen. She looked down and saw the puddle of blood on the landing. She screamed out. That was the scream Dempsey would never get out of his mind. He couldn't look at her, didn't even try, as she wailed. "You did this!" She reached in between her legs. Blood flowed. She looked at the clot, the mass on the landing. She fell to her haunches. She reached for it and scooped the mass in her hands. She smelled it, then kissed it. Dempsey looked up and saw tears fall from her eyes. She lifted it to him and held it for Dempsey.

"See her."

"I don't see anything," Dempsey said. The smell made him feel sick. It wasn't regular blood or even menstrual blood. This thing she held in her hand had a form.

Dempsey sat on the side of the road and thought of the baby crow he pulled from his windshield, that inconvenience that got in his way.

"Of course, you don't," Belinda said. Those were the words he heard as she straightened her broken neck. Those were the words that echoed in his head as she packed her bags. Those were the words that renumerated in his brain as he drove here. Then the memories that followed. Her hair all over her room. He had laid there for days holding those locks. He grabbed them and brought them to bed with him. He had them with him now. He opened an envelope. Her locks that she had shorn before he had struck her before he had sent her down the stairs.

She had left him. He knew it. Now he had found her again. He needed his songbird again. Even though she had risen in front of him, he needed her. She was a bird, a beautiful bird that was happy with the sun, beautiful in the morning. He needed her, needed her life to sustain him. Complete him. Sustain him. Give him meaning and, above all else, save his face. Even though she had shown him that blood clot, that thing, that flesh she was too weak to bring to this life. Even though she had thrown her cut hair in his face. Even though she had said to him, "Reborn in flesh, but not for you."

Dempsey closed his eyes as he turned off his car. He looked at the club his wife was supposed to be in. He heard again as he closed the door of his car. "Reborn in flesh, but not for you!" She had screamed it at him as she threw the blood clot at him. Dempsey was already on his knees.

He remembered holding her cut hair. His foot was still on the clutch. He remembered his lips on her cheek. The skin cold. That cheek, covered with tears, both of their tears. Gas. He needed to remove his foot off the gas. Christ, and the clutch! He held her hair against her face. Clutch then gas with the rolling hills. Sweaty hair and tears. Then her fingernails against his throat. His hands around her throat. His legs between hers. Her knee in his groin and a low cackling laugh as he rolled to his side. Had they made love? Further screams as he felt her fists punch against his kidneys. His body rolled over, and a final blow to his Adam's apple. Dempsey remembered her as he took another turn on the roadway, no it was not a roadway. It was an opened car door, his car door as he vomited bile to the pavement. When did he last eat? Hadn't he asked this question before? Next, it would be when did he last sleep. He knew he asked that as well. As he was wrenching outside his door, he remembered her words," Oh, my, eunuch. You are nothing without me." At that moment, Belinda had a vice grip on his testicles. He wretched again and felt the sweet pleasure of her hands, squeezing his manhood to oblivion.

Dempsey didn't recall parking his car. Did he park it? Or did they just take his car? He remembered being ushered into the club. Drinks aplenty in this speakeasy. He asked for her. He was greeted with laughter. No. It wasn't laughter. It was mockery. He was sure of it. If anything, Dempsey had a false sense of ego, yet he resolved himself to just sit and watch the show. There were several acts. Women singing, some swung on swings throwing garters to the crowd, Men and women alike were there drinking and laughing. Cajoling! A dead end. Dempsey's heart was heavy. This was it. He would never find Belinda. He would return home a laughingstock. The dead wife who wasn't dead and made off with what? Not his money, nor her father's. No, it was more than that. More than money. His reputation. His esteem, what he had left of it. He had decided to give up and just leave.

He stood up, and that is when he saw her standing there. She came down on the stage. The curtains were black. They opened, and a moon descended. It was on that crescent that his wife graced the stage. *A harlot, a trinket on a glittering pie.* He could hear his mother in his ear. Pure white moon with his wife's body adorned in a scarlet dress. Dempsey put aside the cigar and drink the club had provided him. He wanted to see her, this dead woman who left. His exhaustion and his inebriation did not matter. All he could see was his Belinda. There she was on a moon crescent descending to the stage. Her voice rang out:

Dreams sweet drips from lost lips,
>   Fingers curled lost in dreamless grips,
>   Paper rips and lips curl to huddle in yellow,
>   Flesh soils to toil in your rubble.
>   'Til you sweat those sweet dreams.
>   My lips. My lips. My lips.
>   Killee, killee, killee.

He was there, He was here, with her voice ringing out. He saw those lips, those lips he struck, the body he kicked. He saw her landing there on his floor that her family financed. The girl he had to bring back from the bees' knees, the cool girl. Drag her from the stage back to Hudson, New York. Dempsey was dizzy. He looked at a waitress. "I'm in Rochester?" he didn't ask but rather tried to affirm.

The woman laughed and answered, "Yes, The Viper's Club."

"Vipers," Dempsey said. He drank the rest of his drink, and then his world swirled. He looked at his shirt and watched as it blended into the floor, the white of his shirt melting into the marble blue. His mouth drew slack. He wanted to vomit once again as the colors swirled together. Was it possible to vomit again? To be this sick in one evening? He pulled a small pamphlet from his pocket. He looked at the picture of the pamphlet. A woman covered in snakes. He looked back at the server. "Gorgana?" He knew Belinda's new name. His money made sure of that. And that name, idiotic and obscene. Gorgana. Sounded like a large woman, but he knew where the name came from. Gorgans, all knowing and powerful women of Greek mythology. She couldn't be more obvious.

"Oh, yes. She is immensely popular. She's right there!"

"No, I see she is. I need a private meeting."

"That will cost you."

"I can pay," Dempsey said. He felt woozy and faint.

"I'm sure you can," the serving girl said as she smiled and walked away.

Dempsey raised his glass to his lips, but someone jerked his elbow. He spilled his tea-cup drink on the bar. He cursed, yet the arm wore firm on his elbow. There were two other bodies on either side of him.

"What's this all about!" Dempsey attempted to lift an arm to punch but found himself neatly tucked down. Even if they weren't, his head was swimming, and his arms felt like molasses. He was dragged to the back. He saw women half-naked, putting on bejeweled outfits to shine and jump on the stage. They passed through a hallway to a discreet dressing room. Dempsey's head started to spin, not out of amazement, but rather out of sickness, a violent and purposefully instilled inebriation that only can make one feel sick. He felt the urge to vomit but choked on the regurgitation. He looked as they drew him to a couch in the back of the bar. He was encompassed by women scantily clad and thought of his own wife in this despicable bar. He attempted to lift himself then fell backward again against the softness of the velvet pillows. The softness of the chaise lounge and the elevated pillows made Dempsey fall into a deep sleep, devoid of restless dreams and terrors of birds.

Dempsey's head was spinning. How could there be air when these stank billows of clouds abounded him? Dempsey rubbed his eyes and coughed aloud. He saw a gathering of people around him sitting on the floor like weird foreigners on cushions smoking from hookahs. There were four large windows in the front of the room covered by sheer, purple curtains that billowed inward with the evening wind as if that wind desired to be with them. He wished the wind would reach him. The smoke from the room was intense, and his eyes were burning. The people on the floor in front of him were laughing and cajoling, taking no notice of his discarded drunken ass on the chaise lounge. He assumed they thought he was drunk, well, maybe a little drunk, but more than likely, as he knew it to be true, he was heart-broken and sleep-deprived. One of the members of the revelry looked about and offered kisses. Yes, kisses. He held his hands to his lips and kissed those hands, then extended them out. Strange, this young man. He then raised an arm and banged against a thin bronze metal disc. A loud *dung* sound echoed in the changing room. A few of the people before Dempsey fell silent. The same man raised his hand again and hit the disc four more times until all were silent. Then, all turned their gaze on Dempsey's sick and pallid figure.

A gigantic woman came in; bosom hoisted up in what they all now wore, a brassiere. Her breasts appeared as pointed guns, staring at him. She wore thin silky bloomers and thigh-high fishnets. This woman was a giant. Had to be at least four inches taller than Dempsey, and Dempsey knew he was not a slight man. What was this place of liquor and whores and gigantic women unbound? She offered him a plate of pickled pig's feet and chicken heads. Dempsey attempted congeniality. He picked up what had to be a pig's hoof. He raised it to his lips. The crowd in front of him was silent. He tore off the flesh and forced himself to swallow. They stood still for a moment, and upon him choking down the coarse meat, skin and all, they smiled. He'd had enough. He wretched violently on the floor, on the chaise lounge, on his suit. He cursed as he fell to the floor, slamming the entrée of discarded flesh held in front of him.

"Madam, I don't think he approves." The gigantic woman began to laugh. She left the largesse on the floor next to Dempsey.

Dempsey wiped the spittle from his face. He looked away from the meat offered to him and attempted to stifle another retching of his body. He kicked at the platter and pushed himself back on the chaise. He looked around the room only to see countless eyes upon him from the crowd of people in front of him. He looked for a door, but there were too many bodies around, too many curtains, too much to give him discernible sight. He heard a woman clear her throat in the far-left corner of the room. The purple curtain billowed around her frame, keeping Dempsey from seeing her, but then he heard that laugh.

It was the laugh he heard five years ago when he first set eyes on Belinda. The two of them allowed to speak and walk together, with the appropriate guardians in tow behind them. That soft laugh as they walked in his gardens at his home. The gardens kept up even though they couldn't afford it. All a show to acquire new young money, new young blood to bolster their old name. That carefree laugh of hers, not knowing that her parents cared little for her wellbeing, but rather wanted the name tied to theirs. That happy, innocent laugh, female laugh, the laugh who knew the joys of being a girl but hadn't seen the pain and sorrow of a woman. That laugh he had lied to. That laugh he had pretended and dared to be something from his predecessors: great. He was not. That laugh he fell in love with. That laugh who saw him. The laugh who thought he was kind. The laugh who thought he was gentle and caring. The laugh who believed he loved her. The laugh who demanded honesty, integrity, solidarity, and love. The laugh he let down. Dempsey knew that laugh before the curtain had a chance to cascade down from her shadow. He knew the owner of that laugh. Dempsey felt his arms tingle, and his stomach fill with even more bile.

He swallowed the vomit pitting in the back of his throat as Belinda brought the curtain behind her and began to walk towards him.

In Dempsey's mind, Belinda was dressed in the ill forsaken rage of the roaring twenties. Her tiny feet were still in high heels, little white shoes embroidered with pearls into delicate flowerets. Her legs were stockinged but sheer. She wore a low-neck gown which plummeted almost to her navel. He could see the shape of her breasts, unbound by any corset or brassiere. The dress was an opaque white with sequins of silver attached religiously forming flowerets about the piece. Her skin was paler than before, almost shimmering like the moon when full, the same moon he used to look at as a child in his mother's garden before his father made him learn the songs of the birds. They were all at a hush now as she sauntered to him. Dempsey collapsed on this grand dressing room floor.

"I've come to take you home," he said, looking at her shoe as he tried to keep his saliva from leaving his lips. The rot in his stomach was heaving, and the smell in the air was sickly sweet and decomposing all at once.

Belinda smiled. She took her foot and placed it under Dempsey's chin. She raised his head with her foot and made him look up at her. "I am home," she said. Her leg and foot were solid. His chin was shaking. "As you see, we only have truth within these walls. No wallpaper to yellow our veins."

Dempsey pushed her foot away and made a meager attempt to straighten himself up. He felt woozy. Couldn't be the alcohol. He had plenty to drink before. Maybe. Perhaps. He tried to think, but then his head got fuzzy again.

"Are you feeling okay, darling? Should I call the doctor?" Belinda said, then began to laugh. The group around her followed in her laughter. Dempsey brought his hands to his head. He covered his ears, but he could not keep out their mimicking laughter. Make it stop. Make it stop. Make it stop! Yet, the laughter did not stop. Dempsey fell back against the chaise, then brought his knees inward, huddling into a ball.

Belinda shushed the gathering around her. Dempsey looked up at her. She kneeled and placed a hand on the side of his head. "My dear husband, what can I do for you? You know I won't go back with you. So just tell me what I can do... to make you go away?" She laughed again, and her gathering laughed with her.

Dempsey looked at her as tears rolled from his eyes. "I can't save you," he began.

"I don't want you to," Belinda said, then laughed again, and with her laughter, they laughed. She raised her hand, and the laughter stopped. "But, husband, my dear and generous husband, what can I do for you?"

"The child. You didn't tell me," Dempsey said. "You are lost to me. That much is clear. Not our child? All those times you were out there?"

Belinda kneeled to her husband and smiled. Dempsey saw her smile, the white of her teeth, the shining brilliance, and winced. She drew to his ear and whispered, "Oh, my dear husband. I thought you would never ask why I did it." Belinda looked to the door and cleared her throat. "Bring me Persephone."

There were hushed whispers and some laughter. Dempsey fell to his back with exhaustion. Belinda sat on her side and cradled his head. "Oh, no, my dear husband. Stay awake. She is coming."

She was brought forth on a cot, her little legs withered. She was adorned in a beautiful gown, but Dempsey could see that the girl was frail and ill. "She is my child now," Belinda said as she kneeled next to him. "Oh, and dear, husband, she needs a father. She needs your strength."

The child shook with her weakness, but Dempsey could see that familiar look, the look his wife had when he had kicked her down the stairs, that blank look, but rather yet, those eyes filled with silver.

Belinda looked at Persephone. She placed her hands about her face. She kissed her forehead and said to her, "Are you ready, dear."

"Yes, ma'am," the child said.

Belinda pushed the child's head to the right and bit into her neck. She drained her blood. Dempsey screamed and attempted to push his wife off the little girl. The little girl held onto his drug-induced chest. Belinda would not budge. She kept sucking and feeding until the little girl turned white and limp. She heard Dempsey as he screamed. No one in the gathering said a word. She watched him as he shook at the sight of the blood flowing down his wife's lips. As he shit himself, his wife placed the dead corpse of the little girl back against his chest.

"What have you done!" He shook at the sight of her. He shook at the feel of the dead girl next to him. He sobbed as his hands embraced the little girl's body, and he drew her to him. "How could you do this to her! To me! What are you?"

"Oh yes. You. You. You." Belinda stood up. Those in the room stood up as well. Dempsey wanted to stand, but his legs wouldn't let him. The horror in his arms kept him from gaining any strength. He looked at the little girl covered in blood, her blood, that blood that now seeped into his clothing. Before he would have been disgusted to be this close to death or fluids from the body, but now he did not care. He felt her life seep away in his arms. He saw her eyes flutter one last time then close. Flutter as the eyes of the Osprey. Or was he the Osprey?

He looked at his wife. She sat in front of him and appeared to be grooming herself. She took her hand and gently wiped the blood of this little girl from off her lips onto her fingers, then sucked them one by one.

"She's just a girl!"

Belinda stood and laughed. She was the only one who laughed. Those around her were silent and looked at Dempsey. "Yes, and now, she is our little girl, soon to be just your little girl. My little girl was taken with your fists and your feet." Belinda began to laugh. "Oh, you care so much about our wombs as long as we provide an heir. If I were a true heir, I would have no need for you."

Dempsey felt the little child stir on his shoulder. He reached out to Belinda. She retorted with laughter. "Please," he said. "Please," he said again thinking of the crows, thinking of her smiling under black lace.

"Oh, please, please, please." Belinda began to storm her dressing room. "Please! Please!" she stormed and pace.

The girl began to stir. He saw her. He saw those silver eyes. He felt her hunger as she grimaced and drew her lips back.

"Please! Please, please!" Belinda fell to her knees as the little girl opened her mouth.

The child's sharp teeth broke through her baby girl flesh. She screamed out at the pain of the teeth ripping through her gums. The little girl saw her own blood fall onto Dempsey's neck. She smelled her own blood at first. With that first sniff of her blood, she reached out her arms and stretched. She yawned and stretched again, and then she smelled something else. She smelled another. Something not her, something to feed her. She turned, and as she turned on her side, she gathered a scent of him and realized his body next to her. She sniffed his shirt; she smelled his sweat. She gathered his experiences, his day, the images. She also smelled his fear.

Belinda kneeled into her husband's ear. "What's wrong, darling? Guess you didn't bet on this horse," Belinda laughed as the little girl tore into her husband's neck. "Well, I didn't bet on this stallion either." Belinda sat back as she watched the little girl feast on her husband. She knew after it was done, she would have to kill her. Rip her head off. Children could be unpredictable. Everyone knows to always have a safe bet. Everyone knows to cover their asses these days. Everyone knows not to take any wooden dimes.

Lisah Jayne Walden resides in upstate New York with her two kids and three furbabies. She received a double BA in history and English from the University of Rochester and an MA in English from the College of Brockport. Her hobbies include reading and writing horror, watching movies with her kids, trying new cooking recipes, and gardening.

facebook.com/lisahwalden73

twitter.com/LisahZoe974

instagram.com/stillwritinglwalden

VACATIONS SUCK

BY K. MATT

The plan was simple enough. The family would go on a weekend trip to a cabin somewhere in rural Pennsylvania. Spencer had been the one to rent the van that was currently carrying seven adults (including himself) and one child. The doctor would have been content just going with his brother-in-law Travis, wife Gemmy, and his young son Daniel. But in the planning process, they ended up accumulating his mother-in-law Serena, her fiancee Silas, Serena's twin sister Beast, Beast's male clone Tsaeb, and her friend Ivy. It was an *eccentric* bunch, to say the least. After all, Travis, Gemmy, and Daniel all had monkey-like tails and feet. Beast and Serena? Both feline-human hybrids. Not only that, but Beast also had large leather-like bat wings and metal arms and legs. Tsaeb had dog ears and a tail, with huge, feathered wings. Silas was an elf. The only two in that van that looked entirely like normal humans were Spencer and Ivy.

It looked every bit like the circus would be coming to town, and none of them particularly felt like dealing with demands to put on a show for some random person. Hence the trip to rural PA. Besides, he knew some time away from their home city of Hell Bent would do them all some good. It would be nice to step away from the laboratories that sat on practically every street corner.

To reconnect with nature and just be at peace for a few days. Peace was something they didn't get all that much of, the family's collective luck being objectively horrible. It was never just little mishaps like a flat tire here or a poorly timed illness there. It was usually things along the lines of serial killers that *seemed* friendly and helpful at first before showing their true nature, magic instructors that turned out to be much more horrible than they initially let on, arms dealers that just would *not* go away, homicidal fire elementals...

The list was a long one, to say the least. Concerningly so, for just one extended family. But they had dealt with everything life had thrown at them. Sometimes (or rather, frequently), it would leave scars, both physical and emotional. But these people were survivors.

"Hm...tank's getting low," Spencer muttered as he kept driving along."

"Ugh, yeah, I hear that," Travis said, stomach growling a bit, and his hair-topped monkey feet propped up on the dashboard. "Gas stations usually have food somewhere, right?"

Spencer nodded. "Yes, but it's not necessarily the healthiest option. Not everything gets refrigerated for a long enough time...or sometimes the refrigeration just breaks, period."

Travis scoffed. "Dude, I'll be fine. We've all seen what my stomach is capable of handling...like, the only limits I've seen are bananas and Ivy's cooking."

In the back, Ivy had been reading a horror manga and didn't look up from the pages as she pointed toward Travis. "Okay, first off, Trav, you're lucky you're cute. Second, I'll give you that one,"

Ivy's cooking abilities, or lack thereof, were sort of a running joke in their family. She had been banned from getting anywhere near a stove ever since the incident with the orange Jell-O that had become charcoal in her wake. Nobody quite knew how she'd done it. Not even her, and she was the one responsible.

"Anyone else want to grab a bite?" Spencer asked.

"I'll just do some hunting when we get to the cabin!" Beast called. "I've tried gas station sushi before, and things did *not* go well..."

"Ugh, yeah, that was one hell of a weekend," Ivy replied. "Took a few hours to convince you that you weren't gonna die and that the pink, backward-speaking demon baby was a hallucination."

Beast crossed her arms and huffed. "I know I felt it breathing on me from all three of its mouths, Ivy. Can you hallucinate *that?*"

Her friend just kept reading, offering a shrug. "In all fairness, you were pretty messed up that weekend."

Serena shrugged. "I'm good for now. But if I get hungry, Silas can probably use a summoning spell...right?" she asked, leaning against the elven mage's chest.

Silas rested his goateed chin on top of her head before giving her ear a light scratch. "I believe that can be arranged, m'dear."

Spencer didn't have to look in the back of the van to pick up on Ivy's response. He could tell she was rolling her eyes at Silas. It was her typical reaction to him. His son was the one responsible for teaching Spencer magic before revealing himself to be a homicidal luddite of the highest caliber. Said former instructor had become obsessed with Ivy's sister Yvette (who had begun to substitute as Spencer's instructor). After one fateful night, Silas's demon spawn had disappeared with Yvette, leaving no trace of where they could be. Even with Silas's apologies over his son's behavior, it wasn't enough for Ivy to trust him.

"Food sounds like a good idea to me!" Gemmy called.

"Yeah, bring it!" Tsaeb added.

Once again, Spencer didn't have to look back. He knew that Gemmy probably had that latest ultra-thick fantasy novel open in her lap and was about halfway through it by now. He knew for a fact that she hadn't even cracked the thing open prior to them piling into the van. Spencer had a feeling, also, that Tsaeb's tail was wagging. He was pretty sure he could hear it slapping at the air.

"And how about you, Daniel?" Travis asked. "Hungry?"

The child was in the middle front seat between his dad and uncle, and they could hear him say one word with an almost reverent tone: "Food..."

Spencer smiled a bit. The boy looked so much like him, but with his mother's bright green eyes and monkey traits. He wasn't sure which side of the family the gap between his teeth came from but didn't quite care. The kid was (mostly) quiet and of the shy-and-sweet variety.

Travis hit a button on the GPS with a toe. "Hey, we need a gas station," he said to it.

"The nearest gas station is just off the next exit," the GPS's computerized monotone replied.

The drive would continue for a few more minutes before their next destination made itself visible.

"Now, let's try not to get *too* crazy with the food in there, all right?" Spencer said as they began to approach the gas station. "Trav, Gemmy, that especially applies to you two."

"Aw, what's wrong, hon...is my appetite *that* imposing?" Gemmy teased.

Spencer chuckled a bit. "I've seen how formidable it can be...almost as bad as your brother's."

"Hey, in all fairness," Travis began, "it's usually *after* getting my ass handed to me that I need to eat like that."

Yes, he supposed that was a fair assessment. Of those two, one had enhanced speed, the other accelerated healing, and both possessed rather freakish metabolisms. Because Gemmy's ability was more active than her brother's, she didn't use it nearly as often. But Travis may have been the unluckiest of the group. His regenerative properties had been put to the test time and time again, and the more he had to heal, the hungrier he could get.

Pulling up to the pump, Spencer exited the van. He watched as Travis, Gemmy, Tsaeb, and Ivy did the same, the four making their way to the gas station's convenience store. Whistling a bit, he went to refuel the van. He didn't notice the figure in the flowing red and black dress approaching him at first. He was focused almost entirely on the task at hand.

"Excuse me, sir?" a soft female voice asked, causing Spencer to yelp and practically leap out of his skin.

He turned to face the owner of that voice, pushing up his glasses. What he saw was a tall woman, draped in red and black silk with a pair of deep red sunglasses over her eyes. In a lace-gloved hand, she held a black parasol. Her long ebony hair reached her waist.

"Can I help you with something?" Spencer asked.

The woman gave one nod. "Yes. I need a ride to my home. Sunlight is painful to me, and I can't hold my parasol indefinitely. Arm strain is an unfortunate fact of life."

As she spoke, the doctor could see the long fangs residing in her mouth. Rubbing the back of his neck, his eyes ticked downward. He knew that there were risks in picking up hitchhikers and if she happened to be a vampire...

He knew what a vampire's diet consisted of. And that van happened to contain all sorts of unique blood. He had no intention of letting this vacation turn into a bloodsucker buffet.

"I'm really not sure, miss," he said. "I have no idea where you live. Plus, picking up hitchhikers is generally a bad idea."

She pouted a bit before gently dragging a gloved finger down his chest. "I've had no success so far, and you seem like such a trustworthy sort...And if I don't return home soon, Father will be cross."

The doctor continued to hesitate, unsure if he could trust this person. He had fallen into that trap a few times before: someone would come along that seemed harmless, only to make an attempt on his life at some point. Yes, this person was asking for his help as opposed to offering it, but he knew what his track record looked like.

But at the same time, he had gone into medicine for the express purpose of helping people. Someone with intense light sensitivity whose arm was probably tired of holding a parasol? They seemed like they definitely needed the help.

"I still don't really know, I'm sorry to say," he told her. "It's just that there're a lot of people out there that'd use this to hurt someone, you know?"

She gave a resigned sigh. "Yes, I suppose you're right…"

The woman pulled down her sunglasses, her crimson eyes flashing with a brief red glow.

"But please," she stated, "reconsider?"

A slight rush of warmth flooded through Spencer's brain at that point. He wasn't sure what it was, exactly, but his paranoia about this hitchhiker seemed to melt away.

"Fine," he said. "Just hop in the back. It might be a little crowded back there. Where do you need to go?"

"I'll give the directions along the way. And thank you."

She gave him a quick peck on the cheek, the tips of her fangs lightly scraping against his skin. He opened the back door of the van for her before going to pay for the fuel.

Inside the van, the newcomer looked at the others. Her gaze went to the elf first, and then the two cat-women sitting near him. The cat-women especially looked intrigued. The one with glasses seemed to regard her with curiosity, whereas the one with the eyepatch seemed more suspicious.

Crossing her hulking metal arms, Beast leaned toward the hitch-hiker, her one eye narrowed.

"…So, what's the story here?" she asked.

"Your leader agreed to give me a ride home."

Beast chuckled. "Nah, Spencer's not my 'leader.' He's my sister's son-in-law, and he's generally smart enough to be afraid of my temper. If either of us is a 'leader' in that scenario, I'm gonna go with it being me."

"Are you a vampire, by any chance?" Silas asked, stroking his brown goatee in thought.

Serena pushed up her glasses. "Is it the paleness that makes you ask that or the fangs, hon?"

"Yes."

She leaned in to look the woman over. The woman nodded.

"Yes, as a matter of fact, I am," she stated. "I need to return home. Father gets angry when his children are away for too long."

Beast muttered under her breath, wondering if this woman was serious about the whole "Father" thing.

"So, that's why you're hitching a ride…" Serena murmured, her ears twitching lightly. "How far from here?"

"The only one that needs to know that is your leader," their guest replied, somewhat haughty.

Serena groaned. "My son-in-law and I are on roughly equal ground…I may be a little more elevated if either one of us is above the other, but please don't call him my 'leader.'"

"It is my understanding that if a man is either the eldest or in the front of a group, they are a leader."

Beast and Serena exchanged unimpressed glances. They picked up someone with *those* kinds of outdated views? No matter how much time they spent in this vehicle, it was going to be entirely too long. Silas could have pointed out that he, in fact, was the oldest male in that vehicle, at well over a few centuries in age. But he was an elf of sense and knew that doing anything to get himself declared a leader by someone that out of touch would incur Beast's wrath. Also, he respected his future wife and sister-in-law too much to consider himself their leader.

After a while, the back of the van opened up again, as Ivy, Gemmy, and Tsaeb rejoined the group. Ivy bought a bottle of locally created moonshine, holding it in her arms like it was her own child. Tsaeb picked up a huge bag of beef jerky, his tail wagging as he practically skipped back to the van. Gemmy had grabbed a whole medium garlic pizza for herself since it was entirely meatless, and she'd forgotten about breakfast. Travis opened the door with his tail and reclaimed his place in the front seat, arms filled with as many chocolate bars and bags of Doritos as he could carry.

The vampire's gaze fell right on Gemmy and her garlic pizza. She scooched as far from the monkey-woman as possible, muttering about how anyone could possibly put that poison into their bodies. Gemmy had rolled her eyes and just started eating her pizza, with no intention of sharing. She made sure to put some distance between herself and the vampire, not really wanting to deal with being judged for her choice in food from some random stranger.

As the van got moving once again, the hitchhiker was met with the suspicious gaze of Ivy. She popped open the moonshine, taking a swig. There was *something* about the way she was looking at this newcomer.

"She's a vampire, Ivy," Serena stated, reading the suspicion in the psychic's face.

"Explains why I can't read her mind," Ivy replied, tone flat. "But what the hell is she doing here?"

"Spence agreed to give her a ride, I guess," Beast replied.

The atmosphere in the van became tense for a moment, a small dent appearing in the wall closest to the vampire. Those that knew Ivy well enough had seen this sort of thing before, and it was best not to further upset her.

"Spencer...what the hell were you thinking?" she demanded. "I mean, you remember what happened when that 'nice blonde lady' offered to help you with a gift, right?"

Spencer sighed. How could he forget? He still had nightmares about being stalked, tortured, and nearly murdered by a seasoned killer. A few times.

"Yeah, I know," he replied. "It's j--"

"And after that, with Silas's good-for-nothing son?" she continued.

"In Slade's defense, he did kinda teach me magic...but I see your point. But I can't exactly kick her out of the van; I already agreed. Also, um...we've kind of been having this conversation aloud, where she can hear it."

Ivy paused, looking at the vampire. Said vampire didn't seem too horribly put off by the conversation. Instead, she cleared her throat.

"Is one of those how you ended up with the metal leg?" the vampire asked. "I didn't intend to pry...it's just that I saw it back where you picked me up and was curious."

Spencer sighed. He didn't often wear shorts in public, but he figured there was no harm in doing so. And in doing this, his prosthetic leg was in full view. It wasn't that he was ashamed of that leg. In fact, he appreciated the work that Serena put into crafting it. Best mother-in-law a guy could ask for. But for someone to flat-out ask about it wasn't something he was really accustomed to.

"Yes, I did gain it from a prior trauma," he said. "But I would really rather not go into it."

The drive continued, the vampire occasionally giving Spencer the directions he needed. He turned whenever necessary.

"So, like, where the hell're we going, anyway?" Travis asked, munching on one of the bags of snacks he picked out at the gas station. He ended up sharing a few of them with Daniel, who was content with a few of the chips and one of the candy bars.

"Hm...yeah, you never did tell me the location," Spencer said, not having quite realized that little fact until just that point.

The vampire smoothed out one of her sleeves. "Bludburg. We should be there soon enough."

"...So, like, you're a vampire living in a place called 'Bloodburg'?" Trav asked her with a chuckle.

"I feel you're pronouncing it incorrectly," she sighed, "but yes."

Things got quiet for a bit. But eventually, the vampire jumped with a squeak, as Tsaeb had finished his bag of jerky and shifted his attention to her. The dog/bird/human hybrid leaned forward, sniffing their hitchhiker intently. She was taken aback somewhat, gingerly pushing him away.

"What...are you a brother to those two felines?" she asked him before pointing to Beast and Serena. "Or is this your pet?"

"He's my genetically-altered clone, actually," said Beast. "We're still figuring out how that fits into the family tree. Threw me off at first, too."

Three more exits had brought the group into a remote area, lined by stalks of corn. This definitely wasn't the city anymore. It wasn't even the suburbs. Just a bit more driving would bring them to a tall gate.

"We're just about there," said the vampire as they approached. "Pull up to the gate."

As Spencer slowed the vehicle down a bit to inch toward the gate, the whole van was treated to a loud popping sound. The van came to an abrupt halt. Carefully, Spencer got out, going to see what the problem was.

He couldn't believe it. All four tires had blown. One tire, he could chalk up to mere misfortune. Two? A particularly bad day. But all four? This felt just plain *wrong*.

"Is something the matter, sir?" the vampire asked from behind him.

He jumped once again, not having heard anyone else getting out. Panting a bit, he glanced over his shoulder.

"Having a little bit of car trouble," he admitted. "Would you have any idea why all four of the tires burst like that?"

She shook her head. "Not at all."

There was something about her tone that told them she probably wasn't telling them everything. Ivy's initial response was to pop open the moonshine again and take a hearty swig.

"If my knowledge of horror movies has anything to say about it," she said, re-capping the jug, "that's outright sabotage, and we'd better watch our collective ass."

Serena took off her glasses and cleaned them off before putting them back on.

"Ivy, you can't compare everything to a horror movie," she sighed.

"Mom, I'd probably listen to her by this point," Gemmy added, her tail curling around her own leg. "Our lives have come *very* close to being horror movies, themselves. There's some precedent for it."

By now, everyone had gotten out of the van, Beast holding onto Daniel. Sighing, she looked at the others. Travis and Spencer stood close to each other, one looking annoyed and the other mildly concerned. Serena and Silas were next to them, the mage's arms around the cat-woman. Gemmy stood beside them, partly worried/partly stress-eating the last slice of her pizza. Ivy just looked irritated with the whole situation. Tsaeb's ears, tail, and wings were twitching as he wondered what they'd do about this.

"Welp, might as well call for a tow truck," Beast said.

Serena was the one to pull out her phone, preparing to call AAA. But when she looked at her phone, her eyes narrowed.

"Odd..." she muttered. "No signal out here."

Spencer, Ivy, Travis, and Gemmy had likewise gone to check theirs, only to find no signal. Tsaeb would have checked his, but he didn't have a phone. He'd been offered one but turned it down a while back. Instead, he had a different means of going to get help.

"Want me to fly off and find someone?" he offered.

The others tried to think of any other options. None came to mind. Spencer seemed in favor of the idea, though.

"Just make sure you don't get lost, alright?" the doctor said.

Gemmy had finished off her snack, wiped her hands off on her pants, and put a hand on Spencer's shoulder.

"Want me to go with him, Spence?" she asked. "I can follow from the ground."

He nodded, putting his hand on top of hers. "That would be great, thanks," he said, giving her a quick kiss on the cheek.

She returned the kiss before turning her attention to the rest of the group. Her gaze settled on Beast and Daniel.

"All right," she asked the child. "Would you like to come with me, or you good staying with Auntie Beast and Grandma Serena?"

"Would we go fast?" he asked Gemmy, his green eyes wide.

He liked seeing his mother's speed in action and had always wanted to go on one of those runs with her. And for a few moments, he seemed to think about it before reaching toward Gemmy.

Beast gave him a quick nuzzle before handing him off to Gemmy. She watched as her niece held the child as close to her chest as possible. And from there, Tsaeb took to the air, Gemmy breaking into a sprint as she followed him from the ground.

And that left just Spencer, Travis, Silas, Ivy, Serena, and Beast to wait for their return. They had no idea how they would pass the time, or for that matter, how long they would actually be waiting.

"If you would like," said the vampire (who they had all temporarily forgotten was there). "You can come in and explore the town while you wait for your friends."

On the one hand, they weren't entirely sure if that would be the greatest idea. After all, the demise of all four of their tires at the same time was much too suspicious to be a coincidence. But on the other hand, it wasn't like they had much of anything else to do. Silas could have done a bit more magic training with Spencer, but they didn't quite feel like it at the moment. If worse came to worse, Spencer knew some simple but effective spells for combat usage. And Serena had to admit, she was quite curious about this town. Beast wasn't about to let her sister go in without someone that could effectively murder most threats.

Ultimately, the group had decided that checking the place out couldn't hurt too badly. It may have seemed like a suspicious place, but they were survivors for a reason. In their group were two magic users, two trained assassins, and one guy who was effectively immortal. Serena was the only one without some kind of powers or combat training, and even then, she was close enough to the others that any threat against her would end badly for whoever dared hurt her.

The gate swung open, their hitchhiker entering first. Spencer was close behind, Serena walking with him. Silas walked behind her, followed by Trav and Ivy together. Beast was ready to follow, but the gate had slammed right in her face.

Beast hissed as she went to try opening the gate. It wouldn't budge. She kicked at it a few times, hissing some more. If she wasn't already suspicious of the place enough, this really set off the old alarm bells.

On the gate's other side, those that had made it through began to take a good look at the area. Roaming the cobblestone streets were pale figures clad in similar black and red garments to their hitchhiker. Nobody was using a parasol, as the sky in here seemed to be black. The only light came from lanterns on the sides of the streets. When they were outside of that gate, the sun was at its apex, but here in Bludburg? There was no way it took hours to get from outside that gate to this side of it.

Small dome-like dwellings lined the streets, and there were posts on each street corner with large speakers at their tops. But what grabbed their attention above all else was the huge structure in the very center of the town. It was a hexagonal building with a statue on its roof. The statue was of a slim, almost impossibly beautiful man. Or rather, vampire.

Ivy's attention had gone to the statue, feeling that she needed a closer look at it. She couldn't quite put her finger on what, but there was just something about it. She thought it might be a good idea to go in for a closer look and intended to ask Beast about going with her.

But there was one little problem.

She couldn't see Beast anywhere. Unsure of who was in charge around the area, she walked up to a pair of locals who were in the middle of discussing something. She didn't quite listen to their conversation as she cleared her throat.

The two looked at her, tilting their heads in unison. It took all she had not to cringe at that.

"Father welcomes you, Outsider," they said.

She tried not to dwell on the unnatural unison between the two, putting on her best smile.

"Hey…um, you see, I think a friend of ours got locked out. There any way to let her in?"

They did not answer right away, one of the pair leaning toward Ivy's neck and giving it a little lick. They backed away as if burned and looked at one another as if trying to decide what to make of this outsider.

"Well? Is there?" she asked, a little impatient and wishing they didn't get sidetracked by her scent.

"That is for Father's Proxy to decide…Tell me, why do you smell strongly of alcohol?"

Ivy shrugged. "Body's, like, sixty percent booze," she said. "So, maybe avoid my blood unless you wanna get tanked."

They walked away without any further word. Ivy watched them go, shaking her head as she looked at that statue again. She needed to get a better look and figure out why this was bothering her so much. But for now, she'd stick with the group.

Speaking of the rest of the group, Silas and Serena had joined hands and started roaming through the streets. There were signs every so often of things that were not allowed in Bludburg. Stuff like Holy Water, wooden stakes, garlic, silver, and sunlight was depicted.

A full moon shone down from the probably-magically-generated night sky. The cat-woman would have found the place almost romantic were it not for the leering gazes from a few of the locals. She didn't quite like the way a few of them were looking at them both, seemingly focused on their necks. In the darkness, their red eyes almost glowed, making their gaze a teensy bit more unnerving.

It just made her hold onto her elf's hand that much tighter. Silas noticed her tension, reaching up to scratch her ear.

"It's okay, Love," he told her. "You're not here alone."

She wasn't sure how well he would do if a fight with a vampire or twenty broke out, but she smiled either way, giving him a lick on the cheek with her sandpaper-like cat tongue.

One of the locals had been staring at them from a small shop nestled between two of the dome-shaped dwellings. He leaned over, calling out to them.

"Hey! I couldn't help but overhear, but are you two married, by any chance?"

Serena groaned. As much as she loved Silas, she preferred to be known for her achievements as a geneticist or in the field of cybernetics as opposed to "this guy's wife." But in spite of her irritation, she nodded.

"Not yet, but we will be in a few months," she said, a smile crossing her face.

"If you haven't got any rings yet, I invite you to come see my wares. Fair prices!" The vampire called.

They did have rings for the event already, but it probably couldn't hurt to see what this guy had available. The couple reached this vampire's little booth and could see a wide arrangement of black metal bands with reddish stones mounted on them. Serena had to admit, the rings were quite beautiful.

"How much would one of these cost?" she asked.

The vendor gave a fanged smile, red eyes narrowed. Serena immediately decided that she did *not* like that look. And for that matter, Silas appeared a bit unsettled, as well.

"If it's anything involving my immortal soul..." Serena began, clutching Silas' arm like her life depended on it. "Well, the rings are pretty, but they're not *that* pretty..."

The vampire vendor never bothered to argue that he didn't want their souls, making things even more troubling to them. And so, the pair backed away from the booth, continuing their exploration. As they walked along, Serena kept looking over her shoulder. The sooner Tsaeb and Gemmy got back there with help for their van, the better.

Strolling through another part of the small town, looking up at the darkened sky, were Travis and Spencer. The condition of the sky rubbed them both the wrong way, though Spencer would be lying if he said he wasn't curious as to what sort of magic could cause that.

Travis had found himself watching some of the citizens. All of them were dressed the same way, and he kept hearing mutterings of someone called "Father." All in all, it reminded him of a few of the movies he'd seen with Ivy. Or a few true crime things he'd seen while working at the comic shop. Though maybe he was jumping to conclusions. An entire population dressing the same way and worshipping a guy they had a statue of didn't necessarily make for a cult, right? But just in case, he figured it would be a good idea to turn down any offerings of a drink.

"So...what do you make of this place?" Spencer asked.

"Kinda gives me the creeps, to be honest," Travis replied. "So, what happened back there, anyway? Like, did you give her a ride because she needed the help, or was it something else?"

Spencer sighed. "I'm not actually sure entirely what happened. I know I was hesitant, but then my hesitations melted away."

"Isn't part of the vampire mythology hypnosis or some shit like that?" Trav asked, an eyebrow raised.

Spencer froze. So that was what happened. It was one thing if that was just a case of his own crappy judgment making another reappearance. But it was something else entirely to have his mind hacked by a complete stranger.

"That would make sense..." Spencer murmured, not noticing the woman approaching them both.

Before Travis could respond, the woman cleared her throat. She placed a cold hand on his shoulder, disrupting his current train of thought and forcing his attention right to her. Spencer's eyes also snapped right to her.

This woman's black and red outfit was a bit different from the others' they had seen. It had a few symbols embroidered in gold along the hems. Neither could translate those symbols, exactly, but they had a feeling this woman held some degree of power.

"...Need something, lady?" Travis asked.

The woman flashed him a small smile. She played a bit with his hair. "You just seem interesting, is all," she said. "I've never seen anyone quite like you."

Well, that was just the slightest bit unnerving. Travis had been told that sort of thing many times before, usually leading to him being thrown in the back of a van and ending up in a lab. It had happened all too often for his liking.

"Eh...thanks, I guess?" Trav replied, going to brush her hand from his shoulder.

She hurriedly grabbed both of his hands, her red eyes taking on a solid glow for a moment. Her smile never broke.

"No, you *need* to come with me. It's for a good reason!"

He ripped both hands out of her grip, her long fingernails slicing into the skin. The scratches healed within seconds, and he was muttering in annoyance, glaring at her.

"The fuck is your deal?"

He didn't get an answer...not in words, anyway. What he got instead was a woman of supernatural strength going to put him in a headlock. He tried to fight back, but he only had the muscle tone of a relatively normal guy that worked out every so often. She had the power of vampirism on her side.

"Hey...*hey*! Get away from him!" Spencer called, aiming a spell at the vampire to try knocking her away from his best friend.

It took three blast spells to get her to release her grip on Travis. He fell to his knees, and she turned her attention toward Spencer instead.

"Please, stay out of this," she said, her eyes taking on that glow again.

Spencer paused, his eyes briefly flashing that same red color. That brief moment was all the symbol-bearing vampire needed to return her attention to her real target.

Travis had pushed himself back to his feet, rubbing his neck a bit and glaring at his assailant.

"What do you want with me?" he asked.

"For you to come with me," she stated. "And if you don't, I'll bite your friend. His blood doesn't smell quite as lovely as yours, but it would have to do. Your choice."

He tried to find some argument against it. On the one hand, he didn't particularly want to go with her. On the other, he especially didn't want her to view his best friend as a walking juice box. So with a sigh of annoyance, he nodded.

"Fine. Whatever. Just don't hurt Spence, alright?"

She grinned at him, her ice-cold hand snatching his wrist in an iron grip. Looking at Spencer, she issued a command for him to stay there and let her leave with Trav. As for Trav, he didn't fight back, and it made him sort of sick not to. But he knew that if he did, she would have targeted Spencer. And then who was to say she would stop with that? She might have gone after Serena next, as well as Ivy. He wasn't quite as worried about Silas, figuring that his centuries of experience with magic usage would beat anything that tried to come for his blood.

He would wait to fight back until they were far enough away from Spencer. Or until whoever this vampire was was distracted.

Meanwhile, Ivy had started climbing one of the dwellings, wanting to get elevated. That, she thought, could get her a better view of the statue. The surface of this domed building was slightly rough, but not enough to get a proper hold. The psychic had to use her telekinesis to help pull herself up.

The turquoise-hued glow that came from her using that ability was not what one might call "subtle." Rather, it was a beacon to those within a few feet of the building. Not that she particularly cared right now. Let them watch.

She reached the roof soon enough, looking around. Many of the locals were going about their business, and a handful of them were watching this outsider as she stood on the roof. One of them stepped forward, calling up to her.

"Excuse me! New Blood, what exactly are you doing?"

She glanced down at him, eyes still glowing, and an eyebrow arched.

"I wanted to get a better look at your statue, there," she said. "It really is beautifully carved."

"That is a visage of Father!" he replied. "He was staked many years ago, but without His influence, none of this would be possible."

She nodded, returning her attention to the statue's face. It was still somewhat distant, but she could make out enough of its features. And it was a face she definitely recognized.

That was the face of a vampire known as Victor Lupei. Back in the early days of her career as an assassin, she and her sister Yvette had been tasked with taking out a vampire that had been preying on innocent people. She recalled Lupei coming after her, specifically. He'd separated her from Yvette. While with him, he had sampled a bit of her blood. The pure concentration of alcohol in her system had sent him stumbling backward. He had called her a monster over that and was ultimately dispatched by Yvette once she'd found them. His judgment over her blood had sort of hurt for a few years after the incident.

She was there for this "Father's" death and was now essentially surrounded by people that worshipped the guy. Taking a few breaths, she carefully made her way back to the ground, going to track down the others. If there was ever a time that they needed to stay together, it was now.

Walking along, a few of the denizens of Bludburg stopped her. One woman grinned, gripping her arm.

"Did you enjoy basking in Father's glory?" she asked, crimson eyes lighting up.

It took all Ivy had not to kick her and run. Instead, she smiled back. "I could definitely feel something there, yeah," she said. "If you'll excuse me, I need to go find my friends and share this elation with them."

The vampires released her, and she fast-walked away from them. The first ones she came across were Serena and Silas. The couple looked a bit uncomfortable, as a pair of vampires had stopped to chat with them. Ivy could hear little snatches of the conversation, which seemed to revolve around "joining" and "Father's love."

They stepped away after Serena said that they would consider the offer. And once they were gone, Ivy approached the couple. She leaned forward.

"All right, we need to get Trav and Spence and get the hell outta here," she whispered. "I don't know how much they know about their leader's death, but I was kinda there when it happened...I wasn't the one that staked him, but I share a face with the one that did, and they might want revenge."

"They kept trying to convert us to their beliefs," Silas replied. "And we're fairly certain they wanted at least one of our souls. Getting out of here would be ideal."

"But we can't go without regrouping with Beast," Serena added. "I think she's still outside. And there's the matter of Tsaeb and Gemmy, and them returning with help for the van..."

Ivy nodded. "We'll cross both of those bridges when we come to them. Let's just focus on finding the guys right now."

Out of the corner of her eye, Ivy could see a figure running toward them. Tall, built vaguely like a stick, shock of light brown hair...

Well, then. They had found Spencer, at least. Though the panic he gave off told her that something had gone wrong. Turning to face Spencer, Ivy pulled her flask from her hip and took a swig. She'd finished the moonshine somewhere in her travels through the village.

"All right, Spence...what happened?" she asked.

He came to a stop, panting a bit.

"One of them dragged Trav off somewhere," he stated, breathless. "I tried to stop her, but she got into my head a couple times, and...I have no idea where she went with him. I'm so sorry..."

Serena shook her head before putting her arms around him. "It's not your fault, Spence. We'll get him back like we always have."

He nodded, returning the hug. "Thanks...I needed that," he said. "I'll give you all three guesses as to why they wanted him."

The others took a moment to work that out, Ivy groaning in annoyance. "Any idea what exactly they'd want with his blood?"

Tapping her chin, Serena muttered under her breath a bit. And then she shared her thoughts with the others.

"Well, we all know how strong his regeneration is," she said. "Know how a stake through the heart will kill a vampire? Travis can shrug that off in roughly a minute at most. So his blood could possibly enhance their own abilities."

"Think they'd be all on-board the 'Convert Everyone' train in that case?" Ivy asked.

"Oh, I don't doubt it," Silas muttered. "I've seen groups like this many a time before."

"We should really start hunting right now, then, shouldn't we?" Spencer asked.

Ivy nodded, and the four began patrolling the area for any sign of their friend.

Travis took a look at his new surroundings. He'd been dragged into the temple in the middle of town. Inside, the walls seemed to be made of gold, as did all of the furniture. Any cushions were of a deep red velvet. Even the table he was currently being chained to was made of this combination of gold and velvet.

He had tried to fight the woman off as soon as they set foot inside, of course, but she had been quickly flanked by two others dressed similarly to herself. One opponent with supernatural strength was difficult enough to deal with. But bringing in two more? Travis may not have been the brightest crayon in the box, but even he understood when he was horribly outmatched.

"Hm...least it's not as bad as your standard-issue lab table," he muttered to himself.

Watching the area, he focused all his attention on the woman that had brought him there. He figured that this had to be some kind of temple. But he did have a few questions for her.

"Hey...mind telling me what this is about and who the hell you are?" he asked.

She nodded. "Yes, I suppose you do have a right to know. You see, I am Victoria, Head Priestess of the Lupeinites. Also known as Father's Proxy. Our aim is to restore Father's life to him, as it was so unfairly torn from him well over two decades ago."

"...And let me guess, you're planning to use my blood to pull that off, right?" he asked with a groan.

Victoria gave another nod. "Yes, that's exactly right. Your blood has the most robust smell I have ever experienced. I have never before met someone so well-suited to our goals. You're, I suppose, our Chosen One."

Travis was quite unimpressed. He hadn't made it to his thirties just to be some vampire cult's "Chosen One."

"There any way to get you to let me go?" he asked. "Like, is this one of those 'virgin blood' things?"

"Yes, virgin blood is preferable."

He laughed. "Welp, sorry to say, but you're shit outta luck in that department. I lost *that* a few years back."

Victoria crossed her arms. "When I say 'virgin blood,' I don't mean it sexually. I mean, your blood has never been used in a ritual."

With a shrug, Travis chuckled. "Yeah, even that one's not guaranteed. Do you *know* how many people have been coming for my blood over the years, lady? I have no idea if experiments count as 'rituals,' but it's been used so many times it's not even funny."

The High Priestess patted his head. "We'll find out for sure, then, won't we?" she said in a sickeningly sweet tone. "Even if we have to drain every drop of it from your body, we're going to do what we can."

"And if it fails?" he asked, doing his best to avoid biting the wrist of the hand she'd used to pat his head, glaring at the offending appendage.

She shrugged. "Then those friends you came with will serve as our blood farm. If it works, they might be turned."

Well, neither of those options sounded particularly ideal. Travis bit his lip. "Uh...there a third option, there?" he asked.

He didn't receive an answer. Instead, being left on his own as Victoria and her associates walked away. The second they left his line of sight, he began looking over the chains, trying to figure out how to get himself out of there. He had no intention of sticking around.

They returned moments later, however, to begin hooking him up with needles and tubes.

The escape attempt was about to get a bit more complicated, then, wasn't it?

———

Outside of the gate, Beast had been pacing for a while. She had tried to jimmy it open, but it wouldn't budge at all. She tried kicking the gate down, but it withstood even her heavy barrage of punches. At one point, she had taken to the air to see about heading in from above. But as she reached a high enough altitude, she could see nothing but an empty field below.

So, what did this mean, exactly? Was she going crazy? Did that last bit of catnip she'd had before they left for the trip have some weird effects? None of this made any sense to her.

Perhaps she should try the overhead option again. Illusions were a thing, right? She had seen every mage she'd known use them from time to time. Nobody said that vampires couldn't utilize that same sort of magic.

Stretching a bit, she backed away from the gate before breaking into a running start. Beast jumped as high as she could, her wings soon catching the air. Moving herself higher in the air, she flew a few feet above the gate. She then flew a little higher than that, looking down at the apparent empty field.

Taking a deep breath, Beast went into a dive, metal feet first, and closed her eyes. She had no idea if it would result in her landing in the grass or smashing into a barrier that would cause all sorts of pain.

What she got instead was the sensation of plunging into something warm and somewhat viscous. The heavy smell of blood surrounded her.

When she opened her eyes, she was standing on a street. Black and red-clad figures were standing there, all facing a pole with a speaker attached to its apex.

"Rejoice, Children!" a female voice bellowed through it. "A new era will soon be upon us, for we have a means to revive Father to rule over us all! Come to the temple for the ritual in ten minutes! I repeat, a new era will soon be upon us..."

The message continued, and Beast shook her head. Some kind of necromancy ritual? Every mage she knew looked down on the art of necromancy. It was seen as going against every law of nature. It was part of why one of her family's enemies had called Travis an abomination.

As she listened to the message repeat itself, she thought of what could possibly be used to reanimate the dead. Silas would be powerful enough but was one of those against the practice. Spencer was indeed skilled, but probably not skilled enough. Travis had come back from the dead a few times before, and that ability was carried in each and every one of his blood cells. And vampires dealt in blood, and--

Beast shivered at the realization of what this woman had been getting at, soon running through the streets to see if she could find the others. If she had to storm this temple alone to retrieve family members, she would. And she would mow down all who dared to stand in her way.

Her run ended after a few minutes, as she saw the thick black and brown waves of hair that could only belong to Ivy. She wasn't alone, as she saw Spencer's tall slim frame next to her and her sister's ears and tail. Silas was at the back of the group, and Beast decided just to slip in with them.

"So, what's the plan, here?" she asked.

Ivy turned her head to see her there.

"Hey, Beast. Glad to see you made it in, finally," she said. "Could use the extra manpower. Heading to the temple to get Trav."

"So, I was right, and they plan to harvest his blood to bring this 'Father' guy back."

Ivy nodded. "Yep..."

The plan was for Ivy, Spencer, Silas, and now Beast to plow through any sort of resistance while Serena went to find their target. They wouldn't stop until they had him back. If that meant leaving a trail of undead bodies in their wake, then so be it.

Leaving a member of their family in any sort of blood-draining situation was something they were all vehemently against.

By now, a crowd was gathered around the temple, and the small group began trying to push their way through the crowd. There were mutterings about apparent rudeness, but nobody tried to physically stop them.

The first actual resistance they met came when they charged through the temple's entryway. Standing there, armed with halberds, were ten guards. And all of them had their weapons pointed at the intruders.

"Turn back and take your place with the others," one commanded.

The group looked at each other as Spencer stepped forward. He focused entirely on the male that had just told them to head back outside and aimed a spell at him, blasting him into a wall.

From there, all hell broke loose as the other nine vampire guards rushed at the two magic users, the psychic, and the cyborg. Serena had managed to slip past them all, keeping an eye out for any sign of her son.

The interior of the temple was comprised of multiple corridors, and Serena found herself getting quite turned around as she rushed along. A few times, she came close to running into one of the temple's priestesses but had managed to evade them.

She drew closer and closer to the temple's inner sanctum, and two scents grabbed her attention: blood and burning candles. The smell grew stronger as she advanced. But she could go no further, as a strong arm hooked around her waist, yanking her backward with a yelp.

"And where do you think you're going?" a voice asked.

She looked at the vampire that had grabbed hold of her, pushing up her glasses.

"You need to stop your ritual," she said. "No good can come of it."

The vampire chuckled, pulling her further away.

"No," she said, "I believe it will do nothing but good. Father will be revived. We can spread his love to all. Do you not wish to see this love?"

Serena shook her head. "I think by 'love' what you really mean is 'deprivation of the soul.'"

The vampire ignored her reply, instead choosing to focus on her neck. She squirmed against her grip, even as the fangs brushed against the side of her neck. But the vampire was too strong for her. She squeezed her eyes shut and prepared for the bite...

The bite ended up being more of a light scratch, and the vampire cried out in pain. Hearing a growl, Serena opened one eye.

Standing there, his own teeth having sunk into the back of the vampire's neck, was Travis. In shock, the vampire released her grip on Serena and turned her attention to Trav.

The half-monkey was pale right now, and a bit unsteady on his feet. Serena's best guess was that they had already gotten a good amount of blood from him. She saw the vampire rip him off of her back and throw him to the floor.

Without a moment's hesitation, Serena reached down and grabbed her son's arm, pulling him upright and rushing toward the exit with him. The pair were pursued by three of the other vampires inside of the temple. And these three were particularly quick.

It took little time at all for the two to be surrounded by the trio.

The three fast vampires advanced on them, fangs bared, and a murderous look in their eyes. Serena and Travis stayed together, Travis ready to fight to the end, even as his legs threatened to buckle beneath him. Serena wasn't much of a fighter but would give it her all. This was all in the name of survival, after all.

"I CALL FORTH THE LIGHT!" Silas's baritone bellowed from the distance.

Before anyone could question what that was supposed to mean, rays of pure sunlight appeared, bursting through the temple's ceiling. Serena and Travis's would-be assailants hissed, their skin starting to burn right away. A deafening hissing/screaming sound resonated from all around them, mother and son both covering their ears as they moved forward to rejoin the others.

Making their way through the throngs of deteriorating vampires, they saw Ivy and Beast both covering their own ears, both looking at Trav and Serena with relief. Off in the distance, they could see Silas and Spencer, both standing back to back. Blue and green magic swirled around them. The pair were bathed in pure light. The hitchhiker that had brought them here in the first place had been trying to hide under her parasol, though it was all in vain as she began to burn in agony.

The screams and hissing died off within moments. When the group uncovered their ears, all was quiet. Almost eerily so. The dust had settled soon after. Travis had taken a few steps toward Spencer, collapsing after those first four. Beast caught him before he could hit the floor, soon just lifting him into her arms. Serena watched as he dozed off right then and there.

"What happened there?" Beast asked as Serena approached her.

"My best guess is that they harvested some of his blood, but he got away before they could drain him entirely."

The group started leaving the temple, making their way through the mounds and mounds of dust left from Silas and Spencer's attack. It would take a bit more walking before they reached the gate. Ivy was the one to rip it open. She had to use her powers on it, but the gate was torn straight off of its hinges and tossed aside.

As they stepped outside, Spencer was the first to collapse near the van they had rented. So much for a nice peaceful vacation.

Ivy settled beside him, as did Serena and Silas. Beast remained standing, not wanting to wake Travis. His body had a bit of blood to recover, so he needed his rest.

"Well, this was a disaster," Serena muttered.

"Yeah, I hear that," Ivy replied. "Think anything'll go right today?"

"I wouldn't bet on it," Spencer said, going to try cleaning some vampire dust from his glasses.

He couldn't find a clean spot on his shirt to use for that task, just rummaging through the van for his cleaning cloth.

They waited a few more hours for help to arrive for their van. By the time Tsaeb, Gemmy, and the tow truck arrived, the sun was beginning to set. Travis had revived in that time and was a bit hungry.

Spencer and Ivy had gotten into the tow truck, Spence taking Gemmy's place in one of the seats. Daniel had been waiting there, clearly happy to see his dad.

The plan, for now, was just to get home. With their collective luck, their time at the cabin would result in them somehow managing to summon demons or something like that. Beast would fly Travis there, Tsaeb would fly back, himself. Silas would merely teleport himself and Serena home.

This vacation was just the latest addition to the long list of horrifying incidents to befall their family. But if there was one thing that helped them get through it, it was one simple fact.

These people were survivors.

K. Matt is both an author and illustrator living in a rural part of New York state. When she's not drawing comics, she's writing stuff that may eventually become a comic. Sometimes, she's been known to procrastinate (her favorite procrastination activity being baking). Fairly often, she's known to be better communicating through text as opposed to verbally.

Website: https://kaylamatt.wordpress.com

facebook.com/HellBentBookSeries

twitter.com/MarieTwixie

instagram.com/kmatt666

SHADOWS OF BLOOD

BY AIMEE SHAYE

Prologue

Draupati lay in her bed, waiting for her husband's return. This battle was not one she could fight in her position. While normal vampires were unable to get pregnant, she was far from normal. She was the strongest type of vampire there was: a Prichasa. There were no other creatures quite like them, and they were superior of all vampire races. Perhaps that was why Rome's leader wanted to unite with them, whatever his reasoning, she was glad it led her to her husband. She prayed for him to come home safe and sound as she rested her hand on her stomach. It was too early for her to start showing, but she could already feel the life force growing inside her.

She wasn't sure when she had drifted off to sleep, but she awoke with a start to her husband standing over her. Only, something was amiss. When her eyes focused, her heart beat wildly in her chest as she caught a glimpse of fire-red eyes she had never seen in her life. "Who are you?" Her shrill voice masked the fear in her heart. She immediately jumped out of her bed and willed her sword to her hand. As it materialized, she gripped it tightly and held it out toward the stranger.

"Don't you recognize me?" His voice taunted her as he manifested an ax.

Anger and fear swelled in her being at the smirk that played out on his lips. How could she forget the monster who had tried to murder his own brother on his wedding day? She prayed to the gods to aid her in this battle and come to her rescue, but none of them had responded. Of course they wouldn't. *Please,* she pleaded, *any of you. Please help me.* But again, she was met with only silence. She was completely and utterly alone. She closed her eyes and thought of the life growing inside of her. *I do not suppose you can help your mother from in there, can you?* She didn't expect an answer, and yet, the silence she was met with left her hollow.

"What are you doing here, Caelus?"

A sinister smirk spread across his lips.

"Putting an end to my misery."

His misery? What misery could he have had? He was the next in line for their father's throne, a position his brother gave up after marrying her. Was that not enough for him? What more could he have wanted?

He stalked toward her, and she walked along the wall, trying to make it to the door of her bedroom, but before she could, he seized her by her hair. He should not have been able to overpower her, to control her like this. But then again, something wasn't right. She knew it deep in her bosom.

The red eyes. His ability to summon the ax. His strength. These were not abilities that humans possessed. Even Decimus hadn't been able to do any of it before he fed from her.

That was when it dawned on her. He was no longer human. He must have killed.... "It was you!" The words were out of her mouth before she could think. "You were the one who murdered my father in battle! You drank from him!" The blood must have been poisoning him. Large amounts of their blood would do that if humans weren't careful.

He laughed maniacally and hooked his ax on his shoulder. "So I did." He licked his lips. "And now, my queen, it is your turn."

Before she knew what was happening, he was at her throat, and everything turned to black around her.

Chapter One

He sat on a rock, watching the waves hit his and the other rocks around him. Not a drop of sweat dripped down his smooth ivory face, yet he was dressed all in black, no shoes or socks on. And maybe that's why he wasn't hot. After all, the water was cold and reaching up to his toes. At six feet two with biceps that anyone would die for and a six-pack that the ladies would love to touch, this man looked lethal, as if he were out for blood, but this was his outside. Sitting there, he looked as if one touch would turn him to ash. And that's all that he yearned for, just one simple touch.

He stared out at the nothingness of the ocean. Where would it lead to eventually? There was no land in eye view; it almost looked like you would swim right into a cardboard sky if you continued out so far. Would anyone be so stupid to try? He probably would if only he could touch it. It was surprising that he could even sit on the rock when he was supposed to go right through it. Maybe it was his imagination that created the rock for him. What a cruel imagination he had!

Walking along the shoreline was a beautiful girl with the prettiest strawberry blond hair that he had ever seen. It fell in curls to the small of her back and highlighted her caramel skin against the beautiful white gown that she had on. The gown was a light material, much like a curtain's material, and the end of it went in the direction of the wind as she walked against it. When she turned to look at him, his only focus was her beautiful blue eyes. It was like looking into the water around the Island of Capri, only in the depths of those blue eyes was a beautiful sapphire soul so warm, it could melt anything as cold as ice and maybe even colder.

She removed a stray strand of hair from her face as she looked over to him and smiled. That smile was striking and captivating. What he wouldn't give to touch that face! "What are you doing over there?" She punctuated each word carefully and strongly. She was trying to be fierce, but it didn't work because of her indulgent expressions.

He looked behind him, wishing to see someone else, but it was only them on this beach, and he instantly knew this wasn't reality. He was in his memories. God, why couldn't he stay out of them?

"Decimus, what are you looking for, my love?" She walked over to him.

He took her hand in his. "Nothing, my love." He drew her nearer and kissed her forehead. Oh, how he ached for this moment to last, but it couldn't. He needed to awake from this dream. It wasn't good for him to be locked here. He had to get over this once and for all.

She hugged him tightly as she, too, realized that this was just a dream. Soon he would awake, and she would be gone, but both of them knew that this moment together would put them both at peace for a moment of eternity. "Why haven't you come yet?"

He pushed out of her hold and turned away from her, refusing to let her know the reason for his existence this way. "I haven't been judged yet," he whispered. The truth would kill her, and she'd be trapped here with him as well. He wouldn't do that to her. It would be wrong.

"There is something you're not telling me. What's wrong?"

"I have to go." He walked out into the water. "We'll meet again, Draupati, I promise." Tears pricked the back of her eyes.

"You'll drown," she said.

"Here, yes. But there I shall awake to horrors I wish you will never awake to. Wait for me, Draupati. Promise me."

She showed him her wedding band. "I've waited all these centuries. What's a million more?" She forced a smile

"I love you."

"And I love you, dear Decimus."

He waded out into the water until it consumed him and all that was left was bubbles in his wake.

She awoke with tears streaming down her face and an ache in her heart. What the hell was that!? She was tired of that guy being her dreams and calling her Draupati. Her name was Ahana, for crying out loud, and she swore that if she'd seen him on the streets that she'd be able to pick him out. If only she could only get her hands on him for invading her sleep! But her rage against him didn't change the hurt in her heart and the hollow feeling in her stomach. Every part of her knew that she knew this man, but from where? That was the only question that weighed heavy on her mind. Surely, he was someone who lived close by. It had to be. She hadn't gone out that much, and she didn't know millions of people. He could only be out of the select few that she met in this crazy world. But finding him wouldn't be so easy.

She sat up in her bed and wiped her tears. Her dreams were getting weirder; she wished they would stop. It had been about a few months now that she had been having these dreams, and it wasn't like they stopped and came back. She had a different dream every night. In one of the dreams, she was in bridal attire waiting for him. She couldn't shake the notion that something weird was happening to her.

There was no real explanation for it, and she refused to believe in reincarnation and the supernatural. She believed that those things were all lies, myths of the past that needed to stay where they belonged. But then what was that connection that she felt? Maybe it was no connection at all. Maybe it was just as if she were watching a sad movie. Things like that happen. She's read so many books with supernatural heroes in them that it was about time she started to dream about them.

Either way, she felt uneasy and decided that she wasn't going back to sleep, so she got out of bed and made herself a cup of coffee and grabbed her history textbook, and started to read the next chapter for the lesson that the professor would be babbling about later on. She got up to the part about Plato, literally four pages into the chapter, before sleep claimed her again. She wasn't even aware of the fact that she fell asleep, not until she woke up, that is.

She startled awake to her alarm was blaring her room, and when she got there, she realized she only had an hour before class started, so she rushed to get everything done. She jumped in the shower and cooked breakfast as she got dressed, it would have been dangerous had it been her first time doing it, then threw everything in her book bag that she needed while she ate and ran out the door with her book bag in her hand.

When she got downstairs, her best friend Brad was waiting downstairs for her. "I was just about to ring the bell," he said. "You're late. You're never late."

"Tell me about it." She sat on the back of his motorcycle and fastened the spare helmet before wrapping her arms around his torso. The building their classes were held in wasn't too far from the apartments, but with the way they walked, they'd never make it on time. There was hardly any other reason for the otherwise ten-minute motorcycle ride.

"Did you do the reading?" he asked her as he stepped off the motorcycle and took his helmet off.

"I got to page four and fell asleep."

"Was it really that boring?" He narrowed his gaze at her. "I kind of liked it."

"I don't know," Ahana admitted with a shrug. "I don't even think it registered in my brain. I was reading, but the only thing I could think about was what I dreamed of last night."

"Are you having those dreams again?" he asked.

The first night she had the dream, she immediately called Brad even though it was three in the morning. They had been friends since they were in diapers and told each other everything. So, naturally, when she woke up from the dream heaving and crying, he was the first person he thought of.

"Yeah," she sighed. By this time, they were outside of the classroom. "I'll tell you after class though. We're late enough as it is." She opened the door and held it open behind her for her friend to follow.

They sat next to each other during class, and although Ahana was hearing what the teacher was saying, she wasn't listening. She was copying the notes, but she wasn't retaining the information. Her mind kept going back to her dream and wondered who the guy was. Who the hell in the right mind would name their child Decimus? Why the hell would she know anyone by that name? She had to admit, though, he was gorgeous. She smiled at herself while thinking about his body and the way he just sat there, then her eyes began to close, and she drifted back into the dream world.

Draupati... It was his voice...or what sounded like his voice. She couldn't be sure, but he sounded as if he was in pain, tormented even. That sadness she saw in his eyes in her dream now transpired into his voice. Just what was this? She was surrounded by nothing but darkness and emptiness. No matter the direction she reached out into, she only felt air. Not a single wall or person. *Draupati...* His voice was louder now, an echo bouncing off the walls, surrounding her...encompassing her. She wanted to turn around and run, but she couldn't. Something pulled her further into the darkness; it controlled her every move.

"Where are you?" she asked the voice, playing along to decipher between the dream and reality. But he never responded. *"Who* are you?" Again, no answer. "Please, tell me. I am trying to understand..." Only her voice echoed around her, and then her entire world started to shake, but nothing fell around her. She could only feel the rumble in the ground, and suddenly everything flashed white, and her eyes opened; she was back in class, and Brad was shaking her.

What happened?" She rubbed her head.

"You just...blanked out." She looked at him and was met with dreaded concern.

Ahana ran her fingers through her hair and groaned. "I can't take it anymore." She groaned and put her head down on the table. "These dreams have me losing sleep. I don't understand a thing that's going on."

Brad grabbed Ahana's bag and helped her out of her seat. "Let's get you some coffee and some decent food before your next class starts. You have two hours."

Ahana took a deep breath. "Class is over?" She shook her head. How on earth did she miss a three-hour class? She had only been in that dream-like state for a few minutes.

"Uh...yeah." He picked up her notebook, and his mouth dropped, leaving her in suspense of what it was looking at. "When did you start drawing?"

"When did I—What?" She grabbed the notebook from him, and clear as day was a picture of the man in her dreams, Decimus. Only he wasn't in a suit like he usually was in her dreams. Instead, he was dressed as...She wasn't quite sure, actually. "Are these Roman clothes?" She handed the book back to her friend.

He took the book and scrutinized it. "Could be Roman. Could be Greek. Why are you asking me? You're the one who drew it."

Ahana shook her head. "I did not draw that...At least I don't remember drawing it." She took a deep breath. Whatever was happening, she certainly did not like it.

Chapter Two

Decimus wandered the streets. There was no other word for it. What he was doing wasn't considered walking. To walk, one needed a destination. Right now, there was no destination in sight. He could go back home, but for what? There was nothing there for him but an empty bed and candlelight that danced on the walls and mocked his loneliness. He was disgusted with it all. He wanted to go back to his time and his place...if that wasn't all so far away and if it wasn't unbearable to go back there. It was haunted by too many betrayals, too many deaths. Going back there seemed unlikely; this would have to do...if he survived.

He was lonely...isolated, devoid of so many things in this form. He wasn't even sure why he kept himself clean if there was no hope in ever getting free from this. There was one hope...one small, tiny silver lining...but he was sure that that hope would go away the minute he walked into the room. No one would give him back his body. It was near impossible.

He walked down the street when he noticed that there was a pier ahead, at least the water would give him some kind of solace; then he could make believe that he was back in his time on an isle with...No! He didn't want to remember that. There was no reason to because that was gone. That was no longer coming back. That was why he was like this. But one thing was for sure: if he could get his hands on it...*Calm down, Decimus...you're never going to get your hands on it.* He had to remind himself of that regularly.

Once by the fence that was the end of the pier, he looked down at the water. It wasn't clean like the water that he used to know, but it was better than nothing. It would have to do. He needed to relax, and if he couldn't relax this way, he wouldn't be able to relax at all. He got lost in the small waves of the water. He wanted to pick up a rock and throw it into the water so bad, but he couldn't. His hand would just go right through it. He started to remember the day he was condemned as *this,* but then he suppressed it to the back of his mind. It wasn't worth remembering. But then again, it was the only thing he had to give him strength.

None of that should have happened though, that was the only thing about it that he regretted. He could've walked away; he could've let it be, but no...he just had to fly in and ruin everything...including himself. The day he became a Silhouette was the day that he began to hate himself. He was able to live with being a vampire but being a Silhouette...he couldn't do that. Silhouettes were the lowest of the low. They were condemned to a ghostly shape until they were judged. Once they were judged, they could either go back to being a vampire, or they were erased out of existence...every existence from their human life to the vampire life and every good thing they did would be erased. No doubt it would leave a void in time, but that's why there were so many distractions, so many things to fill the void. The gods knew what they were doing. Only the real murderers, the ones who betrayed their kin, the ones who killed out their families...they were the ones who were turned into silhouettes.

But he hadn't done any of the sort, so why he was turned was beyond him, but then again, he had so many enemies that it was possible it was all just a set up by all of them. That's the only thing that seemed logical.

If only he could figure out a different way to get out of this body before Judgment Day.

"You are a hard man to find."

His body went rigid when he heard the voice behind him, a voice he hadn't heard in ages. There were few who were able to enter his realm and only for a limited amount of time and for no reason other than to bring bad news.

"And yet, here you are." He would have rested his arms on the railing if he knew his arms wouldn't go right through it. "What do you want?" He knew he should have been ecstatic to see his best friend, but whenever he came around, it was never for anything good.

"You have awakened Draupati's memories."

Like he thought. Never anything good. He rolled his eyes. He knew nothing good was going to come from this. It was true. He had been trying to reach her for months now. Perhaps she was the only one who could help him out of this form. She might have been his last help. But he wasn't sure it would work. And now that it had...if Balthazar could feel her memories awaken, then he was sure the Eyes could as well. This wasn't good.

"How can you be sure?"

The man reached into his pocket, handed Decimus a folded piece of paper, and took a deep breath. "I'll come back later to finish this conversation. Let that sink in."

Before Decimus could utter a word, the man was gone.

Chapter Three

"Where the hell have you been? I have been waiting out here for thirty minutes! No way in hell was the line to the men's room that long!"

Brad shrugged. "You're right. The line to the woman's bathroom was, and you know I can't resist flirting with the prettiest thing that walks by." He flashed her a smile displaying his dimples.

She shook her head. "You know, I have little patience for your antics today. I am losing my mind over this dream guy!" She groaned and banged her head on the restaurant table.

"Doesn't your religion say something about reincarnation?" He stuffed his face full of a meatball.

Ahana picked her head up from the table and gave him a droll stare. "This is definitely not that."

Brad shrugged and wiped sauce off his face. "Then how else would you describe it? You drew the man perfectly, for God's sake! If this is not reincarnation, then I don't know what is!"

Ahana shook her head. It was true that Hindus believed in reincarnation and marriage for seven generations. What her friend was saying wasn't far from what this could be, but she refused to believe that's what this was. Sure, the idea was beautiful, that in every birth, she would find her soulmate and marry him for the next seven generations. But all it was, was a comfort of sorts. Things like that didn't really happen, did they? Then again, vampires and werewolves existed, so why not this?

She knew her mother would say yes, and her grandmother wouldn't deny it either. They had told stories of their ancestors long ago who had been reincarnated. Yet why was it so hard for her to believe that something like that could happen to her?

Probably because she refused to even think of marrying, let alone loving someone. She saw the way her mother treated her father. Like he was nothing more than a wallet that needed to cater to her every whim. She didn't want to end up like that. But still, what Brad was saying wasn't too out of the way for what her religion believed in.

"Okay. Let's say, for a mere second, I believe you. What could I possibly do with this information? All I have is a face and a name...Decimus. It's not like I can shout his name from the rooftops, and he'll come running."

Her friend slurped the rest of his spaghetti and wiped his face with a napkin. "While that is true and completely absurd that you'd even consider screaming his name from the rooftops, we do have search engines. Maybe you could search for him."

Ahana rolled her eyes. She couldn't think of anything more stupid than researching a man named Decimus. "A name like that is going to turn up thousands of results probably from ancient Rome or ancient Greece. Which will fuel your theory, and I definitely won't buy it."

"And why not?" He leaned back in his seat and flagged a waiter. "Think of the picture you drew. Was it not of a man in Roman or Greek garb?"

Ahana leaned in and narrowed her gaze at her best friend. "Why do you seem more interested in pursuing this than I am?"

Brad shrugged and sipped his drink. "Nothing exciting ever happens around here. This is the first man of yours I've been interested in since your first boyfriend."

"One: he is *not* my 'man.' Two: you promised you would never bring up Yogesh again."

He busted out laughing, and she really hoped he would stop because all eyes were on them. "No offense, but the guy quoted Bollywood movies every time he spoke to you. It was hilarious!"

Ahana shook her head. Her first boyfriend was less than a boyfriend and more of a match her parents were thinking of pursuing when she turned eighteen. She was a freshman in college, and they thought it would be a good idea to start thinking of her marriage, especially since arranged marriages take some time to find the perfect match. Yogesh was her father's friend's son, and he was studying to be a teacher. She was expecting him to be in a different field like business or a doctor, a lawyer even, so she respected the fact that her parents' views were the same as her own: as long as he was well educated or had an honest profession, there was little she would refuse. Not once did she think about entire conversations revolving around lines from Bollywood movies.

She had to admit, it was romantic at first. He would send her cute texts from her favorite films, but then it just got weird. He literally tried to have the *exact* conversations from films! And when she didn't answer with the next line, he got upset. That was definitely not the life she wanted for herself.

But this wasn't either.

She couldn't pursue a man she had only seen in dreams. Could she?

. . .

Chapter Four

He paced back and forth in a fitful rage unbecoming of himself. Never had he been so angry, so undecided in his life. At one point in time, when he was a general in the Roman army, he would not have thought twice to just march up to Draupati and tell her like it was. But this was entirely different. The woman he had to talk to was not the Draupati he knew and loved. Was not the Draupati who loved him. This was another woman entirely, and he could *not* just march up to her and say: "You are my beloved wife, Draupati, to whom I married several hundred years ago. My head is on the chopping block for a murder I did not commit, and you are the only one who can prove me innocent." To which she was then likely to respond: "Whose murder?" Then he would have to reply: "Yours." To which this new version of Draupati would probably kick him where it hurt, run for her life to the police station, and he'd likely be in more shit than what he was in at this present moment. There was no scenario in which the end result was his life granted back to him. *You might as well give up while you are ahead.* And he was just about to when his friend's corporeal form showed up in front of him. "The Judge wants to see you."

Decimus immediately scoffed. He absolutely despised Balthazar's jokes when they revolved around The Judge. Lustitia was *not* a goddess to be taken lightly, nor was she one to actually take a joke. She loathed vampires, and the very thing they all stood for and looked for any reason to condemn them all. She had waited ages for his Judgement Day on purpose, and now that it was close, he wanted to murder his friend for making such lighthearted jokes about it. "If you like living, I think it is best you leave."

His friend ran his hand through his messy hair and stood up straight. "Look, I'm not messing with you. I *might have* told Lustitia that Draupati was starting to remember."

Decimus' vein popped in his head as fire rumbled within him. "You did *what?*" He barred his fangs at his friend. If he wasn't this body-less shadow, he would have seized the man by his throat. How many times did he have to tell Balthazar that he didn't want Draupati in the middle of this? Even if she was starting to remember, what she would ultimately remember would only mean his demise and nothing more. Nothing good was going to come of this.

"I know that you want her to stay out of it, but if it will save your life…"

"It will *condemn* me!" Decimus balled his hands into a fist, wishing he could punch something and get all of his anger out, but that wish was useless.

"What are you talking about? If Draupati remembers, she can clear your name."

Decimus closed his eyes and forced his anger down. He *really* didn't want to relive this part of his life. But he didn't have a choice now. He had to tell Balthazar.

"In Draupati's memories, *I am* the one who murdered her. Caelus pretended to me and lured her to bed, where he slowly tortured her and then drank her dry. The last thing she will remember is my face hovering above hers."

His heart clenched within his chest as bitter memories surfaced. When he got there, it was much too late. Her blood was *everywhere*. The sheets, the cot…everything was soaked in it. He wished it was him who died on that very bed. He should have been there for her. With her. He should have never gone out to hunt alone. She was never against his vampiric nature. She even allowed him to feed from her to satiate him between hunts. He cradled her in his arms and cried until Morta appeared by his side. That was when it was all said and done. After Caelus fled and left his life soulless. They had bound their lives together the minute he drank from her. Unbeknownst to him at the time, Draupati was a pureblood vampire of the highest royal vampire family in India. Caelus must have known that which was why he had to torture her first and then feed from her. She would have never willingly let him.

The complication came from Ahana, though, not from Draupati

herself. If Ahana's memories were only *now* starting to come back, she wouldn't remember Caelus. She would only see Decimus' face in her mind. There was no telling what that memory would do to her.

"So, you see, Balthazar. You have now put both of your best friends at risk."

Balthazar cursed under his breath. "Now what?"

"Now, I go to Lustitia and see what she will do with me." Decimus hung his head and imagined the goddess of justice's temple. He wasn't sure what exactly to expect, but he was certain it was not going to be pleasant.

Chapter Five

Thick, dense fog surrounded her as crows and ravens cawed in the distance. She tried to reach out in front of her to see what was there, but even her hand disappeared. She called out, hoping someone, anyone, would hear her, but she was only met with an eerie silence that made her insides turn. She was trying to visit the historic part of town, the one where the apothecaries still ran shop and where there were underground taverns and shops. How she ended up in this dense fog was beyond her. She wanted to go back the way she came; only the fog made it impossible to see which direction that had been. One thing was for certain: the ground beneath her feet was cobblestone, just like the historic part of town ought to be. Maybe this was it, after all.

Against her better judgment, she continued to walk forward, and after several minutes the fog seemed to lift. When it cleared completely, a shiver ran down her spine, and she was face to face with a large mansion. If she had to guess, it covered at least three blocks. The gate in front of her ran the length - and possibly the width - of the property and was at least three times as much as her height. From what she could tell, it was at least a football field's length to the front of the house. In the front, where there should have been rows of cars, the land was completely devoid of them. There was a grass area, complete with a statue of what seemed to be a goddess of some sort and what should have been spouting water. The harder she looked at it, the more it seemed familiar to her. Like she had seen the face of the goddess before, but it was too far for her to truly see who it was. Instead, it was covered in moss. In fact, now that she looked closer, the entire cobblestone leading up to the mansion seemed to be covered in moss as if the person who lived there hadn't been taking care of the property. Yet, she noticed, the mansion itself was in good condition, from what she could tell anyway. The brick foundation didn't seem to have a single crack in it, the windows weren't boarded up, and the brown door was as modern as the one on her single-family home she inherited from her parents after they retired and moved further down south.

"What do you think you're doing?"

The deep, masculine voice came from directly behind her and made the hairs on the back of her neck stand up. She knew that voice anywhere. *Decimus*. Licking her lips, she prayed that it was a dream. That the moment she turned around, she'd wake up, and this would all be over. But when she turned around, she came face to face with the man from her dreams. His eyes were as clear blue as the water he waded into in her last dream. His skin was olive, clean-shaven, and devoid of any scars. He was almost a whole head taller than she was, and his aura was lethal. She had to get out of here, and yet she had so many questions for this man.

"I...um...I..." She didn't even know why she opened her mouth to speak when she could barely form her own thoughts.

"It is dangerous for you to be here. You need to go."

Ahana shook her head. She wasn't going anywhere without answers. "Who are you?" The courage in her voice did not do justice to the rollercoaster in her stomach.

"You are on *my* property, and yet you ask *me* who *I* am? You humans are so strange." Decimus flashed his fangs at her, and she rolled her eyes. Of course he was a vampire. The fog, the crows, the ravens. It all made sense. She wasn't oblivious to the vampires who lived in the historic part of town, but she was oblivious to her own religion. Reincarnation was not proven as vampirism, werewolves, and witches were. There was no set proof of reincarnation. And yet as she stood there, looking at him, she knew she had been wrong all along.

"Your name is Decimus, is it not?" Now she was getting brave. She could feel it crawling through her skin. Where it came from, she wasn't certain, but she was glad it did. She would need to put this man in his place if she was going to get her answers.

"And you are Ahana Vaikar."

Ahana's eyes went wide though she knew it would make sense that he knew that just as she knew who he was. "What is our relationship?"

"Our relationship is nothing," Decimus responded. "Now leave."

"I'm afraid I cannot do that. You see, I've been having these crazy dreams, and you're in them, and the fact that you know my name tells me that you know the connection between us, and I am *not* going to leave here until I get my answer from you."

Decimus sighed, but not in defeat. Instead, it was a sigh of utter annoyance. "You ought to have thought of a better line than that. Seriously. The human who dreams of the gorgeous, brooding vampire. It's so cliche. I only knew your name because I can read minds, not because you are anything special. Now, if you will leave me to my abode..." He pushed past her and unlocked the gate.

"The moss on your property shows you have not been here for ages, so just where have you been, Decimus?" She didn't know why, but she felt the need to question his whereabouts as if he had been gone from her life for far too long, and she needed to understand why and where he had been all this time. It wasn't just a coincidence that she wandered into his property. Something larger was at play here. Brad was right.

"You humans are really something else." He shook his head and extended the distance between them.

Her heart shattered into splinters as the distance between them increased, and before she could stop herself, she screamed his name. "Decimus, please! I need to know what is going on!"

She wasn't sure if it was his conscience or the way she pleaded with him that made him stop, but her heart fluttered to life as he did so and motioned for her to follow him.

"Do *not* touch anything."

She didn't care about anything enough to want to touch it. All she cared about was getting the answers she deserved.

"*Let. Her. Go.*" Her heart dropped into her stomach as fear crept up her being. The male voice behind her sounded *exactly* the same as the one in front of her, yet how could there be two? What the hell was going on?

The man in front of her growled a guttural growl that sent her running for the gate, but before she could reach it, it slammed shut. "*She* is not going anywhere, Decimus." *Decimus?* Was the first one not Decimus? If he wasn't Decimus, then who was he?

"You are not going to win this time, Caelus."

She took a deep breath. *Okay. So, the one I thought was Decimus is actually Caelus, so are they...twins?*

"You always have to get involved, don't you? You just can't let it be, Decimus, can you?"

"Draupati was never yours to begin with. I will not let you have her. Not when she is innocent and remembers nothing of her past. Have you no shame?" The real Decimus was definitely not someone to be messed with. The way he curled his lip in disgust and sent the front gate flying as he said those words was enough to make her want to roll up in a ball and cry. But she didn't. Instead, she stayed frozen to the ground, watching the two men.

"She was never supposed to be yours. You knew that, and still, you fell in love with her."

The real Decimus threw his head back in laughter. "You were always so naive. Did you really think you were worthy of the Red Bloods? You? A Black Blood? A good for nothing creation of the devil himself. A demon disguised as a vampire. Did you really think she wouldn't see through you? What love had you for her? To torture her to death and drain her of her life."

Ahana's head reeled as she watched the two men arguing before her, and all at once, the world spun. The last thing she felt was the ground beneath her head.

Chapter Six

"Who said it was love?" Decimus wanted to punch Caelus where he stood. The devilish sneer on the demon's face said all it needed to. He never cared about Draupati. All he cared about was the power her red blood could give him.

Draupati's powers were ancient. More than being able to walk in the sun, her powers allowed her to see the past and future. They made her invincible and immortal while most vampires could burn to ash in the sunlight, die from not feeding, and could be fatally wounded. None of those ailments pertained to her. It was an honor to feed from her and not one that should have been taken lightly. Yet Caelus took advantage. And all for what? A power that was useless?

"What do you get from killing her...again? Was the first time not enough?"

"Why do you want to know? So, you can do it yourself?"

Decimus seized the demon by his throat and held him against Draupati's statue in his garden. "I demand you to tell me what it is that you got out of murdering my wife!"

A sinister smile spread across Caelus' lips. "Blood magick."

Decimus' grip tightened around the man's throat. Blood magick was one of the darkest magicks to exist. It allowed anyone to manipulate blood and create hexes and curses. It could bring demons to life, summon demon lords. Some spells could even kill gods.

Just as Decimus was going to snap his neck, the man head-butted him and made his grip loosen. A second head butt made Decimus stumble far enough back that Caelus was able to deliver a kick to his ribs.

While it didn't shatter them, it was enough to bruise him. It took him several seconds to catch his breath, and in that time, Caelus had Ahana over his shoulder. Decimus refused to lose his wife again and summoned all the strength he could muster and charged at the demon.

He lunged at Caelus with everything he had. He was *not* going to lose his wife again and definitely not the same way he lost her the first time. This time he was going to fight with everything he had in him. He had a fortnight to prove to Lustitia that he was innocent, and by the gods, he was going to keep his promise. He had to make this right, or he would lose Draupati forever. If he didn't prove himself innocent, she would never be born again, and his love would have failed him. The seven rounds for seven lifetimes would have proved useless. He *had* to win her love back at any cost.

He summoned his ax to his hand just as Caelus summoned his sword to him. With a battle cry, he ran toward him and sliced his ax through the air, only for Caelus to teleport behind him. "You have grown weak, *brother*."

"Don't you *dare* call me your brother." Decimus charged at him again, and this time his ax caught the man's arm and sliced his skin open. Caelus screamed out in pain and held his hand over his arm as Decimus smirked, waving his ax in the air. "Pure silver and sharper than a vampire's fangs."

If anything could kill more beings than a sharp blade by itself, it was silver. Many beings were weak toward it, vampires, too. The only thing that kept Decimus from being harmed was his bond with Draupati. One that would wear off if he didn't get her to remember who she truly was. *Two weeks...I can do this.* He hoped.

"You are going to regret the day you came back into your corporeal form."

"You can't threaten a man who is ready to lie down on his deathbed. But *I* certainly can threaten a man who thinks he is above death. If I *ever* see you near her again, you'll be seeing your father sooner than you wish. And may he eat you alive when you get there."

"This is not over," Caelus growled before disappearing.

Sighing heavily, Decimus ran to where Ahana lay on the ground. After listening to her faint breathing and checking her body, which was devoid of any blood and scratches, he thanked the gods she had only passed out. He gathered her into his arms and carried her into his mansion, one he hadn't seen the likes of in ages. As much as he hated to admit it, he was grateful Balthazar kept it spic and span. Though, he would have to give him hell for letting moss cover the front pavement and statue of his beloved wife. The most important thing right now was her health. He wasn't sure how he was going to tell her everything or how she was going to take it. Did she even know that her best friend was an immortal thrall who had been enslaved by Caelus and was saved by Decimus? How would she react if she didn't know?

Gods, he should have never lured her to this place.

Chapter Seven

Ahana came to in a room she did not recognize lit only by candlelight. The bed above her had a beautiful canopy, and the bed seemed to be made of dark wood, probably mahogany or cherry wood. Further inspection in the candlelight revealed a desk in the far corner, upon which seemed to be paper and an old quill pen. Next to it was a trash bin. On the wall opposite the bed was an armoire whose wood seemed to match the bed and large wooden doors, which probably led to a walk-in closet. On the ceiling was modern lighting, so why the candles?

Getting out of bed, she searched for the switch to the light above her and immediately found it next to the door of the room. After switching it on, she blew out the candles and whistled low when she saw everything else the room had to offer. Opposite the armoire, on the other side of the bed, was an open wooden door which led to a beautiful white and peach tiled bathroom. There were two large sinks against the wall with storage, a large bathtub in the middle of the floor, and a stand-up shower to her left, next to which was the toilet. Soft, plush brown towels hung on the handle of the shower door. A note was taped on it:

The bathroom has everything you could need: women's toiletries, shampoo,
conditioner, soap of every womanly scent I could find, shaving cream, razors,
lotion. You name it. It's here. Feel free to rummage through the cabinets to
find everything you need. There are fresh clothes in the wardrobe. Your friend
Brad brought them for you. You are not a prisoner here. You are free to leave
at any time you wish. Just do not leave without talking to me.

Yours,

Decimus

Her heart leapt into her chest. Decimus. The man from her dreams. This was his place? And how did Brad know where she was? Did Decimus call him? He must have. But why? What happened?

Suddenly, her memory came back to her. Her visit to the historic part of town, the fog, the fight between him and his lookalike, Calcium? Caleb? *Caelus*, her mind reminded her. Gods, what did she get herself into? She really hoped it was all a dream, but now that she was awake and saw that it was, in fact, reality, she wasn't sure how to feel. The only thing she was certain about was that she wanted to talk to him, too. She needed to know what all of it meant. Who he was. Who she was. If Brad was right and she was reincarnated, then that could definitely make him her husband. Her presence here was more significant for him than it was for her, and she would definitely hear him out.

She took a quick shower and got dressed in the clothes Brad brought for her because, of course, he would bring the oversized long-sleeved t-shirt and black leggings. Well, she supposed, it wasn't like she wanted to impress a man she knew nothing about, and yet, it seemed, he knew everything there was to know about her.

When she stepped out of the room, she wasn't exactly sure which way to go until she noticed notes taped to the wall with arrows on them. The note on her right read, "To Leave," and the note on her left read "To talk to Decimus." Her mind screamed for her to leave. It would be the right thing to do. After all, she knew nothing about this man. Staying would have been insane!

On the other hand, this was the same man she had seen in her dreams. If Brad was right and she really was reincarnated, this man's memories were all of her as his wife. The least she could do was listen to what he had to say. Maybe he could explain it all, or maybe there wasn't anything at all to explain. Maybe he just wanted to tell her what happened and let her know how long she had been here. *How long have I been here? Where's my phone?!*

Panic immediately set in on her. She didn't know how long she had been here, if he had taken advantage of her, where her phone was, or if anyone was looking for her. Sure, Brad knew where she was but were her parents aware? What if they called the cops? What if people were looking for her?

She immediately set off in the direction of talking to Decimus. She needed to know exactly what happened while she was out cold.

When she followed the last arrow, she ended up in the kitchen. There were various breakfast dishes out on the island, and Decimus was drinking out of a black cup. She didn't even want to think about what was in it. Bike rose in her throat as she accidentally imagined it.

"It's just coffee." Decimus' voice was deep and low as he spoke. "Despite what people think, some vampires do have a taste for certain foods and drinks other than blood. I usually have the taste for coffee." He took a sip from his cup and gently put it down on the table. "I wasn't sure what you liked, so I made it all."

She could definitely see that: eggs, bacon, sausage, hash browns, waffles, pancakes, and a box of cereal with milk were all waiting for her on the table.

"I know I could have asked your friend Brad when he called to see how you were, but I didn't want to keep bothering him. Here's your phone." He slid it over to her side of the table. "Don't worry. I didn't go through it. I asked Brad if he wouldn't mind calling your parents and letting them know you weren't feeling well, and he was watching over you. They texted early this morning. I'm sure you will want to talk to them."

He took another sip of his coffee and took a deep breath before speaking again. "Also, it has been five days since you've been out, and before you ask me why I didn't wake you, I tried. I even had a doctor come look you over. Doc said you were in a state of shock, most likely from my argument with Caelus, and needed as much rest as possible. She said she was certain you would come too soon. She was last here last night. I am glad you are awake and will inform her so she can check you over before you leave."

Ahana was shell shocked. She heard everything he was saying to her, but she wasn't completely processing it. How could someone who didn't know her go to such lengths to make sure she was comfortable?

"Why?" It was the only word that came to mind. Why was he doing all of this? Why did he need to talk to her? Why was all of this happening?

"Why what?"

"Why are you doing all of this? Who are you?"

Decimus threw back the rest of his coffee and got up to place the cup in the sink, and for the first time, she was aware that she was alone with a stranger. If he wanted to, he could kill her and make it seem like she never woke up from the shock she was in. He could suck her dry, and no one would ever know the truth. And yet, she couldn't stop herself from pulling out one of the stools and sitting at the island across from him. Something within her drew her toward him, and for the first time, she realized there might have been truth to what Brad had told her.

"Do you want the whole truth, the semi-truth, or a fraction of the truth mixed with lies I've told myself to make me feel better?"

Ahana considered all the options. The whole truth could mean an end to the perfect world she created for herself. Would she be able to handle it if it turned out there was more to the supernatural world than she was already aware of? The semi-truth could be a risk. What if someone was out to kill her, and he was the only one who could save her? Would he omit it? And a fraction of the truth mixed with lies was definitely not the way to go. She sighed. "I've come this far. You might as well tell me the whole truth."

"Are you sure? I am going to warn you ahead of time that once you know the whole truth, there is no going back. This truth could make or break you...could make or break *us*."

She thought for a moment. The truth was that she was already knee-deep in this. The man from her dreams was right before her eyes. In the flesh. She had seen him argue with someone who looked as though he might murder her, so if that was the case, she needed to know. How were they all connected? *Why* were they all connected? "I understand, and I am ready."

Decimus nodded and told her the whole truth, leaving no parts of it out. He told her how he was a general in the Ancient Roman army. He told her how she was an Indian Princess of one of the strongest vampiric bloodlines there ever was. He told her how Caelus longed for that power. How they both fell in love with her, but she chose Decimus. He told her how they had not only taken the seven rounds around the fire but how they bonded their life force and how *this* was *the last* lifetime they had to make it right. He told her how Caelus murdered her wearing his face. Told her how Brad was really a thrall he had rescued and had befriended her to ensure her safety. Told her how her parents were aware of all of it, and that was why they left her here. For him to find. And all of a sudden, everything hit her all at once. So many questions with so little answers, and nothing made sense. *He had killed her.* And yet he had *the nerve* to sit here and call her his wife and beg for her to set him free?

No. This wasn't happening. This was a dream, and she would wake up from it. All she had to do was leave the manor. So that's what she did. She grabbed her phone and ran out, running as fast as her feet would carry her until she couldn't run anymore. She wasn't sure how far she got, but when she stopped to catch her breath, Decimus was right behind her and caught her in his arms before she collapsed.

"Let go of me!" she screamed out while struggling with all the remaining strength she possessed. Of course yelling at the guy practically dragging her down the street would only make him more agitated at her than he already was. His grip tightened on her wrist, forcing her to wince slightly.

"You're lucky that I followed you, you know that, right?"

That much is true, I suppose. If the other one was still around, I would probably be a goner.

She muttered a few incoercible words under her breath and eventually stopped her pointless struggles. Her right hand swept the few dark brown curls that had fallen in front of her shoulder to her back again and allowed her mud-colored eyes to scan the slowly darkening street. The streetlights began to flicker to life-and continued to do just that, flicker. This part of town always sent chills down her spine at night. Each of the old brick buildings looked as if they would crumple to the ground at any moment, while some had already been conquered by gravity.

Stares burned into each part of her body, but no eyes could be found, and strange noises echoed from within the buildings, down the alleys, and behind them. Occasionally, she would jerk her gaze around to look behind her to try and catch a glimpse of anyone who might be following them. *No one within sight-but they're there, I know it.*

Her heart rate accelerated with each step they took further into the Valor territory. Decimus glanced over towards her once again before coming to a halt. He turned to fully face her but kept his grip on her wrist as tight as it had been since he forced her to come here. It reminded her about the day they first met-when it all began.

"You're safe with me. Keep your nerves low-they can feel your fear and thrive off of it. By now, you should know that." He kept his voice as powerful as it has always been with as little emotion as he could manage to keep from leaking into his words.

"Well, if it weren't for you, Decimus, I would not be in this position in the first place, would I?" She perked a single eyebrow and kept her hard gaze locked on his. An annoyed sigh rang from his throat.

"Ahana, if not for me, you would have been dead five days ago when I first came across you, remember?" His grip loosened a bit while his eyes seemed to lose a little of their coldness.

"Did you ever consider that that might have been better than getting me dragged into all of this?"

"I did!" His voice was shrill with anger and hurt. "By the gods, I did! But I just...I couldn't. I can't live life this way. I have stayed away from you for *six* lifetimes already. I do not expect you to understand, but for me to see you die *six* times and for me to not be able to hold you, to love you like I have wanted to for all of these years...It is a torture I wouldn't wish on Caelus! I know this all sounds insane. If I thought myself human my whole life, I would think it, too. But this is the *truth*, Ahana. I have so many pictures, memories, drawings. Anything you could possibly want to see for me to prove that I am telling the truth. I have accumulated all of it for this moment. Just please come back inside, or those demons will tear you to shreds!"

She didn't protest this time or speak for once. It wouldn't make much of a difference since she could see the entrance getting ever closer. A stinging pain washed over her leg as she heard a slight ripping sound. "Ow," she hissed while coming to a stop and jerking her gaze to my leg. A small tear in her faded blue jeans rested on the back of her leg while the fabric was slowly being coated with a crimson liquid that now drained freely.

Small, disturbing laughter rang into the flickering darkness, and her heart dropped to the ground. She hadn't noticed that Decimus had turned to face her and was looking at the blood coating leg. Her eyes roamed over the empty streets and begged to see what was actually there-though she knew she never wanted to see those that actually lived deep within the streets of the Valor.

The Valor. Damn the day I ventured too closely to this place.

Chapter Eight

Decimus hated himself for what he had done to Ahana. She locked herself in her room and refused to come out and eat a single morsel of food from him. Balthazar even came by and tried to talk to her, but she wouldn't have it, and rightly so. He had been her best friend since they started high school. He was her ride or die, and for Decimus to make him hide the truth from her was not fair. He knew she would need time to get over it. But time was not on his side. He now had only nine days before he had to appear in front of Lustitia, and if he could do it sooner, he would love to, but it had to be on Ahana's terms. If she didn't want to tell Lustitia the truth, he was as good as dead.

"Look, I know Ahana - Draupati - whatever you would rather call her, and I'm telling you that she will do the right thing. She may not remember her feelings for you now, but she will remember them in due time. Just give her the space she needs."

Decimus sighed. He wanted to, he *really* did, but he didn't have time. If she didn't tell Lustitia that Caelus was really the one who killed her, Lustitia was going to erase him from existence. While most days he hated living, he found it worthwhile to at least be able to see his wife from afar. But to die for something he didn't do was -

The click of the doorknob turning set his heart into overdrive. He was certain she was never going to emerge from the room. When she gently padded down the steps, uncertainty in every step, he did every-thing he could to keep himself from scooping her in his arms and hugging her.

"You said you had proof that I am truly your wife. I'd like to see it."

Although his heart was beating with joy and wanted to leap out of his chest to embrace her, he forced his happiness down and stood. "Follow me."

He led her through his mansion, through a large, gilded door, and down a winding staircase that led to a long corridor. He could feel her fear as he did so and tried not to turn around and frighten her. On this level, there were tapestries which showed their life together, busts of the both of them which had been in their ancestral palace, and a room with just her clothing and jewelry. Things he swore he'd never get rid of. As he showed them all to her, he watched as the different emotions played across her features, but they always went back to one: confusion.

He couldn't tell if she remembered anything, but if there was one thing that would jog her memory, it was her sword crafted by Tvastar himself for the sacrifices her family made to aid in the battles of the gods. He had fought many battles alongside her when he was a Roman general and wanted to fight many more. If it wasn't for Augustus, they may have never met.

When he stepped foot into the armory, Ahana stayed at the door. When he turned around, he caught tears streaming down her face. He immediately crossed the room to where she stood and placed his hands on her cheeks, and wiped her tears away with his thumbs. "If you want to stop, I understand," he assured her.

She shook her head and wrapped her arms around him. "I cannot believe you kept all of this."

Decimus took a deep breath, unsure whether to wrap his arms around her in turn or leave it be, but when she kissed his cheek, all sense left him, and he lost himself in her hold.

"By the gods, I have missed you *balaam*." Her voice was barely above a whisper, and Decimus wasn't sure he had heard her correctly.

"Did you just....?"

Ahana pulled away from him, leaving only a minuscule space between them, and wiped her eyes. "Look at all of this," she gestured with her hands. "It's a room straight out of our palace. *My favorite* room in the *entire* palace. How could I ever forget the first time Tvastar handed me my sword, and you demanded a twin to it?" Her lips turned up into a smile. "It has been far too long, Decimus. I feared I might never remember."

Tears swam in his eyes as he gathered her into his arms again. He didn't know how he got lucky or how she remembered so quickly, but none of it mattered to him. All that mattered was that she remembered.

Chapter Nine

Ahana's breath caught in her throat as she stared at the armory before her. Rapid scenes of her and Decimus flashed through her mind. First was the day they met. He was sent to her palace to forge an alliance between Augustus and her father. Little did she know the alliance would have been finalized with their marriage. Not that she had any qualms. The memory of their wedding night and his chivalry warmed her to the core. The next memory was the first time they made love. It was sweet, sensual, slow. Heat crept up her neck and flushed her cheeks and ears. She hoped he didn't notice.

The next memories that followed were intimate moments the two of them spent together, followed by a war they fought side by side. Tears filled her eyes as she watched her father collapse in a heap of blood at her feet, several arrows lodged in his back with scars too deep to be healed. Though they were vampires, she remembered, and little could kill her bloodline, there were ways to do so.

Cursed weapons coated with human blood were a sure way to get the job done quick. Only a handful of people knew it, and she knew *exactly* who his murderer was.

The next memory which flashed before her was the last memory she had of her life as Draupati: Caelus drinking her blood and killing her mercilessly with the cursed ax. Unable to bear the pain of it all, she closed the distance between herself and Decimus and wrapped her arms around him. It had been far too long that they'd been apart. No more.

She would march herself to Lustitia this very moment and demand her husband's life returned to her. He would no longer live as a Silhouette as the goddess deemed.

"Are you sure you don't want to wait?" Balthazar's face lit up with excitement.

Ahana shook her head. "The longer we wait, the longer she has something to hold over on him. I am the proof she needs. Only I have what it takes to defeat Caelus once and for all. Let her judge as she will."

She turned to Decimus and kissed his cheek. "You did love to dress me in my warrior's gear. Will you help me for old time's sake?"

· · ·

Chapter Ten

Decimus paced back and forth as they waited for Lustitia to come to the gates of her temple. He always knew the goddess to be punctual, so what was taking so long? Patience was not one of his virtues, and it took all of him to not break through the gates and demand a retrial this very second.

"Breathe." Ahana's voice was steady and stern. "You know she *despises* having to turn a judgment and admit she was wrong. She is probably thinking about how to face the rest of the gods."

Decimus stopped for a second and fixed his beautiful turquoise eyes on her. "I hope you are right, amore mio."

He watched as his beloved blushed and brushed his thumb against her cheek. It had been ages since he heard her voice, and now he didn't want to stop hearing it. But for that, he needed Lustitia to grant him his freedom. *Gods, where is—*

The doors to her temple flew open as she emerged in a long gold gown. Her milk-white eyes bore into his soul as if she could truly see him.

"This had better be good for you to *demand* to be seen." Her voice was laced with contempt as if she already knew what he wanted.

"I demand you to release my husband, Lustitia!" Ahana came between him and the goddess and held her head up high. "He is not guilty of the crime you hold him accountable of."

Lustitia took a step toward her, and Decimus clutched his sword tight. While normal swords were useless against gods, this one was not. And he certainly was not afraid to use it.

"Draupati," Lustitia sneered. "My, my, my, it has been *ages*. I was hoping you'd *never* regain your memory." She sighed deeply. "Well, since you are here. I hope you have proof that he is innocent, or there is nothing more I can do."

Ahana turned back toward Decimus, and he caught a glimpse of the uncertainty in her eyes, but with one nod, that uncertainty turned into determination.

Ahana took a step toward the goddess and reached out her hands to touch the goddess' head. "I can show you if you will let me."

"Well, get on with it, then. If you're going to prove me wrong—which no one ever does—it might as well include the theatrics."

Decimus rolled his eyes. At least he didn't have to fight her. As apathetic as the goddess could be, it seemed she had some kind of heart after all. He watched as Ahana used her powers to play her memories out of Lustitia and admired his wife all the more. To relive that memory in full, piece by piece, bit by bit, must not have been easy for her. And yet, she stood still, body rigid, head held high. This was the Draupati he remembered, and this was the woman he wanted to learn all over again.

When Ahana pulled away, Lustitia clutched her chest tightly and took a step back. It took her several moments to regain her breath and speak. "Decimus Vanholsen, I grant you your freedom. No trial necessary. However, we will need you at the trial of Caelus Vanholsen to deliver your wife the justice she so deserves. Do you accept?"

Decimus nodded and took Ahana's hand. They both kneeled before the goddess. "I accept, your grace."

The goddess inclined her head to them both and smiled. "If there is any way I can be of help to you both for the pain you have endured by your gods, please inform me."

Both nodded, but neither said a word for several moments. Then Ahana freed her hand from his and whispered something to the goddess of justice. Decimus wasn't sure he wanted to know, and Ahana assured him he'd find out when the time came, but for now, she wanted to go home and live the rest of her life with him.

"But first," she stated as they teleported home. "I need to feed." Decimus thought he would never hear those words again, and he laid his neck bare as she sunk her fangs into him and drank to her heart's content.

Epilogue

Ahana took a deep breath as she finished feeding from her husband for the second time today. She wasn't sure what kept it at bay for so long, but whatever it was, she was glad she had. If her own husband's blood wasn't satisfying her, she wondered if anything would. Currently, they were sitting in Dhanvantari's—the god of healing—temple as he looked her over. Decimus swore to her that his blood should have been enough to satiate her.

It took Dhavanatari several minutes to look directly at her, and when he did so, it was with a smirk and raised eyebrows.

"You are going to be a mother."

Ahana did all she could to contain her excitement. So Lustitia came through after all! When Ahana believed she was merely human, the doctors told her she couldn't have children. She now knew that was due to the way she died at Caelus's hand. She took the opportunity to ask Lustitia if she could fix that. Clearly, the goddess was able to do anything.

"Wait. What?" Decimus turned to her with love, hope, and admiration on his face. "But I thought with the way Caelus…"

"This is what I asked Lustitia. She followed through with her promise that she would help us." Ahana smiled and wrapped her arms around her husband, not wanting to ever let him go.

"I am many things but normal is not one of them," says Aimee Shaye when asked to describe herself. She is a novelist whose genres include Fantasy and all its subgenres. When asked what drives her, Aimee says, "The world around me. The people I know. The love and support of my family." Aimee is a family-driven person and enjoys meeting and getting to know her readers. She is full of life and down-to-earth. She has a personality that fills the room. More than that, Aimee is someone people easily open up to. Her passion for life, reading, and writing are evident in her novels and she leaves no stone unturned in showcasing real emotions even in a fantasy world.

Readers from all of the world enjoy reading her novels which are suitable for all ages, despite her characters being in their late teens and early twenties. You can find all of Aimee's Social Media at the following link: http://linktr.ee/AimeeShaye

facebook.com/AimeeShaye08
twitter.com/aimeeshaye
instagram.com/aimeeshayeauthor

SCARLET CLAIMED

BY DORA BLUME

Chapter 1

"Damn, Hope, you're one hell of a shot," Carson shook his head as he dismantled his weapon. His sandy blonde hair fell into his eyes as he carefully placed his gun in the box.

"Whatever, Carson, you just need to work on your reflexes." I jabbed his arm as I walked past him. I pulled the clip from my own gun and placed it in its case.

"So, do you have big plans tonight?" Carson glanced over at me as he holstered his gun.

"Nah, I'm looking forward to some uneventful time at home." I slipped my leather jacket onto my shoulders and turned toward the door of the training room. "What about you?"

"Marissa is making dinner tonight. She'll kill me if I miss another family dinner." He leaned back against the table. "I can't believe your man doesn't have anything big planned."

"Why would he?" I asked.

"I don't know, cause it's your birthday. You don't have a single thing planned?" His eyes bore into me, and I could feel his judgment.

"I don't make a big deal of it."

"It's your birthday, you should make a big deal of it." He shook his head. "Do you want to come have dinner with us? I can call Marissa right now."

"No, I'm fine. I don't really want to spend my birthday with you and Marissa, no offense."

"Oh, none taken," he laughed.

"I just don't see what the big deal is about birthdays. I've never been one to celebrate them. Now can we drop it?" The cold, stale air of the room hit me, and I shivered. I knew it wasn't as cold as it suddenly felt in the room.

"Message received, so, what are you thinking about the case?"

"I think we need to go back and talk to the coroner. Something about their bodies doesn't add up." I had been thinking about the case since we got the call this morning. There was something niggling at the back of my mind. I just hadn't figured out what to do about it.

"What are you thinking?" Carson asked.

"Well, there wasn't that much blood at the scene. But based on their wounds, they would have bled out." I tapped my finger against my lips. "Where did the blood go?" I turned to look at Carson.

"Are you sure there wasn't a drain nearby or something? Blood doesn't just disappear." Carson held the door open for me.

"No, there weren't any drains close enough to the body. It was in an alley." I gave him a duh stare before continuing. "There was nowhere else for the blood to go. Maybe I'll pay a visit to the station before I head home for the night." I pulled out the keys to my Dodge.

"Call me if you come up with anything." Carson's phone buzzed. He pulled it out of his pocket and looked at the screen.

"Marissa?" I asked.

"Yeah, on second thought, I'll talk to you tomorrow. Will you at least do something fun tonight? It is your birthday, after all. And don't stay at the station. I know how you like to think you can pull all-nighters, but then I have to deal with your crabby ass the next day." Carson narrowed his eyes at me. He was dead wrong; I could go at least two nights of no sleep before I was crabby.

"Okay, Dad, I'll try." I smirked, knowing I had no intention of listening. If the case led me down the rabbit hole, I had no problem following it.

Carson hit the button on his phone and turned away from me. "Hey, honey, I'm just finishing up at the range with Hope."

I shook my head and walked to my car. I wasn't sure how Marissa put up with him sometimes. My latest failure of a relationship proved no one was really willing to put up with me that was for sure. Long hours and my inability to leave my job at home certainly affected every relationship I'd ever been in. I wished there was one person out there who was willing to understand my passion for what I do. Michael certainly hadn't understood. We got in regular fights about me staying in the office. He would get mad at me anytime I talked about work. He used to tell me it was just a job, and I shouldn't be so wrapped up in my job. He didn't understand. He never understood. It was too bad. He certainly knew how to please a woman in bed. Damn, I was going to miss that part of our relationship.

I pulled up to the parking lot near the coroner's office. I had to get answers for the victims. There had been two similar murders in the last few weeks. I wanted to know if these murders were committed by the same perpetrator. There was something about the wounds and the blood that was niggling at the back of my mind. Something told me this was an important detail. I had a feeling the connection was in the blood.

I walked through the door to the coroner's office. Laura had her feet up on the desk, a sandwich in one hand and her mouse in the other. A game of solitaire was on the screen. "Hard at work, I see." Laura started and dropped her sandwich onto the desk.

"I'll have you know I'm on my lunch break," she shot back and turned to look at me, her cobalt eyes sharp.

"Oh well, sorry to interrupt your precious lunchtime." I crossed my arms over my chest.

"Careful, Hope, I could make you wait for whatever it is you came here for, considering your shift was up, what three maybe four hours ago." She flipped her blonde braid back over her shoulder. She lounged back in the chair, taking another bite of her sandwich. I knew she was bluffing.

"Okay, Laura, I am deeply sorry for disturbing you. I only have a few quick questions about the man who was brought in this morning. I know you're not the one who completed the autopsy, but you're the best, so I was hoping you'd have a second look." I fluttered my lashes and gave her my award-winning smile.

"You're insufferable, you know that." She rolled her eyes at me. "Fine, let's go take a look." She stood up from the chair and headed into the lab. She signed into the computer and pulled the notes up on the screen. "Did you change your hair? It looks nice," she commented as she read over the notes.

"Thanks, I got some layers and highlights the other day. So, I have a few questions about the wounds." I tucked a piece of auburn hair behind my ears.

"Yeah, it looks like there were jagged knife wounds across his neck. He noted it was rather messy. Let's take a look at the body." She glanced at me and walked over to one of the doors. She pulled the handle and grabbed the table to glide the body out of its compartment. She carefully pulled down the sheet to examine the wounds. With a gloved hand, she touched the jagged lines on the neck. "It's weird how these cuts indicate the killer wanted to really slice up the neck. It looks like they cut several times over the same spot." She stretched out the skin and moved her head closer. "It almost looks like they used the tip of the knife to make sure they punctured the artery."

"Okay, so the victim should have bled out at the scene?" I looked at Laura as she stood up straight. Her hand was still against the man's neck. He couldn't have been much older than eighteen.

"Yes, the artery is punctured. They would have bled out within minutes." She dropped her hand. "Where are you going with this?" Her eyes narrowed as she walked back over to the notes. She pitched her bloodied glove on the way.

"There wasn't much blood at the scene. Certainly not enough to indicate the victim bled out from a punctured artery. Are you abso-lutely sure they would've bled out from the neck wound?" I asked.

"Positive, there are over two liters of blood missing from the body. The cause of death was exsanguination based on a cut to the carotid artery. There should have been a lot of blood at the scene." Laura shifted her weight from one foot to the other.

"So, the question of the hour, what happened to all that blood?" I blinked up at Laura.

"Maybe a vampire drank it," Laura's eyes sparkled.

"A vampire, really?" I rolled my eyes. "You've been watching too many of those vampire shows. Who's the flavor of the week?" I asked, knowing she was watching one of the many shows about vampires.

"Damon," she answered automatically.

I shook my head. "I think it's more likely we have some weird sicko out there with a blood fetish. I'm going back to examine the evidence. Any other weird things noted about the body?"

Laura glanced back at the notes. "She had a good dinner about an hour before her death. Looks like she had lobster. How often do you eat lobster?" Laura dipped her head.

"Not very often, it must have been a special occasion. I'll look into it. Thanks, Laura."

"You are very welcome, so why aren't you out with Michael tonight?"

"He's busy," I headed toward the door.

"Oh no, you don't. He's too busy to spend time with you on your birthday. That's not like him, spill." She grabbed my arm and turned me to face her. She's lucky she's a friend, or I would have knocked her on her ass for grabbing me like that.

"Michael decided he didn't want to be with a workaholic." I looked into Laura's eyes. I watched as her face softened into a look of pity. "It's fine. I didn't want to be with anyone who didn't understand my passion for the job anyway." I pulled my arm away from her, and she let me.

"I'm sorry, Hope. That's shitty. What kind of guy dumps his girl-friend right before her birthday?" She shook her head.

"What's the big deal with birthdays? Everyone acts like I should be out getting drunk or something. What if I like investigating? This is absolutely how I would choose to spend my day." I pulled on the sleeve of my jacket.

"Examining dead bodies in the morgue is your ideal birthday. Oh honey," she patted my arm before shaking her head and turning away.

"I need to go follow up on this lead. I'll talk to you later."

"Sure, call me tomorrow. I have the day off. We can have a girls' night out or something." She gave me a sympathetic smile. Seriously, the pity thing was getting a little annoying.

"Yeah, I'll call you." I turned and walked back out the door. Laura and I were friends, but we weren't that close. Most of the people I hung out with were the people I worked with on a regular basis. My shoulders slumped a little as I thought about that. Maybe I needed to find some friends outside of work. I drove back to the station and opened the file on my desk.

Looking over the photos, I knew it. There wasn't enough blood at the scene to support the victim bled out there. There also wasn't anything to suggest the body was dumped. So, what happened to the blood? I went into one of the layout rooms. I pinned up all the photos from the case on the corkboard. I took a step back and stared at the photos. There had to be something here I was missing.

The door opened behind me. "Aren't you supposed to be at home, celebrating or something?" Reed stood in the doorway.

"No, I am exactly where I should be." I looked at Reed over my shoulder.

"Well, since you're here, you need a fresh set of eyes?" I couldn't help but notice how nice his muscles looked against his blue button-up. His dark hair fell slightly over his eyes, and he brushed it back as he walked up to the photos. He tapped the photo with the body sprawled out on the pavement. "It looks like a straight robbery. Did you search the area for her ditched wallet?"

"What makes you think it was a robbery?" I asked. I wasn't ready to move from my seat yet. I tilted my head as he turned back to stare at the photos. Damn, his ass looked nice in those tight black jeans. I had a rule not to get involved with anyone I worked with, but I might make an exception for Reed.

"Well, he was found in a back alley without his wallet. What else would it be?" he blinked, looking back at me.

"I'm not sure yet." I stood. "Notice the lack of blood in the photo. The coroner ruled it was exsanguination from the knife wounds. If that's the case, where's the blood?" I tapped the photo. "There's not enough blood at the scene to support him bleeding out."

"Maybe it washed down the street or something." Reed turned, facing me. He was close, close enough I could smell his mint and eucalyptus aftershave.

"It didn't rain that night. If the blood flowed somewhere else, there would be evidence of that. There isn't any. I'm starting to think the killer drained the victim somehow before slicing open his neck. The coroner also noted a weird puncture mark in the neck that looked like they stabbed the tip of the knife straight into the artery. I can't imagine why someone would do that." I shook my head as I glanced again at the photo with the man's body.

"Okay, are you sure the blood didn't soak into his clothes?" His eyes shifted to me.

"No, it's not at the scene, and it's not in the body. Someone must have drained him."

'Okay, but why? I've never heard of a case where the killer drained their victim before killing them. What would be the point of that?" Reed scratched the stubble on his chin.

"I don't know why. I just know the blood that should be here, isn't. I can only assume it went with the killer. Until the evidence shows me something else, I'm going with it." I went back to the table where I had all the notes from the scene. "You want to go over these with me? See if we can find something to either support or disprove my theory." I began pulling out the different sheets.

"You don't think I have my own cases to work?" he moved to stand behind me.

"I'm sure you do. But you also came to ask about my case, which means you find this one much more interesting than yours." I smirked up at him. I watched as his head tilted slightly. I knew I was right. He found something about this much more interesting than his own work.

"All right, you got me there. I'll take some time and go through this with you." He pulled out the chair and rolled himself closer to me. I passed over one of the pages from the file. He smiled and dipped his head. He began reading, and I grabbed up the next.

After an hour, I handed over the last of the sheets from the file. "There's nothing to indicate where the blood could have gone." I pushed the file to the side. "I think I have to go back to the scene," I huffed.

"Yeah, I'm not sure I can join you at the crime scene." He paused, glancing out the window. "I don't think you should go alone, either. Where's your partner?"

"His wife made him dinner. There's no way I'm pissing off Marissa for a hunch that probably won't lead anywhere. I'm just going to stop by and check it out. I shouldn't be long." I stood, slipping on my coat.

Reed stood, "I'd feel better if you had a black and white with you on this excursion. You know the killers often visit the crime scene after the murder is committed. I don't think you should go alone. I'll go see who's available." Reed opened the door and looked around the station. I stepped behind him. The few officers that were in at this hour were either typing at computers or booking someone into custody.

"Reed, I don't need anyone to take care of me. I'll be fine." I squeezed past him and headed for the back door.

"Hope," Reed called. He closed the distance between us. My breath hitched as his arm rested on my shoulder. "Will you promise me that if you notice anything out of line or get a bad feeling, you'll get out of Dodge? No chasing after a killer on your own."

"Come on, Reed. I'm not that stupid. I'd never go after a dangerous suspect on my own."

"Okay," he let out a deep breath. "Are you coming back here after your errand?"

"No, I'm told I should be spending some time out or relaxing or something." I shrugged. His hand moved from my shoulder to squeeze my upper arm.

"That sounds like a good idea. You should do something that doesn't involve work. You hitting up the regular spot?" he asked. All the police at the station had a regular watering hole. It was a rustic bar and grill a few blocks from the precinct. I liked to stop for a whiskey every now and then. My apartment wasn't too far, so I could walk home if I decided to have more than a few. Not that any of the guys in the place wouldn't offer me a ride if I lived further. It always amazed me how many offered to get me home safe. Of course, they may have wanted to make sure I made it all the way into my apartment. The disappointed look on their face when they learned I was a short walk from the bar was always amusing.

"Yeah, maybe."

"I hope to see you there." The corner of his mouth turned up.

The crime scene was a little over a mile away. There shouldn't be too much traffic, so I should be at the scene in a few minutes. I kept racking my brain, trying to figure out where all the blood could have gone. I pulled up and parked near the alley where we found the last body.

The tape had been long removed, but the alley was still devoid of any people. The homeless who had frequented the alley had moved on to somewhere new since they had lost access during the initial investigation. I bent to examine exactly where the body would have been lying. The grit and rocks from the street gave me no clues as to where the blood would have flowed. The drains were at the end of the street. A dumpster was a few short steps from where the body was found. I bent to glance at the bottom. Not even a speck of red remained. Either the cleaning crew had been thorough, or the blood hadn't even made it this far.

"Ugh," I lifted the lid to the dumpster. The crime scene crew had already checked the dumpster. If they had found any blood, it would have been collected. There was nothing in the file about the blood. I studied the inside of the dumpster. Besides the foul smell of rotting food, there was no indication anyone died here. I stepped back, glancing around one last time at the scene. There was nothing. My hunch was definitely leading me somewhere. I just didn't know where yet.

Why would someone drain a person of blood, then cut their throat?

The cuts were jagged across the throat, leaving a mangled pattern. The coroner said it was done with a serrated knife that had been used several times. It was messy. Some would think that it was because it was someone who may not have known what they were doing. I disagreed. I think the unsub knew exactly what he was doing.

I just needed to figure out who they were before they did it again.

There wasn't anything else I was going to learn here. I had no idea why someone would drain another's blood. There were a few diseases that required regular transfusions. Someone without insurance might get desperate enough to drain someone. Maybe some creep needed blood for a ritualistic sacrifice. Those were the only two things I could think of off the top of my head. Either way, I didn't understand what they would need the blood for. I got distracted as I thought about it. The type of person to do something like that would be a real sicko. I sighed. I might as well head to the bar to have a drink. There was obviously nothing else I could do here for the night.

The sound of pebbles skidding across the pavement drew my attention. I thought I was alone here. My hand instantly went for the gun in my holster. It was a habit. I turned to see Reed standing at the entrance to the alley.

"Reed? What are you doing here? I thought you said you couldn't come with me tonight." I furrowed my brow as I dropped my hand from my gun.

"I know, but I didn't feel right with you being here by yourself."

"Oh, well, I already finished up. I was just leaving."

"Excellent, are you ready for that drink?" he asked.

"Yeah, I could really use one." I gave him a weak smile.

"Come on, I'll walk you to your car, and we can head over to Bernie's."

"Sounds like a plan." I began walking in the direction of my car, and Reed was a step behind me. I turned my head to look back at Reed. His hand was in the air seconds from hitting me with the butt of the gun. I blinked in surprise before I felt the sharp pain from the hit and wobbled. My head felt heavy, and the world spun.

"You just had to dig into the blood, didn't you?" I heard him mumble before I lost consciousness.

Chapter 2

The pain in the back of my head was the first thing I was aware of when I gained consciousness. I wasn't ready to open my eyes, so I listened to the room around me. The events from the night were coming back to me. Reed had knocked me out at the crime scene. Why the hell would he do that? Unless he was involved with the murders somehow. I tensed as I thought about the possibility. How could he be involved? What was it he said before I blacked out? Something about the blood? Shit, what the hell had I gotten myself into?

"I know you're awake. You might as well open your eyes." Reed's voice was sharp, and I blinked open my eyes. I tried to raise my hand to my head, but both my hands were bound in front of me with zip ties.

"What the hell is going on, Reed?" I asked. I pulled my wrists against the restraints.

"Isn't it obvious? I kidnapped you." He was sitting in a leather recliner across from me. I was lying on my side on the brown leather sofa. At least a pillow was tucked under my head. My shoulder ached from the angle of my hands.

"Did you bring me to your house?" I asked. I stared at myself on the black screen of the television. I didn't look any worse for wear. Too bad he'd hit the back of my head, not the front. I wouldn't be able to see any bumps from this angle. I could certainly feel one, though.

"Yeah, I didn't want to chance bringing you anywhere else. My house is sound and light proofed. No one will hear you if you scream." There was an edge to his voice. "While it's daylight, no sun will seep through the windows either." His eyes met mine across the room before he focused back on the book that lay open in his lap. A wine glass filled with a red liquid sat next to him on the twisted metal end table. It was a weird piece with jagged lines like the designer couldn't decide which way they wanted the metal to go, so he chose all of them. Reed took a sip from the glass. The liquid stained his lips red. Even now, a heat rushed through me as I watched his tongue glide over his bottom lip. I shook my head to clear it of the absurdity.

"No sound or light? Why would you do that to your home?" I asked. I couldn't fathom the need for a sound and light proofed house.

"How unfortunate? I always thought you were the smart one on day shift. You haven't figured it out yet, my dear, Hope." His eyes never left the book. I watched as he used one finger to turn the page. I was beginning to think I was an annoyance to his reading.

I thought back to what he'd said, my investigation, and the previous murders. "Was the blood missing from the previous victim?" I asked. I didn't like this train of thought. But Laura would be damn proud. It was because of her and those damn shows that my mind even traveled there. Okay, I may have watched an episode or ten of True Blood, but that was it. Those were my kind of vampires. Oh god, what the hell was I thinking? Vampires, was I really going there? The investigator in me was screaming at the ridiculous train of my thoughts.

"Ah, now you're piecing it together. Yes, both victims were drained of blood. I took precautions to make sure no one would think anything of it and only assume they bled out. How is it you were not convinced?" His eyebrow arched as he lowered his book to study me.

"I noticed there wasn't enough blood at the scene. I told you this while you acted like you were helping me with the case." I rolled my eyes. "I should have known. Murderers often insert themselves into the investigation. I thought you were being my friend." I sighed and tried to sit up without the use of my hands. It was difficult, but I managed. I didn't like being lower than he was. I tried to shift to see what was behind me. I needed to figure a way out of this place. Away from Reed. "So, now that you have me here, what are you planning to do with me?" I asked.

"Oh darling, you will be my progeny. You're smart and more than capable of living in this world than most. I knew that the day we met." His eyes sparkled. "I have to get the approval of the council first, of course. As I was not prepared to turn you quite so soon, I thought I would have time to groom you first." His finger traced around the rim of the glass before he lifted it to take another drink. By the look of the stain on his lips, he was drinking blood. My stomach lurched. It was probably the blood from the crime scene. His eyes met mine, and his lips curled into a wicked grin. I pressed my lips together to hold back my nausea. He gave me one last cursory glance before he resumed reading.

"Progeny? What does that even mean?" I asked. I thought it was weird how his speech had changed. In the office, he seemed like a regular cop. Now he spoke as though he were older, more refined. It was giving me whiplash. I needed to get the hell out of here.

"It means, my dear, that as soon as the sun sets, I will go to the council. I will ask their permission to turn you into a vampire. I believe I've made a fine choice in a new progeny. I wasn't planning to turn you quite so soon, but your voracious appetite for investigation has necessitated immediate action from me. I couldn't exactly let you go and tell others what you've discovered, now could I?" He tapped his finger on his lips. "Did you tell anyone besides me what you were investigating?" He closed the distance between us and took a seat on the couch next to me. His eyes locked on mine, and he spoke again. "Hope, dear, who else knew about the missing blood?"

I felt mesmerized by his intense gaze. "The coroner," my mouth moved automatically to answer. I knew I shouldn't be saying anything to him, but I couldn't control my mouth.

"Does your partner know?" he asked.

Again, I felt my control over my answer disappear. "No, I hadn't gotten a chance to tell him at the range earlier. I wanted him to enjoy his dinner with his wife." I blinked.

He smiled. "Good girl, I don't believe the coroner will dig too deeply into it. You were the only one who seemed to be engrossed in discovering where the blood could have gone." His fingers trailed a line down my cheekbone and stopped under my chin, lifting it to meet his eyes again. "Why couldn't you let it go?" he asked.

"It was the only thing that I didn't understand about the case. I am an investigator; it was a lead. I followed it," I answered simply. I was trying to find the killer. Apparently, I was on the right track.

"Hmm, well, that's good. I would hate to have to hurt anyone you care about." His finger felt like acid against my skin as his threat rang through my head. I would find a way to kill this man if he ever went after anyone I loved.

"I'll kill you if you hurt any one of them," I spat back at him.

"Ah, there's the spirit and fire I so adore. I intend to mold that fire in you for my own purposes. Before long, you will have the ultimate gift from me. Immortality. I can only hope you treasure it, as I have treasured my own."

"You know that they're going to ask questions when I don't show up to work today." I probably shouldn't have mentioned that, but I hoped people noticed. Carson, at the very least, would notice. I said I'd give him an update today.

"Oh?" His eyebrow rose. "The guys at Bernie's last night watched you have a few too many drinks for your birthday. The Captain said it was the least he could do since he hadn't actually seen you celebrate in years." His mouth curved into that wicked grin that I was beginning to hate. "Sorry, princess, but they think you'll be in bed all day nursing a wicked hangover." He stood; a self-satisfied smile plastered on his pretty face.

I wanted to punch him. "No one's going to believe that. I wasn't even at Bernie's last night." I narrowed my eyes at him.

"Oh? But they believe that you were." He tapped his temple. "A few well-placed memories into an already inebriated mind is child's play." I scowled. He could manipulate people's minds. Shit, what else could he do? I let out a breath. I didn't know what else to say. He'd obviously covered all of his bases. I couldn't exactly say he'd been a bad cop in the time I'd known him. He nodded once and strode down the hall.

I whipped my head around, trying to find a way to get out of here. He talked about immortality as a treasure. I assumed he was planning on killing me. He was obviously delusional about having immortality. He was just another sicko murderer who thought himself above everyone else. I saw the door on the far side of the room behind me.

"You'll never be able to open that door. You might as well get some rest before tonight. You're going to need it for what I have planned for you." His voice rang clear down the hall. How did he know I was looking at the door? He must just assume that since I'm trapped here, I would be trying to escape. I pulled on my wrists, trying to loosen the zip ties. I felt the blood as I pulled harder, and the hard plastic bit into my skin. I loosened them slightly but not enough. I yanked harder and tried to slip my hands through the plastic. The blood flowing from the cuts was helping to lubricate my wrists. Maybe I would be able to slip my hands through the small space I was making. I kept trying to yank my hands apart.

I felt his presence before I heard him. "Are you trying to tempt me, young one?" Reed made his way around the couch and knelt before me. He lifted my wrists to his nose and inhaled. I yanked my hands back against my chest, and his mouth broke into a vicious smile. He pulled my hands back toward him. I jerked my legs up and kicked him. The impact of my feet on his calves hadn't even phased him. He licked where the blood was oozing out from under the restraints. His eyes lit as he tasted my blood. My stomach lurched at the hungry look in his eyes. He slid the zip ties down my arm and licked around the wounds. I watched as they sealed before my eyes.

"What the hell?" I asked as I stared wide-eyed at where my wrists had just been bleeding. There was nothing but a small pucker of a line where the plastic had cut my skin. I watched as even that disappeared.

"I told you. I'm immortal. With the blood of immortality, comes certain gifts. I can heal your wounds with my saliva. Do not do that again. Though, I do enjoy the exquisite taste of your blood. It's like a fine wine. I find you to be quite delectable. I can't wait until you trust me enough to share my bed." He licked his lips again, and his eyes darkened with a hungry desire.

"Never gonna happen." I spat in his face. He lifted his hand to wipe away the saliva and blinked down at me.

"That's not what you were thinking at the station. You liked staring at my broad chest while we were working together. You wanted me, for more than just the assistance I was offering." His eyes continued to bore into mine.

"That was before you kidnapped me against my will. I thought you were being a nice guy. I didn't think you were a murdering sicko." I sat back, trying to get further away from him. I didn't want to be this close to him. My heart ratcheted in my chest, and I knew I was in danger. More danger than I may have realized. He was a predator, and I was prey. I needed him to turn his focus on anything else.

"I only kidnapped you out of necessity. Please, you need to rest." His eyes locked on mine. He spoke one word, and my eyes drifted shut. I was going to figure out how he was able to do that to me.

Chapter 3

"Wake up, Princess. It's time to meet your destiny." I felt a hand on my shoulder and jerked away from it instinctually. "Come now, the council awaits." His smooth voice soothed over me. I felt instantly relaxed before a jolt of shock hit me.

"What? What council?" I blinked my eyes open in the dim room. "Where am I?" I didn't recognize the living room. I blinked a few times before it all came rushing back to me. I yanked on my arms. The plastic bit into my wrists, and I sighed. I was hoping it was all a dream. Reed stopped before me.

A lock of his dark hair fell into his eye. He was wearing a tailored black suit with a thin burgundy tie. I had to admit, he looked dapper in the suit. "My dear, I must present you to the council before they will approve your transformation. I laid out a dress for you in the bedroom. I expect you to be impeccable." He took my wrists and broke the bindings.

"You expect me to put on some gown and accompany you to my death. Uh, no, I don't think so." I sat back against the couch. There was no way I was going to volunteer for whatever he had in store. "I think you forget that you kidnapped me." I crossed my arms over my chest and stared back at him. I didn't intend on letting him bind my wrists again. I was going to exploit a weakness the next chance I get.

He bent so his eyes were level with mine. I looked away. "You will put on the dress."

I narrowed my eyes and glared at him. "No, I won't." I tried to look away from him, but I couldn't manage it. It was like he had trapped me in his gaze.

"You will go put on the dress and join me for the council meeting."

I stood without thought and walked down the hall and into the bedroom. There was a rich burgundy gown on the bed. It matched the tie Reed had on. I didn't want to put on the dress, but my hands moved without my permission. In a few minutes, I was standing in front of a full-length mirror wearing the long dress. It had a slit that went all the way to my upper thigh. It was elegant and sexy. The thin spaghetti straps ran to the two triangles holding in my breasts. It was good I was well-endowed to fill out the dress. I glanced around the bedroom. The charcoal gray bedspread matched the manly feel of the room. The headboard was a rich black leather with a footboard that reminded me of a sleigh. I hated that I was standing in the bedroom of the man who somehow could take complete control of me. I clenched my hands into fists.

The door opened behind me. "Ah, I knew you would be lovely in that dress." He closed the distance and stopped behind me. His arm skated around my waist, and my whole body stiffened at his proximity. My skin crawled where his fingers grazed along my stomach. He looked at me through the mirror. "I can't wait until you welcome me with that fire. You are such a beautiful woman."

"Don't touch me," I stepped to the side and out of his grasp. I turned on him. "I will never welcome you. I don't know why you think I ever would. You are holding me against my will." I stormed out of the room and back into the living room. With my hands free, I went for the door. He was in front of it before I had made it a few steps. He moved so fast he was a blur. "What? How? Uh, how were you able to do that?" I sputtered.

"It's all part of the gift of a vampire. By this time tomorrow, you will know everything," he said. He whispered something into my ear before I could move away. My knees weakened beneath me. I fell into his arms, and everything went black.

I blinked my eyes open in the middle of a dim-lit room. I was stretched out on an altar. There were six people looking down at me from their dais. Reed was standing next to me. I shifted, so my feet were away from the people and stood, brushing my hand down my dress. I couldn't believe I woke up on an altar. It was like I was about to be the sacrifice, and the group was waiting to watch my suffering. By the looks on their faces, maybe they were. I noticed that each person wore a mask of boredom, but something behind that spoke of intrigue. One woman with long hair that flowed over her breasts licked her lips when our eyes met. What the hell was she so excited about? A shiver ran down my spine at the possible answer for her excitement. Reed hadn't exactly filled me in on what was about to happen here. I was surely the sacrifice.

"Progeny, what is your name?" A stern woman looked down at me. She had the strong jawline of Mediterranean women. She wore the mask of boredom like she'd seen this many times before. "Speak, girl," her voice boomed in the open room.

I took a step back, startled. "Hope," I responded. Reed's hand slipped to my lower back, and he guided me forward. I scowled at him. He touched me as though we were intimate. Did these people know he kidnapped me? Was this the standard for vampires?

"Hmm, interesting, Is this the detective we spoke of, Reed?" The woman tapped her finger against her thin lips. I wasn't sure what she thought was so interesting about my name. Her focus turned to Reed.

"Yes, ma'am, she is the detective. She has shown promise in the field and will be a welcome asset to our council and the collective." He squared his shoulders after he was finished. I narrowed my eyes. So, I was here because I was a good cop? I thought it was because I discovered his secret. Was he keeping that from them?

"And you Reed swear to teach your progeny the way of our world. You will take responsibility for her actions, all of her actions? She will live with you for no more than five years in which you will train her and educate her to be an asset to our collective."

"Excuse me, don't I have a say in this? You actually want me to live with this repulsive man." I turned my head and spat on him.

"No progeny understands the choice and gift we offer. Therefore, no, Hope, you do not have a choice. You would not understand the choice you were making regardless." She waved her hand flippantly. "Reed Longfellow, do you agree to the terms?"

"I do, mistress. I will take responsibility and educate my progeny for a period of up to five years. As soon as she is educated and ready, I will bring her back to the council." He bowed his head. "Thank you for your kindness in allowing me to bestow my gift upon another worthy progeny." He lifted his head, and I noticed him make eye contact with one particular woman on the council. I saw her nod imperceptibly toward him. What was that about? I promised myself I would remember and look into that later. I wondered about the formality of whatever was happening. They were talking about my death, yet they were so formal about my being educated. What happened after I left Reed? Not that I planned to stick around him for that long. There was no way I was staying with my kidnapper for five years. I'd heard plenty about Stockholm syndrome, no thank you. I was not that girl. I planned on getting the hell away from Reed as soon as I possibly could.

"So it is decreed, Hope Matthews will now be, Hope Longfellow, under the guidance and protection of Reed Longfellow." She bowed her head, and her hair fell forward, obscuring her face. I felt my heart race in my chest. What had just happened? Did they really think they could make me stay with Reed for five years? No way, I would escape this madness the first chance I got.

The rest of the council spoke in unison. "So, it's decreed."

Something fundamental just happened. I looked between the members. Reed took a step toward me. His arms came up to wrap around me. I held my arms out and backed away from him. I really didn't want him touching me. I didn't know how he kept knocking me out, but maybe I'd be able to leave. I needed to get the hell away from him, from this, whatever it was. I didn't like the way Reed was looking at me. It had my stomach tied in knots. I glanced at the dais. There were six other people here. They wouldn't help Reed keep me against my will, would they? "You can't do this. You're holding me against my will. You have to let me go. I'm a cop."

A perilous laugh came from the dais. "Oh, how I do love this part." The woman who'd looked so stern earlier now had a delighted smile on her face. What was about to happen that she looked so happy about? I wasn't sure I wanted to find out.

My eyes widened as a realization hit me. They weren't going to help me. I was on my own here. I held my hands in front of me, ready to fight. I spent years in the gym combat training. There was no way I was going down without a fight. Reed advanced on me. His arms went for mine, and I jumped back swiftly out of his reach. I kicked my foot up before he realized what was happening and made contact with his chest. It was like kicking stone. He didn't even budge. He grabbed my ankle swiftly, knocking me back on the floor. I hit with a loud thump as my shoulder crushed into the red carpet. He dropped my ankle, and I spun onto my back. I reached my hands to flip myself up. Before I could get my hands in place, Reed was on top of me. His knees moved to straddle me; his weight pinning me to the floor. I lifted my leg to kick him from behind, but his hand reached back and caught it before I hit his back.

"Mmm, I like it when you're feisty." He dropped his head, and his nose moved up my body, taking a deep breath. I was so startled by the motion I didn't move. "You smell good enough to eat."

When I recovered, I tried to punch the side of his head. My knuckles connected with his jaw, and I cried out as I felt the bones in my hand break against his skin. I had thrown a correct punch, so why the hell did my hand break? "What the— " He grabbed my hands and held them firmly above my head. He shifted his weight back to my thighs so I couldn't move my legs. I was trapped. The realization had me panting, my heart already racing in my chest. I tried to pull and struggle against him, but it was no use. He was much stronger than me.

His mouth descended on my neck, and I felt the sharp puncture of my skin. I screamed. It sounded like there was water rushing through my ears. My head began to throb as I felt him pulling against my neck. I tried to jerk my body, but Reed was an immovable force. Something changed after he punctured my neck. My limbs felt heavy like I couldn't move them. I was screaming in my head to fight, but physically I couldn't do anything. His knee moved between my legs, sliding against the apex of my thighs. He rubbed himself against me, and I could feel his hardness against my stomach. My skin crawled, but I felt his arousal as if it were my own.

His mouth left my neck, and he looked down at me with such admiration. It was hard to look away from him. His arms slipped below my back and legs. I was lifted onto the altar when I had awoken. My stomach flipped at the idea of being on full display for the council. I couldn't even move my neck to look at them. Reed moved back over me, his erection resting against my core. I was relieved I was still fully clothed, or he'd be dangerously close to my entrance. For some strange reason, a wave of desire washed through me at the thought. What was happening to me?

His eyes locked on mine as he took something that was handed to him from the right. I saw the glint of the knife as he used it to cut through the skin on his wrist. He pressed the cut to my mouth. I felt my heart flutter in my chest. I could hear the darkness welcoming me like a warm blanket on a cold night. My eyelids drooped. He pressed his skin harder against my mouth. Copper filled my mouth, but I was too tired to drink. I wanted to follow the darkness. Everything felt so light, like I could drift away. Flashes of Carter at the range, talking to his wife. The guys at the bar, roasting me for my last failed boyfriend. Image after image of my failed life filled my head. What was I really holding onto?

"Swallow, Hope, you need to drink," he commanded. My eyes stayed closed. I knew he couldn't compel me with my eyes closed, or at least I hoped that was the case. I would rather die than become like him. His lips pressed against my ear. "Taste the sweetness of my elixir. Drink, Hope, it's delicious." Suddenly, the copper changed to the sweetest thing I'd ever tasted. I couldn't not drink it. I sucked hard against the sweetness filling my mouth. I needed more. My strength began to return, and Reed wasn't holding me down. I gripped his wrist and pulled it tight against my mouth. I swallowed each mouthful of the delicious liquid. When it was taken, I gripped at the air, grabbing whatever I could get my hands on.

"You liked that, didn't you?" a deep voice rasped against my ear. I couldn't think of anything beyond the sweetness. I wanted it back so badly. I was so aroused, my heartbeat pulsed between my legs. I wanted to find the pleasure my release would bring. I ground my hips against the hardness between my legs. My head swam, and I continued to rock my hips. Searching desperately for anything that would provide me relief. It was useless. I wasn't going to find my release that way. I was driven by carnal desire.

A soft chuckle sounded next to my ear. "This is my favorite part."

Lips pressed against mine. I flicked my tongue out and tasted the sweetness. I wrapped my hands around Reed's neck and pulled him closer, gripping his hair between my fingers. When he growled, it reverberated through my body. I wanted more. I rubbed against his hardness, creating a delicious friction. I tasted him with a hunger I couldn't seem to satiate. My tongue explored as my hips ground against the harness between my legs. Hungry, I was incredibly hungry for him. It felt like every nerve ending in my body sparked to life at the same time. Every touch ignited the fire within me. I needed more, so much more.

"Do you want me to soothe that ache inside you?" I felt a hand move down my body. Fire licked every place his fingers grazed the thin fabric of the dress. I moaned, reaching my mouth toward those delicious lips again. I didn't feel like myself. I could think of nothing beyond the desire pulsing through my entire body. I'd never been so filled with need. There was a desperation that I needed filled.

"Yes, oh God, yes," I cried out. My fingers curled around his shoulder, pulling him closer. I needed his body closer to mine. My other hand drifted down yanking open the buttons on his pants. I kept grinding my hips against his leg. I felt like a wild animal, ready to have her way with her prey. Yet, I didn't feel like the predator here. I yanked at his belt, but his hand stopped me from going further. I stared wide-eyed at those dark soulful eyes. A small smile curved his lips.

"Patience, you will be rewarded." I felt myself being lifted from the altar. "If you'll excuse us," he said. My head still swam, and a wave of dizziness hit me. The dim-lit room disappeared, and I was being carried down a dark hall. The door opened, and Reed lowered me onto a soft mattress. His lips lowered to my neck, his heavy body pressed against mine. I relished in the weight of him pressing me into the mattress. It had been too long since I felt the weight of a man on top of me. Oh, God, I was desperate. My head swam with desire. My core ached for a release. I'd never been so desperate. "Hope, I knew you would be delectable. I can't wait to be inside you." A hand slipped the strap from my shoulder, and the soft press of lips moved down my arm. My nipple puckered as soon as it was exposed to the cold air. The cold was quickly replaced by the warmth of Reed's tongue. He lapped at my nipples, sucking them each into his mouth. I moaned at the sensations pulsing through me. I felt ripples of energy running from my nipples to my core. I wasn't sure I could get any more aroused, but as he sucked on my nipple, I knew that was untrue. How was he doing this to me? I felt every lick, every suck as though he were attached to some wire that sent pleasure through me with every touch.

"Oh God," I arched up into his mouth. I wasn't sure how much more I could take.

"Hope, I've wanted you since the moment you walked into the precinct." His mouth made its way down as he slid the dress off my body. There was something about what he said that had me trying to focus around the blur of desire. Precinct, what about the precinct? There was something I was supposed to be remembering. Lips moved down my body, and my back arched again. "Say you want me." His voice sounded pleading. "My blood and passion run through your veins." His head rested between my legs. He licked between my folds, and I moaned, throwing my head back. Finally, I would get what I needed so desperately.

"Oh, God." I cried out, all the sensations hitting me at once. His tongue was amazing. It moved so fast in all the right places. In moments, I was crying out as my climax hit me like a freight train. He kept going, prolonging my orgasm. My hands gripped his hair as he continued to pleasure me. When a second orgasm hit, I pulled his hair and clutched him against me.

"Tell me you want me. I'm not doing anything more unless you tell me, Hope." His mouth left me, and I felt the absence immediately.

"Oh, God, I want you. I want to feel you inside me." I ran my fingers through his lush hair.

"I need you to say my name, Hope," he growled.

"Fuck me, please," I begged.

"Damn, you make it so hard. Just say my name. I want to know that it's me you want. We're going to spend five years together. This is your first lesson. This is what the transformation does to you. I transferred my emotions to you through the blood. I need you to consent before I go any further. Tell me you want me, Hope. Just say my name." His lips found my ear, and he nipped the lobe.

My eyes snapped to his. My head was clearing since I'd gotten the orgasm I so desperately craved. I felt my body relaxing as he kissed down my neck. My mind was returning to thoughts beyond desperately needing release. My hands roamed down his chest. The buttons were open on his shirt. I wasn't sure when that happened. My fingers wandered lower. The button was pulled free from his pants. This was Reed, the man who kidnapped me. The man who just agreed to kill me. He probably did just kill me. My body no longer felt like my own. Something was changing. I could feel it. But did I want this with him?

He stopped and looked down at me. I watched as he bit his lip. "Do you want more blood? I could tell you enjoyed it." His eyebrow rose.

I cringed. "No, I don't want blood, Reed." My voice was surprisingly steady. I looked down to his bare chest. I had to admit I liked the feel of his taut muscles beneath my fingers. He'd already made me come. I could let him finish what we started. It didn't seem like that big of a deal. But something inside me told me it was. I could feel his erection through the fabric of his pants. I lay bare to him. My dress was discarded somewhere on the floor. I felt vulnerable under his penetrating gaze.

"What is it you want, my dear, Hope?" his voice was rough. I could hear the strain of holding back. He wanted me. The desperation in his voice was telling. He wanted to be inside me. I wasn't sure what had stopped him. He could have easily been inside me while I was so lost to the pleasure of my last orgasm. Yet, he stopped. I flipped back to what he'd said. He needed me to say his name, to consent to him. I shook my head to clear it. I didn't want this. I didn't want him. My stomach clenched at the realization of what just happened. Why was I so willing? What was it that made me so desperate? He mentioned transferring his desire. How? How was he able to transfer his desire so that I wanted him beyond all reason? There was so much about what just happened that I didn't understand. "Come on, Hope. I can make it so good for you. I will always make it good for you." His voice came out rough. He was struggling to hold back. A ran my hands over the muscles of his chest, licking my lips.

It was tempting. "I want to go home, Reed. I don't want this."

He froze. Disappointment flashed in his eyes. "Are you sure? You don't know what you're missing. I can give you what you want, Hope. I can give you everything."

"I'm sure I want to go home. You kidnapped me. You think I'm going to want you after you took me against my will. What was it about your blood that made me ravenous for you, anyway? That was not my desire." He cursed and got off me. I shivered at both being exposed and at what just happened between us. My body, my desire, didn't feel like my own. I didn't mind the satiated feeling I had afterward. My body was humming post-orgasm. Reed wasn't wrong about giving me what I needed. He was magnificent, but it was hard to look past the fact that he kidnapped me.

"It's the blood. It makes you aroused. I was aroused by you, so I transferred that feeling to you. Apparently, it didn't last." He smoothed his hand down his trousers.

I smirked. "Wasn't what you were expecting? Did you think your little arousal trick was going to last longer? Were you hoping I'd beg for you?" I smirked, watching the annoyance play across his features. "Too bad, I'll never want you, Reed. Now, are you going to bring me home or what?" I swung my legs over the side of the large bed. I remembered starting in the council room with six people at the dais, watching. I was glad not everything happened with an audience.

He turned on me, pulling his coat taut over his shoulders. "Yes, my dear, I'll bring you home." His lips curved into a coy grin. "We have five years to get to know each other, intimately. I'm sure you'll love it." There was an edge to his voice that had my stomach flipping. *Five years, he thought I was sticking around for five years. Was he delusional, or did he hit his head?*

"No, I'm going home, to my home. Back to my life." I grabbed my dress off the bed and slipped it back over my head. I hated wearing dresses of any kind, and this was the worst. Who went out in gowns beyond those on the red carpet?

"You can't go back to your life, my dear. You are a vampire. As soon as the blood works its way through your body, you will be turned. The life you had before today no longer exists." His voice held a bit of amusement. I wanted to wipe that smirk off his face.

"So, how does it work exactly?" I asked. I wasn't sure what to expect. Would I get that craving for sex again, like when he'd given me his blood? I shuddered. I didn't like feeling like I wasn't in control of my own desires. I wanted to be in control. I needed some of my dignity back. Not that I regretted what just happened. I was a girl. I had needs. He provided for my needs. It wasn't much different than any other one night stand I'd had. Hell, I probably would have taken Reed to my bed at some point if it wasn't for the whole kidnapping thing. I certainly enjoyed admiring him at work. I wasn't going to be a victim here. I wasn't going to regret the fabulous orgasm he had given me. I was in control. He stopped when I asked. That was the end of it. Now, I just needed to understand what was going to happen next? Not that I actually believed I was turning into a vampire. Maybe Reed was more delusional than I first thought.

"There is one small thing that needs to happen for the full transformation. I wanted to have some fun with you first." He pulled down the collar of his shirt. "Fulfilling your desire and sex is part of the ritual, but you have to ask for me, willingly. Most do. Most actually beg the way you did at first." He licked his lips. My eyes narrowed. I hated that I'd begged him. It was part of it. I couldn't help myself. My core clenched at the reminder of how badly I'd needed him and how well he delivered. Dammit, I needed to get that out of my head. I would not beg for him like that again, ever. A sly smile curled his lips, and I hated that he probably knew what I was thinking.

"What's the small thing?" I asked.

"Your death." His smile turned devious, and he stepped closer to me.

Chapter 4

My eyes widened as the realization hit. I needed to get the hell away from him. I flew off the bed and to the opposite side of the room. I didn't realize this was going to be dinner and a show. I held my hands out in front of me, ready to move into action if I needed to. I had fought him earlier and knew I was outmatched, but damned if I was going to give up. He just said he needed to kill me. I needed to stall him, so I could get the hell out of here. I didn't actually want to die. "Um, so when you say my death, do you mean you're going to actually kill me?" I backed into the wall behind me and flinched. I tried to side-step, but Reed was there in an instant. His finger trailed down my jaw, my neck, my chest. My breath caught in my throat.

"You, my dear, will be a magnificent vampire." He breathed against my neck. "You'll beg for me soon enough. You won't be able to help yourself." he chuckled darkly. "Although, I do love a good chase." He inhaled deeply against my neck, and I stiffened. "I love how you smell with my blood coursing through you. It's intoxicating." My stomach turned, and bile rose in my throat. I couldn't die. Not like this. I had to fight to get away from him.

I jerked my knee up into his groin. He groaned, but it didn't have the effect I was hoping for. Most men were crippled by a knee to the family jewels. Not Reed. I tried it again, jerking my knee up with all the strength I had in me. "I'm not going to be a vampire. Not if you don't kill me."

"Oh, my dear, I'm going to kill you. I've already started the process. You're weak from blood loss. The only reason you feel strong right now is because my blood runs through your veins. I have to say, I love the effect I'm having on you. It doesn't make me want you any less." His finger ran over my neck as the other hand gripped both my hands above my head. I felt his sharp nail scrape down my neck and the trickle of blood in its wake. His tongue slid up my neck. "Mmm, you taste so good, Hope." My name came out like a prayer on his lips.

"You're repulsive," I cursed, trying to yank my hands from his grasp.

"Mmm, I like you in this position." His hands tightened on my wrists.

I jammed my knee up as hard as I could. I watched him wince at the contact for a millisecond before his satisfied mask returned. I was starting to think he liked it when I hurt him. Like he was getting off on it. "I like watching you wince in pain. I know it hurts a little. Otherwise, you wouldn't grunt every time I made contact." I looked back at him, defiantly. "Maybe I'll keep doing it until you let me go. It's not like you can have kids or anything." I jammed my knee up again. A smirk lit my face as he winced. He couldn't hold both my hands and my legs. Could I hurt him bad enough to be able to get away?

"You're enjoying my pain." He licked up my neck again. "I like this side of you. I knew you were devoted to your work, but seeing you in action is inspiring." He licked the crook of my neck, and I shivered. "It feels good to cause pain, doesn't it, Hope? You want to hurt me. Come on, Hope, admit you enjoy causing me pain." He pressed himself against me. I could feel his erection against my stomach. He was getting off on this. I was arousing him by hurting him. My stomach rolled.

He was right. I enjoyed hurting him. I wanted him to suffer at my hands. He kidnapped me. Anything I did was a result of being taken against my will. I was trying to survive. The fact that I was enjoying his pain didn't change that. I wanted to see him suffer. I fantasized about hurting him even more. I hated having my hands bound. I hated how he pressed up against me. I hated how much I didn't hate feeling his body pressed against mine. There was something seriously wrong with me. "I can't do anything with you binding my wrists."

"We both know that's not true. You were doing just fine with your legs. I enjoyed having my head between them, giving you pleasure." His mouth moved to nip my earlobe. "You can't hide how you feel from me, Hope. I felt your heart rate increase. I can hear it flutter now with every touch. I know you're not as repulsed by me as you're letting on."

"You're mistaking adrenaline for attraction. You just got me off, and now you want to kill me. I think you're the one who's confused." My voice rose. "Do you normally kill the women you've been with, or is it my sparkling personality?" I rubbed my knee up the inside of his thigh. Maybe I could play on his desire for me. Get him to let me go long enough for me to run. He was talking about killing me. I didn't really want to stick around for that part.

"You haven't seen anything, yet." He dropped his hands to my neck, squeezing. I tried to push him away with both my hands, but he was an immovable force. I clawed at his hair, yanking out the strands as I tried to get free. "Although, I do love to feel your fiery passion as you try to fight me off, I'm getting rather bored. I need to be done with this already. I have a job to get to in a few hours." He pressed his lips together. "Sorry, I couldn't enjoy this any further. You're a wildcat I look forward to taming. You are mine." He cupped my face in his hands, and I was mesmerized by the sparkle in his dark eyes. I hadn't noticed before how dark they were. He smiled, and in a flash, his hands moved cupping my head. A sharp crack sounded, and darkness descended on me. In the few seconds before I died, I vowed revenge on Reed. I would make him suffer if it was the last thing ever I did.

I woke cocooned in satin. My arm stretched out and felt the smooth fabric of the sheets beneath me. I moaned, my head spinning with the flashes of memories. Reed's hair between my bare thighs, me crying out as an orgasm rocketed through me. Reed's tongue licking up my neck as he held me bound against the wall. The devilish smile that curved Reed's lips before everything went black. I shook my head. What the hell happened?

My body felt strange. I stretched my arms above my head, feeling each of my muscles uncoil as I pulled them. The room around me was strange. The sheets were ruby-red and matched the thick curtains on the windows. A mahogany armoire was directly across the room. It matched the vanity dresser. I focused back on the window. There wasn't even a shimmer of light coming through the drapes. Everything here was so dark. It seemed unlikely that not a single stream of light would penetrate through the dark room. I rolled onto my back. A deep red canopy was above me. What was the deal with the different shades of red?

I threw my legs over the side of the bed. I was dressed in the gown from last night. How did I get here? I couldn't remember anything after Reed's hands were on my throat. I furrowed my brow, thinking. He said he'd gotten bored with me fighting. Did he kill me? I vaguely remembered the snapping before everything went dark. My stomach turned. I couldn't believe how caught up I'd gotten in the pleasure that I forgot about him kidnapping me. I told myself I wasn't going to regret it. Being with Reed was like a one-night stand. He hadn't even really penetrated me, so it was fine. I was chalking it up to it being too long since I'd last gotten laid. It had nothing to do with how sexy Reed looked without a shirt or the fact that his blood made the desire within me insane. What was that? A little attention and arousal, and apparently, I'd forgive anything. I didn't mind the orgasm. It was earth-shattering. I would never regret that part. I licked my lips thinking about it and my core clenched. Damn, I would need to get that under control.

There was a dull ache in my stomach. I got up, glancing back at the room. All the red was bothering me. I would never decorate a room in different shades of red. It was weird. I headed for the kitchen. Something smelled delicious. Reed was sitting at the kitchen counter, a paper in front of him. "I called the chief for you. He hopes you're feeling better soon. He also took your request for the night shift." He didn't look up from the paper. "He agreed that you could switch immediately. Looks like we'll be partners in more ways than one, Matthews. I can't tell you how much I'm looking forward to it." His eyes flashed up to me, and a devious smile split his mouth. I hated him. I hated him so much. How dare he go behind my back to speak to the chief?

I narrowed my eyes at him. "What the hell did you do, Reed?"

"Well, I couldn't exactly have you working on day shift when you can't go out during the day, now could I? You have to earn daylight privileges. I have to be sure you're not going to use the sun to kill yourself." He bent the newspaper to actually look at me when he spoke.

"What the hell, Reed? Why can't I go out during the day?" I asked.

"Oh, my dear, you can't be that incompetent. You understood every facet of what happened last night. Even while you were screaming for more, you knew." His eyes narrowed on me. I didn't like the flutter I felt at his intense gaze. "What we did, there's no coming back from.

We're connected. You will be my progeny for the next five years, or until I decide you're fit to go out on your own." He paused, watching me. What did he mean there was no going back? How could one night change so much? My throat felt tight. He nodded as though he understood what I was experiencing. "I explained to the chief that you had the flu, so you won't be expected back for a few days. You'll need to control your bloodlust before you can return." Reed pushed a glass filled with a red liquid toward me. The smell hit me, and I wanted it, desperately.

"What's that?" I glanced down at the glass. The pang in my stomach grew. I needed whatever was in that glass. A small voice in my head already knew what he was going to say. I just wasn't ready to accept it.

"Blood, it will fill the ache you're feeling." His eyes flicked up toward me. His eyebrow quirked up. I could almost see his intrigue. He pushed the glass closer. "Come now, love. You need to control your thirst. You won't be able to be around humans until you're satiated." I licked my lips involuntarily and flinched back. I couldn't drink blood. What the hell was I thinking? Why did I want it so much?

"I prefer coffee in the morning. Maybe some eggs and bacon." The reality of everything that happened hit me all at once. Reed had fed me his blood and snapped my neck. That was the sound I'd heard before everything went dark. This bastard actually killed me. Now I had to drink blood, and I couldn't go out during the day. I hated him. My blood boiled beneath my skin with my hatred. It enraged me that he was right. I could smell the blood in the glass, and my mouth watered. I wanted to drink it. My body craved it. I licked my lips slowly as I stared at the dark red.

"Come on, Hope, you need to drink it. You'll feel better once you do." He stood up and walked around the table, stopping in front of me. He picked up the glass and held it in front of my mouth. He'd reduced me to a whimpering fiend, desperate for the satisfaction only he could bring last night. Now, he was trying to reduce me to a damn toddler by feeding me. No, I was not going to let him debase me like this. I was still Hope Matthews, the baddest bitch of a detective. I was good at what I did because I was strong. I could handle his bullshit. I grabbed the glass out of his hand. His eyes widened in surprise.

I watched the liquid slosh against the sides when I took it. I wanted the blood in this glass as much as I wanted air. I couldn't stop myself. My eyes focused on Reed as I gulped hungrily. I licked my lips and set the empty glass back on the table. My glare never leaving Reed. "I hate you for what you've done to me. I will always hate you." I clenched my hands into fists. I wanted to pummel him until I couldn't feel anything anymore. He killed me. He took everything away from me. I knew without a doubt that everything he had told me was the truth. I just didn't know what that meant for me now. How would I continue to live my life as a vampire? Reed took a step toward me. His proximity both made my skin crawl and my core clench. I needed to stop remembering how hard he'd made me come. My eyes narrowed. "What?"

He ran the back of his hand down my cheek, and I stiffened. "I knew you'd make a magnificent vampire. This, my darling, is only the beginning." He paused, his hand still resting on my cheek. Then in a second, he turned away. "We'll begin your training right away. You need to get acclimated to life as a vampire. The sooner, the better. Today is the first day of your immortal life. I can't wait to see how you honor me." He turned back to look at me. His eyes shined with pride. I wanted to wipe that smug look off his face. He was such an arrogant bastard.

"I will never honor you. I hate you." I spat.

"Oh, darling, you will grow to love me, or your life will be increasingly difficult. As I said, this is only the beginning." He walked around me, stopping behind me. I could feel him against my back. He whispered next to my ear. " I promise you, little one, you will honor me. I will break that fiery spirit of yours one way or another." A chill ran up my spine. I wasn't sure I wanted to know how he planned to do that. He'd shown me the night before just how much he enjoyed my pain. Would his training be about breaking me with induced pain? I closed my eyes. I could still feel his breath on my skin. I needed to pull it together. I couldn't think of him as an enemy while my traitorous body heated every time he came near me. My body reacted to every memory from last night. Was that on purpose? Did he want me to react to his presence with desire? Everything felt like a manipulation with him. I needed to be careful. I would not give anything of myself to this man. He would never break me.

"You will never get what you want. I will find a way to kill you." I said between clenched teeth. He let out a laugh.

"Oh, darling, you will never kill me. Not if you value your own life." He stood before me again, his teeth scraping across his bottom lip. "Like I said before, this is only the beginning. It's going to be a long five years if you spend it trying to kill me. We could be spending our time in much better ways." His fingers skated over my arm. "Besides, the vampire council will end your life as surely as you would end mine. It is our most vital law. You cannot kill your maker." A devilish smile broke out over his face. At that moment, I knew my life had changed forever. I vowed to find a way to hurt this man. I would be the one who killed him, so help me God. I wanted to feel his immortal life slip away beneath my fingers. Somehow, I would make that happen, even if it meant giving up my own life.

Epilogue

Six-months later

Reed threw another punch at my face. I ducked it just in time. "You know I already spend hours in the gym working out. Why do you insist on doing even more training after work?" I ducked another of his punches before dropping and swiping my leg in a circle and watching as he fell to the mat. I climbed on top of him, holding his wrists down on both sides of his head. "You forget that being newly made, I'm stronger than you." I gave him a wicked smile.

He catapulted into the air, flipping me over in the process. He landed on top of me, moving his legs fast enough to straddle me on the floor. "Never let your guard down."

"Whatever, Reed, I'm sick of this. What am I even training for? I'm already stronger than anyone on the force." I slid out from between his legs in seconds and stood behind him. I couldn't help but show off with Reed. Our relationship had always been a volatile one.

"You are training to fight vampires. At some point, you may need to fight your own kind or other breeds. You have to be able to fight the way we do. The council wouldn't be pleased if you weren't able to fight one of your own." Reed flipped himself into a standing position. "You've had enough for today. We'll pick up again after our shift tomorrow."

"Seriously?" I rested my hand on my hip and glared at him. "I would rather be spending less time with you, not more. You're already my partner on the force. You changed my shift because you don't want me to go out in the daylight. Now, you want me to spend all my free time with you, training? Are you fucking kidding me? I don't want to spend a second more than I have to with you." I began unwrapping the bindings on my hands. I didn't really need to do it anymore, but it was a ritual I had from sparring in the gym. Reed kept telling me that my human habits would fade with time. I wasn't sure I believed him.

"Oh, my darling Hope, those changes were necessary. How many times must we go through this? You are a vampire, not a human. Changes must be made to protect our secret, our legacy. You wouldn't want the council to end your life before it's even begun, would you?" He leaned against the wall next to the door. He didn't need to prepare to spar with me. He would fight in his damn suit without a second thought. I suspected he changed after work for my benefit.

"I would like to point out that you kidnapped me and changed my life against my will. I will never forgive you. If I have to live with you for five years, I'm starting to think death may be the preferable option." I tucked my wraps and shoes into my bag. I didn't need the gym bag because Reed had a gym in our house. Yet, I still carried one with me for my sparring lessons. I did it more because it bothered Reed more than anything else. He seemed to take issue with all my "human" habits. He didn't like that I refused to give up the little rituals he deemed unnecessary. I enjoyed anything that bothered him.

"Oh, my dearest Hope, you'll change your mind eventually." He stalked toward me. I hated that my heart raced when he looked at me like that. One thing that hadn't changed after I'd become a vampire. Stopping in front of me, he took a piece of my hair, wrapping it around his finger. His tongue slid over his bottom lip. "I still have an effect on you. I can hear your heart quicken every time I'm near. Stop denying your desire. We could both be more than satisfied if you'd just give in to me, Hope. Let me give you what you need." His last sentence came out husky, and my core clenched. Damn, I hated how he still had that effect on me after only one encounter.

I rolled my eyes. "You haven't gotten any better at convincing me, Reed. I told you. I'm never going to be with you. Currently, I'm your prisoner because of the laws of the vampire council. As soon as I'm free, I'll be long gone. Feel free to lift my sentence anytime now." I flicked his hand away from my hair.

"You are not a prisoner. You may come and go as you please. The council only specifies that you live with me for the first five years to acclimate to your new life. It's really for your protection, darling. I'd hate to have you run into another vampire without my protection." His voice dropped low, dangerous. "As long as you are my progeny, you are safe with me." He stepped back, his eyes darkening.

"I have yet to see another vampire who might be dangerous. The only dangerous vampire I know is you." I flipped my hair over my shoulder and sauntered out of the room. Our relationship wasn't getting any better. I couldn't believe I had another five years and six months stuck in this place with Reed. He wasn't entirely wrong. I felt a strong attraction to him anytime he was near me. It didn't matter. There was no way I was giving into him. He took my human life from me. For that, I would forever hate him. At least I got to keep some of my life intact. My friends, my family, my job were all still a big part of my life. I wasn't sure what it was going to be like to live forever, but at least for now, I was going to enjoy what I had.

Dora Blume is a middle school English teacher by day, writer by night. She tends to write books with spunky, bad-ass female characters, random movie quotes from the 90's, and page-turning adventure. She lives just outside of Minneapolis with her two dogs, Jack and Bailey. Reading is her life's passion. She even gets paid to share a love of reading with others. Fat girl problems is her blog, check it out if you want a good laugh, or cry, could go either way. Check out one of her paranormal books today!

If you enjoyed *Scarlet Claimed*,
make sure to sign up for my newsletter to
get exclusive excerpts, new releases, and more.
And don't forget to my website: dorablume.com

facebook.com/DoraBlumeAuthor

twitter.com/BlumeDora

amazon.com/author/dorablume

YOU GET USED TO THE TASTE

BY TAYLOR J

You get used to the taste.

That's what everyone asks me first, so I figure I'll just get that out of the way. A lot of the disgust toward consuming human fluids isn't much more than a moral high ground; even if the stuff's just sitting around in some cellar, waiting for some asshole to get *some* use out of it, you're still a morally repugnant freak for taking a sip. Naturally, and I don't blame them for it, what my friends wanna ask me is always along the lines of "Don't you hate people staring at you? Don't you hate people looking at you like you're subhuman?" I always tell them the same thing: I seriously don't give a shit. It was always like that. When I was in grade school, I'd eat worms, beetles, and whatever other poor, innocent critter I could find wandering through their home in the dirt, and I'd have the kids give me quarters to watch my little one-man circus.

The first time I came up with this brilliant pyramid scheme, I eagerly rolled out the presentation to my parents. For some reason, I actually believed I could get my parents to put investments in this. I was a fat, dirty, black-haired little pile of needs and demands, and many would've believed there was *ambition* in that hedonistic little shit.

My dad was a soft, melting boulder of a man, but the moment he put it upon himself to *knock some sense into you*, you just happened to forget how doughy he was real fast. Back then, I saw him as nothing more than the personal totalitarian of my young life, and who could blame me? I still hate the bastard, but the more I grew up, I learned the *lessons* he wanted to teach me were perfectly sound no matter how shitty his methods were.

I don't know if I would've been a good person if I actually looked up to the dumb bastard, but I have a feeling that if I did, I wouldn't have wound up doing this forever. I was never an ambitious kid, and when I only lived with my mother, she was perfectly willing to coddle her poor little baby. Of course she was. Eventually, the finances were beginning to bleed out, so I got a job at the convenience store and gave her a hundred bucks a month for being kind enough to tolerate me. That's not so damning of a manifesto until you know that part of the story goes all the way into my twenties. I don't really know what brought it on, but eventually, my mother, with her dying hair and rickety limbs, began to finally realize that if she doesn't do something, this'll be *the rest of her life*. God bless her. She looked like I was going to slaughter her on sight for even having the gall to suggest that I finally take hold of my own life.

Everyone assumed I'd grow out of being nothing but a little ball of desires. So I was just sitting there, brooding over my awful, unreasonable, terrifying assignment of *getting a job*...and then life just decides to roll one for me. The news channel suddenly starts airing a piece on a little town called Hollow Hills, Ohio, a place where all of the supernatural ostracized by general society can find salvation. The vast majority of the population were the usual jackasses you couldn't technically disprove without more than most people cared to give; your typical psychics, fortune tellers, UFO spotters, you know the drill. But then the place also housed the *real* crazies:

People who believed they *were* aliens, big, burly men who insisted they absolutely were werewolves, zealots who believed they were the second coming of Jesus, zealots who believed they were the *antichrist* (don't ask *me* how that shit works out), and everything else under the sun. But then the best part: at the center of the town, they run what they call a "Speculative Investigation" fair.

Yeah, you can imagine where I started to see dollar signs. A place where wackos are paid every day to just be themselves? The seeds of my ultimate, final scheme had been sowed, and I sat there trying to work out what exactly my gimmick for this whole thing was going to be. Sure, it was easy to get those idiots throwing out their wallets, but I needed something that would really get them vomiting cash my way... and then, another roll on life's shitty dice of fate, I saw it thrown haphazardly against the coat rack: my vampire costume from that year's Halloween. I almost laughed, then, already seeing the stacks of green rolling right into my pocket.

Using my inherited money, I bought a house over there. It was a shitty little shack, but we can't count our chickens before they hatch, eh? I barged into the fair manager's little trailer and presented my premise, and the little man was practically trembling, imagining all of the cash that would roll into his pockets over the next few months. Naturally, I was somewhere between cloud nine and the worst trip you'd ever had because what was happening was just not real. I asked the man where exactly he was going to get the blood for this whole gimmick, considering they didn't exactly give away that stuff.

"Not a problem, not a problem," the man assured me, shakily adjusting his glasses, "when you have money, very few things are hard to come by."

To this day, I'm still not entirely sure how that cretin of a man *did* supply what I need for the gimmick, but in retrospect, he must've fit right in with his crew. They made short work of the setup, a stand somewhere near the middle of the fair, with "Meet a real vampire" splattered in paint playing the role of blood. You could pay five bucks to have me drink some of the fair-provided blood, but if you were a real fucking freak, you could shell out ten dollars to make me drink some of *your* blood; many complaints were made about why I couldn't sink my teeth into their arms in live-action, and my favorite excuse was that even vampires need to worry about aids.

You're probably wondering whether or not I was afraid of getting every blood disease on the face of this earth, and my answer to that one's always: of course I didn't. I didn't give a shit if I ended up only living for thirty years as long as I was comfy, and rest assured, I was living the easy life after only about a week. Loads and loads of fish-eyed *Mind's Eye Monthly* readers all threw cash at me to destroy my own body, and soon enough, I moved right into a nice little apartment, where I'd blow all of my checks on the finest Vodka you can fish out of a grocery store.

Now, you can probably guess from my tone that things weren't *always* bright n' sunny. I wasn't sad about spending my time getting wasted and coasting through a pathetic job; I'd develop guilt eventually, but these things take time... No, where things started to go a little lopsided was with the little community I had gotten myself into. At first, I thought I'd encounter nothing weirder than a couple of dipshits insisting their third cousin removed could see ghosts, but then occasionally, someone would really get the shitty little worms squirming under my skin. First, there was this guy in the big black hood... he'd just circle around my crappy little stand, occasionally passing looks and comments my way that I couldn't really read. I'd try to get a good view of the asshole's face, but the man was amazingly proficient about not letting that happen.

I went over to my bossy the next day to file a complaint—essentially, to ask him in no uncertain terms what the hell was wrong with my coworkers. I naturally believed that since I was making big dough, I could probably sway the man into getting rid of anyone I didn't like. The fat little man just bitterly adjusted his glasses—as if by making such a request, I had launched a big, fat, disgusting loogie right in his greasy face.

"I'm going to explain something to you, Francis—something you apparently have not managed to get a grip on with your cold, *undead* hands: I'm running a freakshow. I've had many people just as naive as you come to me complaining about harassment, abuse, whatever other bullshit, and what you need to understand is that *being humiliated is your entire job.* You could easily head to Mickey Dees or Walmart and ask if they need any help, but I think we both know you aren't here because you want to do actual work."

It was all bullshit right up to my ankle, but I was helpless to do anything about it because he was the hand that fed me. So, I just sat at my post, assuming the pestering from freaks and weirdos was just part of the job description, and believe me, I did my best to bear it. I'm sure this is the part where you're screaming, "Get the hell out of there, you dumbass!" and sure, I *get* that, you bet your ass I wish I did, but hear me out for a second, eh? I had a flat-screen TV in my apartment, and I had only been doing this job for about a month; you do the math for yourself, eh?

The job was already busting my ass, but the green was rolling in, and I knew I wasn't ready to do the dreaded *actual work.* Now it's hard to say where shit got *real* strange, but I think in retrospect, I remember the day the first *real* freak had come up to me. He was wearing this real Victorian jacket, along with, I shit you not, a top hat straight out of the fifties; and naturally, I'm thinking the guy must either be a real whack job, or he has to have his head so far up his ass he's seeing his own processed meals. Then he looks at me and then adjusts the damn *monocle* on his face, staring at me like a fresh specimen.

"A new member of our community in our little town of Hollow Hills... we've had quite the boom as of late." He grinned, a grin that I would soon become real fucking intimate with. "I apologize if this comes off as at all intrusive, but my curiosity is simply insatiable. You see, our fangs are one of the biggest symbols of pride among our community, and I would very much like to get a good look at yours."

I squinted. Even among the biggest conspiratorial weirdos, nobody particularly wants to find out how the magician got that rabbit out of his hat because they know, in some choked way, that if they did so, they'd have to admit to being *wrong.* I'd already long-expected someone to come up to me with those sorts of questions, but people like that were typically participating in the joke just as much: *Ha-ha, this freak thinks he's a vampire. Let's see if I can prove this is a scam.* I didn't know what the hell I was supposed to do; I was surrounded by weirdos, but none of them had actively tried to scrutinize whether or not I was *one of them.*

"Well, I'm sorry to say you're gonna be disappointed with a front-row-seat viewing of my molars, my good man. I'm half-human, and thanks to mama's genes, I don't have the fangs you want to see." Once you're in the business of producing pure bullshit for a while, you end up shocking yourself over just how efficient you become at producing the stuff. The man fidgeted with his monocle again and then strained his mouth to create the largest smile you'd ever see.

"Well, I have indeed heard of such conditions among our race, and I do pity you, good sir. Do you require the charity of others to survive? I'm sure you must be starving." He leaned his torso over my table and unwrapped his entire mouth, and dear God, the fangs *were* real; I didn't know how the hell someone comes into a deformity like that, but it made it *really* easy to imagine him tearing into your arm fat like it's Thanksgiving dinner. I could've written that off as some kinda trick, but *all* of his teeth were a row of sharp little daggers, and all together, it was like staring into the maw of a hungry piranha, very ready and willing to put its tools to proper use.

"You'll be very pleased to know that we have effective ways of treating such ailments in our community." He let his fingers dance back and forth on the table, and for a second, I thought this was going to be where I die; the psycho was going to just tear my throat out, and this little adventure of mine would come to a tragic end. The douche must've strained his arm spider-legging his fingers as close to me as physically possible before eventually retracting the thing—oh yes, he wasn't some ordinary psychopath, he had the courtesy to make his prey know what was happening long before they're all eaten up.

Then he started to claw through his coat pockets, and I could only imagine what kind of college funny-dust he was getting ready to shove in my face—but all he had to offer me was a little business card with...directions?

Two miles past the abandoned Rite Aid. You know it when you see it, friend.

My hands quivered under the weight of the shitty slice of paper, and I wondered what the hell I was thinking letting this pack of weirdos get to me. I didn't *have* to go to their shitty cockfighting slash cock eating ring and get shanked. They'd give up on their newest toy and look for some other poor sap to mutilate. But then wasn't it naive to think any of this would turn out easy? Insane people don't give up. It's sorta their whole thing. I don't know what sort of neurological dysfunction makes you *really* get a hankering to try to perform vampire surgery, but with the career path I had taken, was I really anyone to judge?

I tried to just coast through this shit. I knew how my boss would act even if I begged him on my knees to not let the boogeymen kill me, and I knew if I got the police coming to his honest little establishment, he'd have my head by next week. I think it was about a week later when another one of *them* imposed themselves onto me; this twig of woman, wearing funeral clothes that hung over her as gracefully as a garbage bag, rested her elbow against the surface of my stand and gave me a snicker. Her ratty purple hair was the only evidence she didn't come straight out of the catholic church.

"You haven't come to our party yet, son. We were all real sad to see you had not come after so long."

I wanted to give the usual excuses of time constraints and shit like that, but I wouldn't be here if I had anything going on other than an endless stream of drunken debauchery, and I was sure even this group of cranks knew such a thing damn well. The woman cocked her head back and forth before letting me off with a hearty chuckle.

"Ah, I understand...being so abruptly introduced to a new community must have left you horribly frightful. I understand, darling, believe me—when I discovered there was an entire community for our kind in a town like Hollow Hills, I could only imagine they were nothing but a pack of imitators con-artists." I could've *sworn* the woman gave me a look with that one—that, or maybe by this point, I had simply been able to fill in the gaps. "But all of the vampires in the humble little club turned out to be wonderfully welcoming, affable folks. If you're having fears, I recommend you let go of them. "

I was just becoming content in believing this particular pack of crazies had let up on me, and then here I am. Her eyes had begun to chip and crack in her age yet were still acutely active, taking in every twitch on my frame; and, despite the whole persona I've built up so far as a bit of a skeptic, I could feel that those eyes made my skin as thin as paper. Jesus Christ, I came into this whole gig thinking that it was just gonna be the magician's open secret, y'know?

"Cat got your tongue?" The woman asked, and with that, she left. The rest of my...ha-ha, "clients" that day asked me why the hell I was so jumpy, and in my best attempt to be cute, I'd tell 'em that being a creature of the undead is nervous work. It wasn't so bad—having your hair frazzled and your eyes bloodshot is a good look for a vampire—but, you know, it's hard to sit back and relax when you're thinking about all the ways someone can tear out your arteries and have a juicy snack. The days after that went pretty smooth, I think. There were always a buncha clouds hovering over Hollow Hills, and as the day rolled by, I'd try to watch them shift in their rest instead of trying to look out for any sudden knives or some shit.

After work, I headed up to the gun store in Hollow Hills, a little mom 'n pop place called Shoot 'Em and Loot 'Em; ya know the sort, hick enough that you feel like one of those Duck Dynasty beards is just gonna manifest right on your face. There was a wooden backdrop, and against it, there were just as many mounted animals as there were guns; if you were one of the saps who mistook them for a product, the guy would probably have you on the wall too. Trust me when I say I never thought I'd buy a gun in my life; it ain't a political thing, having that sort of power in my hands just seemed real stressful, and here I was feeling like it was the least I could do to not end up at the bottom of some river.

I picked out a pistol, and the duck-dynasty-expy the atmosphere promised at the front raised an eyebrow. Yeah, sure, I could only imagine what other people would be thinking about a relative newcomer to the town buying a gun so quickly; only wants to blow his head off or our heads off, eh? And I was especially sure that if I was honest with the man about why exactly I *needed* one, he'd be the one to personally blow my head off, but when I told him I was being harassed by fellow members of our community, he simply sighed.

"Ah know it better than anyone, my man...this town's got freaks like it's got mites."

"Tell me about it, damn."

The man's pupils dotted back and forth, eyes far too tiny for his fat face, and eventually, he centered back on me. His breath smelled of mustard and beer, and the store itself smelled like marinated wood chippings, but I let him use me as an ear anyway.

"I swears to you, my man, one of 'em got my mother. I dunno how they did it, but one day I wake up just to find her bloodied corpse draped against my couch, n' the couch itself was real nasty. The policeman tells me that he's got it all figured out, but that it definitely *ain't* vampires because vampires ain't real, which is a whole load of shit!" For no reason, he screeched, and for no reason, he slammed his fist against the counter, and for good reason, I was glad I wasn't in uniform. "My mama died of a sudden, totally unexplained blood loss, n' you wanna tell me any old *thug* done somethin' like that?"

Jesuuus Christ...my heart started thumping like it was about to finally break, and my God, I felt like I could just tumble and crash right into those gun racks. Oh, ha-ha-ha, there's a killer going around that just *happens* to really like funneling out blood? Maybe a bunch of 'em, even? Jesus. Jesus, Jesus, Jesus. I knew very well there were freaks in Hollow Hills, but can you blame me for not suspecting them to be the *metal* sort of freaks that actually do the shit they say? I didn't wanna hear any more of the hick's story because I had a feeling that if I did, a blood vessel in my brain would probably violently burst up, at least that's what it felt like. I headed back home and slept, holding my new baby behind my pillow 'case any of those freaks decided to mess with me.

I didn't end up sleeping a wink, as you can probably imagine. Normally, living in a shitty little town, it's easy not to bother being conscious of the cars and the crickets and the squirrels, but suddenly I felt like every car in the nearest mile was ready to crash right through my damn house. It felt like there was an entire boulder piercing through my stomach even though I really hadn't been that indulgent that night. I dunno if anything really happened that night, and I think it'd be fair to say that *then* I was just being a bit of a nut, buuuut...I swear, I started hearing something.

Footsteps—big whoop in an apartment complex, I know—but footsteps off the wall are a little more rare, eh? *Tap, tap, tap, tap, tap...tap, tap, tap, tap*...I locked 'n loaded and sat by the window, but all I got for myself there was a potential night in the slammer. Then the footsteps just started on the *other* wall! How great is that? How great is that?! I was so damn mad I wanted to just smash up my own place, smash these gadgets and these cute decorations that *dirty* money; I was biting my lip so bad it started seeping out the red stuff they love so much, ha-ha-hah. Then it stopped, and I realized I'd let them in my head. Dear God, I let them dance around in my fucking head!

I collapsed onto the couch that night, and I realized for the first time in my life, I was actually *stressed*. If I wanted to fear for my life, I would've become a policeman or something, not risking my life so a bunch of curious mothers can point at me and then forget about it a week later! But then I couldn't imagine myself working some crappy nine-to-five job, flipping burgers, and then eating where I shit, and that'd be it for the rest of my miserable life, wouldn't it? I turned on the TV and left it on for the whole night, imagining it might be the end of my time with the thing.

The next day at work was actually fine. Sure, my eyes were bloodshot to hell, and I was pretty damned jittery, but there wasn't anyone

particularly strange to come and harass me, and we count our bless-
ings in this house! They were around, though, and of course my heart
would light up like radar whenever they were even a mile close to me. I
could see them, wandering in their gothic getup and intimidating the
other guests with their Absolutely Real Vampires stories, because of
course they were. Of course they were! They were always staring at
me, of course I was always the star! Always, always, always! But, hey, at
least they were trying, right? I'm sure the leader of the freaks must've
sat down with them and said, "Hey, we're scaring off the newbie. We
need to chill off the welcome party." Well, fine, fine, I could deal, I
could deal as long as they were ten miles away from me at all times.

Well, I found out why exactly they were so nice to me during work
hours; there was a massive cardboard box sitting right in front of my
place, and on top of it there was a note:

A gift from friends. Join us soon.

Oh, dear God, this is where things start to play out like a snuff film.
It's so twisted you'll probably have me committed on the spot, but
unfortunately, the whole tale doesn't come together without it. Yeah,
you could argue I probably should've either left the thing or take it
straight to the dump, but if someone sent *you* a deranged mystery
package, wouldn't you wanna crack the thing open too? I don't know. I
feel like that's a shitty excuse too.

I began tearing off the tape, the meandering *slick* rumbling through
my chest. My hands were damn ready to just go rogue, every finger
trembling and breaking under the weight of the cardboard, my heart
begging the rest of my appendages to give up on this twisted shit. My
ominous admirer had gone ape shit on keeping the thing secure, and I
took every piece of tape off as an individual act. My pap always would
always give me these bullshit lectures about how it's better to tear off
the band-aid quick instead of making an ordeal of it, but it *does* hurt
less to make an ordeal of it!

But the box was naked of its restraints now. If there was some
kinda boogeyman crouching in there, waiting to gouge my eyes out or
some shit, there wasn't anything more stopping it. The boogeyman

never did show. I mumbled about how I was acting like a child, yet when I clasped the folds, I just couldn't do it. I know, I know, in any sane world, it was probably just a massive mound of dog shit sitting in there, or maybe some kind of threatening message from a local genius about how I wasn't a REAL vampire, you know how this shit goes. Ha-ha-ha-ha, if all I got was some smart-ass's amateur investigation, it probably would've been the most joyful moment of my entire life.

I sucked all the air I could and tore open the box. Under that first layer, there was just...the top of a cooler. And...and oh dear god, that *coppery* smell. I knew it, I knew it so damn well that I could barely stand smelling at after work. That...oh dear god. Oh, dear God, if I didn't know you'd already turned your head to me right now, I'd be *begging* you to let me forget this shit. There was a note...man, I'm not sure I even properly remember what it said because by then, I was already really fucking clocked out.

We noticed you were stalking some game the other day and figured we'd give you a freebie. Drinks on us!

Drinks on us. Ha-ha-ha-ha-ha. Funny bunch of bastards, they were! Funniest group of freaks in this whole damn country. I thought I was going to puke. Seemed pretty likely, in fact. The iron odor was the strongest, but there was a little bit of decay under it...you know, how people always tell you it smells like that dead raccoon you once saw. It was barely there, and yet that smell still lingers in my nostrils to this day—hell, one of my biggest motivations for keeping this job is so that I'll never have to face that smell ever again. But we'll there when we get there, eh? I don't remember a lot of that night, but I am pretty sure that I puked all over that damned cooler, and I'm pretty sure I ejected my entire body's worth of fluids.

So, I'm sitting there with God knows what, and I realize the whole situation has gone so topsy turvy that I can't avoid getting the suits involved anymore. I struggled to hold my phone, imagining that little asshole telling me off for ruining his whole scheme—I took a gamble that the man would have even the *slightest* compassion for his perform-ers. It wasn't a lot of keystrokes, that *nine-one-one,* but when you actually needed it, it felt like you were retyping the entirety of Wikipedia. A raspy sounding woman greeted me, and I instantly imagined the sheer amount of calls this poor police team must've had to deal with. *Help me! There's a zombie living in my fridge, eating all of my raw meat and shitting in the fruit cabinet!*

"Someone left a package on my front doorstep, and in it, there was...a cooler. I think there's a lot of blood inside it, and maybe something else."

The woman audibly sucked in air, and there was a brief delay; she spoke up again, this time at least trying to mask the exhaustion in her voice. I went through the usual routine of forfeiting my personal information, and the woman took a little bit to stir the whole thing up in her head. I tapped my fingers against my hand one by one, my feet following suit until the woman finally spoke up again.

"Yes, we'll have someone right with you in just a moment. Keep the object right where it is, and do not touch it."

I threw myself onto the couch and wrapped my arms around myself until they got here. I realized I was shivering horribly in a way I hadn't since I was a kid, and my chest burned. It was the same feeling I had when I learned of my shitty pap dying; you know you're supposed to be panicking because something bad is happening, and hell, maybe you *are* panicking, but you're never panicking in the *right* way, eh?

I'd seen the TV shows where the hero throws away the body that's been thrown into their lap because they don't have time for the cops, and frankly, I just didn't have the energy for that sort of scheming.

Eventually, I got the old brisk knock. Guy was a frail lookin' thing that, in more ways than one, could hardly fit into the uniform they threw on him; if you were *really* generous, you could say he had the ghost of a mustache over his lips. I pointed over to the cooler, and the poor sap looked just as green about its potential contents as I was. I came over and stood by him as he began to open with barricaded hands, and he eyeballed me quickly before shrugging.

We both blew chunks the moment the thing was open—or, at least, I dry heaved something fierce. "Dear Jesus," the poor man muttered repeatedly. The cooler was just a tub of red fluids, with the occasional *chunk* floating through it. It wasn't smooth. It was somehow *mushy*. *Cherry applesauce, y'all.* Dear God. I could bleakly speculate who exactly this pile of fluids used to be, but I did my best to swallow that lump in my throat anyway—fuck if I needed to know who I'd gotten killed. The cop, trying to reassemble the sanity of the situation to *some* extent, spoke up again.

"Did, this...package...have a return address of any kind?"

I shook my head solemnly. "Nah, only this." I gave him the note, and he looked at me as if I had personally murdered his family.

"Damn, man. You touched it."

"Man, give me a break. I wanted to know what the hell they were trying to send me."

The cop sighed. "Well, because we don't have a return address, we're gonna have to deal with this the long way, fingerprints, and all that." He held his hands in his pockets. "You leave this thing here while I get a couple of buddies to have it hauled out."

"But...but wait! Can't you see how badly I'm being harassed?"

The man's lips curled up into a sad little grin, and I think that was when I knew how screwed I was. *You hear about the poor bastard they found in the river,* they'd all mutter to each other, pretending whatever was twisted about their town wouldn't come up and suck *them* dry so long as they kept quiet about it

"The fuck do you want us to do about it, man?" The cop asked, shaking his head. I don't know what exactly they did with that big tub of guts, but there was nothing hot off the press about a terrifying cult of wannabe-bloodsuckers being exposed. I also didn't get any more *gifts* from my dear friends, but you can guess whether that made me feel better. But the new deliveries never quite came, and my job as a circus freak actor went swimmingly for the next few days.

Sitting in front of my stand with my legs crisscrossed, I drank a pretty bitter coffee, unable to appreciate that it was one of the last coffees I'd ever be treated to in my entire life. The freaks were still around, of course, but they kept their distance; I let myself slip back into that hedonistic comfort. I even started flipping at the newspaper I'd left behind my stand, not concerned with the fact that the thing lacked the usual new-book-smell you'd expect.

Course, good moods are like anything else good; it don't take much to break it.

Local gun store owner brutally killed in breaking and entering. The corpse was discovered without a hint of fluids remaining in his body, which has led investigators to debate the nature of the crime; there were discussions of the crime being political in nature, but the sadistic way the body was desecrated has determined it unlikely.

Let me tell you, my dear audience, by that point I had already been inhaling gallons and gallons of human fluids, and I'm sure I had some cancerous tumor of AIDs, herpes, and HIV growing in my lower belly; and yet for the first time, I felt ready to puke the stuff back up.

I let the paper slip out of my hands; it stank like something foul had grazed it, the sort of thing you only really pick up in your third eye. Damn, I guess I really am going crazy, huh? Don't judge me too much, kid. You would too. I stared at the crowd of gothic actors laughing and have a grand old time on the other side of the fair.

As you've probably gathered by now, the rationality bit in my brain has always been just a bit broken. I want a few more quarters to take to the candy store. I start making myself a good meal of worm soup; I want a piss easy job, and I'm a vampire. So suddenly, an awful, stupid, crazy idea begins to breed in my head like lice, and it's *so* ignorant, yet I can't help but see it as brilliant. *If you can't beat 'em, join 'em.* One of those classic, shitty phrases that nobody actually says outside of those cheesy sitcoms and kid's shows—what was the Goosebumps episode where the kid pretends to be a mutant because he's just *that* ugly?

I threw away that shitty little card the man gave me, but the exact words were long stored in my mind— I knew what I had to do. Well, what I *had* to do was get in my car and zip the hell out of there, but your sanity has a funny way of slipping out of pockets right when you really need the damn thing, huh? I dug through my closet and found a sad-looking backpack, the one I'd taken what little shit I had in my *actual* home, and I threw the gun in it—and, after a moment's hesitation, a couple knives for good measure. I zipped up the bag and threw it on my back, just getting ready to go on a cute little hiking trip. Yessir, I'd go through the woods, all the way to the next town over, see the sights and the birds and the trees, and they wouldn't even have a car to light on fire.

It's been a while now, but I remember I parked my car a good couple miles from the dead Rite-Aid. I must've really been off my rocker at that point because I started to wonder if they'd find a motor vehicle archaic. Can vampires fly? *Are you starting to treat them like they're real, ya fucking nut?*

The moment I passed the place, I felt a hand trying to tear my heart from my chest; my legs shook, and my arms trembled...but it was just the jitters before the show. The first few times I'd drunk blood for a tip, I was pretty freaked out, but I got over that. There probably wasn't going to be some secret hideout just past the dead pharmacy; more likely, a bunch of delirious freaks would drag me into their inner circle and have me drink kool-aid from a nice, innocent chalice; and maybe I'd wake up in the hospital with an ulcer, but what the hell, as long as they get it out of their system, huh? But then I could see something in the distance, a figure that spelled my death without having to say a word—from a distance, it was just a big lump of brown, but I didn't want to see *anything*. I could imagine some poor douchebag coming to ask if they had a permit for this little structure, only to find that his neck had been made into a nice Capri Sun pouch.

I could also imagine *me* meeting some old hick rocking gently in his easy chair, stomping out his cigarette and threatening to shoot my *damn* head off if I didn't run back to my group of freaks—and somewhere else, God knows where, the "vampires" would be laughing their heads off. *Oh, but you haven't forgotten the gift, have you?* It was the middle of fall, and I was still already starting to feel tired of the Dracula costume. The brown figure eventually formed a humble little wooden building—the wood itself looked old and tired, the windows were cracked, and there were splinters just laying all around the porch.

Very classy. I stared through the front window and saw the skeleton of a tavern; there was the bar, high seats and all, and a few booths, but I didn't see any bartender laughing happily about the kid he found wandering route twenty

I leaned against the door and watched the sky. I wondered for a moment if I was going to actually do this, this exercise in madness...and I just shrugged. I rapped on the door. I think all my life I've wondered if I'm going just a little bit crazy—when I was a youngin' mawing down those worms, I was already wondering if I was goin' just a little bit psycho. Course, I always viewed myself as somehow superior to the other freaks—I got good grades, and as an adult, I could shuffle into society's lanes pretty okay, I think.

Eventually, I did hear stairs creak from the far side of the place, and it was one of those moments where you're not sure if your screws got tied back in or they all came exploding out. I think we've all heard the sound before, friends—pressure on wood, the little *creak, creak, creak* that always invites itself in at the crack of midnight, and you're never truly sure if it's the wind or if Texas chainsaw man himself has come to spill a nice bowl of spaghetti all over that couch you just bought. Rude motherfucker.

It was that same piece of shit, that guy with the top hat and the monocle. He shook my hand, patted me on the back, and gave me that very same shark tooth grin that had freaked me the hell out before. Let me tell you, for every movement this man made, there was a little trail of rat droppings behind it; the act wasn't too bad, and he'd probably get somewhere on Broadway, but it wasn't terribly hard to tell it *was* an act, get me?

"Ah, you came, you came! It's a momentous event every time one of our kind comes to greet us." He elongated the last two words with his rumbling voice as if he were a forlorn partner who'd been denied a good rub-down one too many times. I was never one to be particularly capable of shame, as you've probably gathered by this point in the tale, but hell, when you're making your plea to a starving T-rex, you're suddenly a *little* bit more scattered. As I was prepping for the biggest performance in my life, the taste of those worms popped into my mouth; that mushy, slimy paste that never gets any easier. You could get through a gummy worm without much hardship, but I was munching on the real deal. *You get used to the taste.*

I wanted to giggle, I wanted to giggle like when I was five years old, and I wondered if in this crowd of loonies that'd really enhance my performance. Creatures of the night must always have a hell of a lot to chuckle about, hrm?

"Always a little tough for me to meet new folks, you know how it is. My old machine up in the attic always tells me they're a buncha fakers ready to drive a stick in my heart." That funny little phantom taste of worms got thicker in my throat, and I think I realized it was always there— I don't think I'd ever be able to forget it.

"Ah, yes, yes, yes, I understand completely. I've long kept hold of how to step around the peasants, but you seem quite...youthful, what with your dialect and all. Come in, come in." There was a little subtext of distaste in the way he said *dialect,* and that was what really made me want to book it the hell out of there. It reminded me of the way my pap always referred to us children as *"youths,"* the same way you refer to the cat who just did its business on the carpet. There was a nice big sheet of dust over the bar, and were I enough of a man-child, I probably coulda dropped down and made a snow angel in it. He led me down the rickety set of stairs that freaked out before, and I was greeted with a long strip of every kind of blacks, purples, and reds, with an entire party of funeral attendees filling up the place.

I could handle a little pack of the weirdos, trust me, but seeing a good twenty of 'em all lined up like that really freaked me the hell out. They were all staring at me, and in the moment, I couldn't really tell you if they were appraising me as a friend or as a gourmet thanks-giving dinner; you decide what difference it made.

I parked myself in one of the diner seats and greeted the bartender, an elderly looking man in a purple dress shirt. He just groaned and asked me what the *fuck* I wanted. I think of all the bloodsuckers I met on this little adventure, he was probably the most human. The woman in the funeral outfit I'd met at my stand slid next to me, grinning with those piss-yellow teeth. "We've been waitin' for ya, man. What's the holdup been?" She patted my back with increasing vigor, and by the time she was done, I was pretty sure she wanted to smack my spine straight out of my throat.

"Nervous, that's all. I'm still getting used to this whole thing." There's the damn worms again. I ordered a vodka mixed with blood; I knew it'd probably taste like complete shit, but hey, it was my last drink! It freaked me out a little that they had enough of the goop to spare it like that, but hey, I guess there's nothing wrong with being over-prepared.

They didn't bother questionin' the backpack, and at the time, you better believe I thought I was the descendant of mister Einstein himself. I'd nudge it once in a while with the back of my fingers, just to comfort myself with the rattle of the thing. Here's how I see it: the sitch I'd gotten myself in gave me permission slip to spill a little red stuff. We don't ever wanna admit it to ourselves, but the coppers protect who they *like* around. *But that goes both ways, ain't it? If my body ended up in a septic tank, they couldn't pay someone to fish it out.*

I stepped away from my chair and started my routine—I cleared my throat the loudest I could, probably sending spittle into whoever happened to be right next to me. Everyone looked at me, and suddenly I felt pretty damn good about myself; it might've been their turf, sure, but I was getting ready to perform *my* profession. All of the eyes stared at me, those cat eyes that float in the dark when the sun don't shine, but in this context, I didn't have a lick a fear in my heart. They're my buddies, waiting to see me down a whole basket of worms. A nice basket of wriggling, slimy worms...oh god, the taste was the *worst* then.

"Hello, hello, my fellow creatures of the shadows. I'm a newbie to this little community, and let me say I'm very humbled to be of your acquaintance." The idiots at my stand were usually more satisfied Vuck Vyour Vlood Dracula act, so I admit that with the setting change brought a few challenges. I was pretty sure the crowd got out enough to know of the devil machine with the antennae and other such extravagances, but my gram-gram taught me better safe than sorry. "I don't know how you people do it in your community, but I'm afraid there's a few things I'll have to inform you of before I can feel truly comfortable integrating myself. Let me say that I *do* indeed appreciate the generous offering I received at your hands.

"Blame me for this miscommunication, as I was shy; you see, I grew up to a clan of vampires traveling through Virginia, where we were pursued by a hunting clan. As a result, we took great pleasure in ending our pursuers, and my father taught that it was extremely disrespectful to hunt another undead's game, even under the guise of doing them a solid. My good friend, I think his name was..." How do you come up with a vampire name on the spot that isn't some variant of *Vlad...*

"His name was Varnsworth." In my puberty, I thought I was a real intellectual reading goth literature. "You see, he told me this woman, this woman who he found...excuse me, well-fed. Most of us don't particularly desire much meat on our bones, I know. I see this woman sitting on a bench, and there's no one around for miles; I figure I'll show him that I truly appreciate our companionship. I take her life, bag 'er up, and drag her to his living space. When he saw what I'd done, he gave me a bloody nose. Though I don't hold it against you, seeing your gift did rather offend me." Can you believe it? I was fucking *proud* of that performance.

I think I've heard somewhere before that vampires have an acute sense of smell, and that really came into play there because these vampires sure as hell could smell bullshit, no matter how many layers of gift wrap you put over it. They weren't eager to listen to my yarns anymore, they were all just *staring* at me. Then my buddy, the top hat vampire, came up from his seat and clapped, walking towards me. I was never really afraid of bein' caught with my pants down, lemme tell you that, but I really felt like I was getting ready to die. Oh, I wish.

See, this guy was the type to dangle the fish over the fire before he finally fried it, you get me? He patted me on the shoulder and threw his head in front of mine, giving me that God-forsaken shark tooth grin once again. "Ohhh, I apologize, good friend. We have not received a complaint of any kind about our gifts for the longest time, so I'm afraid we hadn't had such a preference in mind. I muuust say, however, that I am very curious about this clan you say you come from."

Some people, I suppose, aren't content with just tearing off the pants when they see the lack of a belt—they wanna milk you for everything you might have. I'd like to say I'm a pretty creative guy, but I was really running out of material for this particular routine, man; back at the fair, I was a "servant of Vacula, vurned for his eternal housekeeping," but somehow I knew I was in front of a wee bit tougher a crowd, eh?

"Oh, we weren't anything particularly special. We were a little group stranded in the Arctic, and though it was quite convenient being away from the eye of hunters, we were starving. A man named Victor Scott rounded all of us up and proudly declared that we would hide under the shadows no longer—under his guidance, we would charge into human territory and take our stake in the world. We traveled through the world under Scott's leadership, hiding out in small towns and feeding off the isolated. Though there were the fair share of hunters and scrutiny, I'd say we got along very well."

His lip curled into a smug ass little grin, and I could swear I saw his tongue do a little dance his mouth—you better believe I was already the Thanksgiving turkey. I was clutching my backpack at that point. It was a new sensation to me, and I think that's because the twerps that'd come and watch me destroy my stomach were *amazed* by even the slightest act of defiance towards **the man,** even if that meant chowing down on some no-no foods. But it's a whole different story when you're in front of a crowd of outcasts, the type who had to actually *fight,* not to stick it to **the man** but keep his shoe off.

"I do have a question about your tale, my dear Francis," the top hat man said, tilting his head and lowering his eyelids. I was so far in the doghouse I'd smell like fur for a month. I dunno if my composure was finally busted by that point, but I could see the stares from the damn freaks go just a touch darker; I swear I could hear muffled little chuckles behind the silence, followed by...hissing? God, I don't know.

"You said you received a bloody nose during your tale. That would be very concerning, considering our kind do not excrete blood in any such way."

I can't really put shit together from there properly because when I do, my mind's much more interested in playing back all the ways I could've crawled out of that hole. Daylight...I think that's what I miss the most. It's sorta shitty to say I miss the sun more than my parents, I suppose, but you can you blame me when the Sun never left for a pack a cigarettes? Sorry, I guess that's cruel, the man is dead. Anyway, I took out the gun. I knew I was screwed, but hey, you don't wanna waste a chance to waste some crazy assholes, aye? You know, the dumb ass I was, I actually did believe there was power in my hands.

I blew a hole in top hat man's chest, as in, an actual fucking hole.

Dust blew out and splattered on his companions, who all started crashing into each other in confusion. I wasn't really concerned about them. What I was really, really concerned about was that the guy didn't flinch. There was a big gaping cavity in his chest, but it's a Tuesday, these things happen. He was grinning, and not the usual serial killer smile; no, I could easily imagine him running his grainy, black n' white talk show, rambling on about gas prices and the war and whatever other garbage.

He started walking up to me with a cheerful swing in his step, and the closer he got to me, the more that damn shark grin started to unfold itself. I had let myself think they all believed my act, that this man earnestly wanted to invite me into his damn cult, but, really, the worst thing in life is finding out you're playing a game you never signed up for.

He started running his fingers up and down my arms, and the cronies stood on either side with those big fangs right out. You go ahead and think they were plastic if that helps you sleep this story down a little better, but I swear they were the sharpest teeth on this planet. I shut my eyes and did my best to let what was coming flow away, and that doesn't work when mister talk show host decides to headbutt me. They all started kicking me right in the stomach, in the knees, my dick, everywhere they could get their dirty feet. The scariest part? I'm pretty sure they specifically didn't *want* me to pass out. I just looked like a dying animal, seeing if it could still feel, and I'm sure that's how my new buddies saw the whole thing. Their leader beckoned the roaring crowd away, and lemme tell you, they all looked at that man like a bunch of sickly little dogs.

He stood in front of me and clenched his fist, then swung it back and forth in the air—I was realizing increasingly that this whole thing was just this man's vacation. I'm not one to discriminate. I'm sure there's bloodsuckers out there who believe torturing their game is inhumane; that ain't these folks. Hell, let's be real, these folks didn't need me at *all.*

"I'm sure you've been anticipating it throughout these weeks—I'm going to begin the operation. We can't afford pain medicine in this humble abode of ours, which I'm sure you understand. On the bright side, the entire process is free."

Before I knew it, the bastard was mashing on my jaw, taking every single God damned tooth out of my mouth. I thought of the freak show I'd joined, and suddenly everything seemed just a little bit claustrophobic; it was a home for the ones who had none, and if I came out of this, it'd be my home forever. I still had that dream of everyone oogling at me through the *big screen,* not through the glass of the asylum. I think, by that point, I was going to just a bit loopy. I guess maybe I shoulda wished I talked to my mother more or wrote that book everyone thinks about cooking up, but really I was thinking about how I never tried that breakfast crunchwrap. Cry for me.

I was crying and choking on my own sobs. I won't act like I was some stoic sitting there all peacefully as I guts get knocked out. I guess, by that point, he decided to start wrapping things up because he pulled a red sharpie and drew a line down my neck. I feel kinda sick talking about myself like that, but what's the point in not being perfectly candid at this point? I wasn't a person anymore then, and I wasn't gonna be after.

I think I can describe what the man's breath smelled like, and that freaks the hell out of me more than anything. He kneeled next to me and started licking my neck, up and down, up and down—and, let me assure you, I'd never let anyone fuck with me like that. I think I first truly understood when I felt how dead his tongue was. I'm sure you don't really know what having a dead snake rubbed against your cheek feels like, but let me tell you, it ain't my favorite feeling in the world. Now, I'm sure if you're wanna those Bella Swan freaks, you probably think this whole thing sounds real romantic, and I hate to break off any potential hard-ons, but it wasn't a polite little nibble this guy gave me. Nah, he just tore right into my neck, sucking with the ferocity of a man who just got out of the desert. It sorta felt like a thousand bees colonizing the side of your face.

It was all starting to get real gray, real mushy, and I guess I thought that was it. I think I wished that was it. But I woke up back in my apartment, and I had a bitch of a headache; everything in my stomach was ready to come hurling out too. I checked the mirror and, sure enough, my teeth were back, the whole party! I'm usually a pretty pale guy without really trying, but here I was suddenly...suddenly I looked like a corpse! A corpse! Isn't that lovely? And suddenly I was really looking forward to going to work. I really wanted a nice, refreshing gulp of that red stuff, let me tell you! All the kool-aid a man can ask for —real thirsty, good old me.

I sat out there with a big grin on my face, day after day. I told my boss that I could only work the night shift, and he didn't mind. Made my act make a little more sense anyway, so who gives a shit. I grinned at every person who came up to me; my mama always told me you make the best of it when things go a little bit rough. I guess I never had dreams, and I never really wanted 'em, and...and, you know what, who needs 'em anyway? Never liked the sun anyway. Asshole kept getting in my face. I grinned cause I had a long-time career ahead of me, and the cash was going to just keep rolling in. My friends would come and glance over at me once and awhile, but I didn't mind. Water under the bridge, as my dad always said after he smacked my ass.

And the worms were gone! I can't even remember what that shit tasted like. Hell, I can't remember what *anything* tasted like, but so what? I don't need any of that broccoli or cauliflower because my good old blood's all I need anymore. Saves a lot of money, too.

You get used to the taste!

My name Taylor, and ever since I was a child I've had stories I've had a yearning desire to express my creativity any way I can. Around my teenage years I developed an interest in horror fiction, with authors like Stephen King, Neil Gaiman and Bram Stoker quickly becoming some of my biggest influences. My current dream is to finally share my work with the world, with opportunities like this anthology to hopefully prop me up enough to get myself out there.

A TOUCH OF JADE

BY LYNN MULLICAN

THE EVIL

Jade parted the leaves and peered into the darkest part of the forest. It was here where night turned to evil, where the forest was the thickest and hid the evil lurking within it. She, like the others in her village, mourned the loss of their loved ones, but Jade took it upon herself to search out the killer. Armed with her sword and her fae abilities, she pulled the sword from its sheath, her gaze shifting toward the entryway. Her long dark hair brushed against her bare shoulders.

Then, something pricked her, scratching her delicate pale skin. She touched her cheek. Blood stained her flesh. She frowned and flicked her wings in frustration. This area of the woods was fenced off with large needle bushes, as if guarding anyone from entering here, but Jade was determined to go inside.

Legend in the fae kingdom spoke of a sailor who had crash-landed here about twenty-seven years ago. It was said he wasn't human, that he had fangs and a lust for blood. Her elders called him a monster.

Jade slinked toward the entryway and peered inside. The trail went around the large tree, which obstructed her view of the forest beyond. She cautiously moved inside, surveying her surroundings. What was once a passageway into the evil was now covered in thorny vines and needled bushes. Trees obstructed her view of the outside world. Her heart raced.

An owl hooted above her. Then, movement in the brush caught her attention. She spun, her sword raised, ready for attack, but nobody was there. She made her way around the tree, keeping her back to it until she stood before the trail that led further into the evil. *Maybe this was a mistake. Maybe, you shouldn't be here.*

The scent of blood awoke Kane. This wasn't an animal. This was human, and not just any human, it was a fae human. He drew in a deep breath. Her scent filled his nostrils, the aroma of heaven, something he longed to get closer to, yet something he feared. Kane rolled over and dug his fingers into the dirt. This one was special. She was not like the others.

Kane crawled atop a rock and remained hunkered down. She had ebony hair, the eyes of night, a curvaceous body, and the clothing of a warrior. Yet, here she was seeking … *what? Why was she here? Nobody came here willingly.* The sword shone in the moonlight. *She was here for him! Not Kane, but his alter ego, Vlad.*

Kane grinned. *He would not let Vlad have her.* Kane turned and scrambled through the brush, staying low to avoid her gaze.

Something scrambled through the brush to her right. Jade hissed, raising her sword as she ran, chasing it past tree after tree. She whacked at the branches, cutting them, as she raced after it. It was an animal, not a human, but that didn't matter. Maybe it was the killer and not the sailor. Another whack took a branch off. The branch rebounded, striking her upside the head. She halted, taking a moment to steady herself. The monster stopped up ahead of her, its head turning to glance back at her. She narrowed her eyes in on it. Her jaw dropped. It was human but ran like an animal. Her heart thumped harder in her chest as she charged at it. It dove to the left, avoiding her, but the danger wasn't in the creature, but what lay below her.

One more step took her off the edge of a cliff. Her wings fluttered as she spun around. A high wind struck her, pummeling her into the side of the mountain. Below, ocean waves crashed onto the coastline. She scrambled to grab onto the rock when she lost grip of her sword. It tumbled to the ground below. Then, his hand caught hers. The wind slammed against her, bashing her against the rock. This was a fae's worst nightmare.

Jade glanced up at him. His bald head shone in the moonlight. She reached up and latched onto his arm, allowing him to pull her up onto the top of the cliff. She sat up and studied him. His skin was pale as if he had never seen the sun. His chest was bare, his dirt brown-colored pants were shredded just below the knees, and he wore no shoes.

Their eyes met, then he turned and started to scramble away.

"Wait!" she screamed.

He stopped and glanced back at her.

"Thank you …" she said, breathless. "For saving me."

A moment of silence filled the air.

"You could have let me die."

Hesitantly, he turned to face her.

"After all, I was going to kill you," she said. "That is if you are the one killing the faes."

He stood silent before her, moving toward her. Scars adorned his chest. Then, he offered his hand. She took it and allowed him to help her to her feet.

"What is your name?"

His silence worried her. *Was he a monster? Or was this even the man she sought?*

"Kane," he answered. His voice was deep and throaty with a strong accent.

She raised an eyebrow. "You're not from around here."

"No," he answered, moving away from the cliff. "I'm not."

She didn't move.

He stopped and gestured toward her. "You really should move away from the cliff. You could get caught up in the wind again."

He was right. Hesitantly, she moved away and nonchalantly ran her hand over her knife. The handle was cool against her hand. *But, if he was the killer, why would he save her? He couldn't be the killer.* She glanced around.

"Where are you from?"

"Romania," he answered. He sat down on a nearby rock, facing her.

"I've never heard of Romania. Did you travel alone?"

Kane glanced at the ground. He was hungry, very hungry. He peered up at her. *Do not let Vlad out.*

Jade looked him over again. "Maybe I can get you some clothes, something to replace what you're wearing. You look like you've been wearing those clothes for years."

"I have," he said. *Her lips were enticing. Hell, she looked tasty.*

Their eyes met.

She smiled. Her hand moved to her knife. "I'm sorry if I'm too inquisitive."

Kane smiled. "You're not." He could feel Vlad rising to the surface of his being. "By the way, has anybody ever told you how beautiful you are?"

She blushed. *Not much,* she thought. The men in her kingdom were scared to approach her. They thought she was too masculine. *A sword-wielding fae? How dare she want to engage in warfare and the protection of her kingdom?* She glanced away. She felt for this man, but he said he had been here for years.

"No," she answered.

She glanced up at him to find him inches away from her. She recoiled, taking a step back, her hand still on the handle of her knife. *How had he done that?* It took him a millisecond to approach her. His hand grazed her cheek, where she had been pricked by the bush earlier.

"You've been hurt."

"It was just the thorns, no biggie." She brushed past him.

As she moved past him, Kane ran his tongue over his fingertip, where her blood had been. She tasted sweet and spicy. This one was delicious. Kane closed his eyes. He could feel Vlad pushing to get out. He bit his lip, drawing blood. *No! He would not allow Vlad out.*

Jade glanced back at him, her gaze shifting over his face. Something about him was changing, his facial features, and his demeanor.

"Listen," she took a step toward him. "If you know who's killing the fae, please tell me."

The muscles in his jaw twitched. "I don't know," he lied.

His eyes darkened.

"Are you all right?"

"Yes," he hissed.

Jade took a few steps back, turning to look around her. "Well, if you find out, please let me know."

Kane advanced quickly on her, alarming her.

"How do you do that?"

He chuckled. "I have special talents like you."

"I don't know what you're talking about."

"What's with the wings?" he asked, touching one.

She jumped and spun around. "Please don't touch them. I don't like that."

He grinned. "I like them."

"I'm glad you like them, but you mustn't touch them."

"You have lips like rose petals."

Before she had a chance to respond, he leaned over and kissed her, eliciting a spark at the touch of her lips, causing the two of them to recoil. Jade stared wide-eyed at him.

"What happened?" Kane asked. Vlad backed off, leaving Kane to take control of his body. He stared at her, his jaw hanging open.

"You can't be the one," she stammered.

"What do you mean?" He cocked his head.

"That only happens for a fae when she kisses her future husband. It only happens once in a lifetime."

Kane grinned. He leaned against the tree next to her. *She was the one.* It looked like the devil, and the angel were meant to be married.

TWENTY-SEVEN YEARS AGO

"Boris!" Hugo yelled, his Romanian accent deep and rough.

Boris didn't hear Hugo above the storm. The ocean waves slammed against the ship, but it didn't stop Boris from transporting the boxes onto the ship. As he stepped down, the ship shifted, knocking Boris onto the deck. The box crashed and tipped over—a dark liquid leaked within the box, staining the outside of it.

Boris hissed, straightening his glasses.

"Dammit!" He flipped the box upright and stared down at the liquid. It was dark, possibly red, but it was difficult to tell within the night. He dabbed his finger in it. *Wine?*

"Boris!"

The wind blasted past him, and the ship shifted with it. Boris held on, his grip on the box tightening as he tried to keep it from sliding.

"Boris!"

A hand fell on his shoulder, alarming him. He turned to stare up at Hugo. With a thick British accent, he spat, "Oh, bloody hell! Don't scare me like that."

Hugo stood above him, straightening out his cap. "My apologies, but they will be here soon."

Boris scrambled to his feet with the help of his friend. The pier was dimly lit, but the shadow of four men appeared in the near distance. They carried a long box with them.

"What the ..." he began. "We don't have room for that."

"We told them we would," Hugo said, his eyes focusing in on the box. "They paid us good money to transport it."

Boris squinted, his gaze narrowing in on it. "That's a coffin."

"That's not a coffin," Hugo replied.

"Yes, it is. Look at the size of it. I'm not transporting a coffin." He stepped over the box and gestured toward the men. "Tell them to take their money, their boxes, and get the hell off of my ship. I'm not interested."

"Boris!"

He snapped his head around and, with an intense gaze, yelled, "No!" He straightened his glasses and his cap as he turned away. "Get this box off of my ship!" he yelled. "Roman!"

Roman, Boris' seventeen-year-old son, ran out of the cabin. His thick blonde hair swept up in the wind.

"Yes, sir!"

"Take the rest of the boxes off of the ship!"

Rain poured down on them.

"But, sir, we just put them on the boat."

The older man inched in closer to Roman. "And, we're taking them back off. We're not going anywhere."

As Boris gave orders, Hugo stepped off of the ship and approached the men. The four men wore dark overcoats and hats, their faces nearly hidden within their large upturned collars. Hugo stopped before them and held a hand up.

"I'm sorry, gentlemen, but we're not going to be able to ..." *Well, I'll be damned if it wasn't a coffin.* He looked up at the men, a grim look on his face. Boris was right. They shouldn't be transporting a coffin. A dead body was most likely within it. "We can't transport it for you."

He reached within his jacket and pulled out the money the men had paid them. As he handed it to the man in the lead, the man's gaze met his.

The man glared at him, his eyes red with fury. He wasn't about to take the coffin back to the house. He paid the men to do a job, and by damned, they were going to do it.

The man spoke with a Romanian accent. "I paid you. You do the job."

Hugo backtracked, becoming nervous. "We can't transport a body."

That was the truth. Unless they had written permission, they couldn't transport the body.

The man in the lead left position fidgeted. "This thing is heavy. Please let us put this on the ship. We must get back. We have other work to do."

Hugo glanced at him. "I'm sorry, I can't."

A blow to the side of the head caught Hugo off guard. As he turned to gaze back at the other lead man, the second lead man dropped the coffin and came at Hugo with a police baton, striking him repeatedly.

"You will take this coffin."

"Hey! Hey! What's going on over there?"

The men turned to see Boris and Roman staring at them.

Hugo dropped to his knees and fell over, the cash he had in hand spilling out onto the pier. The wind picked it up and washed it out to sea as the second lead man grabbed the coffin. They headed toward the ship.

"Oh, bloody hell!" Boris spat. He turned to Roman. "Turn it loose!"

Boris and Roman ran for the ropes and began unwinding it from the dock.

"Hurry!" His heart beat fast in his chest, his breathing becoming labored. A sharp pain filled it. He clutched onto his chest. "Roman!"

Roman spun around. "Dad!"

He ran to his father's side, and before he knew it, the men stepped onto the ship, dropping the coffin on it.

The second lead man turned to Roman, a scowl on his face. "Take it out to sea and drop it overboard!" he snapped. He looked Boris over before dropping cash on the man's chest.

His gaze shifted to Roman. "That's for your father and his stupidity. He could have cost more lives because of his reaction, but you listen to me!"

The wind whipped past the men, whisking their overcoats around their bodies.

"Go to hell!"

"Listen to me, Roman!"

Roman's eyes teared up.

"Don't open it! Just drop it in the sea and let it die!"

Roman was afraid to ask, yet he did. "What's in it?"

"The devil!" he answered. The men turned and stepped out onto the pier, the ship shifting beneath their feet.

Roman stared after them. One of the men almost took a spill, but the first man in the lead caught him by the arm. They disappeared from sight. Roman turned to his dad.

"Dad!"

"Sit me up!"

"What?"

"You heard me, help me sit up!"

Roman helped his father sit up. They leaned back against the boat and stared at the coffin.

"Do what they say! Do you hear me?"

"Yes, father."

"Do not open it!"

"But, how could the devil be in there?"

Boris looked to the sky. The rain fell harder.

When his father didn't answer, he said, "I'm going to move you into the cabin!" He grabbed his father and stood him up, holding as much of his father's weight as he could, and walked him toward the cabin. "How could the devil be in there, father?"

Boris glanced back at the coffin and grunted. "Just get me into the cabin."

Once they were inside the cabin, the rope snapped, and the ship shifted, the storm dragging it out to sea. Boris fell onto the couch with Roman almost atop him. Roman threw his arm out and caught himself against the nearby wall.

"Promise me you won't open it, son." He winced, the pain in his chest two times worse than when it struck the first time. The pain moved down into his arm. "Did you hear me?"

"Yes, sir."

"Take the ship out to sea. You'll have to hook it up to the crane and drop it overboard."

"Yes, sir. I'll take care of it."

Boris teared up. The pain wasn't getting any better.

"Father, aren't you a bit curious though?"

"No," he lied. *Whoever was inside must have been a monster. Why else would those men want the coffin buried at sea?*

BURIED AT SEA

The storm continued, whipping the ship about the sea as Roman took it further out. By the time Roman stepped out onto the deck, he was already tired from fighting the storm. His father was holding on but barely. Boris had been falling in and out of sleep while Roman steered the boat further out. Roman had tried to wake him up several times to make sure the old man was alive. Thankfully, the old man was a tough old bird.

Roman stared at the coffin. From this angle, he could see the locks and chains on it. He inhaled deeply and exhaled. The chill of the air allowed him to see his breath. He drew his coat in tighter and glanced up at the crane.

It was a bit old, but it should be strong enough to do the job. Since there were chains on the coffin, he reckoned he would be able to loop the hook around the chain and lift it.

Snores echoed from the cabin onto the deck. Roman snickered. The old man was out, but better alive than dead. He headed toward the crane when a noise caught his attention. He stopped and glanced back at the cabin. Boris was still snoring, yet the sound continued. Slowly, he turned his head and glanced back at the coffin. A scratching noise came from within. His heart thumped in his chest.

He took a step toward it, holding his breath. As he drew nearer, the sound became clearer and more prominent. Roman halted. The devil was scratching at the coffin. *The devil?* Those words churned his stomach. *Who was he kidding? The devil didn't exist, and he surely wasn't a man. Even if he was, the devil couldn't be contained within a coffin.*

Roman moved closer toward the coffin. A bang echoed from within it, forcing him to recoil. *Bloody hell! It's only a man inside.* He ran up beside it and dropped to his knees, taking the lock within his hands. The scratching within subsided. *It wants out. It's a man, only a man. The devil can't be contained.*

"No, Roman!"

Roman spun around. "But, dad, there's only a man in here."

Boris stood in the doorway, holding his chest. His hair was frazzled. "You heard those men. There's a monster in there."

"But, sir, had bad can a man be that he must be buried at sea, *alive.*"

His brows furrowed in. "Oh, son."

Their eyes met.

"If you only knew the horrors some men commit."

"But, he's alive, dad. He's been scratching at the lid. How can we let him die like this? We would be killing him."

Trembling, Boris moved out of the doorway. He braced himself against the post on deck as he walked toward him.

Eyes wide, he said, "If he's still alive in that coffin, then he must die. Those men said he was a monster. He must be a brutal murderer or something equally as horrendous." He glanced back at the crane. "Come, let's get this hooked up and get it overboard. Let's be rid of this horror. We must put this behind us."

Roman stared up at him, his breathing labored. "I can't."

More scratching came from within the coffin. Boris stared at it, his heart beating faster. Though it was cold out, sweat emerged from his pores.

"Roman, now!" When Roman didn't move, Boris grabbed the ropes to lower the crane hook. "Fine, I'll do it myself!"

A blast of wind struck the side of the ship, driving it sideways toward the ocean floor. Water splashed up over the side, throwing Roman sideways onto the ship's side. The coffin slid backward and into Roman, pinning him to the side. He screamed.

Boris held tight onto the ropes, his body becoming airborne. Below him, the coffin slammed into his son, and as the ship side struck water, the coffin tumbled onto its side, crushing Roman. As the ship rotated back, the coffin crashed onto the deck, cracking the locks. Boris slammed into the crane post, cracking his glasses as he fell onto the deck. He slid forward into the opposite side of where his son had fallen, rolling sideways, his back striking the ship's side. Roman rolled forward toward his father, his body limp.

"Roman!" Boris reached out as his son struck the crane post, landing in an awkward position. His mouth dropped.

A clanking sound came from the far right of him. He glanced up at the coffin. The chains lay loose around the coffin.

"Oh, bloody hell!" he muttered.

The lid fell open, exposing a man dressed in brown pants and a white button-up shirt with only socks on his feet. His clothing was tattered and bloody. His dark hair was a mess, some of it missing as if it had been ripped from his head. He lay unmoving on the deck.

Boris peered over at his son. "Roman," he whispered. "Wake up."

Roman didn't move.

"Roman, please wake up."

The devil moved. Boris' heart skipped a beat. He closed his eyes, praying he had imagined it. It had to have been dead, but no, the moment he opened his eyes, the devil appeared in his face.

Startled, he gasped. Then, it struck, driving its elongated nails into his chest, pulling him closer—close enough to sink its teeth into his flesh.

The wind and ocean tossed the ship again. The devil flew backward off of Boris. Both he and the devil plummeted down the deck and onto the opposite sidewall of the ship. Roman's lifeless body flew past him, over the side, and into the water.

"No!" Boris screamed.

Boris scrambled to grab Roman, but it was too late. Roman's body disappeared into the water. Tears welled over his eyes. As he tumbled forward onto the side net, the devil scrambled for him. Boris clutched onto the net as his body struck water. In his attempt to latch onto Boris, the devil slid past him and into the sea.

The waves shifted again, tossing the ship back onto its other side, rocking the ship back and forth. Boris let go of the net and slid halfway down, barely managing to grab onto the door. He grunted, the weight of his body relying on his shoulder. Pain settled deep in his muscles. Again, the ship shifted, throwing his weight backward. The door struck the cabin, slamming him against the cabin. He wasn't going to give up, though. Beside him, the crane rope lay next to him. He grabbed onto it and held on tight.

HOME, SWEET HOME

Sometime later, Kane drifted in and out of consciousness on a piece of driftwood. He drew in a deep breath. The taste of saltwater filled his mouth. He gagged, coughed, and spit-up seawater. He gazed up at the moon sneaking out from behind the clouds. Its light illuminated the water. *Why was he out here in the ocean?* He couldn't recall what had happened. Vlad must have put him in another predicament. He grunted in frustration. Kane was sick of this hell. If only...

In the near distance, he saw land. *Britain! The land he moved to, his new home!* His eyes lit up. Kane pulled himself up higher on the wood and began paddling. Then, he looked down. Where had the driftwood come from? He glanced around him at the dark water. Debris lay scattered on the water a few miles within distance of him. He snapped his head around. *Was there a downed boat nearby?* Behind him, a ship stood on the horizon, but it appeared to be farther than land.

Kane glanced up at the moon before paddling toward home.

A celebration was in order in Fairyland, the birth of Jade, elder Oribis' second daughter. It was a full moon, and as Oribis held Jade high, her wings fluttered. Oribis smiled.

The wind picked up again, howling past him. Lightning struck on the furthest side of the island. Jade's eyes opened wide with fright. Then, rain fell from the sky. The first plop landed on her head, and then her eye. She wiggled in his hands.

"I announce the birth of Jade."

The fae community stood nearby, applauding the newborn child. Music, singing, and cheers filled the air. Thunder boomed overhead, bringing lightning with it. At first, the child cowered in Oribis' hands, but when the light struck, she glanced in the direction of it.

As Kane climbed ashore, he stared around absently at it. This was not Britain. His surroundings were vastly different. He had to swim around a massive cliff to find the beach where he could climb ashore. Atop the cliff appeared to be a dense forest, but as he swam toward the beach, the forest grew thinner as it descended out toward the ocean.

Once on land, he stripped off his waterlogged shirt, revealing the scars that turned him into a vampire. The scent of wildflowers filled the air. He drew in a deep breath and exhaled slowly. He smiled. *Now, this was heaven.* This was what he wanted. He didn't want any more death. He didn't want to kill anymore. He dreaded the taste of blood, but his alter ego, Vlad, loved it. Vlad relished in it, Vlad the Impaler, the killer.

Kane drew in another deep breath. Maybe this was where he belonged, secluded in the dense forest. He flipped his dark hair and ran his hand through it, stopping where his hair had been ripped from his head. He huffed, his thoughts racing back to the men who invaded his home.

Kane had tried to isolate himself in his house to avoid killing, but it was too late. His victims had been traced back to him.

He grunted, taking a moment to try to calm his nerves. He closed his eyes and let his senses take over. Ever since he had been turned, his sense of smell, hearing, and taste were keen, more so than the average human.

The faint sound of music filled the air. Kane felt a sense of relief as he proceeded up the embankment. Another deep breath drew in the scent of something fresh and new, human, yet not human. He knew not what it was. He found himself scrambling through the brush with Vlad on the verge of emerging. Vlad was also interested in this new scent.

No, no! Kane stopped, trying to force Vlad back inside. He did not want the monster to emerge. The monster was the reason he was here in this position. From somewhere in the near distance, a female giggled.

He froze, his gaze shifting to the young couple in the bushes.

"We can't," she whispered to the teenage boy. Again, she giggled. "Stop, Hedrick. We can't. My father will be furious."

Kane watched from afar, his curiosity getting the better of him. He hunkered down and circled around to the left, creating a wide berth. Vlad was even more curious than Kane. He stopped behind the brush, not too far from them. He grinned, his fangs glistening in the moonlight.

Kane tried to push him back down, but the boy's actions were irritating Vlad even more than Kane.

"Shh, Alda, your father will never know." Hedrick pinned her arms down and began kissing her. She struggled within his grasp as he fought to control her.

Vlad stood, catching Hedrick's attention. Hedrick recoiled, backing away from Alda.

"Who are you?"

Vlad didn't answer. Instead, he proceeded toward them, his eyes intent on Hedrick.

"Look, you need to back off. Alda and I were having a good …"

Alda scrambled to her feet and turned to gaze back at Vlad. He looked her over, revealing his fangs. Alda did a double-take as she ran away.

"Wait for me." Hedrick turned and gestured toward Vlad. "Thanks for ruining everything." Then, he caught sight of the man's fangs. "What the …?"

He turned to run when Vlad ran up behind him, grabbed him by the neck, and cranked it to the side, breaking his neck.

Alda glanced back, her eyes wide with fear. Her heart leapt into her chest as she ran off into the darkest part of the forest, scraping past the thorny brush. She gasped and grabbed at her arm. Blood leaked from the wound, but she carried on, past the large, thick tree which divided the path. She took refuge behind it, glancing back in the direction she had come from. She didn't see the stranger.

From behind her, something warm touched her neck, and as she opened her mouth to scream, Vlad covered her mouth and sunk his fangs into her.

Hours turned into days, weeks, and then months as Kane found himself a home within a cavern in the dense part of the forest. It was here where he found nourishment, more so of the animal kind and not human. For this, he was thankful, but Vlad's curiosity was growing. The fae humans were also growing more curious about the area he called home. They referred to it as *the evil*, primarily because they found a few of the animals Vlad had fed on. The faes had never seen such an attack before, so they had decided it was in their best interest to form an army for protection.

Kane snickered. Despite the fact he didn't like killing, he knew the faes were useless. Vlad would tear them down in seconds flat. Little did they know Vlad had led an army, and he knew how to kill. He and his army had been efficient in killing. But Kane didn't want to die either. He knew that Vlad would keep him alive. With ever-growing remorse, Kane allowed his alter ego to kill the faes and anybody else who threatened his life.

. . .

THE PRESENT

Kane leaned against the tree, a grin on his face. He had killed enough faes to fill a river with their blood, but this one was special. Vlad hid just below Kane's surface, unsure of what to do with this one once he heard the words *future husband* and *marriage*. For once, Vlad was at Kane's mercy.

Jade stared at him, her mouth open, her hand still on the knife's handle.

"Are you wanting to catch flies, or would you prefer to get to know me before we get married?" he laughed.

This fae was a shifty one, a fighter, and a bit edgier. He liked that. Slowly, he reached out, his gaze shifting to her hand and the knife, as he pushed her chin up.

She closed her mouth and stepped away from him, her eyes moving to his hand.

"Personally, I would prefer to get to know you first. I don't just marry anyone." He smiled. "I know us men have a history of womanizing, but I'm not into that."

Her eyes narrowed in on him.

She wasn't falling for his sense of humor. *She was a tough cookie.* Maybe in due time, he would charm her.

Jade glanced around. It was getting later, and her father would soon be checking her bed to make sure she was in it. Ever since some of the faes had been killed, he would do his nightly rounds to make sure everyone was home, in bed, and safe and sound. She couldn't blame him, after all, her sister, Alda, had been found, drained of her blood, the day after Jade's birth.

"I must get home. My father will be worried sick about me." She took one last glance about and headed back in the direction she had come from.

"Would you like me to walk you out? It is quite easy to get lost in this part of the forest."

She had wanted to find the killer, but now she wasn't so sure she wanted to tangle with him if this man was the killer. She was sure he was.

"No, thank you."

He was quick, stealthy, and quite different than she expected. *Future husband? How could she marry the man who killed her sister? Killed the faes? What would possess her to be attracted to such a man or monster?*

She stepped into the brush, finding the urge to hurry along. She snatched the knife out of her sheath and swiped at a branch. The branch snapped back and narrowly avoided her face, thanks to Kane, who caught it.

Jade whipped around, holding her knife up. Had he been any closer, she would have stuck him with it. Instead, he smiled and held the branch.

"Why? What kind of thanks is that?" he asked. His eyes glistened in the moonlight.

Her heart raced. "Thank you," she said nervously. Her voice shook. "I appreciate it."

Quickly, she turned and raced toward home. At the fork, she halted, ready to take a left when his voice boomed behind her.

"Go to the right. It will take you out of here."

She glanced back at him before fleeing the evil.

Once back at home, she quickly jumped into bed, sweat beading on her skin. She threw the blanket over her and closed her eyes.

A moment later, her father stepped inside, leaves crunching beneath his feet.

Jade pretended to be asleep, but then he touched her shoulder. She jumped.

"Father?" she bolted up to a sitting position.

He smiled as he took a seat beside her. "I'm sorry to wake you."

She rubbed her eyes. "That's all right. I haven't been able to sleep well tonight."

"Oh, is that why you went for a walk?" he asked, pulling the blanket aside to reveal the dirt on her neck.

"Father!"

"Now, now. You just jumped in bed. I saw you. You didn't have time to change."

She sighed. Jade knew her father better than that. *What else did he know? Did he follow her to the evil?*

"I'm sorry, Father. I couldn't sleep, so I ..."

He put a finger on her lip. "I know. You are restless at heart. Always have been since the day you were born. It must have been something in the air that night—the loss of your sister, Alda. I wish you would have known her. She, too, was restless at heart, but you must remain vigilant, cautious, and strong. There is a killer out there, and until we kill him, you must remain here at night. The killer has yet to strike here in our village."

Her heart sunk. *Did she lead the killer here? To their community? To her home?*

"What is it, my dear?"

"It's nothing, Father."

He frowned. "Something is wrong. I can see it. I can feel it."

A moment of silence hung in the air. "Get some rest, and do not leave again, do you hear me?" he asked sternly.

"Yes, Father." She pulled the blanket up as she laid down.

Her father stood and then halted, turning back to her. "Where is your sword?"

Oh, no! She cringed. *He saw that it was not put away.* She didn't know how to answer him. She closed her eyes and then glanced up at him. She would have to go to the beach in the morning to look for it.

"I lost it in the woods."

His eyes grew angry and red.

"You lost it?"

"I'm sorry, Father."

"I ..."

"Tomorrow, you will look for it," he demanded. He stomped out of her hut.

She stared after him. He was not only mad at her but disappointed. She knew better than to go looking for trouble, but as he said, she was restless at heart, always had been, and always would be. Tomorrow, she would find it. She closed her eyes and drew in a deep breath. The scent of wildflowers was in the air.

STALKER

Jade awoke in the middle of the night to the killer hunting her in her nightmare. She bolted upright, trying to catch her breath. She had never felt so haggard and out of breath from a nightmare before. She brushed her hair back and glanced at the empty space behind her door. The sword wasn't there. For some odd reason, she had half expected it to be there as if she never lost it, but as she struggled with the blanket, which was lying halfway down her body, her eyes fell to the object at the end of her bed. Her heart leapt into her throat. There lay her sword, shiny, clean, and dry as if it had never left her side.

She bolted out of bed and glanced around the hut, snatching the candle from the wooden bedside table. Nobody stood in the darkness. Only the shadows remained. She had led the killer to her community, to her home, to her room. A chill ran up her spine, creeping her out. She had never felt violated before until now.

Why had he not killed her? Still dressed from the night's previous hunt, she threw her boots on and grabbed her sword. With it in hand, she stepped out of her hut and glanced around. Only the sound of an owl echoed in the night.

Jade took a step in the direction of her parent's hut as the distant echo of an animal howled. Quietly, she crept up to her parent's hut. From outside, she could hear her father snore. Though she was still troubled, she snickered. But, as she turned to gaze out at the meadow beyond, something moved in the distance. She stopped, her breathing becoming labored. It stopped. It was him, Kane, the killer.

She drew in a deep breath. They stared at each other for what seemed like minutes but lasted only seconds. Then, she wondered, had he visited others within her community? She glanced around. Nothing seemed out of the ordinary. No cries. No screaming. No sign of violence or otherwise. *Did he really only come to bring her sword? Why not wake her? Was he the same man she was looking for? Was he the killer? Or was it somebody else?*

She swore he smiled. In turn, she faked a smile, though he had saved her. He couldn't be the killer, but what kind of man snuck into a woman's hut to return a sword. She broke out in goosebumps thinking about it. Then, he turned and walked away, disappearing into the darkness.

Jade walked around the community, surveying it, making sure everything was in order. As she returned to her hut, she stopped in mid-stride. Her father stood in front of her hut, his arms crossed over his chest. She dropped her head and continued toward him.

"I see you found your sword."

"Yes, I did." She couldn't lie and look him in the eye.

"You also disobeyed my orders."

"But, Father, I knew you would be ..."

He put his hand up. His eye twitched as he looked at her. "You will not participate in tomorrow's events."

"But, Father, I ..."

"You heard what I said. You will remain in your hut when not helping with the food and cleaning."

She frowned, her eyes tearing up. "But ..."

"You heard me. You also will not partake in the sword training, not like you should be anyway. You should be doing what good female fairies do. You will help the other women around the village."

"I'm a grown woman," she whispered.

"And, grown women do what grown women should do. I will find you a suiter."

"Father, no, ..." she stammered.

In the distance, Kane caught her attention. He grabbed onto a tree branch and pulled himself up. He sat back against the tree and pulled an apple from his pocket. He bit into the apple, and it was as though she could hear the crunch of the apple as if he was standing beside her. She stared absentmindedly at him, her mind wandering.

"Jade!"

She snapped to, her attention back on her father.

He turned to gaze into the forest when she grabbed his hand. Instantly, he stared down at her. Jade's mother stepped out of the hut, her long golden hair draped over one shoulder.

"What is going on out here? It's the middle of the night."

Jade glanced back at her. "Go back to sleep, Mom. I couldn't rest, so I took a walk."

Her father exchanged glances with them. "Go back to bed, Jade."

"Goodnight, Mom."

She headed to her hut as her father escorted her mother back inside. Once they were inside, Jade stopped before her door. Behind her, something hit the ground. She looked back over her shoulder. Less than two feet away was a partially eaten apple. She peered out at the tree Kane had been sitting in. He was gone.

She glanced down at the apple and then grabbed it. She brushed it off, and after one long look around her, she took it inside with her.

Once inside, she put her sword back into its sheath and hung it on the wall behind the door. Then, she washed off the apple, and after carefully studying it, took a small bite. She hadn't had an apple in a long time. It was sweet and refreshing. She closed her eyes and savored the moment.

Jade rolled over, the sunlight beaming through the hut walls. It was dawn. It was time to get up and get some work done. She threw her blanket off and sat up, tossing her hair over her shoulder. She froze. Her gaze fell on her bedside table where several apples lay. Her jaw dropped.

Kane did it again. *How did she not hear him enter? How did she not wake up?* That was it. She had to sneak out of here and find him, find out why he was stalking her, but that was not going to be easy. The men were training in the meadow, and the women would be waiting for her to come help them. As she mulled over her options, she pulled her boots on, then strapped on her sword and knife.

As her mind raced, she stepped out of her hut and glanced around. The men were already training for battle, their swords clashing, echoing within the meadow. With a quick glance, she turned to her left, ready to slide into the brush, when Lily stepped before her, a clay pot in hand.

"Are you ready to help? Your father said you would be helping us with the food."

Jade fake a smile. "Yes, I will. I will join you in just a moment. Can you give me some privacy? I need to relieve myself."

Lily frowned. "Really, Jade?"

"Yes. I just woke up."

"I'm not supposed to let you out of my sight," she said with a smirk.

"Sorry, but you are not watching me. I'll come join you in a moment." She leaned in closer to Lily. "I promise."

Lily sighed. "Don't let me down. Don't let your father down. He will reprimand you."

"I'm twenty-seven years old. I'm not a child anymore," Jade said.

Lily walked away, leaving Jade alone.

She took one last glance and disappeared into the brush, making sure that nobody was watching or following her, as she wouldn't put it past Lily to sneak up on her.

She moved into the thickest part of the brush, trying to hide within it, as she moved around to the opposite side of the meadow, past the warriors, hoping to find Kane. She presumed he would be lurking within the evil.

On the way, she stopped to relieve herself, as she had said she would, and then once done, proceeded onward, managing to keep herself hidden within the brush. Once past the meadow, she moved through the forest, sticking to the trees to maintain some discretion. It was at the pathway leading into the dense forest where she stopped and glanced around—no sign of him.

One more step took her inside, where the large trees hid the sunlight from her. Darkness overwhelmed her. Then, a hand appeared before her, an apple in hand, Kane's breath hot on her neck. She gasped, her wings fluttering as she stood, trembling, her hand moving to her sword.

"I see you accepted my gift."

Her voice shook. "Gift?"

"The apple? The one I shared with you. You ate the rest of it."

She peered over her shoulder at him. "I brought you more."

"I saw that."

She moved away from him, snatching the apple from his hand. He had not eaten from this one. She turned to face him.

"How is sharing an apple a gift?" she asked, rolling the apple over in her hand.

"It's a gift of friendship and marriage." He smiled. "Of trust and of caring for one another."

"But you don't know me."

"Does that matter?" He moved closer. "I see that you're a caring person, or should I say fae." He began to pace. "You know, I never believed the fairy tales. I didn't think faes actually existed, especially a fae human. I find that interesting. I'd like to get to know you better."

Their eyes met. "Do I get to know you better then? Find out who and what you are."

She thought back to the stories her father spoke of the killer, the monster. She thought back to the way he ran when she first saw him. He ran on his hands and knees, much like an animal, but faster, like that of a wild cat.

"Of course."

"I get to ask my questions first," she began.

He shook his finger. "Uh, uh, uh, I said I wanted to get to know you better first. So, I get to start with the questions."

"Fine," she said, leaning back against the tree.

Kane paced before her. "How old are you?"

"Twenty-seven," she answered.

A look of surprise spread across his face. "Wow! And, your father still treats you like a teenager? How absurd?"

"I know," she agreed. "I know there are traditions in our community, but I'm not a child anymore. My dad told me he wanted me to marry, said he would find the right man for me."

He rubbed his chin. "But, shouldn't that be your decision, not his?"

"Yes," she said with confidence.

"And, what would he say if you told him you didn't want to marry the man he chose? What if you stood your ground, forced him to treat you like the woman you are?"

She stared at him.

"What I mean is, you're an adult woman. You should make your own decisions, even if you chose to leave your village ..."

"But I don't want to leave the village." She folded her arms across her chest.

"What I'm saying is, you have your own mind," he gestured to his head and then moved in closer, touching her on the forehead. "Your own thoughts, your own brains, you have things you want to do, and not necessarily in the fae traditions. That's why you are your own person. I respect women like you."

A faint smile spread across her face. "Really?"

"Yes. You're independent." *Oh, how he wanted to kiss her again.* He was close enough to do it, but he refrained. "Independence is beautiful."

She was taken aback, surprised by his remarks. He made her feel good about herself and not so wrong in her father's eyes.

"You're beautiful," he added.

He wasn't the most attractive man, but his heart was in the right place. He would stand by his woman and any decision she made. He would respect his woman.

Then, she blurted out, "Are you married?"

Their eyes met.

Then Kane laughed. Vlad laughed. "No, I'm not, my dear. Why? Would you like to get married?"

"Yes," she answered, not realizing what she was saying.

His smile faded. "Do you want to defy your father and marry someone who is not fae?"

Her heart leapt into her throat. "Yes."

A moment of silence hung in the air.

"Do you want to leave your village?"

She couldn't breathe. *Did she want to leave her village?* She was a rebel. Everything she had done was against her father's words from the day she was born.

"I don't know. Maybe, maybe not. I'm not sure."

Kane stood before her, inches away from her. Jade was his. He licked his lips.

"Can I kiss you again?"

"Yes," she whispered.

He leaned in and kissed her, that spark sending a tingle through his lips. Though he wanted to stop, he didn't, and neither did she.

She had only ever kissed one man before, and it was only out of curiosity. There was no spark between her and her first love. This man raised her curiosity, though. He couldn't be the killer.

Vlad rose to the surface despite Kane trying to keep him restrained.

As Jade pulled away, she peered up at him, their eyes meeting.

"Were you serious about wanting to marry a man who is not a fae?"

"Yes," she answered.

"Good." He looked past her into the near distance. "We have visitors."

Jade spun to find her father and the other warriors approaching the path, which led to the evil.

Kane suddenly grabbed her hand. "Come with me."

"What?"

"Come with me."

Jade glanced back at the warriors. With a faint smile, she turned and ran with him deeper into the forest and into a cavern. She felt like a rebellious teenager again, defying her father's orders and traditions. She wasn't about to marry a fae. She wanted to venture out into the world and experience life.

Once inside the cavern, Kane slowed his pace, leading her further inside.

"It's dark in here." She glanced around.

He halted. "Are you scared?"

"Should I be?" She was beginning to rethink her actions. "I'm not used to being away from my family and friends."

He led her deeper inside the cavern. "Do you realize you accepted my proposal?"

"Did I? I've never been proposed to."

Vlad rose to the surface, a grin on his face. His eyes changed.

Jade took a step back. "What's wrong with your eyes? You seem different."

Kane fought to maintain control, but Vlad had become vigilant.

Kane's voice grew deeper. "Why Jade, come to me, my love. I can give you eternal life."

As Jade took a step back, a voice boomed from behind her, frightening her. She jumped back in Vlad's direction. He grabbed onto her and pulled her back into him, swiping the sword from its sheath.

Jade's father stood at the entrance to the cavern.

"Jade!" Oribis yelled.

"Father!"

"Have you come to congratulate the bride?" Vlad asked. His eyes turned red as he held her tight against him.

"Bride?" Oribis glanced at Jade as the sword moved to her neck.

"Look at the lovely ring she accepted." Kane held her hand up, showing off the fiery red stone that had appeared on her hand.

Her father's mouth dropped.

Jade stared at it in disbelief and squirmed within his grasp. "How dare you, Kane? I did not accept your proposal."

"Oh, yes, you did," he answered. "You accepted it when you bit into the apple, my love. Now, you are my wife."

He stepped further into the cavern, swept her up, and took a couple of steps back, jumping into the cave below.

"No!" her father screamed.

TIL' DEATH DO US PART

Jade scrambled out of his arms, her gaze shifting upward. The opening was probably fifty feet in height. She turned, looking for her sword, and then realized Vlad still had it.

"Looking for this?" he asked, sword in hand.

A glimmer of light reflected off of it, catching her attention.

"I'm not your wife," she snapped, trying to pull the ring off of her finger. It remained tight around her finger, unmoving.

Fine! She didn't need to remove it yet. Her priority was getting out of here.

"I liked you," she said. "I was starting to think you were a good guy, but you proved me wrong and manipulated me, turning me against my father. How dare you!"

A snicker escaped his lips. "You liked Kane, not me, not Vlad."

She eyed him curiously. *Vlad? Who was Vlad?*

"Oh, did Kane not tell you about me?"

She shook her head. "No."

He took a step toward her, holding the sword out.

"Of course, he wouldn't." He shook his head. "Because he wanted to gain your trust. Did he tell you that he killed those fairies?"

She took a couple of steps back, her hand moving to her knife. She unlatched it. Again, she shook her head. Another step back took her up against the wall.

"Did he tell you that he killed your sister?"

Again, she shook her head. *Vlad and Kane were one and the same man. How could this be? She didn't understand.*

"Kane, can you hear me?"

A hearty laugh escaped his lips. "Oh, do you think you can get through to him? Sorry, my love. You only have me, not Kane." He leaned in closer. "I can destroy, Kane. I can tear him down."

Vlad pressed the tip of the sword against her chest, and with a flip of the wrist, he arced the blade across her flesh, cutting her. She winced. The sight of her blood drew him in.

"I'm growing hungry, my dear." He moved the sword to his side as he neared her.

It was then she knew what he wanted. She remembered her father had mentioned the fairies were drained of their blood. Vlad was the killer, the monster he spoke of, and that included Kane.

"Very hungry," he whispered in her ear.

Jade gripped the knife tight, and as she welcomed him into his arms, she told him, "Go ahead, feed from me."

As he lowered his head to her neck, she drove the knife into his back. He reared back, screamed, and went for her neck again. She kicked him, her foot connecting with his stomach, as he swung the sword. She narrowly avoided it as she threw herself to the ground and rolled away from him, grabbing a rock with the other hand.

He swung again, his face decaying. He was dying. She threw the rock, hitting him in the head. The sword fell from his hand as he stumbled across the rock.

Jade dove for the sword and caught it by the handle. She rolled onto her back and sliced the air with it, connecting with his body, taking him down. As she bolted to her feet, she spun, ready to fight again, but Kane's body fell, his body turning to ashes.

She was out of breath when Oribis touched her shoulder.

"Jade."

She spun, eyes wide, tears brimming at the sight of him. "I'm so sorry, Father. I'm so sorry. He manipulated me, he ..."

He pulled her into his arms and held her tight. "I understand. Listen to me." He pulled her away and looked her over. "All the training you have ever done served you well today. I'm proud of you, and I'm proud to call you my daughter. You're a strong woman."

Lynn Mullican was born and raised in Phoenix, Arizona, where she currently resides with her husband, three children, and five grandkids. She has woven her fascination with the paranormal into written works including short stories, dramatic plays, poetry, screenplays, and full-length novels. In her Bad Elements series, she incorporates years of knowledge in self-defense and martial arts.

As of 2018, Lynn has published several short stories, including; Raven's Hill, Raven's Hill 2: The Ritual, Sacrificial Blood, The Awakening and The Awakening II: Nexus. She also has three published novels; Bad Elements series, Crystal Dragon, Blood for Blood, and The Hybrid Unleashed.

Website: http://lynnmullican.blogspot.com

facebook.com/Author.LynnMullican

twitter.com/lynnmullican

instagram.com/mullicanlynn

MORE BY FICTION-ATLAS PRESS

Fiction-Atlas Press releases two anthologies a year. We hope you'll check out some of our past anthologies or sign up to be notified about future ones on the next page!

Chasing Fireflies:

A Summer Romance Anthology

A Twist of Fate:

A Twisted Fairy Tale Anthology

Counterclockwise:

A Fiction-Atlas Time Travel Anthology

Beyond the Mask:

A Fiction-Atlas Superhero Anthology

Unknown Realms:

A Fiction-Atlas Press Anthology

The Devil You Know:

A Fiction-Atlas Press Anti-Hero Anthology

THANK YOU

We hope you have enjoyed our anthology.
It would mean the world to us if you had the time to leave a review!
Reviews are what keep us writing!

FOLLOW FICTION-ATLAS PRESS FOR INFORMATION ON FUTURE PUBLICATIONS.

FICTION-ATLAS
PRESS LLC

http://fiction-atlas.com

facebook.com/fictionatlas

twitter.com/fabookbargains

instagram.com/cl_cannon

youtube.com/clcannonauthor

ARE YOU A FAN OF BOOK BARGAINS? WE ARE TOO!

Fiction-Atlas has launched our FABB bargains newsletter.

Get the best free and discounted books, plus awesome giveaways delivered straight to your inbox!

FICTION-ATLAS BOOK BARGAINS

Get the best free and discounted books, plus amazing monthly giveaways, delivered straight to your inbox!

Sign-up here: https://bit.ly/fabbreaders

We also post daily bargains on our Facebook and Twitter pages!

facebook.com/fictionatlasbookbargains

twitter.com/fabookbargains

www.ingramcontent.com/pod-product-compliance
Lightning Source LLC
Chambersburg PA
CBHW071158100726
47908CB00002B/427